NEXT SEASON

To Shirley

NEXT SEASON

a novel by

MICHAEL BLAKEMORE

with an introduction by
SIMON CALLOW

APPLAUSE
NEW YORK • LONDON

NEXT SEASON a novel by Michael Blakemore

© 1968, 1988, 1995 by Michael Blakemore
Introduction © 1988, 1995 by Simon Callow

First American Paperback edition published by Applause in
1995

Library of Congress Cataloging-in-Publication Data

LC Catalog # 95-79044

British Library Cataloging-in-Publication Data

A catalogue record for this book is available from the British
Library

ISBN: 1-55783-223-4

APPLAUSE BOOKS

211 West 71st Street
New York, NY 10023
Phone: (212) 496-7511
Fax: (212) 721-2856

406 Vale Road
Tonbridge KENT TN9 1XR
Phone: 0732-357755
Fax: 0732-770219

Introduction

When I first read *Next Season*, its jacket had been replaced with brown paper. It was being passed around the box office and front of house at the National Theatre like a samizdat. This was 1969; though no more than a year old, it was already out of print. It was widely rumoured to be a *roman à clef*, although no one seemed very clear as to who precisely the characters were based on. 'Sir' (Laurence) was one of the models, said some; Peter Hall, another, according to the head usher. The events referred to the Nottingham Playhouse, if you believed one lot; no, said a different crowd, it was Stratford-upon-Avon. We faintly knew who Michael Blakemore was: he ran the Citizens' Theatre in Glasgow, where Albert Finney had gone after his film, *Tom Jones*; and 'Albert' (we felt we owned him) had just opened on Broadway in Blakemore's acclaimed production of *A Day in the Death of Joe Egg*. All I really knew was that it was about the theatre, and it had been written by an insider. That was more than enough for me.

The sensational aspect of the book went right over my head. I tried, from my tiny store of theatre lore, to identify the characters, or at least Braddington, where the novel was set. It was hopeless; but after a very few pages, I had ceased even to try, because something far more important was coming through: this man was telling me what it was like to be an actor. I had found what I was looking for. The other books – I'd read them all – told you *how* to act (Stanislavsky) or mused (Michael Redgrave) on the *meaning* of acting, but this one was about the demands and the rewards of acting, what it takes from you, what it gives you back. Acting as work, work as passion. I cried for joy. A way of life existed which would use my energy, my brain, my bursting heart; and which was useful and important. Somehow, never having set foot on a stage, I knew that Sam Beresford/Michael Blakemore's experience was authentic; knew all about his fear that his small part would be cut, his elation at finding a characterization that released the scene's wit and menace, his obsession to find and if necessary make the right kind of glasses for the part, his despair at failing to triumph when called on to take over from another actor. Above all, I knew exactly what he meant when, running through the part of Hamlet in his mind, he felt "an absolute certainty that he could play the bloody thing, that if a stage were to materialize at that very moment, he could step on to it and astonish any audience, any-where". He was speaking directly to the as-yet-unrealized actor in me.

Everything that I encountered when I eventually escaped my integument and became what I always was, confirmed what Blake-more had written. Re-reading the book the other day I was struck all over again by the precision and vividness of the observation; but now I saw that I had been too swept away by the revelation of acting to see: what a very good novel it is. Sam Beresford, the central character, is mercilessly exposed in his emotional con-fusions and calculations, trying, in a rather cold way, to organize his sexual relationships, angry and frustrated when they don't work out. The milieu of a young actor of the late fifties is excellently evoked, its greyness and dinginess the more sharply perceived in the light of Beresford/Blakemore's Australian back-ground. "Grey towns drowning in lakes of smoke; hills plowed into rows of terraces that presented against the sky silhouettes as sharp and ugly as blades of rusty serrated saws." And Braddington, the theatre and the social life of the company are all well done. But the novel's great triumph is to have placed an actor's work, his professional and creative processes, at the centre, and to have made the artistic vicissitudes of a young man who is not yet and perhaps never will be a great artist, so enthralling. The sense of uplift achieved at the end of the novel because that young man is going to continue to try to make theatre, is an exceptional achieve-ment. Why should we care? But we do; desperately.

The conviction of ours, twenty years ago, that the book contained thinly veiled figures from the real world is not strictly true; Blakemore has transmuted his raw material into art, and conflated and refashioned his originals. If there is a *clef*, it is probably the Stratford season of 1959, in which the author played, but that legendary season in which Olivier, Robeson, and Edith Evans all appeared, was a very different affair to Braddington's. Touches of those great individuals can be seen here and there, but his major achievements of characterization, Ivan Spears, the old classical star, and Tom Chester, the young director of the season, are so fully presented as to be archetypes rather than life-sketches. Spears, who has some traits of Charles Laughton, to whose 1959 Lear Blakemore was Knight, to whose Bottom he played Snout, distills practical wisdom to the point of genius, betraying deep understanding of the text with profound experience of realizing it. "Freddie, if you do get into difficulties, look, I think I have the trick of this scene. I think I could help you," he says to his co-star, and we understand that the 'trick' is the master-craftsman's deep intimacy and ease with the play and the author. "This particular play (*The Duchess of Malfi*) was Ivan's. Everything he said about it, and everything he did in his own performance, had an immediacy and a vigour which claimed the material as his own. Webster had found a spokesman, one who responded not so much to the formal qualities of his play, anchored in their own time, as to that enduring impulse that had led to the writing of it, and which, centuries later, in the terms of his own experience, Ivan was able to affirm. The play was his by right of talent, and he was there to turn its pages for the entire company."

In the character of Ivan, Blakemore affirms the actor's contribution both in himself ("in the terms of his own experience") and in his intuitive ability to release the play's (temporarily) frozen life – the profoundly creative coupling of the actor's inner universe with that of the play. In the context of the novel's action (the author metes him out a drastically symbolic fate), Ivan comes to embody the passing order. Tom Chester is what replaces him and

3

his kind; Tom Chester, the prototypical directocrat, manipulator of destinies, coiner of clichés, the new man. It is a devastating portrait, bred of deep resentment. Blakemore shows the invisible processes by which the politician director, equipped with a few borrowed insights, a little oily charm and unlimited faith in his own indispensibility, hijacks a complex craft from its true practitioners, replacing the living organism which was the end of their labours with a product which satisfies critics and Arts Councils and has every appearance of the real thing, but on closer examination proves to be only a plastic facsimile.

Blakemore's ear for the director-speak invented by Tom Chester and his contemporaries, part-matey, part-schoolmasterly, is flawless: "Well, everybody, that was awful, absolutely awful. I can't tell you how bad it was. You've simply got to be better than that. And I know you can be." And: "This is a play about horror . . . we've got to create this atmosphere of darkness and cruelty, and really use the stage to suggest currents of evil moving through this enclosed Renaissance world." More sinister, though, is Tom's power over careers and lives. In a chilling interview towards the end of the book, Tom tells Sam why he won't be in the next season: "Talent's important, of course. Of primary importance. But talent's nothing without – well – ferocity. That's what makes it interesting. Class has gone. Race is going. You can't be above the battle any more. Which I sometimes think you try to be? . . . That's what I look for first in an actor. Determination is the polite word. Your trouble is you're a bit too nice." These conversations continue to the present day; not even the script has changed. The important point, as Blakemore makes clear, is that Tom Chesterism has made the discussion of whether work is good or bad irrelevant, because the discussion is always conducted in their terms. They have won; and there will be no more Ivan Spears. Unless . . .

The reprint of *Next Season* is timely, because it coincides with a resurgence of the independent spirit among actors. And this novel is the finest fictional celebration of the passionate craft of the

4

actor. There have been remarkable novels of the theatre – from *Wilhelm Meister* to John Arden's magnificent *Silence Among the Weapons* – but no other book has so truly depicted the creative anarchic excitement of acting. Perhaps that's the real reason it was under brown paper covers for so long.

Simon Callow

Play-in

A FALSE SKY, he thought, for February, and declined the rise in spirits which traditionally accompanies a change in the weather. Through the windowpane and beyond the gabled roof of the big red-brick house next door touches of white cloud fled across a blue sky. Shielded by glass, he contemplated the first naked sunshine of the year, of 1959. It was the ninth of February, 1959. He was twenty-nine years old, at the end of his ninth year in England. He lay in bed and tried to think of other nines. One thing it certainly was not; it was not nine o'clock. His alarm had rung in vain an hour ago, and now he had a stiff neck, a fuzzy head and guilt. This physical remorse would probably be with him all day.

Tea, then! The day was not yet lost. If he took it quietly over a pot of tea, and let the sap rise in its own time, things might improve.

He opened the door to his "kitchen," a converted cupboard with a window, which alone entitled his landlord to call the room a flat, and put a kettle full of water on the gas. He paid four pounds a week, too much his friends said, considering he had supplied some of the furniture himself, but it was worth a pound to have the landlord off the premises.

From somebody's wireless upstairs he could hear *Housewives' Choice* and was pleased when he recognized a tune he liked. He was very susceptible to popular music at this hour of the day. Usually he resented its triviality, but this morning the bouncing song went down to his stomach with a swill of tea and his spirits quite suddenly revived. He hummed an accompaniment with shamefaced glee. He poured himself a second cup of tea and began to think of the audition he had done the previous week. He ran through the words again, first in his head and then out loud. "You common cry of curs . . ." He hadn't done at all badly; better than usual. Perhaps it was the speech he'd chosen, from *Coriolanus*, heavy with appropriate irony. This was the third time he'd auditioned for the Braddington Playhouse, and this year he had been determined not to care. Enough, but not too much. He thought he'd almost succeeded. "Very good indeed," a voice had said from the back of the theater. "And thank you very much for coming." He made his way to the stage door past five young men, younger than him, probably fresh from drama school. They were pallid and solitary with nerves, one of them mouthing his lines like a prayer. They invited sadism, he reflected sadly; the profession does. Comparatively he was a veteran. At auditions his knees were still inclined to shake without warning, and when it was all over and he stepped out of the stage door into indifferent daylight, he still felt a sort of incredulous shock as if through his own stupidity he'd been narrowly missed by a bus. But he no longer felt humiliation. To this extent he was professional; anguish had become cautious hostility.

Each year Braddington auditioned about five hundred actors. They sent them a form letter a fortnight before, allotting each a day and a time and suggesting that they choose "two contrasting pieces of not more than two minutes each." He could never understand the theory behind the audition system. The best parts were already cast, and all that remained was to recruit the odds and sods, the bit parts and walk-ons. They might just as well pick them out of a hat. Perhaps it was a gesture of recognition on the part of the management toward the great unemployed. Perhaps it was a way of reminding both parties that it was a buyer's market. Certainly the actor who emerged triumphant from this rugged lottery rarely quibbled about salary.

He washed up his cup and set about tidying the room. He pulled the bedclothes into a roughly "made" position, then smoothed the bedcover over the whole. He put away two pairs of shoes, and in the same cupboard studied a mounting pile of dirty clothes. He would soon have to go to the Bendix. Perhaps today. What was the program? Well, there was that letter home to Australia. And his part to study. Three hours' work on that (or anyway two) had to be fitted in somewhere. The Bendix might provide a temporary reprieve.

In spells out of work, as a kind of therapeutic discipline, he made himself study the great parts. A month ago he had finished seventeen weeks in a well-paid TV comedy series. It had been a job with many pleasant distractions: a cheerful indolent cast, a good-natured crew, and the long tightrope of Tuesday transmission day with its bracing sense of crisis. A week after it was over he had realized what a vulgar and hopelessly unfunny show it had been. He needed badly to renounce his allegiance to it, so he had started work on another part. At other times he had learned Malvolio, half of Macbeth, Oswald in *Ghosts* and Marlow in *She Stoops to Conquer*. Now he was pitching in to Hamlet. And why not? If he couldn't entertain grandiose ambitions in his own room, where could he? From the battered cabin trunk under the bed he had ferreted out the scripts of the parts he had previously studied, much annotated and interleaved with pictures of notable actors who had played the roles. Now he kept them by him on the table, lucky charms, not to be looked at but to remind him that his task was neither impossible nor too absurd.

Well, there was the Bendix. What else? He suddenly remembered it was Friday. He was due to sign on at the Labour Exchange at 10:30, in precisely three minutes. With relief and a certain muddied gaiety he hurried to dress and shave. A sense of urgency, however slight, had entered his day. He had something to do; or rather something else, something to do with other people. A plan was formulating. He would go into town, sign on and collect his money, drop in at his agents' before lunch, eat in town, then come home and do some work. He was not prevaricating. The work would get done sometime before midnight, and he knew quite well the longer he put it off the more painful it would be. But just now at this hour of the morning by himself in this room the postponement was too sweet to resist.

The Labour Exchange was half an hour away by tube, from Hampstead to St. James's Park, with a change at Charing Cross. It

9

was foreign territory to him now, but during the four years he had lived in Victoria he had got fond of it and was loath to change. He liked the air of tolerance about the place. There was a lady with a hearing aid whose whole manner was a smiling wag of the head. She could never quite accommodate herself to the fact that the face she saw last week on TV was the same as the one now queueing up for unemployment benefit.

Outside the Exchange a pair of Jamaicans were making the best of the sunshine, and he nodded to them as he went in. The day had put the lady with the hearing aid in good humor, and her official inquiry—"No work?"—emerged gay and rhetorical. He answered a plain "No." Often he found himself qualifying it with a cheerful "unfortunately" or "any day now." There was a blunt reality about the query that always shook him slightly, and it needed to be promptly smothered in whimsy.

The sun was now as high as it would get, cool and brilliant in the winter air. He squinted at its beauty and decided to approach his agents' on foot by way of St. James's Park. He walked briskly and had soon generated a feeling of exceptional well-being. He was going to enjoy this walk. He started thinking about *Hamlet* and the well-being became excitement. That was interesting: that Ophelia should supply such a detailed description of Hamlet's appearance during one of his longest absences from the stage. Change of costume intended perhaps? He's just told Horatio he's going "to put an antic disposition on"; then we don't see him again until he feigns madness with Polonius. Change of makeup, even. Maybe to match his bedraggled appearance he should have started growing a beard. It would certainly give that line later on, "plucks off my beard and blows it in my face," an astonishing point. Suddenly, it seemed, he had turned a corner of his mind and stumbled upon the part laid out before him. He passed the other people in the park with a secret, riotous sense of liberty. Gladly he let his thoughts consume him along the Mall, up the steps to Lower Regent Street, and under Piccadilly Circus. In Shaftesbury Avenue he was stopped short by the sound of his name. He turned to see an acquaintance of four years ago, a tall gregarious actor named

Cook with whom he had been on quite good terms in rep. He felt as angry as if he'd been physically sprung on from behind, but swiftly accepted the necessity to mask this sense of inexplicable outrage. His friend's next remark only added to his irritation.

"What are you looking so serious about?"

"Was I looking serious?"

"Like the wrath of God."

"Oh, I was just thinking."

"That won't do you any good. Come and have a drink."

"No, I don't think I'd better."

His friend took him by the arm. "Come on. You need it."

"No, I can't. I've got an appointment," he answered with a shrill firmness that surprised him. Cook looked a little hurt. "Sorry. Look, I'd love to. Only I've got to see my agent, and I'm running late as it is."

"Your agent? Well, that explains it. Who are you with, by the way?"

He gave his agents' name, Kelly and Constable.

"They're good, aren't they? Up and coming."

"Everyone says so. They haven't done a damn thing for me."

"Mine either. Busy at the moment?"

He was relaxing into the comfortable fatuities of a "pro" conversation. They moved out of the way to the side of the footpath and chatted for five minutes. He felt the need to make up in some way for his initial hostility. They'd really been quite close in rep, and had in fact shared a girl friend, or rather he'd taken the girl friend over when Cook had moved on to another job. They sometimes went out drinking, the three of them together. He was beginning to remember it all. He wanted to ask about her.

"How is Jill getting on? Have you heard?"

"She married, chum. Been married a long time."

"No, really? I had no idea."

"Yes. Not long after we left. She gave up that flat and got a job in Nottingham. Was married almost immediately."

"God, I wish I'd known. I'd like to have sent her a present or something."

The marriages of old girl friends were always so final. In a way they were a little like death: the opportunity for a kindness or a shared adventure suddenly withdrawn. In the last eight years he had worked in a dozen or so provincial cities and there were girls in all of them to whom he sometimes felt he could have been nicer.

"She was a really marvelous girl," he said a trifle sentimentally.

"She certainly was. Do you still see Sally?"

"Oh yes, that's still on."

"Well, give her my love. It's time you married her, isn't it?"

He thought he might blush. Perhaps it *was* time he married her. How long had it been? Five years getting on for six. Yet somehow the idea of marriage, *his* marriage, was never quite real to him. He regarded it with something like a child's sense of impropriety when it first applies its knowledge of generation to its own parents. The deductions were indisputable and yet for all that inacceptable. Before parting, the two friends exchanged telephone numbers. It was more a gesture of good faith than a practical step toward keeping in touch. Neither would probably ring. Each new job meant new people; it was foolish to hang on after. The common interest of work and shared ordeals was often all there was.

His agents' offices were in Greek Street. He climbed the two flights of stairs, inwardly preparing himself for fifteen minutes of discomfort. He had been with them two years, but it had taken the best part of that time to feel remotely at ease in that busy den of show business. His visits had only one meaning—he needed a job—so once a week as a matter of principle he stood about the office for a quarter of an hour or so in stubborn if ineloquent testimony to that fact. It was the only way to get things done. After a time his presence would receive uneasy acknowledgment, and a token telephone call would be made on his behalf. Just occasionally there was a job on the other end of the line. The usual climate of the office was of a frantic and resonantly hollow cheerfulness. The girl with the puffy face whose name he was always forgetting was at the switchboard, vaguely out of it; Mildred Kirby was at the reception desk shrieking away over the phone with a ritualistic theatricality that she felt was part of the job; while in the safety of their twin offices the partners, plump ginger Kelly and starch-collared Constable, pursued the immensely busy and mysterious rites of the middleman.

He had long ago made up his mind about agents. Their job consisted of two things: making money out of the theater, and disguising even from themselves their essential redundancy to it. In the case of his own agents Kelly handled the first, Constable the second, which explained why, though Constable was the smoother and better-groomed of the two, it was in the person of Kelly, tie adrift, often unshaven, that the real power of the office was vested. Everyone knew it, including Kelly. He had once been an actor at the Gate Theatre, Dublin, and had worked up a personality of exuberant stage Irish. But he could well afford the role of buffoon. His prosperity told him so, and in any case he despised actors; they persisted in an occupation he'd had the good sense to give up.

From time to time the partners would emerge from their offices to consult Mildred about a telephone number or some detail of a contract. The waiting clients responded to these entrances like a litter of puppies, in a quite defenseless bid for attention. The partners would move through them with the bonhomie of gangsters, blocking overtures with brisk smiles and greetings of exaggerated cheerfulness.

Today he was relieved to find himself the only waiting client. He could almost like Mildred when she was by herself, and began to talk to her about rates and taxes, a subject he knew she was interested in. Constable's head appeared round the door.

"Mildred, darling, what's the name of that producer doing *The Gay and the Damned* for ABC? Why, hello, old lad, just the man I want to see. Come on in."

Constable, too, could be extremely cordial when the pressure was off. He lost a little of his suspicion and gave in to his natural yen to be well-liked.

"Sit down. Make yourself comfortable." It was impossible really to dislike Constable. Often enough he was ushered into this tiny paneled office, seated in the old velvet armchair, and pressed to accept a cup of tea with two sticky chocolate biscuits melting in the saucer—usually when things were slack, but at least it happened. Today the dome of his totally bald head, supported as it were by the twin columns of his elegant silver sideburns, gleamed benevolently in the light of the tiny Czech chandelier.

"*Just* the man I want to see. Are you interested—only as a fill-in, you understand—are you interested in doing a screen commercial? Very nicely paid."

"What's it for?"

"Neutrodor."

"What's that?"

"I gather it's a new deodorant just coming on the market. This could mean a very well paid series, what with repeats and so on . . ."

"No . . . I don't really think I want to do that. Maybe four years ago. You know, you can get typed in that sort of work; I don't think it does one much good . . ." He was struggling to find some practical reasons for declining a job just the mention of which shamed him.

Constable interrupted tactfully. "I understand, old boy, I quite understand. And I agree with you. Completely. I was just thinking about the old bank balance."

"You're right about that. Any TV plays coming up?"

Constable became grave. "I know, old lad. I really do. Things have been a little quiet for you lately, but we'll soon get things moving; don't you worry about that."

The telephone rang. It always did during these chats. He would be with Constable perhaps twenty minutes, and for at least fifteen of them the agent would be on the phone. Safely engaged, Constable could then look his client square in the eye. It was an intimate conspiratorial look, as if they were both handling the phone call together; the client was forced into a sort of charade of participation, smiling at unfathomable jokes, acknowledging subtle shades of guile. It was a performance that left the muscles of the face fatigued and the palms damp.

14

Constable hung up, sighed, and rose abruptly, offering a warm hand. This was a favorite device he had for ending a chat, based on the assumption that business had just been concluded prior to the ringing of the telephone. Whereas in fact business had just failed to begin. With a smile that he tried to make indulgent he took Constable's offered hand and said goodbye.

"I'll come and see you again, next week then."

"Do that. By all means. We're sure to have something on the boil for you in a day or two. So keep your pecker up."

"O.K. Will do," he said, adopting the jargon he detested in order to smooth his departure. "Thanks a lot. Bye, Mildred."

"Bye-bye, darling," said Mildred in a high-pressured whisper, cupping her hand over the telephone receiver to interrupt a conversation of feverish importance.

He was practically out of the door and gone when he heard Kelly's voice behind him. "Mildred, when in God's name are we going to get these letters done?"

With a willingness he immediately regretted he had swung round and greeted the Bigger Noise. "Hello, Kelly!" Everyone called him Kelly.

Kelly walked past him, appearing not to hear while he enlarged on his question to Mildred. Then quite suddenly he turned to bestow simultaneously a broad "Hello" and a sharp slap between the shoulder blades.

"Jesus, boy, what's the matter with you? You're as nervous as a mountain goat. Uncle Kelly won't hurt you."

Mildred's shrieking laughter filled the office.

"You gave me a shock, that's all," he said, rather too quietly.

Mildred again became convulsed over her typewriter. Kelly terminated the fun. "Quick as you can, darling; we've got to get the buggers in the post by tonight." And he shot back into his office.

Once again he said goodbye to Mildred and made decisively for the door. He found himself running down the two flights of stairs to the street. It was no good. He would never manage it. He would never be comfortable with Kelly. It was a pity he depended on him, because at times like this he realized he was one of the few people he really hated.

Anyway, it was over now. He wouldn't need to go back there for another week. Now it was five to one, he was standing in Charing Cross Road feeling a little better in the open air, and wondering what would be the best way to tackle lunch. There was the Curtain Club in Cranbourne Street, where the food wasn't bad but the atmosphere depressing: a cellar full of unemployed actors. His visits to the Curtain Club were like his visits to his agents: achievements of will to give some definition to the limbo of unemployment. He rarely enjoyed them. When out of work he felt spiritless and withdrawn, when in work aggressively genial, and both states of mind had a bad taste afterwards. Still, he went. But only on the days he felt up to it, and this wasn't one of them. He decided he would catch the tube to Hampstead and eat there. Then walk down the hill and do some work. He felt he wanted something nice to happen to him, something unexpected and exciting; he wasn't sure what. If only he could run into some girl, have an adventure, have something happen to him quite gratuitously without labor or connivance, some assurance of a charitable deity. But it wouldn't. He would have to content himself with lunch. When he was out of work his meals propped up the day; they became treats, comforting indulgences, temporary escapes from the dull anguish of inactivity.

He was back in his room by mid-afternoon. The big bed, the armchair, the typewriter on the table—all had been waiting for him with the malign patience of inanimate objects. He suddenly detested his room.

Now that he had been robbed of even the automatic distraction of walking, he found himself overwhelmed with a feeling of petty wretchedness. He tossed himself on to the bed and lay with his hands behind his head staring at the ceiling. He wanted to fall into a deep stupid sleep, to get drunk, to masturbate: to subside out of his own life. He considered in turn these possibilities and dismissed each, not from a position of strength, merely from a weary acknowledgment of their price. There was no point in making things worse. He was going through a bad patch but he had known more unpleasant times. He began an orderly appraisal of his present situation, and after a while felt better. True, he had had a long spell out of work, but he still had money in the bank. Sally was out of town with her parents and he missed her. He was without a girl and this in itself was enough to wreck him. Sometimes he had had three on his hands at once and there had been a different set of problems. Now he had none. Well, things would change. It was just a question of patience.

His thoughts floated in ragged succession between his mind and the ceiling, and their rough design brought with it a nibble of purpose. He lay on his back carefully nourishing this sense of growing impetus. Quite suddenly he swung himself onto his feet, walked over to the table and sat down. Vague temptations assailed him: to walk once around the room, to make a pot of tea, polish his shoes, go to the lavatory; but he had already opened the script and felt himself comparatively safe. He stared at a passage but the words remained obstinately words, so he turned back to the pages he had studied the day before. He started reading and felt a tingle of satisfaction as he realized that most of it had stuck and that he knew it by heart. He stood up and moved about the room muttering the lines, suddenly caught up again in his purposes for them.

Very faintly a noise reached him. It had traveled along the hall, up a flight of stairs, across the landing and through his door. His head rose sharply in response to it. It was the barely perceptible tap of letters falling through the front door onto the hall linoleum —the afternoon post—and it was a sound that had broken the back of many dark afternoons. He dropped his manuscript on the bed and left the room.

There were four letters in all, two for Hess on the top floor (bills by the look of them) and two for him. One looked like the new program for the National Film Theatre, and this pleased him. But it was the second letter that had arrested him. He had recognized at once the rich stiff gray envelope with his own name

B

and address in a fancy red type. Most actors would. Feeling uncomfortably excited, he weighed it in his hand. There was a possibility that it contained his future.

Walking slowly up the stairs, he opened it and read:

DEAR SAMUEL BERESFORD,

Thank you very much for' coming along to audition for us. I am delighted to be able to tell you that Mr. Tom Chester is very keen for you to join us for the season and has you in mind for the following parts:
The Doctor in "The Duchess of Malfi"

Donalbain in "Macbeth"

As regards the final play of the season, "The Way of the World": the casting of this play is still in a very fluid state, and I think you would be advised to leave it with us for the moment. Certainly the part would be a reasonable speaking part, and there would be no question of doubling or walking on for someone of your experience.

As regards money: As you know, the budget with us is strictly limited, and after careful consideration we find we can offer you £16. a week. We regret that this is not open to negotiation. However, from a career point of view and in all other respects, I am sure you would find that a season with us would be immensely rewarding, especially as this season will be Mr. Chester's first as Director of Productions.

If you would like to discuss this offer please ring us at our London office above. If the terms suit you we can draw up the contract immediately.

We look forward to hearing from you.

Yours sincerely,
JOHN MACLACHLAN
Executive, Braddington Playhouse

Sam reentered his room and stood by the table, calming himself. He was on the verge of an absurd frantic excitement, and he suspected it. After all, the parts were not particularly good and the money quite dreadful. He walked the length of the room twice, then sat on the bed and began to read the letter for the second time. "Very keen for you to join us." The hackneyed phrase sparked with possibilities, and his mind went spinning after them. A year's work, a summer by the sea, a stage shared with the princes of the business. It could mean an entirely new life. This indeed was the bait and the hook with which the theater played you: the chance that around the very next corner lay a glittering deliverance. At twenty past three on an afternoon like this he seemed to hold the proof of it in his hand.

1

THE LUGGAGE LABELS, each complete with its flimsy twist of fresh string, sat propped on the shelf above the gas fire. He had found this supply by chance three weeks before in one of his trunks, and had decided to address them then and there: Samuel Beresford, The Festival Playhouse, Braddington Spa, Yorks. His job seemed then a vague general comfort, like a diploma or a medal, and he had inscribed his future across the luggage labels with the solemn idleness of a child bemused by its own name. It had been a pleasant month and an active one, lived in the warmth of exciting prospects. He had found energy for all sorts of things; he had finished learning Hamlet; he had seen friends and gone often to the theater. The new job, too, seemed to attract more work, and he had made a hundred pounds doing four days on a film. Also he had had the contrary pleasure of turning down a television—a well-paid part in a bad play.

Now, however, the new job had become untidy demanding reality. It was twelve o'clock on Saturday night and his train left at 9:30 in the morning. With Sally he had been packing his things and preparing his room for the friend who was to be his subtenant, and they had at least two hours' work before them. As usual he had left it all too late. He stood in the middle of the room, holding the labels in his hand, suddenly exhausted and without will. The accumulated junk of three years had to be accommodated into two trunks and four suitcases. They had sorted it out into three piles: "Braddington," "Stored," and "Thrown Out."

Sally, kneeling by the "Stored" trunk, looked up. "What are you doing?"

"Thinking."

21

She picked out an old cotton sweater from a pile of clothes waiting to be packed. "Look, Sam, do you honestly think you'll ever wear this again?"

He studied the garment. He had worn it as a student and it had faded with many washings. Thus faded he had kept it unworn for seven years. "Might be useful."

"You'll never wear it again."

"Throw it out, then!" He immediately regretted the sharpness of his tone. Sally had returned swiftly to her work, eyes lowered and jaw thrust slightly forward. He had become very familiar with that expression, but it had not yet lost its power to both alarm and enrage him. They had worked all evening in an atmosphere of unspoken constraint and he felt a storm imminent.

Neither had forgotten the row of three nights before. As now, they had been working in the flat, cleaning the small gas cooker. In silence they scrubbed at the dismantled stove, dissociating it, on behalf of the new tenant, from the many meals they had cooked on it together. For the first time the practical implications of Sam's going away seemed real and brutal. She had been very generous about his new job and had tried to share his excitement, but now, he realized, she was about to submit a bill in full for all that it would cost her. Nothing he could say or do could mitigate the scene she was about to embark upon, governed as she was by an implacable female sense of emotional justice.

He had left her for a moment to collect some dirty cups from his room. When he returned he found her standing by the stove, head bent and quite still except for two huge tears gaining momentum in a grievous contest down her face. There was nothing he could say; the wrong and the benefit were all on his side. Their relationship (a word for which a love affair finds a use only when the best is over and a poor consolation for permanent loss) had been phased by scenes such as this. A tour, a season in rep, had taken him guilty and glad like a sailor to sea, leaving her in London to reconsider her evenings and plan other weekends. Often it had seemed that they were on the point of breaking it off completely, but though they discussed it at length, something always restrained

22

them from taking so decisive a move: a kind of fundamental goodwill toward each other that made the idea of a final parting a shade excessive and self-important. Some months later he would return, always to be astonished first by how pretty she looked and second by how capably she had managed without him. Wryly, knowing each other too well, they would begin again.

So once again he was packing, hoping that this time perhaps Braddington would lead the way to the Big Break (absurd but nonetheless expected), and at the same time ashamed that if and when it happened he wanted it to be without Sally. It was an unfair and bitter thought, and he despised himself for it, but she had been the witness to so many disappointments (their attenuated relationship itself seemed to mirror postponed success) that in some primitive part of him he almost regarded her as unlucky. He looked at her now bent over the trunk and searched for at least the reassurance of a pretty face; but all he could see in her was an attitude of clumsy dependence of which he was both afraid and resentful. Was she going to cry again? He softened toward her as he saw her struggle to control herself. They continued silently with the packing. Sally spoke first, and he could tell by the careful pitch of her voice that she was about to say something considered and important. He had misinterpreted her expression.

"Sam. I've been thinking. I don't think I'd better see you this time. I mean come and visit you at Braddington."

What was she about to say? He felt himself shocked into attention as he recognized the approach of what could be for both of them a critical moment.

"How do you mean?"

"I've been thinking—since the other night—and I think we should separate."

"For good?"

"While you're at Braddington. I won't visit you, and you won't see me when you come to London. I think we should try it and see how we get on."

"A sort of trial separation?" The understanding tone he seemed to have adopted sounded awkward and false.

"Yes."

She had surprised him. He had been crediting her with one set of thoughts, sad and rather pathetic ones, and all the time she had been pursuing a line of her own. Ever since their row, in fact, she had been computing the matter with feminine thoroughness and now she had come up with her answer. He suddenly admired her, and felt a rush of gratitude that she should suggest what he secretly wanted. Or did he? The huge affection that he now felt for her seemed to contradict it.

"Will we see each other after the season's over?"

"That's six months away. And in any case you said there might be a tour, and you're almost certainly going to be asked back for another season."

"Sally—do you want us to split up? Completely?"

Her eyes abruptly filled. "You know I don't. It just seems fairer to you, that's all. You want to be left alone to really get on with some work—"

He wished his impulse to escape her for a while had truly such an honorable basis. He recognized her first rationalization on the subject. Then she added, "But we will see each other eventually. I couldn't bear it if we never saw each other again. We'll always know each other, won't we?"

Why had she chosen him, he wondered, why him, to make this precious unacceptable gift of humble love? With other men she had had more than her share of pride and independence.

They had finished packing by a quarter past one. Sally sat on each of the three pieces of taut luggage in turn, while Sam guided and clicked home the fasteners. They blinked at the cleared room, quite gutted of identity, then collapsed with relief and fatigue on the bed. The most tedious, dangerous part of his going away was over. The rest would unroll inevitably like a movie: this last night, a taxi to the station, the train pulling out in the morning. From now on he could safely submit to these events, distilled, as it were, out of the past three weeks. The sharp feelings of departure, buoyed upon the elusive significance of all such events, would sustain them both.

24

Sam took some pennies downstairs to inquire about a later train. Nine-twenty in the morning seemed unnecessarily Spartan. There was one possibility, the ten twenty-five to Birmingham, but it meant changing trains twice and once changing stations. With two trunks and three small grips in his charge this was not a very attractive alternative. He discussed it with Sally. She pretended to be impartial, but he knew she wanted him to catch the Birmingham train and he decided upon it. It was a small enough concession to make, and hardly a concession, he reflected, if it meant she would be in a good mood in the morning. Though this was unfair. She was usually wonderful when it actually came to the train on the platform. And of the two of them he would be the one to value that extra hour in bed. He set the old red alarm clock for nine (made in England, bought in Australia ten years ago, and still laboriously ticking), and they undressed for bed.

The alarm broke their sleep at nine o'clock, sounding louder and more urgent than on other mornings, and they rose quickly with a hollow sense of business to be done. Sam washed and dressed while Sally boiled water. She had brought over from her own place small quantities of tea and sugar with some milk in a medicine bottle to make this last morning cup. They sat in silence drinking it.

"Would you like me to come to the station?"

"Would you like to?"

"If you want me to."

"Of course I do. But don't if you don't want to. You could go back to bed."

"No, I don't want to do that."

"Well, then, come. Lovely."

They arrived at Euston with twenty-five minutes in hand. The taxi driver had contrived a formidable list of extras, strapping three cases at sixpence each into the luggage space beside his seat where at least two would have been comfortably situated inside with the passengers. A porter relieved the cab of its luggage while Sam paid the driver. He felt his usual impulse to overtip, restrained it and settled for an exact fifteen percent. They walked along the platform behind the drumming iron wheels of the porter's barrow. The big trunks were stowed in the luggage van; the smaller pieces the porter hoisted into the rack of an empty compartment. Once again there was a tip to be negotiated.

"What did you give him?" asked Sally.

"Half a crown."

"Oh, Sam. I never give more than a shilling!"

Undoubtedly women were better at this sort of thing. They kept their pride out of it.

Sam began to tease her about the horrors of the journey ahead of him, about the earlier train that he had been foolish enough to be persuaded to miss, and now she was displaying one of her nicest traits. It was something she always saved up for the last few minutes of a departure such as this, a harmonizing of herself, in which was implicit a kind of blessing of what he was about to do. He felt suddenly touched by the huge preserve of goodwill that in spite of everything still existed between them. She looked very pretty, both gay and grave, and entirely relaxed.

"I hope you like your lunch. It cost a fortune."

The day before she had bought him a chicken leg, an avocado pear (to remind him of Australia), a few black olives, an apple and a slice of cheese cake, and she had packed them in a tin to eat on the train.

Her ability to leave such a last impression of herself when they separated was one of her sweetest woman's gifts. She was as good when the train pulled out as she was bad when the train pulled in. He frequently dreaded being met by her after an absence. (Meeting *her* off a train was all right for some reason.) She had a way of walking down the platform toward him against the drift of disembarking passengers that almost seemed a deliberate provocation of his misgivings. Some infallible instinct prescribed the wrong clothes, the wrong expression, and his heart would fall as a host of unwanted memories roused themselves.

Sam glanced out of the compartment window at the clock, whose huge hands, chopping off the minutes in tiny visible jerks, made time suitably portentous.

26

"Two minutes left. You'd better get off."

"Yes," said Sally, not moving.

"Go on, nitwit. Unless you want a Sunday in Birmingham."

"Yes, please. Lovely!"

He pinched her and she jumped up protesting. She left the train and they talked through a window in brief general sentences, glancing up and down the platform in the pauses for a sign of departure, careful to safeguard the fragile gestures of affection until last. Along the length of the platform doors were slamming; then the guard signaled. He leaned toward her and kissed her.

"Goodbye, kitten."

"Goodbye, cat."

Their familiar endearments shed the weight of habit and doubt and sounded as fresh as they might have five years earlier. The train shuddered, then began to move.

"Hope you like your lunch."

" 'Course I will. Look, get in touch if anything goes wrong."

"All right."

"Let me know how things are going."

"Do you think we ought to write?"

"God, yes. If it's anything important."

"Good luck with the season."

"Thanks."

"I'll save the notices if you like."

"All right."

The train was gathering speed and she stopped walking with it.

"Bye."

"Bye."

"Bye."

They waved, and he watched her diminishing down the curve of the platform. He lost first her expression, then her face, then the colors of her clothes, and marveled as he always did at the superb melodrama of railway farewells: that incomparable tracking shot. Just before she was out of sight he saw her turn and swiftly walk away. Even in miniature, a tiny speck, her personality was apparent in the act of thus making up her mind. The train pulled clear of

27

the shadow of the station, was severed from it by some morning sun which cut into the compartment, and he fell back into his seat alone with his desolate puzzled affections. Sooty brick walls topped by the backs of neglected houses moved solemnly past the window.

The journey would not be a boring one. A sense of loss more painful than he had expected had sharpened his responses. Beside him were his two Sunday papers, and he knew in advance that today their contents would seem urgent and important. Then there was his lunch to look forward to. For the moment, though, it was enough to lean his head against the glass of the compartment window and allow the tattoo of the swiftly passing landscape to set the pace for his own bestirred thoughts. He had much to think about.

The route of his journey was practically a map of his first six years as an actor, and the towns the train would pass through represented six months, a year, sometimes only a fortnight of his life. Leeds, Sheffield, Derby, Birmingham: all had had their reps, some good, some appalling, all as he had known them changed and largely forgotten. He would remain grateful for the employment they had given him, but it was less easy to be charitable about the sour lessons they had had to teach. He had felt as much a foreigner among the lines he had to learn as he did walking to work in the mornings through the somber streets. Sometimes late at night, when after the evening performance he returned to his room to work until two or three learning an act of next week's play for rehearsal the following morning, the appalling emptiness of the drawing-room comedy he labored to memorize and the gray town it was expected to amuse had seemed to exist in sinister reciprocity. Usually, he found himself straight lead in such plays. People said he had the face for it. "You remind me of the Prince of Wales that was," a town councilor's wife had once said to him, as if she had put her finger unerringly on the true source of his talent, and Sam had been embarrassed to the point of horror.

But it was not the memory of the bad plays that now in some way troubled him; it was the occasional good one. The week the company had spent rehearsing *The Glass Menagerie* had been a prodigy of work and expectation. What had they expected? God knows. What do actors ever expect when they put passion into their work? Something not much less than a Second Coming. It had been the middle of winter, and the management, sensing a bad week, had economized on heating. Those who came sat huddled in overcoats while a cast in shirt-sleeves, trembling in the wings as in a huge icebox, readied themselves to suspend disbelief. Nonetheless there had been three really fine shows that week: the first night on Monday, the Friday night and the first house Saturday. The applause had had the authentic shock behind it, and one man had cheered. Months later, recovering from the season on an Atlantic beach in Spain (so essentially like an Australian beach that he might never have left home), he looked back upon that week as he might upon a fever. What had they been hoping for in the middle of winter? He felt hot sand yielding under his bare feet, and felt a little foolish.

There had been other reps, of course, to which he had eventually graduated, which had done good plays well and had them justly received, companies that offered two weeks to a month to rehearse. But any memory he had of the provinces was always overshadowed by his first two and a half years in weekly rep, and more particularly by the first job of his career. On another Sunday, not unlike today, he had made his first train journey north, and had been introduced through a compartment window to another England. The North: unlike Parliament Square, the Sussex Downs, even the East End, it was not a reality with which he had been familiar, even by hearsay, since childhood. In Australia it had been the vaguest of rumors, an image not exported. Now he was journeying through a terrain of such bleakness that it unrolled before him with the definition of melodrama, and melodrama apparently of which he alone was audience. Was no one else on the train stirred or troubled by what they saw? Gray towns drowning in lakes of smoke; hills plowed into rows of terraces that presented against the sky silhouettes as sharp and ugly as blades of rusty serrated saws. He had been astonished by it. His own country, he realized, had been largely populated by Englishmen

29

rebelling from this. He was not to know, of course, that his indignation was some years too late, that the worst abuses were long over. However, his outrage, as the train carried him toward a destiny of country houses built of trembling canvas flats, with entrances through french windows with no panes in them, was no less sincere for being mistimed. He was not so much discovering England as discovering himself: a Rip Van Winkle waking after a hundred years abroad to the great slumbering crime of industrial England.

At 6:58 that night, only a few minutes late, the train pulled into the terminal station of Braddington Spa.

There were no porters waiting along the platform or hawking their services down the corridors as there might have been in London, so he had to go in search of one. Near the ticket barrier he found a cheerful old man wearing the right cap, who seemed quite surprised that his help should be asked for. They set off along the side of the emptying train toward the luggage van.

Some thirty yards away Sam saw a leg and a back dismount in grave isolation from a compartment door. The man wore a belted camel's hair coat and had heaved an expensive piece of luggage onto the platform. He straightened up and Sam recognized the back of a celebrated head: it was Ivan Spears. He was facing them now and, to Sam's astonishment, had raised his hand and was signaling him. Bewildered, Sam continued to walk toward him. Once again the famous actor waved, and this time he opened his mouth to accompany the gesture with a single word of anxious command. It sounded like "poor." They were almost face to face before Sam understood: he had been hailing not Sam but Sam's porter.

The porter explained that he was with the other gentleman, whereupon for apparently the first time Ivan turned his attention on Sam. There was something glazed and hostile about the look. Sam sensed the mind flick behind the eyes, and was certain he had been recognized as an actor. They would be working together tomorrow; should he introduce himself? He hesitated, mesmerized by the proximity of so famous a set of features. Sam had seen this face measuring six feet across in the first film he had ever been permitted to attend: Ivan Spears starring in *Cromwell* at the Rose Bay Wintergarden the Christmas of 1936. Now he was making some rapid new discoveries about it. The face was somehow smaller and, even in its celebrated coarseness, more delicate than he would have expected, and more vividly tinted. It was rather like looking at a perfectly executed miniature—that happened to smell of whisky.

They had faced each other no more than a couple of seconds when Ivan turned away. The porter led on toward the luggage van and Sam followed. He felt disturbed. He could easily have offered to share his porter with the older actor; perhaps they could have shared a taxi. It would have been politic no less than thoughtful. Instead shyness and pride had made him behave clumsily. His anxiety seemed as trivial as the incident itself, and this further exasperated him. But the idea persisted that he had made a poor start with this his first encounter of the season.

He was soon preoccupied with his luggage. He counted five pieces into a taxi and searched for the crumpled letter bearing the address of his digs. The driver took him by way of the waterfront. As the car turned into its length, the abrupt smell of the sea was unmistakably there, keeping them company on the right. Sam was deeply excited. He had been brought up on the beaches around Sydney, and there had been times of the year when he was more of a fish than a boy. Once the sea at noon had beckoned out of sight to an immensely distant Europe. Now the same presence brought messages from an even remoter shore, that of his growing up. He felt the stir of innocent predatory expectation. It had become thrilling to be in a strange place with new people to meet and new work to grapple with, to sit mute in a taxi while strange lights passed by outside. Priorities began to sort themselves out in his mind. First he would locate his bed for the night; this would rid him of his principal anxiety. Then during the next few days he would begin to hunt out the better eating places. By the end of the week, doubtless, he would have started looking at the girls. Various jobs had accustomed him to this instinctual program, but he had rarely anticipated it with such relish. It gave loneliness a wolfish pleasure.

The Ozone Private Hotel was situated not far from where the Parade, after proceeding a mile and a half beside the sea, turned inland. A steep grassy embankment continued the line of the Parade, and on top of it was built a row of curiously exposed Edwardian terraced houses. The Ozone Private Hotel was the third along. With the driver's assistance Sam got his luggage stacked outside the front door and rang the bell. He had the letter in his hand and checked it again for the landlady's name. In the illumination of a well-weathered glass panel proclaiming OZONE HOTEL OYSTER BAR he read:

DEAR MR. BERESFORD,
   re your advert in the Braddington Herald I have a flatlet which may suit you but the builders are in at the moment. I could let you have a room in the hotel until the flatlet is ready when you could view. My terms are three pounds ten bed and breakfast.
                                         Yours truly,
                                         DOREEN SHRAPNEL (Mrs.)

The door opened, and landlady and guest confronted each other. Sam was aware of a small woman (why had he expected her to be large?) wearing a red overcoat and a small black cloche hat. She looked as if she had just returned from a day directing some small but prosperous provincial business—a hat shop, perhaps, or a dry-cleaning establishment—except that today was Sunday. She had startling eyes, which Sam guessed must always carry that glint of outrage, even, as they were now, when glazed over with genteel welcome.

"Mrs. Shrapnel?"

"Yes?"

"I'm Samuel Beresford."

"Oh, come in, Mr. Beresford." She spoke a careful refined Birmingham.

"I've got rather a lot of luggage."

"Well, put it in the hall for now."

Placing his bags in pairs on the linoleum floor was rather like staking a claim; one worry was nicely out of the way—a roof for the night. However, Mrs. Shrapnel's best behavior was still disturbingly infectious, and he followed her in a kind of polite tiptoe into a room on the left.

"Sit down. Make yourself at home."

"Thank you."

"I was expecting you earlier," said Mrs. Shrapnel sweetly but steadily.

He pictured her sitting here in her black hat, face carefully made up, since midafternoon, and he hastened to explain. "Yes, I had to catch a later train. I hope I haven't upset your Sunday."

"Oh, no! I was staying in all day in any case. We're very quiet this time of the year."

The room they were in had a little pink bar at one end on which stood two lamps made of Chianti bottles. The wallpaper was of a bamboo design, and by the door was a large colored print of a young beauty with a green skin, indeterminately Oriental. Here and there signs of an earlier taste stubbornly held their ground. There was an upright piano against one wall notwithstanding the presence nearby of a large TV set, and half a plaster mallard took wing eternally on the wall above the beige-tiled fireplace.

"I haven't been here long, you know," said Mrs. Shrapnel, apropos of nothing save his thoughts, and Sam jumped slightly. "Three years next August. I wanted to redecorate the whole place. Throw everything out and start from scratch. But it takes time."

Sam agreed. She pointed to the pink bar and eyed it critically. "I had that built the year before last," she said. "But you can't get staff, you know. Not when you need them. It's useful for storing magazines. In any case we have the Oyster Bar facing the front. You'll see that later."

Sam said he was looking forward to that.

"Do you know Owen Digby?" Mrs. Shrapnel was dispensing topics of conversation like a card player revealing his trumps, one at a time. Owen Digby, once moderately successful in British films, was, he felt, the ace.

"Don't know him personally. Know *of* him, of course."

"Owen Digby? You don't know Owen? I thought you were sure to have bumped into him on your travels."

"There are so many actors . . ." said Sam weakly, sensing he had failed her.

"He's a *great* friend of mine, is Owen. He used to stay with me. Not here. When I had the flat in Birmingham. Such a nice man. Such fun. Had me in stitches from morning till night. He was working at the Rep there."

"He's done very well, hasn't he?"

"Oh, yes. Film star and all that. But you could always tell, you know, with Owen. I always knew he'd do well."

Sam wondered what he could do, right from the start, to indicate similarly sure prospects. Then he remembered Owen Digby had gone to Hollywood four years ago and hadn't been heard of since.

"Laugh! Dear me! I used to lie on the kitchen floor, my daughter will tell you, lie there on the lino laughing. I still get a card every Christmas."

Sam nodded.

"I've got a photo upstairs. I'll show you one day. Nice one smoking a pipe. Signed, of course."

They sat in silence for a moment, then suddenly Mrs. Shrapnel was on her feet. "I'll show you your room, then."

She led him up one flight of stairs, then another, describing the room and its facilities as they went. "There's the bathroom and toilet one floor down. I've put you at the top so I won't have to move you at the weekend. There's hot and cold in all the rooms. The flatlet should be ready in about a fortnight's time. I think you'll be quite comfortable here till then."

She had ushered him into a very small attic room with a window above his head that levered open onto the roof. It seemed clean and well-equipped, and its confined comforts quite appealed to him

"This is fine. A womb of a room."

To his astonishment Mrs. Shrapnel laughed loudly. He felt the shade of Owen Digby retreat a step.

34

"Now what about the flat?"

"The flatlet? You'd like to see that now? There's no light. It'll be a bit dark.'

"May as well."

Mrs. Shrapnel seemed delighted at the prospect of some night exploring. "Come on. We'll get the torch."

United now by a common interest and one successful joke, landlady and guest made their way out into the black back garden. A cat leaped off a wastebin and brushed past them.

"All right, Majesty, all right," said Mrs. Shrapnel. "Only the cat."

Ahead, intercepting the line of the sea, Sam made out the bulk of what appeared to be a garage. The beam of Mrs. Shrapnel's torch preceded them, so that the source of her conversation seemed now to be a paving stone, a flower bed, a concrete gnome and finally a newly painted green door.

"This used to be a garage," she was saying, "but the Corporation took away the road so they could extend the front. There's only a footpath there now. So we thought it might convert into a nice little flat."

She unlocked the door and Sam smelled fresh cement and brick dust. He thought of the building sites that as a boy he had helped to explore at dusk when the workmen had gone home.

"We've put in a new floor, and built a wall at the end there for the toilet and basin. Then there's a recess here for the cooker. We're getting a nice new bed as well. The window has a nice view of the sea."

The torch played over various signs of incompletion and came to rest on a mute pile of tools and materials in one corner. In the weak torchlight they looked as if they had been left there undisturbed forever. It struck Sam that it was extraordinary that any human undertaking ever managed to elude the frightful risks of inertia. The making of a window frame became a skill full of mystery. He decided he would enjoy living here.

Mrs. Shrapnel locked up the flatlet and they started toward the house.

"There's a door in the wall leading to the front that you can use in the daytime," said Mrs. Shrapnel, "but we have to bolt it after dark because of the Teddy boys."

Sam was on his guard. "How do I get in, then?"

"You'll have to come through the house. I'll let you have a front door key."

He began to brood. Were his visitors to be vetted? Were there rules? There were some questions he would have to ask. They were back in the hall now, standing by his luggage, and he braced himself to put them.

"You don't mind visitors after the show, I suppose?"

Mrs. Shrapnel endeavored to conceal the close attention she gave this question. "Visitors? No, I don't mind visitors."

Sam continued, laying his questions carefully, one topping the other like bricks. "I may have friends coming up from London to see the plays, and I'd rather like to be able to put them up overnight."

Mrs. Shrapnel smiled a smile of noncomprehension. "But where would they sleep?"

"Well, I thought I might buy one of those cheap camping beds that come to bits when you're not using them . . ."

Mrs. Shrapnel didn't answer. Behind a blank expression he knew she was thinking furiously. He improvised. "You know, they've got bits of wire like a 'W' underneath and stand about six inches off the floor."

"It's a bit crowded down there for two," she said at last.

"It wouldn't be often, mind you. Just now and then, when a friend came up from London."

There was another long pause, then very slowly she spoke. "I expect that would be all right, then."

"Oh, good," said Sam so casually it was almost inaudible.

"You wouldn't make too much noise," she added hastily. "I mean, I have to think of the other guests, you see."

"No! No! I hate noise myself."

"As long as you don't expect me to buy another bed. I mean strictly speaking that's a flatlet, not a flat. I only wanted to let it to one."

Sam felt much relieved. Her concern, it seemed, had been chiefly economic.

"Good heavens, I'd have no one to *stay*. Just occasionally overnight."

"That'd be all right, then. Of course there might be a spare room in the hotel. That'd be more comfortable for them, wouldn't it?"

Sam conceded that it might be. The agreement was mainly in his favor and he gladly allowed Mrs. Shrapnel her escape clause.

"Well!" He slapped his hands together. "I'd better start getting this luggage upstairs."

He felt positively high-spirited, and even forgot for the moment that though he had the flat he had yet to find the girl.

"Have you had anything to eat? I could bring you a sandwich into the lounge and you could watch telly."

"That's very kind of you. But I think I'll go out. I want to explore the town. Then I've got some more work to do before tomorrow."

"They certainly make you work, you theater folk, don't they? Even of a Sunday! Owen was always having to go to his room and learn plays. I don't know how you do it, honestly, I don't."

Sam had forgotten about Owen. Surely he must have created a favorable precedent where actors and their sexual needs were concerned. Mrs. Shrapnel was sure to understand.

It took him four trips to get his belongings upstairs, but he had energy to spare and enjoyed applying it. As he heaved at the baggage, his thoughts grazed happily on the possibilities of his new life. Rehearsals began tomorrow; he felt ready for them. In a week or two he would be in his flat. He sat on his bed and panted. At the moment all he had was a small attic room and his own company. Temporarily, though, it was enough. This was where he belonged, in a room like this, adrift at the beginning of a new job. The slate was clean again, and there were some lovely exciting things waiting to be inscribed upon it. A new job, a new girl; he submitted entirely to whatever this latest stretch of his life had to offer.

37

2

HE WAS AWAKENED by a bar of sunlight above his head. The sea was there, and, hardly awake, he wondered if the others were going down to the beach for a surf before breakfast. What others? With a blink he was properly awake, aware that his landlady had failed to provide his roof window with any sort of curtain. The attic room was oppressively brilliant and warm. He reached for his watch and was exasperated to find that it was barely eight o'clock. He had stayed up till one-thirty studying the play and had set his alarm for nine-thirty. He climbed out of bed and tried to rig up his bath towel as a curtain, but blazing sunlight penetrated the room on either side of it. He returned to bed, his towel swung above him like a luridly striped hammock, and he knew he would not sleep again. He cursed and put the pillow on top of his head, but he was too wide-awake and out of temper even for sexual reverie. He stubbornly refused to get up, however, and lay there awake until, just ten minutes before the alarm went, he fell into a sullen doze.

Mrs. Shrapnel had his breakfast waiting for him at ten o'clock as arranged. He took his time over it, savoring the novelty of such an unexpected quantity of food at this hour of the day; once installed in the flatlet at the bottom of the garden, he would doubtless revert to his customary pot of tea and two buttered digestive biscuits, but for the present he ate well, balking only at a smear of solidified yolk on the edge of his plate. Extra food went some way toward making up for lost sleep. He sipped the dreadful bottle coffee and luxuriated his way through Mrs. Shrapnel's *Daily Express*. She cleared away the plates, noticed the uneaten yolk but decided not to comment on it (a week from now, thought Sam, such commendable reticence would be forgotten), and left him with forty-five spare minutes before the day would start to move. He decided to have a look at the sea.

There it was as calm as a lake, and he knew he might wait forever before any waves disturbed it. It was the ocean, but not the one he knew. He tried to imagine a hundred yards out to sea a steep green bank sweeping stealthily in a great line toward the beach, then breaking with a clap and a roar, then unrolling like a white carpet all the way to the sand. But this emasculated sea seemed to deny even the possibility of such a thing. He looked along the beach; it was fenced across every fifty yards or so by black wooden groins that made of it a series of orderly pens, a kind of stockyard for seasiders. How long would the groins last if a Pacific storm blew up overnight? He felt privy to arrogant secrets. Nonetheless, it was very good to smell the salty wind and feel the absurdity of wearing shoes to walk on sand. He stood gazing out over the blank sea, and ten minutes quickly passed. The set of his face began to have a familiar feel about it. It was a sea face, not expectant, not resigned, but idling intently in a zone between. Something caught his eye. Far away, almost at the horizon, a small crease of white had appeared and as quickly gone. Except that it was unlikely, he could have sworn that it was a wave breaking. He waited three or four minutes and the same thing happened again. He waited a third time and was certain that he had seen a wave. There was probably a shallow sandbank out there acting as a sort of harbor and keeping the inshore water calm. He wondered how big the waves were (probably small though it was hard to tell) and if one could take a motorboat out there and have a look. Once again a mile away a breaking wave blinked white.

It was time to go to work. He left the beach and set off toward the theater. He wondered what was ahead of him. By the evening he would be exhausted, not by work, of which there would be little done today, but by the hundred subterranean adjustments and tiny alarms that were part of the first day in any new company. He was not nervous at the prospect; curiosity and the usual wayward hope had made him impatient to get on with it; he was tired of seeing his new job in terms of rosy expectation. It was time reality offered its stern corrective (and he had no doubt that it would).

Braddington was not unfamiliar to him. He had visited it on four occasions, overnight sallies specifically to see the plays, though now the performances were dim beside his other memories of the town. All too often they had secretly disappointed him. He recalled instead spending half an afternoon in a tea shop reading a paperback of *Howards End,* and on another occasion buying a cheap plastic mackintosh and going for a long walk in the rain along the coast. These were his ways of filling in the day as worthily as he could while waiting on the evening performance. After it was over he would summon up his resolution and go backstage. There were generally a few friends or acquaintances in the company for him to approach, though he hardly relished doing so. What had a great play to do with this narrow world of rumor and grievance? He envied the actors their jobs, but dreaded the betrayal that seemed implicit in the bias of their judgments and the look in their eyes that begged for indiscriminate approval. It was no comfort to know that in the same position, taking off makeup after a show and hungry for some vague reward, he would be behaving in just the same way.

Sam left a street of prosperous red-brick Victorian houses and mounted the raised footpath of a Georgian terrace. He had approached the Old Town. Braddington was really a town in two. To the south was the celebrated eighteenth-century Spa, with its terraces, its Parade, its Royal Crescent and its Playhouse. To the north, where once a fishing village had huddled in close dependence about the small harbor, was the New Town, a minor Blackpool that had mushroomed up at the turn of the century. It had a pier of sorts, many amusement parlors, fish-and-chips shops, and rows and rows of jerry-built seaside lodgings.

When Virgil Graves had rescued the Playhouse from its fate as a furniture repository in the late twenties, one of his hopes had been to join hands with the two towns, and he always insisted that the national success of his venture was its greatest failure. Before the London press discovered him, his theater had been entirely a local affair. Then a famous German producer touring England on holiday wandered in to a matinee, returned to London and acclaimed the production in a newspaper interview. The little theater in Yorkshire became news. In the last month of what up till then had not been a particularly well-attended season the Playhouse was packed, and the residents of South Braddington found themselves the beneficiaries of the smartest theater in England. Originally they had petitioned against the reopening of the Playhouse on the grounds that it would attract the wrong element of person; now their complaint was that the London demand made it impossible for local people to get seats. As for the holidaymakers in the north town, they soon caught the scent of parked Bentleys and evening dress, and decided if they had not done so already that it was not for them.

Virgil Graves worked at his theater for ten seasons. Though the theater had a small capacity and seats were cheap, the productions were lavish and meticulous. It was rumored he had sunk as much as a quarter of a million pounds of his own money in the Playhouse. (His father had owned a mill, if not mills, and no one knew how rich he was, especially as he preferred to dress like a clean-shaven tramp.) He had wanted a theater for the North, a regional theater that would become as much a part of the annual holiday by the sea as the disconsolate donkeys tethered in a line at the north end of the beach. Instead, he found himself with a theater where evening dress was becoming de rigueur. So, baffled in his attempts to return something to those people whose lives the building of his family fortune had helped to suck gray, Virgil Graves gave his theater into other hands. The standard and the reputation were maintained, though eventually all pretense at serving a regional need was abandoned and it was decided to make the price of seats economic.

Sam had arrived at the stage door. The adrenalin started to flow. Nerves were so much a condition of his job that he was able now to disregard all but the most serious crises. He could not escape the symptoms of nerves—in his case a dampening of the palms—but he paid them no real heed. A motor scooter drew up and the helmeted rider dismounted. He was stocky and young and a stranger to Sam though obviously a member of the company. He tried out a smile, bold and insecure, and Sam smiled back. Three other young men were approaching the stage door. One of them Sam remembered from drama school nine years ago; Richard Jones had been his name then, but he had changed it later to Richard Wayland and as such had been doing rather well. This was his third season at Braddington and he had graduated to quite good parts. Sam remembered him as a good actor, though temperamentally rather too bland. Today he was very glad of the familiar face, and together they entered the stage door. There was Alfred, the stage-doorman, sitting behind his counter and nodding a greeting to all who came through. He was seventy-three, snowy-haired and benign, quite flawlessly cast, and this was the most taxing part of his year: fixing new names to strange faces at the beginning of the season. Sam asked after mail to facilitate an introduction. He saw Alfred's attention carefully focus as he gave his name, and he found himself pronouncing it as over the telephone to assist the old man in his courteous task.

"First day we all meet on stage," said Richard Wayland. "After that we mainly work in the rehearsal room. The stage is clear then for work on the set." He seemed to enjoy knowing his way around, and the newcomers were only too glad to play up to it. Would one go off him, thought Sam, the way one always did with the boy who seemed so friendly on the first day of school?

They climbed a short flight of stairs, turned left, then abruptly right, proceeded along a passage, then down another flight of stairs to face two heavy swing doors. It was the usual backstage maze, and he felt impinge upon him the metallic clap of their footfalls on the cement stairs, the smell of disinfectant, and the complex of pipes running above their heads along the passage. A couple of months from now this obscure journey would have become so much a matter of routine that he would forget even the color of the walls. Now they lowered at him inescapably: two shades of gray, dark below, light above, glossed over corridors of bare brick.

A heavy swing door led them onto the stage. There, suddenly facing them, was the great shadowy cavern of the auditorium, with the company down by the footlights cut out against it. Sam walked down the raked stage toward it, much as earlier that morning he had walked down a beach to look at the sea. There it was: part challenge, part promise, part threat, the focus of all these people's lives for the next six months. It was a beautiful eighteenth-century interior, and he found it very exciting. There were stalls, then up a few steps the old pit, and above two sweeping horseshoe circles. Very high up and precipitously tilted was the gallery. Even unlit, the elaborate gilt work glowed from pink-and-gray walls. It was like the interior of some huge exquisite seashell.

"Nice, isn't it?" said Richard Wayland.

"Fantastic."

"Not so good to play in, though. Tricky acoustics. There are dead patches under those circles. You have to bash it out more than you'd think."

Sam found he knew about half the company; some, like Richard Wayland, were friends stretching back to drama school, others people he had shared jobs with at one time or another. These familiar faces constituted the solid middle of the company where he himself was placed. Unknown to him for the most part were, on the one hand, the top of the company, the established stars, and, on the other, the bottom of the company, the twelve men and three girls nearly all under twenty-five who would spend their season carrying spears or (if lucky) gasping out with rather disproportionate intensity a solitary line or two.

A plain girl with a keen stage-management look approached him bearing a tin tray, on which, in a puddle of coffee, stood a number of hot full cups. He chose one with a broken handle which happened to be larger than the others, commented on his guile, and the girl—not really hearing but smiling strenuously, her top lip bright with sweat—moved on. Sipping his coffee (too much Nescafé, too much milk, not enough sugar), he eddied in among the new company like an iron filing into a magnetic field.

As he greeted the people he knew, he fought to maintain an attitude cordial yet calm and not too impressed; in the circumstances it seemed the civilizing one. Inwardly, however, he felt the pull of a less sober configuration of feelings. His curiosity about the famous faces was violent and, he felt, a little obscene. He eyed them now, greeting each other with baroque gestures of affection, much as they might at a garden party, strolling about the stage as though it had all the welcome and spring of green turf. One thing he knew: when his generation of actors was middle-aged and successful, they would not choose this particular way of being insincere. Their way would be all their own.

Equally unreasonable, he was sure, was his impatience with the faces he didn't know at all. The spear carriers were scattered about the stage like statuary, and statuary monotonously the work of a single hand. The fervent intention of each to be different rendered them all identical. They were frozen in poses of studied relaxation, each bent on projecting an image of talent and keenness, each, in fact, padlocked deep inside a pretense and miserably constrained.

First days were dreadful. A good director would take these same people, gently strip them of their defenses and within a week return their individuality to them shining, so that they surprised themselves with it, surprised him, surprised an audience. But good directors were rare. Sam knew with what impossible hopes each was beginning the season. Today was the first assault on those hopes.

Someone clapped his hands for attention. Abruptly, the stage was silent. The stage staff, whispering fraught instructions to each other, tiptoed through the still company setting up rows of chairs. First the stars, then the rest of the company began to find themselves seats. Left standing and facing the assembly with their backs to the auditorium were the stage manager, whose name Sam had yet to learn (Terence Someone), then Jock MacLachlan, the producer, and beside him—assuming a demeanor of extreme modesty which Sam could hardly believe he felt—stood Tom Chester. Some little distance away, dictating pad in hand, and caught, it seemed, in a moment of indecision as to whether to sit or stand (a pose which lent itself to a vulgar interpretation), was the senior secretary of the organization, Olive Delmer.

Jock MacLachlan began to speak: "Now, I won't keep you long, but there are just one or two things I'd like to say before the real business of the morning begins." Here he gave a deferential look to the director, who managed to accept it and shrug it off in one boyish gesture. "First of all I want to say welcome to the entire company. We hope—no, we believe—this season is going to be one of the most exceptional we've had. The company is a very strong one indeed"—Tom Chester nodded—"and we hope it will be a happy one as well. Those of you who don't know where my office is—well, anyone will tell you. I want you to feel free to come and see me whenever you like, and for whatever reason." Although Jock's remarks were spoken at large, it was obvious that they were intended for the lower half of the company. He continued. "Any of you, for instance, who are having trouble with digs, don't forget we have a digs list upstairs. Now two important points. Insurance cards as soon as possible, please. And, this is vital, measurements for the wardrobe. If any of you haven't given measurements, could you go to the wardrobe, 24 George Street, just as soon as possible, and Eric there will look after you. Well, I think that's all, and once again welcome."

He smiled at Tom and resigned his place. He would now return to his office.

"Thank you, Jock," murmured Tom. "Oh, and thank you, Olive. There's no need for you to stay if you don't want to." There was indeed no need for her to stay except that in the past this had been her privilege, on first days at least. For a moment she seemed nonplused but soon rallied, and with a big wagging public smile that sought to explain everything she followed Jock off the stage. Tom watched her go, then took a small step forward.

"I'm Tom Chester. Well, I think we may as well get straight down to work. Oh"—he paused and smiled broadly—"welcome, of course." The company murmured amusement. Jock was not present to share the joke, which could conceivably be construed as at his expense. Sam was uncomfortable. The last thing he needed to begin the season was a sharp dislike for the director. He was hardly in a position to afford it. He turned his head, and across the assembly his glance collided momentarily with that of a small excitable character actor he had worked with in a television play.

A like mind, apparently. This was some comfort, though not much, if, as he now suspected, the look had been observed.

Tom Chester continued. He spoke at length about the play, and it was obvious that he had done his homework, at least the academic side of it. He spoke of dates and sources, referred to Webster's other work, drew attention to the similarity of the characters in *The White Devil* to those in *The Duchess* and explained that for this reason he felt free to borrow a line or two of text from the earlier play. He read passages of criticism from Eliot and F. L. Lucas and concluded with Rupert Brooke's dictum about maggots writhing in an immense night. Sam listened and was much relieved to find himself interested by and at peace with what was being said (though admittedly it provided little room for contention).

Tom next dealt with the treatment he had in mind for the play. "This is a play about horror. And unless every member of the cast, right down to the spear carriers, feels that horror, we won't succeed with it. You've all got to be writhing maggots!" He laughed, but it was obvious that he had found his text for the production and would stick to it. "We've got to create this atmosphere of darkness and cruelty, and really use the stage to suggest currents of evil moving through this enclosed Renaissance world." Sam caught sight of Ivan Spears sitting on the extreme left of the front row. The star had been listening to Tom with what appeared to be approbation. With these new generalities, however, he seemed less comfortable. He was staring intently at the toes of his shoes. Tom went on to talk about the set, the costumes and the lighting. He then discussed the characters, designating a certain specific "humour" to each: the Cardinal, for instance, was to mirror Worldly Corruption. It was essential, he explained, that they be strongly contrasted.

"Drama is conflict," he said with an air of finality, "and conflict is what we must find in this great play." But he hadn't concluded. Almost as an afterthought he added, "Oh, about the cuts. What with the new stuff we're putting in and the play being long anyway, there may have to be a few more cuts than those marked in your scripts. Otherwise the audience will never get home." Sam felt his stomach drop. He was sitting bolt upright with attention. "Anyway, you'll find a complete breakdown of the play on the rehearsal notice board, and the scenes that may have to go are marked in red."

That was the end of the morning's rehearsal. They would meet again after lunch to read the play, and in the meantime use what was left of the morning to have measurements taken, to supply biographies to the publicity department and so forth. Sam left his seat and went straight to the rehearsal notice board. He fumbled for the script in his pocket and carefully flicked through the last act to find his scene, doing his best not to panic. But inwardly he had already begun to curse. He found it, Act V Scene 2, and turned his attention to the board. His finger ran across the headings—Act I, Act II Scene 1, Act II Scene 2—but his eye had hastened ahead and was already resting on Act V Scene 2. There was a note in red, "First three pages cut." He stared at it, then checked with his script, then looked at the board again. His mind fumbled among the implications, not quite believing. It seemed impossible that those three pages were cut, because they were the reason he was here at the moment, the reason he had accepted the job in the first place. Into this momentary vacuum of feeling something shattered and it was his peace of mind. He watched it almost as if it were something outside himself being casually blown to bits. Warfare. Yes, he was back in the theater again, and that meant at the mercy of other people's frequently mediocre decisions. He despised himself for ever forgetting that fact. He was not yet thinking legalistically; over lunch he would wonder about breach of contract and redress. Now he was cursing what seemed to be the sheer artistic ignorance of cutting his three pages. To begin with, the Doctor was a marvelous part, short but written with great comic concentration, and he knew exactly how it should be played. He could be really good in it. But, more important, the scene was the only really funny one in the whole play. Bosola's comedy, savage and mordant, was of quite a different kind. This short scene coming where it did, like that of the gravediggers in *Hamlet,* was a wonderful preparative and rest before the final movement of the play. Why had they cut it? They were damaging the play, and, what he was realizing with a growing depth of misery, they were utterly destroying him. Without those three pages it was a lost season. And this was only the first day! He began moving about the hall with a broken restlessness, feeling his bitterness almost as something physical from which there might be a physical retreat. But like a dog on a chain he was tethered to the news on the notice board. It was there in red and there was nothing he could do about it. Of course he could complain, but when unproved actors made a fuss they quickly acquired a reputation as difficult. With success, "difficult" became "talented," but then success translated most things. He could always leave, throw the job up and go back to London. Except what did he have to go back to? That sort of action was rarely interpreted in an actor's favor. He had said his public goodbyes, and people like Kelly and Constable didn't want to know about him for at least six months. Standing by the notice board, he wondered if he had ever felt more expendable and wretched.

Someone touched him on the shoulder and he started. "Coming to lunch?" Richard Wayland asked him pleasantly. It was a simple enough suggestion but Sam was horribly moved by it.

"Sure," he said, distorting his face into a smile.

At the stage door they joined two others. "Let's try the canteen," said Richard, and they set off toward the front of the theater. The others talked but Sam was silent, his mind throbbing with grievance. If he was to talk there was only one thing he could possibly talk about. To have done so, to have gushed out the whole thing, would certainly have given him relief, but he hated to do it. He wondered if his face looked as ruined as it felt. The others would sympathize, but they would not care. He had no right to expect them to. If anything, they would feel secretly relieved that bad luck had passed them over in favor of another. This was much too early in the season for actors to start licking each other's wounds, faking concern with another's woes to gain a listener for one's own. By autumn they would all be doing it, but not now, for Christ's sake, not on the first day. He realized he would have to eat alone. If he ate in company, eventually his silence would produce a comment, and this would give him the cue to launch in with his story. He wanted to avoid that.

"I've suddenly remembered some shopping I've got to do. See you all later." He had broken away from them before there was time for anyone to argue otherwise. Around the corner from the theater he found a Tea Shoppe and tried unsuccessfully to nibble his way through a lunch. It was not much better being by himself, but it was preferable. He left his treacle pudding uneaten and in the street immediately bumped into Richard Wayland again, on his way to the wardrobe to be measured. Sam joined him. He held his silence walking to the wardrobe; said nothing while Eric deftly entwined him in lengths of tape measure. His face in the long mirror stared back at him pale and inanimate. Why did misery make one so anonymous? With a future like his all this measuring seemed as distasteful a refinement as a hangman politely calculating the drop.

Even the curiosity of the workroom girls, lifting their heads from their sewing to guess about a new member of the company, ordinarily rather flattering, was today a sly humiliation. On the way back to the theater Richard asked Sam if he was feeling all right. Restraint became impossible. He surrendered to a passionate expression of his wrongs. Richard was a good listener and afterward Sam felt weary, better and a little abashed.

At two-thirty the company were reassembled onstage, waiting for the reading to begin. Sam, still bruised, had just settled into a seat on one side and somewhat out of the way, when Ivan Spears, arriving a shade late, chose to sit down in the unoccupied seat next to him. He had a moment of irrational alarm. The star's proximity seemed to demand some gesture, though he had no idea precisely what. He found himself stealing surreptitious glances at the backs of Ivan's hands, long-fingered, pale and surprisingly delicate, and listening to his after-lunch breathing, astonished that he was still capable of making the vulgar and self-evident discovery that a celebrity was mortal.

Tom had risen. "Are we all here?" he said, and the stage manager shot to his feet and, head bobbing, went through a mime of checking the numbers. "Good. We'll just read the play straight through, then. And without the new cuts for the moment."

A breath of cautious hope alerted Sam. He thumbed rapidly through the pages of his text for his scene, but had barely arrived at it before someone started to read. It was Richard, for whom Antonio was the best part Braddington had so far put in his way, and a big opportunity for him. He read confidently and well, with the security of three seasons behind him. Then a voice at Sam's ear, in accents familiar yet deeply astonishing, said, "I do haunt you still." Ivan had spoken Bosola's first line, and the play stirred in its sleep. There was no one on the stage for whom that voice had not associations, and whether it was simply this or whether in truth the line had been superbly read, a tremor of excitement united the assembly. For the first time that day they were a company. The actor playing the Cardinal swiveled in his chair to catch Ivan's eye, and answered him with a frugal "So." Bosola replied, "I have done you better service than to be slighted thus. Miserable age, where only the reward of doing well is the doing of it!" The bitter comforts of the text seemed so apposite to his own situation that Sam began to smile. Antonio's lines soon followed:

> This foul melancholy
> Will poison all his goodness; for, I'll tell you,
> If too immoderate sleep be truly said
> To be an inward rust unto the soul,
> It then doth follow want of action
> Breeds all black malcontents. . . .

Sam smothered a rueful chuckle. The play might have been written for the dispossessed. He had always liked it, but this afternoon it was yielding a special measure of somber delight.

One by one each part found a voice. Sam gave the actors in their professional capacity a more level and generous attention than he had been able to give them as people earlier in the day. Rachel Frost was playing the Duchess; at forty-six she still had the trick of looking a sumptuous twenty under the lights. One had only to see her walk across the room to know that she understood her entire physical presence the way most people know only the backs of their hands. She had established her niche in the classical theater playing high comedy. Her present casting was audacious, though there was a quality to her personality of slightly predatory candor that, when you thought about it, seemed exactly right. Her reading was intelligent but mannered. It would take some persuasion to make her forget the expertise which she and her audience remembered confidently from past performances. Ferdinand was being played by Frederick Bell, and no actor could have looked more right. He had a magnificent El Greco head and, in the right part, a presence onstage that was hypnotic. At the moment, however, he was conforming to his reputation for ineptitude at the early stages of a play's rehearsal. He stumbled frequently in his reading, misinflected his lines and often appeared in ignorance of their meaning. But this was his way, and if past results meant anything, it was as good as any other. There was something extraordinarily shrewd in his frequent protests that he lacked intelligence, something rigidly determined behind his gentle, courteous ways. There must have been. There was no other explanation for his superbly managed career, which for ten years or so had kept him alternating between prestige stage work in England and epic films made on exotic location abroad. He earned thousands, some small part of which had found its way this afternoon into his handmade shoes, one of which now hung displayed in elegant suspension from a crossed leg. Sam couldn't help wondering if part of his confusion at these early well-dressed rehearsals was due to the fact that, like most gentleman actors, he was bent on playing two roles at once.

They were reaching the end of the third act, and the company were beginning to weary. The excitement of the first act had spent itself and the play was now sinking out of sight among complexities and improbabilities of plot. Tom called a halt for tea and the company broke ranks, some to stretch their legs, others to remain gossiping where they were. Sam decided to have a quick look at his scene. He had barely found the page when he realized he was being addressed by Ivan Spears.

"You find this a funny play?" the older man had asked in an insinuating whisper. Sam looked at him speechless. What did he mean? But Ivan went on to insist, "Plenty of laughs?"

Sam was suddenly enraged. After everything else that had happened that day, to find himself without explanation or reason the object of a star's dislike! He blurted out, "For Christ's sake! I think it's a marvelous play!"

They looked at each other in silence, both startled by his vehemence. Sam added in a different voice, rather lamely, "I laughed because it seemed true."

"I see," said Ivan quite amiably, and went away to get a cup of tea. To Sam the incident could not have been more shocking if his chair had collapsed beneath him, but apparently it had had few observers. One of them was Tom Chester, and Sam found a not entirely unsympathetic eye upon him. He raised his eyebrows to show his bewilderment as to how he had offended, and was relieved when Tom shook his head, smiled and mouthed the words "Don't worry." It seemed that the two of them had at least one very important thing in common: they were much the same age.

After tea, Sam wondered if Ivan would return to the same seat, but he did, giving nothing away. They sat side by side staring straight ahead, and it seemed an interminable time before the reading got under way again. Sam had been looking forward to the fourth act, so full of wonderful things, but now with his own scene approaching, his concentration was becoming erratic. So much was at stake. Irrelevant thoughts kept tripping him up. Would he be able to read it well enough to make them change their minds? Would it help having had that momentary unspoken exchange with Tom Chester? A couplet from the text suddenly mirrored his condition, and he grinned again.

While with vain hopes our faculties we tire
We seem to sweat in ice and freeze in fire.

They had reached the fifth act, and over the page he would be speaking. His palms were damp and he felt his heart begin a violent pumping. It seemed an absurdly spectacular demand to make on the body's resources for such a brief responsibility. Suddenly, taken almost by surprise, it was his turn to read. He gave an involuntary pitch forward from the waist, and his first three lines were out and over before he had considered properly what they meant. Bloody small parts. He was more in possession of himself for his next bit:

A very pestilent disease, my lord,
They call lycanthropia.

"Lycanthropia" came out with a meticulous pedantic pronunciation, and somebody laughed. That was good. He felt his grasp of the work in hand grow sure. During his next speech, the long one, he knew exactly what he wanted to do, and felt a thrill of pleasure as he realized he was doing it. Two big laughs came where he expected them. It seemed he was in command, and he read to the end of the scene on a wave of tense nervous enjoyment. It was as much a shock to stop reading as it had been to start, and after it was over he had to keep his script resting on his knees because his hands were shaking. Ivan Spears gave him a long enigmatic look, but whether of approval or hostility he did not care to investigate. However, he had satisfied himself, and he felt they would have to have a good reason now for doing without his scene. He tried to concentrate once more on the text, but again found it difficult. Beforehand his mind had skipped on ahead; now it kept jumping back, going over the lines he had just spoken like a schoolmaster correcting work, awarding a tick here and a cross there. He felt a blushing, prickly self-congratulation overwhelm him, somewhat disproportionate to his contribution but beyond his power to resist. The scene had taken about three minutes to read, yet it was becoming the very center, the bull's-eye, of his entire day. He noticed Ivan Spears was smiling, and not unkindly.

The reading was over. Tom jumped to his feet. "Right," he said, and paused a full five seconds in thought. "I found that *most interesting*. Really." This observation, hardly remarkable, was spoken with the authority of an insight, and many of the company seemed prepared to accept it as such. "We'll begin setting the play tomorrow. I think we'd better have a full company call for ten, because some of you will be making a few more appearances in the play than you thought." This called for a keen laugh fom some- one, and someone supplied it. Tom then continued. "At the moment I see the play in a very free fast-moving way. I think it's very important to be in the right gear to rehearse. I think the girls should borrow long dresses from the wardrobe as soon as possible and I'd like to see the men in jeans and gym shoes." Some of the men, thought Sam, and he knew which ones. He could not visualize Frederick Bell in gym shoes, though the theater had seen stranger things.

The company disbanded. Friendships had yet to be established, and routines of work and leisure quarried from the unfamiliar environment. The stars vanished upstairs for a drink with Tom in his office, cohesive with status and responsibility. The rest of the company drifted out of the stage door in tentative groups. Five of the more gregarious men had already discovered each other, and were laying plans in cheerful hollow voices for coalescing later on at a pub. Others went their separate ways, disguising their listless- ness. Sam was luckier than most. He had his purposes, pressing ones, and he was eager to be about them. He knew from the slight smiles of accord that he had received as he left the theater that he had read well, and now it was important to follow up this advantage. By tomorrow morning he had to have his scene learned and sufficiently rehearsed to speak for itself. It was not his favorite way of working, but for the moment it was the only way, and he wanted to get on with it. The size of his part did not spare him from his usual misgiving that somehow the lines would be im- possible to learn.

He walked briskly home to the Ozone Hotel. Mrs. Shrapnel was nowhere in sight and he hastened up the flights of stairs in great hushed strides to avoid her. He closed the door of his small room behind him, and collapsed thankfully upon his made bed, his weight distributed along its length like a felled log. He felt totally exhausted. His mind was stinging with fatigue, and his feet, still shod, prickled in sticky socks. He lay face down on the cheap bedspread, smelling new cotton and remembering dread and curiosity: it was the smell of the new shirts that he had once had to wear as part of a school uniform. His thoughts grew vivid and remote. With a swift change in gear his body had adapted for sleep, and for an hour and a half he was unconscious.

He woke alert to a darkened room and remembered at once the work ahead of him. It seemed as imperative as ever but quite unreal. Beyond the window was the evening sky, and he saw his task suspended against it lonesome and small. And silly. The bedspread beneath his cheek was damp with saliva and he wished he was still asleep. However, he rose, washed his face and hands, did his hair, and the feeling receded. He checked that he had the script in his pocket, then set out to find a restaurant where he could eat and study between courses.

Two hours later he was back in his room. In the restaurant he had found that there was no need to actually learn his lines; he had read them through so often that they were more or less in his head already. Now he wanted to discover as much about them as he could before he finally fixed them in memory. He was surprised how many possibilities there were in the text that he had missed that afternoon, and grew quite excited. With study he was getting a proprietorial feeling for the part; he knew about it now and had a right to it. The night sky was no longer a threat; he was making a center for himself. What a sublime idiot the Doctor was. He had found a way of saying the lines

> . . . Straight I was sent for,
> And, having minister'd to him, found his grace
> Very well recovered.

55

on a kind of modest sigh that suggested just what he wanted to in the way of unassailable professional conceit. He tried the reading out loud a couple of times to the empty room, and succeeded in vastly amusing himself. He sat on the bed and chuckled. It was like a conspiracy between himself and the part to make an audience laugh, and at the moment the conspirators were laying their plans in a mood of giggling self-congratulation. He felt impatient to get rehearsals over and his performance on display as soon as possible, but caution and superstition restrained him. There were still a number of tests to which he must submit before he could safely risk that one. Rehearsing a part in some respects was like undergoing inoculation against the hazards of public performance. Gradually, day by day, you built up a resistance to its varying dangers. One danger was the kind of excitement he was feeling now; it tended to vanish treacherously at rehearsal the next morning. He continued working for a further hour and a half, taking care not to waste too much energy on the fantasies of Success that were inclined to accompany his work in a manic phase; then, having wearied himself into a kind of sobriety, lines well learned and homework done, he closed his text, went to bed, read a copy of *Woman's Own* that Mrs. Shrapnel had thoughtfully put out for him, and slept soundly.

3

THE NEXT DAY at rehearsal Sam had two surprises. The first was that Frederick Bell was wearing jeans and gym shoes, and the second that he was down to play a further part: a courtier, with nothing to say, in Act I.

And later, in the Duchess's death scene, one of the madmen. Though it carried few lines, it was this second part that worried him; it was not so many pages from the Doctor, which could mean that they had made up their minds to do without him. However, he decided to bide his time and for the present not challenge Tom on the matter. At the rate this first walk-through was proceeding, it would be at least three days before they reached his scene and until then he would do his best to create an impression of willingness. He turned himself into a chess piece for the day's work.

Tom's way with his walk-ons was not quite the obedient milling about that Sam associated with an older generation of director. He was careful to learn names and said more than once that he wanted everyone to feel free to voice opinions or suggestions. Perhaps he was remembering his predecessor, Virgil Graves, whose way with a company had been to treat the walk-ons like stars, and, if necessary, the stars like walk-ons, maintaining that discrepancies of talent and salary were usually handicap enough for those with little to do. Tom was eager to pay his respects to this doctrine (popular with actors), but temperamentally, and notwithstanding jeans and gym shoes, it did not suit him. There was no disguising the fact that when he looked at an actor below a certain rank the curiosity went out of his eyes. Sam reckoned he was just about at the dividing line. In most respects, though, it was a peaceful day, and the newness of the company, eyes like restless

c*

fish in a new bowl darting silently round the room, prevented it from being a boring one.

It was obvious that Sam would not be needed at all the following day, so he asked the stage manager what was the call. None had been prepared, and Terence, already saturated with responsibilities, went off to point this out to Tom. They whispered together, then Sam was told he had the morning off.

The next day Sam rose to face a decision which could no longer be postponed. It was the question of jeans and gym shoes. When Tom had first issued his edict, his instinct had been one of open rebellion. He was suspicious of any kind of uniform. On the other hand it was sensible and sort of liberating to work in regulation old clothes, and Tom had a point about being properly shod. One of his anxieties at the early days of rehearsal was that somehow his feet weren't gripping the floor properly. Very well, then; he would accept a compromise. He would buy gym shoes but wear his own trousers. He set out to find a shop that sold them. In the Parade he met the motor-scootered actor he had nodded to the first morning. He had just mounted his machine, behelmeted and further invested with what were obviously brand-new blue jeans and gym shoes.

"I see you've got the school uniform on. Where do you get it?"

"Just around the corner. In the market. Robsons and Sons."

"To the left?"

"Yeah. Bloody silly, isn't it?" Nevertheless the purchase on his right foot, which he had extended and was now wagging to and fro, seemed to give him some satisfaction. "They'll be useful, though, you must admit."

They were both showing extreme cordiality. This was one of the better things about the beginning of a new job.

"Look, I'm afraid I don't know your name yet. I'm Sam Beresford."

"I know. You're playing the Doctor, aren't you? Lovely little part."

"I hope so."

"I'm Toby Burton. No, no relation. He's from Wales; I'm from

Manchester. If you haven't guessed already. Well, I'll be seeing you, Sam. Don't forget. First on the left." His machine farted in affable confirmation and he drove off waving.

It had been a pleasant encounter. In Robsons' he met another member of the company, also, it seemed, buying gym shoes, but for whose name he did not have to ask. He saw her just before he entered the shop, in profile, leaning over the counter briskly finalizing a purchase, and even through a haze of plate glass there was no doubt at all whose child she was. Amanda Maitland was smaller than her mother but the features were all Ruth Durrell's, less beautiful though perhaps for that reason rather poignant. Her coloring was probably her father's, a pale skin and hair straight and black and worn like a neat little cap. He had seen her father only in photographs. Not only did she have a Dame for a mother, at this moment acting in London, but miles away in New York a playwright for a father, reputedly alcoholic now but a great stayer with hits, a triennial event going back to 1936. It was difficult to assess a stranger with this kind of public lineage, and Sam approached her cautiously. He had an ambivalent attitude toward her which he didn't much like. He had to admit that on the one hand he was very curious about her, but on the other he was ready to resent at the first sign any manipulation of her advantages. Poor girl; this must have been the way most people approached her. He tried to forget about all that.

"Hello," he said.

She turned, startled, looked at Sam a moment, then—recognizing him as one of the company—returned his greeting with an enormous smile that turned into a gasp of laughter. He had expected her to be coolly theatrical, but this was something different: it was a loyal greeting to someone on the team such as one would expect an expensive, liberal, upper-middle-class education to produce.

"What have you been buying?" he asked.

"Oh, I've been getting my gym shoes."

"You? But I thought it was only the men."

"I thought I'd like some, too."

Sam wanted to smile. Amanda buying gym shoes seemed only too consistent with her reading on the first day. She was playing Julia, the Cardinal's mistress, and she had read her part with nothing if not keenness, tackling the sexy bits with special determination. It was pretty silly casting, but touching, too.

"What are you smiling at?" she inquired, also smiling.

"Nothing. Nothing at all. I just think its admirable, your buying gym shoes, that's all."

"Aren't you buying any?"

"Well, I was thinking about it." He turned to the young assistant with the middle-aged expression behind the counter, who had been privy to this exchange.

"What size, sir?"

"Eight and a half, I think."

The assistant frowned and bit his lip with a seriousness which would not have been out of place if he had just learned that typhoid had broken out on the other side of town. "Oo, sir. I think we're right out of that size. The nearest I can do is nine and a half."

"Oh."

"Or seven and a half," he added helpfully.

"Maybe if I took one of each . . . it might sort of average out."

Amanda laughed and the assistant's eyes frosted over. Sam made reparations. "Anyway, thanks very much. I expect you've had quite a demand for them the last couple of days. Will you be getting any more in?"

"We can easily order you some, sir."

"How long would that take?"

"Ten days. A fortnight at the most."

"Bit late, I'm afraid. I really need them now." He turned to Amanda. "Well, that's that."

"What about jeans? You could get them."

"No, I didn't think I'd wear jeans."

"Why not?"

"I wasn't even going to get gym shoes! I think what one wears at rehearsal is one's own business."

She looked at him a moment. This idea had obviously not occurred to her, but she seemed to have no difficulty in accepting it in someone else. She started to grin. "Mutiny?" she inquired.

"Certainly not. Look, I was all ready to compromise on the gym shoes."

"Yes, but they're out of them. Why not compromise on jeans instead?"

It was Sam's turn to hesitate.

"They're cheaper," she prompted.

"All right. Good idea. Thank you." He ordered a pair of jeans.

"Thanks for waiting," he said to her, accepting his change and his packaged jeans, intricately trussed with blue string, from the assistant. "Which way are you walking? Down toward the theater?" He had originally thought of going back to the Ozone, but company seemed pleasanter.

They walked down the Parade carrying their shopping and chatting about the play. Sam liked her. They had, as the saying goes, much in common. Assumptions which he had thought dead apparently still had some life in him, and for the moment he was not prepared to resist the bland pleasure of their reassurance. Most of the girls he had grown up with were like this, in most respects, save perhaps the celebrity. And the thing that pleased Sam most about her was the fact that the celebrity seemed not to have altered her at all. An earlier conditioning held sway. She had yet to learn how good-looking she could make herself—a dominant beautiful mother probably had a lot to do with that, or perhaps she just wasn't interested in clothes. Even so, it was clear that all the details of her appearance had been carefully monitored by a certain sort of selectivity, an idea which she had always been encouraged to have about herself and which she now took entirely for granted. She was a bit too skinny to walk the way she did, leaning forward with her chin in the air; it made her look more flat-chested than she was. But it was a walk with certainties to it.

Similarly the slight self-conscious lift of the eyebrows—which contrary to intention, led the eye direct to the source of anxiety, a very mild rash of spots at the hairline—had more pride in it than apology.

They decided on coffee in the Tea Shoppe where Sam had unsuccessfully attempted lunch the first day. They weren't talking shop, which was surprising, but had got around to basketball, a topic which now seemed the inexorable consequence of shopping for gym shoes. Amanda was describing a victory for the Harlem Globetrotters that she had seen in Philadelphia. Her manner of speaking was perceptibly mid-Atlantic, and Sam remembered reading somewhere that she had done some of her schooling in America. All her acting had been done over there. For two years her name had been featured in one of those little ads in *The New Yorker* proclaiming a Broadway run. The play had been her father's (it was said he had written it for her) and she had been a great success in it. Braddington was her first job since returning home. They finished their coffee, and Sam was about to suggest a second cup when he sensed that perhaps both were thinking that it was better not to overdo a good thing. Instead they rose.

"Well. That was lovely! Now I must get on with my shopping," said Amanda.

"And I must get back to my digs," he replied.

They parted on the corner. Sam felt very pleased. Here was a girl he was going to like but not to want, a fact which a moment later was brought home to him with hungry certainty when a girl his own height with a luminous ivory skin, and bottom and breast with the resilience of a new mattress, bounced out of a chemist's shop, passed him within inches, exuding the authentic smell of Girl, and disappeared into the post office across the street. He stood, looking at the blank post-office entrance, as disturbed as a tree that shivers to stillness again after violation by a great gust of wind. He walked on, trying to reestablish his line of thought. What had he been thinking about? Yes, he seemed to have found a friend, a genuine one; and, come to think of it, possibly a useful one.

62

Sam arrived at rehearsal the following morning knowing that the day was to be crucial. His scene was only a few pages away, and by noon its fate would have been decided. He was not sure that the matter was not under discussion when he arrived; Tom, Frederick Bell and Ivan were in a huddle about something in the far corner of the room. He glanced at them and felt the morning cloud over with familiar anxieties. With experience he was learning to transmute such anxieties to rage, the only neurotic symptom consequent upon his work that was not destructive to it. But probably they were not discussing him at all. He would wait and see. What else could he do?

"Now, about this scene," said Tom when they came to it, "I think it'll have to go."

Sam was devastated not merely by the import of the statement but by the fact that it seemed to have been said without any reference to him at all. Tom was addressing his remarks to Frederick Bell. Ivan stood nearby, half including himself. Frederick nodded his head and turned to acknowledge Sam. His face wore the solemn expression customarily assumed for woes not one's own, in which, nonetheless, Sam detected some genuine sympathy.

"I thought he read very well the other day," he said.

"Of course he did. That's just the trouble," said Tom, giving Sam a smile which he felt the impulse to return but just in time resisted.

Ivan gave a long hum of reflection and they all looked at him, expecting him to speak. For quite some time he didn't. Then he mumbled, "It's a nice little scene, you know."

They thought about this; then Tom said, "There's no doubt about that, though I do see what Freddie's getting at."

Sam had been watching them so intently he found that he'd forgotten to breathe. He made a conscious effort to resume normal respiration. He was not sure yet who was on whose side.

Frederick Bell took him affectionately by the arm. "Look, you know this has nothing to do with you. You read very well the other day. We all thought that." He was trying to be pleasant but was slightly inhibited because he didn't know or had forgotten Sam's name.

Tom helped him. "No, Sam read very well," he said. Then they all began calling him Sam.

"A good reading, Sam," said Ivan.

"Yes, Sam, we're all agreed on that," said Frederick.

"And don't think we're trying to take your part away from you, Sam," said Tom.

Ivan silenced them again with another reflective hum. "You see," he said, pausing an age to screw his face up, "I think we need the laughs."

"Yes," agreed Tom in a noncommittal drawl, "but I know exactly what Freddie means. That scene could leave him looking an awful Charlie."

So that was it. With the issue squarely in the open the debate warmed up. Ivan replied with great friendliness. "With due respect, Freddie, I'm not sure you're right about the scene's being bad for you. I think it can help you."

Tom answered for him. "But I think Freddie's right about the danger of his mad scene's turning into farce."

"Certainly. But remember the Doctor's laughs are all against the Doctor. Up against him, Ferdinand emerges with, well, a kind of dignity."

Frederick had been looking at each in turn. Clearly he seemed prepared to be persuaded away from his doubts. He looked at his feet and grinned. "I wish I could believe that," he said, adding, "I expect Sam does, too."

"Freddie, this is a boring thing to say," said Ivan. "But when we did it before, that was the scene everyone talked about."

"Well, perhaps I don't know how to do it. Perhaps I don't know what the scene's about," he said simply. It was admissions like this that made him well-liked. On the way to success he made sure no one feared him.

"You haven't rehearsed it yet, for Christ sake!" reassured Ivan, and Tom put in "Don't forget we've still got three and a half weeks."

Ivan continued: "But look, Freddie, if you do get into difficulties, look, I think I have the trick of this scene. I think I could help you."

Frederick looked at him shrewdly. The same remark from Tom would not have appeased him. Tom was the director; he would have his say anyway. With Ivan, however, you were with another actor, who knew the risks and wouldn't try to bluff you; his help would be spare and to the point. He had to weigh up the slight loss in prestige such help might involve against what could be the very real advantage to his performance. In calculations such as this he rarely made mistakes.

Tom spoke up quickly. "Listen, what about this for an idea? We rehearse the scene for a fortnight, do our best with it. Ivan can help you if you feel you'd like him to, and then if you're still not happy with it, Freddie, we cut it before we open."

Frederick nodded. "That seems fair."

"Good," said Ivan. The problem was solved and the director had had the last word. Everyone was pleased. Then they remembered Sam.

"Bit hard on Sam," said Frederick, and all turned excessively amiable faces on him.

"At least it's not cut—yet," he said, and wondered if that sounded sour.

"It's up to Sam to convince us we can't do without him," said Tom cordially. "You'd better be good, Sam."

Sam pretended it was funny, too, though the thought of every rehearsal being turned into an examination didn't amuse him at all.

"He'll be all right," said Ivan, patting him on the back.

They began to walk the scene. Sam, book in hand, didn't try too hard. Later there would be time for them to see what he could do. If he got there too quickly there was always the danger that they would scrap his scene out of sheer boredom with it. He mumbled his way efficiently through it, noting his moves, and left it at that.

They broke for lunch at one. Sam was about to leave the rehearsal room when he felt a hand on his arm. It was the stage manager. "Tom would like a word with you if you don't mind hanging on a minute." He sat while Tom and Terence worked out the afternoon call. The room cleared. When Tom came over to him they were alone. He spoke in a hasty intimate whisper: "About that scene. Don't worry about it. I had no intention of cutting it. The thing is Freddie is a bit anxious about his part, particularly his mad scene, and I wanted to keep him happy. He's always like this at the beginning, but he means no harm, and take my word for it, he's going to be a really fantastic Ferdinand once he gets going. There's not another actor in the world more right for it. You wait and see."

Sam nodded, but was given no opportunity to agree with or comment on the things that were being said to him. Having spoken, Tom darted away, leaving him reassured, confided in and "dealt with." For some reason it was the most humiliating thing that had happened to him that morning. But at least he was now sure of one ally, and a surprising one at that, Ivan Spears. As it turned out, Ivan's advocacy of the tiny scene and his offer of help to Freddie were to profoundly affect the whole production.

This development first suggested itself in the middle of the second week of rehearsals. They had been through the play twice, once to block the moves, once to consolidate them, and now, this Thursday, the whole company were assembled to take the play once again from the top. There was a feeling of uncomfortable expectation among the gathered actors, an acknowledgment that the pressure was on for each to show a little of his hand. As much as any public a company, too, had its demands to make; they were an actor's first audience, and they judged each of their number and were judged in turn themselves, with a private tribal severity. Richard Wayland got the rehearsal off to an efficient start. He knew his words well, spoke them loud and clear, and for the moment his fluency seemed achievement enough. Nevertheless for the thousandth time Sam was shocked by the extent of an actor's nakedness. Richard was revealing things about himself that had nothing to do with the play. It all seemed too soon after breakfast. As he acted, he had gone first a waxy pallor; then a deep flushing had overcome his neck and ears. With the text out of his hands for the first time his movements traced out a graph of painful inhibition. He was a sufficiently experienced actor to hide most of his discomfort, but there was an irreducible minimum of insecurity against which he had no protection, and never would have, particularly under the gaze of people like other actors who understood it. Still, as one of the play's beginners, he had done well, and was seen to gain strength markedly when the actor playing opposite him lost his lines and had to be prompted twice.

Ivan Spears slid into the scene. He appeared to concede nothing to the watching company but had retained the book and in contrast to Richard spoke his lines quietly in an intent reflective mutter. After a few lines he stopped to suggest a change in a move. Whatever pressures he felt he was resisting. They carried on till his exit, when he suggested they run his piece again. He had his own rhythm to impose upon the rehearsal, and with great courtesy he was making it plain he would not be rushed. The company, faintly disappointed but also relieved, settled down for a morning's work.

Ferdinand's entrance was approaching, and a knot of actors had congregated around Frederick Bell at the back of the rehearsal room. Sam was among them. He exchanged a glance with the senior actor and received a disquieting smile from him. Frederick was patently nervous, and this seemed inappropriate in a man of his reputation. Sam wondered if his own presence in Ferdinand's retinue was not putting him off. Did he feel guilty about him? He wanted to show goodwill, but couldn't think how. With nothing to say and little to do he was hardly nervous himself, and he felt his ease as an unfair advantage, as though in some way the tables had been turned.

Ferdinand and his followers made their entrance into a non-existent set and took their positions on the bare rehearsal-room floor. Stretches of sellotape, indicating flights of stairs and marble walls, enclosed them. Beyond the skylights above their heads a jet droned. Frederick spoke his first line and Tom clapped his hands.

"No! No!" he exclaimed. "The entrance needs to be much bigger. Much bolder. It's up to all you people following Ferdinand.

I want a lot of laughter and gaiety. Do it again."

They did it again, and again Tom stopped them. It was better, he told them, but still not good enough. They continued with the scene. Frederick had abandoned his book and was having trouble with his words. After a page or two Tom suggested pleasantly to Frederick that it might help him to go over the same ground again. They returned to his entrance. The supporting actors, eager to demonstrate their willingness, had enlarged on the laughter and chatter but it sounded false.

"More! More!" said Tom as they entered. "Lots of ab-libbing." And the falseness rose a degree or two in volume. Frederick tried to speak his first line above the noise, then stopped and appealed to Tom.

"I'll never be heard above all that."

"No," said Tom, addressing the supporters, "that was too loud that time. Take it down a bit. Do it again."

They did it again, and again the crowd noise refused to take on meaning. Tom took pains to disguise his impatience, which he knew in any case was not really justified. No one was disputing his direction, and a dozen actors coming on stage at once couldn't be expected to find their way to it without a little drill. Sam guessed that Tom knew this; he also guessed that at the moment he had little idea exactly what drill. He could only inwardly curse ·the stupidity of his actors for not showing him.

Frederick was even more uncertain of his lines the second time through. He was deeply uncomfortable but was using all his professional resource to grasp at some sort of harmony. He rallied the shadows of previous successes, trying to fit them like pieces of a jigsaw into the blank spaces of his new part. None fitted. The scene limped to the same place as before.

"Would you like to do it again, Freddie?" Tom asked in a sympathetic but faintly hurt tone. Frederick said he would.

They returned to their places. "Hello, Sam," murmured Frederick, laying a hand on his shoulder. He wagged his head. "That cunning old bastard, Ivan. I wish he'd told me he was going to carry his book."

They made the entrance again. Repetition was not helping them, merely consolidating their mistakes. The actors began to feel discouraged as their error set around them like a cast, knowing what they did was wrong but not knowing how to put it right. Tom said nothing and the scene proceeded. Suddenly Frederick stopped. The prompter's face lifted from the book wonderingly, but the actor shook his head when offered a line.

"What is it, Freddie?" asked Tom.

"I'm worried about my first line."

"It sounds fine now."

"But no one will know what it means. 'Who took the ring oft'nest?' Doesn't mean anything to a modern audience."

"Well, it's simply a reference to the sport on horseback. Running the ring, where they tilted at a ring with the lance."

"Yes, I know that. But how can we explain it? It's my very first line. I feel it's important."

"I don't think it matters, Freddie," said Tom steadily. "The line's come and gone in a second."

Frederick's expression grew stubborn, a characteristic one least expected from him. "Nevertheless, it's my first line," he repeated.

Tom laughed. "I think you're making a mountain out of a molehill," he said.

"I'm the one who has to say this line. I want it to be understood."

There was a pause.

"It will be," said Tom.

"How?" persisted Frederick.

"May I make a suggestion?" Adopting a schoolboy's tentative manner, Ivan had raised his right hand. Both turned to him with relief.

"Sure," said Tom, "please."

"Why doesn't he bring the lance on with him?"

"How do you mean?"

"Well, the scene is all about Ferdinand going off to war, and horsemanship and so forth. They could all come on with armor and swords and military equipment. Maybe they could arm Ferdinand on stage, dress him up."

"I don't think Ferdinand should make his first entrance carrying a lance," said Tom, smiling a little dubiously.

"No, no," said Ivan. "One of the other characters. Sam there on his right. Wait a moment." He walked over to the corner of the rehearsal room and took hold of a long pole used for closing the blinds on the high windows. "Here, use this. Now, Freddie, when you come in and say the line 'Who took the ring oft'nest?' turn round to Sam and feel the grip of his lance with your right hand. You know, like a cricketer being knowing about a cricket bat."

They tried it, and it worked. "Good," said Ivan. "What's the next line?"

" 'Antonio Bologna, my lord,' " said the actor playing Silvio.

Ivan thought a moment. "Good!" he said. "Look, Freddie, before you say your next line take the lance and let the point of it descend slowly to Antonio's feet. Pick him out with it. Make it quite friendly; smile if you like. Try all that again."

They ran the three lines of dialogue.

"Who took the ring oft'nest?" said Ferdinand, and his preoccupation with the lance gave the line a languid imperiousness.

"Antonio Bologna, my lord," answered the flatterer that Silvio had suddenly become.

The point of the lance traced a slow arc and fell at Antonio's feet. Ferdinand smiled and said, "Our sister duchess' great master of her household? Give him the jewel."

The attentive company murmured with excitement. Even Ivan seemed surprised at the effectiveness of his piece of business. It had struck a note of indefinable foreboding. Frederick had executed it beautifully. He looked at Ivan, unable to contain a smile of pleasure.

"What do you think?" said Ivan, turning to Tom. "You may want to cut it later. But I think it helps for the present."

"No, I like it very much. But I'd like to see all the attendants come on with something from Ferdinand's armory." He pointed to various people. "One of you can carry his sword. Maybe you can carry a gauntlet. Someone else a visored helmet."

"Sure, sure!" said Ivan. The stage crew scuttled about issuing makeshift props. The room had become quick with invention. "How does the scene go on?"

They ran some lines which Ivan followed in the text. He interrupted: "Tom, this is a very good idea, this laughter, but I think we need to sort it out a little. Now, it seems to me that what is happening is this. This great prince is surrounded by his courtiers laughing at his jokes. He encourages them, leads them on. Then in a moment or two someone makes a crack and everyone laughs except Ferdinand. Then he says—what is it you say, Freddie?"

" 'Why do you laugh? Methinks you that are courtiers should be my touchwood, take fire when I give fire; that is, laugh but when I laugh, were the subject never so witty.' "

"You see? This can be an icy moment if we can get it."

They went carefully through the few lines of text, deciding where the laughter should come. "If we use it like this during the scene," said Ivan, "we won't have to push it too hard at the entrance. In fact, try the entrance next time without the laughter." He took Freddie by the arm and walked him a little to one side. "Freddie, I think you may be anticipating the villainy a little. This is an immensely powerful young nobleman. He's sure to have all the charm in the world. The wormwood is in the lines. Let them do the work. Trust us to learn about him in our own time. Remember the way you played Claudius? Usually he's a husky-voiced old bugger with a black spade beard and a suggestion of B.O. And Gertrude in a henna wig! Christ! You gave him a silvery plausible magnetism. Marvelous! 'By their works ye shall know them.' Not by their makeups." He gave Frederick a jocular slap on the back and both laughed.

Tom spoke up. "I think I'd like to run all that again."

"Good idea," said Ivan, and the actors trooped back to their marks with renewed spirit. "Tom's quite right about you chaps. We need to know from *you* that Ferdinand is a great prince. Freddie shouldn't have to do a thing. You walk into a room and know who the king is by the way everyone else is treating him. The center of the circle is nothing without the circumference. The circumference creates it." He caught Frederick's eye. "Freddie, I'll give you the cue: 'Here comes the great Calabrian duke.'"

Frederick caught the rolling excitement of the line. This time he walked into the scene with a notion of the part that had become suddenly all his own. He had absorbed the smallest details from Ivan, a gesture slight as a shrug or the tone of a single word, and now he reproduced them extended and changed by his own personality. His audience submitted to him and he cruised to the end of the scene in perfect safety. His lines, soft-spoken, had acquired a smiling disturbed ambiguity. When he jested "I would, then, have a mathematical instrument made for her face, that she might not laugh out of compass," his hand, reaching out with rigid delicacy to touch a nearby face, seemed to be dreaming of some intricate torturing device. The gesture was both surprising and inevitable. Ivan turned to grin at the absorbed company, sharing his relish with them. Now that they had found it, this way of playing the scene seemed as obvious and proper as the key lying brazenly on the shelf for which you have searched in vain all morning.

Nothing else in the day's work was to prove as exciting as Ferdinand's first two pages. For fifteen minutes Ivan had held the company in thrall, taking charge so nimbly and with such certainty that the work was over and accomplished before anyone quite realized what had happened. He had given the day its sense of direction, and now he seemed content to be, as before, just one of the actors. He continued to make the odd whispered suggestion to Frederick, but was careful to leave his other celebrated colleagues alone; at this stage they probably did not need (and certainly did not want) any help from him. Not that his interference was easy to resent. He had the good director's gift of making each direction a compliment, a motion of confidence not only in the intelligence of the actor to grasp his point but also in his special ability to execute it. Under his tutelage the work became as clean and precise as wood in the hands of a wood-carver.

At first Tom had resisted Ivan's interference, but he was too

72

acute not to recognize at once the excellence of what was being achieved. He had hired Ivan's services and this was a bonus. Besides, Ivan was treating him with perfect courtesy, and it soon became understood between them that there was a valid public excuse for Ivan's participation: Frederick had asked for it. Ivan played according to this rule, and was especially attentive when Tom made suggestions about his own performance. One thing, however, was apparent to all. This particular play was Ivan's. Everything he said about it, and everything he did in his own performance, had an immediacy and a vigor which claimed the material as his own. Webster had found a spokesman, one who responded not so much to the formal qualities of his play, anchored in their own time, as to that enduring impulse that had led to the writing of it, and which, centuries later, in the terms of his own experience, Ivan was able to affirm. The play was his by right of talent, and he was there to turn its pages for the entire company.

4

I⊤ wᴀs two days before they reached Sam's scene. He had followed
its uneven approach as they stopped and started their way through
the play. They had begun the morning with Act V and spent three
quarters of an hour on the scene preceding his. With fragmentary
attention he watched it being rehearsed, suppressing nervous
yawns and wondering where all his eagerness and confidence had
gone to. It did, however, give him a chance to study the actor with
whom he would be playing, Francis Roland, a middle-aged man
who had been with the company three years and whose parts were
usually in line with the one he was now rehearsing, aging bass-
voiced noblemen. Sam knew him to be a reliable performer, but he
sensed from the rather sour ease with which he was now rehearsing, book conspicuously in hand, that Pescara was not a part that
much interested him.

The entrance was approaching. He moved to the back of the
rehearsal room and stood waiting. His palms were damp, and at
the moment acting was the last thing in the world he felt like
doing; tomorrow perhaps, or later in the day, in an hour's time,
but not right now. He was joined by Francis and they exchanged
small formal smiles, exorcising mistrust. Sam was going to try it
without his book, and he was conscious of his empty hands. He
stretched, without moving his arms, and breathed deeply twice.
Suddenly he had a moment of panic. Ivan had vanished through
the door leading to the men's lavatory. Sam had wanted him to be
present; the one pair of eyes he could trust to see what he was
trying to do would not be there. They came to the end of the
preceding scene and Tom said, "All right. Carry on." Whereupon
Ivan reappeared, his hand leaving his fly; apparently he was keen

74

to be there for the scene himself. Sam remembered the work he had done on his part, summoned up his courage, and he was on.

"Now, doctor, may I visit your patient?" said Pescara, and Sam listened with all his might. There wouldn't be time to warm up. The part was so small he had to be able to play it from scratch. With irritation he realized that one bent knee was trembling; he was more nervous than he thought. With a part of his mind he wondered if the vibrations inside his trouser leg were visible.

He answered:

> If't please your lordship; but he's instantly
> To take the air here in the gallery
> By my direction.

He struggled to stay firmly in the present and not go jumping into the future, anticipating lines or business. He knew the words backwards and it was absurd to be anxious about them. He had only to do the things he had to do, one at a time, with complete conviction, and the part would unroll with the scene and come to life with it.

They carried on; nobody stopped them. Sam came to his lines:

> Straight I was sent for,
> And, having minister'd to him, found his grace
> Very well recovered.

He heard an abrasive grunting sound from a source out of focus on his right. It was Ivan laughing, and it was one of the most flattering sounds he had ever heard. He broke out in goose pimples of resolution as he attacked his next speech. The intention behind his lines was acquiring the focus and precision of billiard shots. He was still nervous but much happier; the part was working.

They were stopped at the bottom of the page, just before Ferdinand's entrance. It was like a string snapping. Sam allowed himself a look at his small audience and found that people were .smiling.

Ivan came forward. "Very good. Very funny. I like the way you say that bit 'Straight I was sent for,' but why not use that same feeling elsewhere? There's the lines about meeting the duke at midnight with the leg of a man on his shoulder. Don't *you* be shocked. It's all in a day's work to you. Let Pescara be shocked. You're the Doctor. It gives you the edge on him."

They tried it this way and it was better. The Doctor's professional assurance was flowering grotesquely, and Pescara was playing up to it beautifully, with just that degree of assumed humility with which a nobleman might be expected to lend an ear to a technical expert.

"Splendid," said Ivan. "That's exactly what we want to get from you both: the fact that he's a marquis and you're just a doctor. Not forgetting, of course, that you're a doctor and he's just a marquis."

Sam was delighted. The uneasy social station of the Doctor was one of the first thoughts he had had about him, but he wasn't sure whether he would be able to convey this. The Doctor's expansive diagnosis of Ferdinand's madness was on the one hand obsequiousness to a social superior, and on the other a clear demonstration to himself of his own intellectual supremacy. This was what made it so funny.

They continued to work the scene, taking it apart and solving its problems one at a time with a gentle nut-cracking determination. Sam had lost all his nervousness now. His concentration was rigged like a sail to catch the least breath of an idea or an impulse. Sometimes when Ivan stopped him, so attuned were they that he was able to anticipate the suggestion he had been on the point of making. They smiled together like pleased respectful contestants and proceeded. The rehearsal was moving onto the plane of pure disinterested play, and as in the games of children, he had the same sense of flushed prickling physical harmony. He was skipping with the part. It seemed there was no better way of spending time. Finally, they ran the whole scene, putting the bits together to see how they fitted. The run-through lacked the pleasure of surprise, but it was encouraging to see how much had been accomplished.

He wanted to run it again, twice if necessary, to make quite sure of it, but Tom and Ivan agreed to leave it for the moment. Sam reminded himself that his scene was but five minutes in a long play, and set off to have a cup of coffee in the Green Room downstairs.

He had only nibbled at breakfast so he ordered a ham sandwich with his coffee, which Hilda behind the bar served him with the sluggish good nature one comes to expect in organization canteens. Toby Burton waved at him and he joined his table. Sitting there with him were his flatmate, Don Petersen, who wore huge hand-knitted red sweaters and looked sufficiently like Kirk Douglas for one to question his motives for becoming an actor in the first place, and Hugh Beardmore, who smoked a pipe, wore a tweed hat to rehearsals and had been to Leeds University. Like Toby they were both in their early twenties and were walking on. With them was Janet Bennett, a trim intense friendly woman of thirty-five, who had been with the company a couple of seasons playing small character parts and had a reputation for straight speaking. The manners of the company one to another were as good now as they would ever be. Though no longer strangers, they were still on something like their best behavior, and curiosity was generously doing the work that later on in the season a more niggardly respect would have to attend to. Sam was considered to be something of a dark horse among them, an impression he did nothing to contradict.

"How did it go, mate?" said Toby, passing him the sugar.

"I don't really know," said Sam, lying. "Ivan was a great help."

"Darling, he's marvelous!" said Janet. "We haven't had someone like him around the place for quite some time, I'll tell you that."

"It's an entertainment just to watch old Ivan at work," said Toby. He looked at Sam. "He seems to like you, mate."

The remark gave Sam an intense dubious pleasure which he hoped did not show. He was not really present with them at the table at all. His mind was still humming with his rehearsal, and the disturbance it had left behind was, if rather more agreeable, as

77

private as pain. He ached with a waning exhilaration, which, lik᠎
the failing effects of a self-administered drug, he was reluctant t᠎
shake off. The personality he offered them chatting amiably ove᠎
coffee seemed the crudest masquerade.

Don Petersen, wrinkling up his brow in an excess of politeness᠎
was speaking to him. "What were you doing before this, Sam?"

"Mainly TV's. Did a few days on a couple of films."

"Films?"

"Mm. Just a few days."

Don wanted to know all about it. He hastened to explain tha᠎
the parts were tiny ones, but Don insisted upon being impressed᠎
And after all why not? It seemed easier to accept Don's estimate o᠎
the importance of the work than what he remembered of his own
half an hour's work at the tail end of the day as climax to eigh᠎
hours in a windowless dressing room left to himself with a painte᠎
face. But films were films. Maybe it *was* quite a good thing to hav᠎
done. Actors never escaped the suspicion that the important work
the real work, was being done elsewhere. Except, Sam suddenl᠎
realized, with this job. The best thing about these rehearsals of *Th᠎
Duchess of Malfi* was that he was absolutely sure of their worth.

His companions were called to work over the loudspeake᠎
system, and he was by himself. He finished a second cup of coffe᠎
and, still preoccupied with his part, set off to find a lavatory. H᠎
had chosen one that suited him some days before, another of th᠎
small quests consequent on a new job. It was remotely situate᠎
beyond the wardrobe, and at this hour of the day could b᠎
depended upon to be vacant. He found it smelling of fresh dis᠎
infectant and very clean, the corners of the floor still damp from᠎
the cleaner's mop. The satisfaction of being the first of the day wa᠎
his. He sat, thinking about his part. On the wall of the classroon᠎
at his junior school years ago there had been a chart with a smal᠎
picture of a Tudor merchant wearing spectacles. He remembere᠎
the merchant exactly; he had been down in the lower right-han᠎
corner, and the spectacles had been funny square black ones᠎
Maybe some sort of spectacles would be good for the Doctor.

That afternoon he found himself free and he decided to pursu᠎

the idea of the spectacles. For the time being he had exhausted his few pages of text. The hunt for a pair of Elizabethan spectacles might yield some surprising incidentals. He tried the public library but they had no illustrations to help him. Then he remembered an optometrist's shop that he passed every day on his way to the theater. They might have a reference book of some sort. The woman at the desk asked him to sit while she fetched the proprietor, and he thumbed his way through a tired copy of *Punch* as limp and gray as old lettuce. The proprietor had been told by the receptionist that Sam was one of the actors, and this was reflected in his expression, one of amiable curiosity that had yet to make up its mind between awe and contempt. Sam had seen it many times, and it was explicit of the relationship between the actor and the general public.

"Now, what can I do to help you?" he asked, smiling.

Sam explained that he was trying to trace a design for some Elizabethan spectacles.

"Let me see. Let me see," said the optometrist, tapping the sides of his own heavy library frames with an index finger. "This isn't the sort of thing you mean?" He opened a cabinet door and found a fragile pair of silver frames. "Early Victorian. Genuine, you know."

"No, not really, I'm afraid." Nevertheless they talked about the Victorian spectacles awhile to avoid acknowledging a dead end.

"*Just* a moment! Just a *moment!*" exclaimed the optometrist, snapping his fingers and disappearing through the curtains in a purposeful exit of which Henry Irving would not have been ashamed. The fact that some people were on the stage and some weren't frequently seemed quite arbitrary to Sam.

He reappeared with what looked like a collection of rolled-up posters under his arm. "We might just have the very thing you're looking for right here. What about this?" He began to unroll one of the charts. "One of the manufacturers sends us these for distribution to schools."

Sam read inverted OPTICS THROUGH THE AGES. It seemed familiar. Then to his wild astonishment down in the right-hand corner of the chart he saw unroll from the waist onward his Tudor merchant. Even upside down he was recognizable. The chart was the same one that had once adorned his own classroom wall. He explained excitedly. The proprietor seemed quite able to take the coincidence in his stride. "They don't change this sort of thing much, you know. It's just for the kiddies."

"Can I make a little drawing of these spectacles?" Sam asked.

"Take the whole thing. Take the chart with you. I don't want it."

"Are you sure? I mean, can't I pay you for it or something?"

"No! No! Glad to have it out of the shop. Hope it's some use to you."

Sam left the shop cradling his chart as preciously as a map of buried treasure. He would copy the design and make some spectacles himself. In the street he ran into Amanda on her way to rehearsal and stood telling her about his find, torn between the desire to communicate his discovery and the need to act upon it. She released him laughing, and he hurried on to the Ozone. In his room, he unrolled the chart on his bed, and, keeping the four corners from springing up with his slippers and a pair of shoes, he traced a full-scale design of the spectacle frames on a piece of cardboard. He cut this out carefully with a razor blade, and tried it out on the bridge of his nose. The spectacles weren't quite broad enough or perfectly symmetrical, so he had another attempt and then another until he had the shape that pleased him. They looked right, but obviously cardboard wasn't a material strong enough to last the run of a play. With chart and spectacles he set off again to the theater to seek aid in the properties workshop. No one was there except Frank Butler, the stage carpenter. Frank took the cardboard pattern between his thick accomplished fingers, and wheezed cigarette smoke at it for some time without speaking.

"You could cut it out of a sheet of tin," he said finally.

"Would that work?"

"Or a sheet of celluloid."

"That might be better. Thicker."

"Wrong color, isn't it? You don't want them transparent, do you?"

"I can paint them black. They ought to be black." Frank

continued staring silently at the cardboard in his fingers. "Leave it with me, then," he said at last.

"That's marvelous! Thanks very much indeed."

He was about to ask him when they would be ready, but Frank's patient ways rebuked him. However, his expression had apparently already posed the question, for Frank answered, "I'll do 'em now. Come back later in the afternoon."

He thanked him again and left him to his mysterious skills. The problem of how the Doctor should look had become all-absorbing. The spectacles, he decided, were right. And he had a feeling about a wig, dry hair and rather black, and straight. Probably, too, a sallow complexion and a bluish chin.

"What are you frowning about?" said Richard Wayland, appearing around a corner.

"Nothing, nothing at all. Listen, where can you get makeup in the town?"

"There's a shop that sells cosmetics in the High Street. They've got theatrical slap, too. Just opposite the post office. Try them."

On the way to the cosmetics shop he thought about a false nose. He wasn't sure about that, though. He mistrusted noses. But he would buy some nose putty just in case.

The cosmetics shop had an incomplete feeling about it, like a sweetshop. The stock was too monotonously similar. Sam was surrounded by such things as pyramids of soap and lurid cardboard displays of lipstick, and he looked round expecting the qualifying seriousness of a dispensary. A gray-haired woman in a pink-nylon work coat served behind the counter, and Sam took his turn behind two women. He asked about theatrical makeup, in rather ringing tones to explain his presence, and the woman leaned over a narrow flight of stairs leading to the basement and called out, "Valerie."

When Valerie appeared, the line of Sam's thoughts buckled and came to a trembling halt. He had seen her before. She was the same big shining girl who had brushed past him a week ago and vanished across the street into the post office. He had lost sight of her, he had then thought, forever. Now suddenly here she was

D

again, and not only that: Sam knew her name and had a reason to speak to her.

"Do you sell theatrical makeup?"

"What was it you were wanting?" She spoke very quietly with her chin tucked in. Male customers were probably a rarity. There was a woman buying hand lotion whom he suspected of listening to their every word.

"You don't sell theatrical pancakes?"

Valerie moved to the small counter at the end of the shop and Sam seized the opportunity to follow her. Three yards away, they might have privacy.

"What color were you wanting?"

"I thought a kind of sallow color, a bit pinched and academic-looking."

The girl produced a large drawer of assorted pancakes, and one by one she removed each from its cardboard box, unscrewed its lid, demonstrated its color, and when this proved unsatisfactory screwed the lid back on, returned it to its box and placed the rejected pancake to one side of the counter. They repeated this process through a great range of rubicund and sunburn tones, a task which in other circumstances would have made his toes contract with exasperation. As it was, he was content if it took the rest of the afternoon.

He allowed himself to be mesmerized by the movements of her hands, employed among the pancakes as delicately as if the lacquer on her arched nails was not yet quite dry. Each time she stretched out her fingers to dispose of a pancake, four dimples puckered the back of her hand with the silent exclamation of a rocket at night. He looked up at her face dreamy with her task. She wore far too much makeup though its application had obviously been meticulous. She probably spent hours at a time down there in the basement trying out the varying merchandise. The touch of true color at her wrists and throat suggested she would look best of all with a scrubbed face, but then selling the stuff was her job. She probably had some title like Beautician. She deserved it. She was a beautiful Beautician. And her height (which she probably fretted

82

about at home, getting in and out of clothes for a local dance quite blind to her own sugar and spice) made her all the more incredible. That he couldn't lean over the counter and start making love to her immediately quite demoralized him.

They had found a pancake that looked the right color.

"At last!" said Sam, he wasn't sure why. "That looks the right color."

Valerie seemed pleased, so he bought it—as well as some spirit gum, a lake liner, three eyebrow pencils, a packet of orange sticks and several other things he didn't need. His purchases were wrapped up and there was nothing else to do but leave. He looked at her hard to see if she had any inkling of the effect she had had on him. But she refused to be willed into any sort of admission. He turned to go and then remembered: "Oh, what about nose putty? Have you got any of that?"

"No, but we can order you some."

"How long would that take?"

"Ten days to a fortnight."

"That's a bit long."

"We could write off and you could get it in two or three days if you don't mind paying the postage."

"All right. That's a good idea."

It was a marvelous idea. He now had a valid reason for coming back to see her.

"I'll call back in a day or two," he said, and added, "Thanks, Valerie."

She smiled, apparently less perturbed than he was by such ponderous boldness, and he left the shop with hope. Removed from Valerie's orbit, he had a vague sense of risk averted. She was far less of a disturbance when out of sight, and he returned to the thought of the spectacles. They wouldn't be ready for some time, so he decided to see what was happening at rehearsal.

Ivan greeted him as he tiptoed through the door, "Just in time. We're running it again from the end of your scene. You can do your exit for us."

Sam did so, then found himself a seat to watch. They had

reached the scene where Julia endeavors to seduce Bosola, and Amanda was just about to make her entrance. Sam wondered if she was nervous. There was nothing in her resolute expression to suggest it, but he guessed that she was.

She and Ivan commenced their scene. It had difficulties for them both, the most obvious being the forty years' difference in their ages. Her aside, "What an excellent shape hath that fellow," spoken with a faint American cadence, had dangerous comic possibilities. Cast as the great woman of pleasure, she seemed determined to take her unlikely role by storm, and she set about embracing Ivan with athletic zeal. His playing remained as muted as hers was exuberant. Sam admired her courage, though he had to concede it was getting her nowhere. She was providing someone in her small audience with a splendid opportunity for a cruel, funny remark, and Sam felt for her.

Tom stopped them. "That's coming along fine. Much better than last time. I still think you're doing a little too much, though, Mandy."

"Still too much, huh?" said Amanda, nodding her head co-operatively. She was a girl who was prepared to take a lot of punishment.

"What do you think, Ivan?" said Tom.

The old actor seemed reluctant to speak. He hesitated, then turned to Amanda and said rather diffidently, "Languor. Don't forget that sensuality is a languid thing. Not aggressive. That's the fake kind. The cliché."

She nodded her head, but there was no comprehension in her eyes. Either she was too uncomfortable at the moment to attend to his point or she did not understand it, and he did not pursue the matter. They carried on with the scene. Playing opposite the Cardinal, she gained somewhat in confidence and fluency. She kissed the poisoned Bible he offered her and died noisily and effectively.

Ivan seemed pleased. "That's it! Very good. You're beginning to enjoy dying. Cops and robbers. Deaths are always fun to act; no more words to bother with. But don't be afraid to let yourself go.

84

That's what the audience come for. That's what they secretly hope for in their black hearts. Sex and ritual murder. Gladiators and blood. Well, that's what you must give them. Once you've got 'em, you can do what you like with 'em. But hook them first. That's what the theater is: a bullring. And what's wrong with that? Better than a night school for prigs, which is what it'll become if we're not careful."

Everyone laughed, and that was the end of the day's rehearsal.

"I'm depressed. Come and have a cup of coffee with me," said Amanda, taking off her long rehearsal skirt to disclose her new blue jeans.

"Sure," said Sam. "Why are you depressed?"

"I'm so bad in that scene!" she said with a crisp smile and a wag of the head.

"No, you're not. It's coming along fine."

"It's all right; I know I'm bad. But I *can* do it! I know I can!" She turned a frowning determined face on him.

"Of course you can. It gets better each time."

"No, it doesn't. It gets worse."

Sam thought a moment before replying, "I think that was a good point of Ivan's, you know."

"What was that?"

"Well, about the languor."

"I didn't understand that. What did he mean?"

"Well, when you play the scene you want to feel as if you'd like to sink onto a double bed somewhere."

"But I'm not sure I want to sink onto a double bed with Ivan." Her remark was not malicious, simply a statement of fact.

Sam laughed. It shocked him a little that talent and years of achievement could be displaced so effortlessly by a simple sexual estimate. As far as a twenty-one-year-old girl was concerned, he recognized the brutal integrity of it.

"No, that was mean," she added. "He's a marvelous actor and he's still very attractive really. But he's just—so *much* older. The lines don't seem to fit."

85

"I think you'll find a difference in costume. He's very clever with the paint."

"Of course I will. Anyway it's my fault. There's no one else to blame but me." She had cheerfully wrapped the subject up, and that was the end of it.

Sam suggested a diversion on the way to coffee by way of the properties workshop to collect his spectacles. She seemed delighted with the idea. "Let's!" she said. But the workshop was locked when they arrived. Sam gently kicked the skirting of the door, exasperated that behind it his spectacles were probably waiting for him in a state of pristine completion. "What are these?" said Amanda. She had noticed something on the window ledge. There were his spectacles resting on a piece of brown paper, on which Frank had written with a thick stub of pencil *Careful—Wet Paint*. Sam touched them with the tips of his fingers to see if they were tacky, but the black mat paint had already dried. He picked them up gently, smiling with pleasure. The frames were made of celluloid, but the sidepieces, carefully joined with small hinges, had been made of metal, presumably so that they could be bent to fit.

"Aren't they good?" said Sam.

"Try them on," said Amanda. She rummaged in her large raffia bag, containing among other things her script, some sheet music and a copy of *Elle* magazine, and produced a small mirror.

Sam looked at the image jumping unsteadily above his thumb. The spectacles were superb! His face seemed to have grown longer; he looked hawk-eyed and pursed around the mouth. His expression began to alter to accommodate this new look, and the Doctor stared back at him. But he would need a nose. Not a large one; a very subtle one that would extend the tip of his own nose maybe a quarter of an inch. It would give his face just that look of drooping, sniffing pedantry that it needed.

"The rule about false noses," explained Sam, "is that no one must ever be able to tell you're wearing one. You really need a cast of your own nose to sculpt the false nose on."

"Why don't you make one?"

"What?"

"A cast of your own nose."

"How?"

"With plaster of Paris, I suppose. Like a death mask. Make one on yourself."

"On myself? I couldn't do that, could I?"

"Get someone to help you. I'll help you if you like."

"Will you? Say, that's not a bad idea. In any case a cast would be a terribly useful thing to have."

"Richard Wayland's coming to supper on Sunday night. Why don't you come, too? And we can make it then."

"Really? Well, thanks. I'd love to."

"Buy some plaster of Paris."

"Yes, I will."

"Why are you smiling?"

"You seem to make things so simple."

"What things?"

"Things like making a cast of your nose."

"Well, they are simple, aren't they?"

"Yes, they are. Or they ought to be," said Sam. "Let's have coffee."

"Let's!" said Amanda.

In the coffee shop they met Toby Burton and Don Petersen and sat talking with them for almost an hour. Toby suggested they all go back to his and Don's flat, have a salad dinner, then watch the play on the landlady's TV downstairs. They trooped through the dusky streets, Toby twisting back and forth across the road on his scooter, reluctant to be out of hearing. In the attic flat they ate hard-boiled eggs and salad from a huge bowl that had been indiscriminately filled with lettuce leaves, squashy quartered tomatoes, raisins and bits of banana, all of which had then been vigorously mixed. Sam found a small grub in his portion but kept quiet about it. He wondered if Amanda had noticed. If she had, it hadn't bothered her. He liked the way she threw herself so whole-heartedly into one small activity after another—chatting with people, drinking coffee, eating grubs. He ate his salad with a will, washing it down with a sludge compounded of bottled beer and thick slices of buttered brown bread. Afterwards the play was not much good, but they sat it out, then left the house in a rush to catch the last half hour at the pub. Concealed in Sam's breast pocket, like a private thought, were his spectacles, and in the crushed pub he found himself unconsciously protective toward that part of his body as if nursing a bruised rib.

Dosed with two pints of beer, Sam made his way home to the Ozone. The echo of his footfalls clapped him along the empty Parade, briskly proclaiming the town as his. He knew it now, which road was which and how to get where. He paused to look into the weakly illuminated window of an antique shop. A policeman was standing in the shadow of the doorway. "Evening," said Sam.

"Evening, sir," said the policeman. "Rehearsals going well?"

"Not bad, thanks," he answered, surprised. He walked on; apparently the town knew him too. How pleasant it was to be an actor. He had become located upon a map, orientated by work and friendship, going somewhere. London hardly existed. His agents', the Labour Exchange, his room—all belonged to a remote past, like clothes discarded. (Sally, too? he suddenly wondered. He had hardly thought of her in the last ten days.) He quickened his step as if it were possible for the walk home to express and confirm his bountiful new sense of direction.

In his bedroom he tried on the spectacles in the long mirror on the inside of the cupboard door, and allowed the Doctor to caper about the room muttering lines for ten minutes. He began to see the glowing press that awaited his performance, and at this point broke off, sat on the bed and reminded himself that his part was very small.

5

"This," reflected Sam on his way to work, "is the best job I've ever had."

This morning, as on other mornings, he was setting off to the Playhouse wondering if the extraordinary spell of these rehearsals could be sustained over yet another day. So much was right that so much could go wrong. For instance his own part, the Doctor, could go stale on him; each time they came to his scene he had to suppress the dread that Ivan might become impatient with his performance, that he himself might fail to execute it with sufficient style and conviction, and that then it would be altered and smashed. This never happened; the scene changed, but always on the basis of what was already there, as in a process of growth. Another fear was that Ivan and Tom might fall out, their partnership collapse for some small reason of wounded vanity or failing nerve, and the production, rudderless, founder in the last week.

Or perhaps Ivan's extraordinary energies might suddenly wither away. It was hard to explain exactly how he dominated rehearsals, but that he did so no one in the company would dispute. He interfered only occasionally: when his help was asked for, or when someone was in difficulties. Perhaps a couple of times a day he would take a scene in hand. Otherwise he stayed within the boundaries of his own large part. What he offered the company, what had become the catalyst for the entire production, was an ardent, unremitting attention to whatever work was in hand. When he did have a suggestion to make, he interposed it into the scene so deftly (with a click of the fingers and a few spare fervent words) that even the actors were hardly aware of the interruption.

Sam loved to watch him at work, straddling a chair with his chin

D*

cupped in his fist or perched on the edge of a table, as still as a photograph and wholly absorbed in the working actors. The concentration he offered them, transfiguring his lined face with a beatific scowl divested of the least self-concern, was both challenge and reward, and reminded Sam of a definition he had read somewhere of the true function of a director: that he should be an ideal audience of one. As he watched him, Sam's mind took snapshots. He knew that the images he had of this intent figure would be with him long after the details of the production had become faded and confused. His concentration seemed to be an unforced thing. It was as if he sought to recognize in what the actors offered him the outline of some production of the play, the prompt copy of which had been lost as long ago perhaps as Webster's first conception of it. His labor was one of rediscovery. And as one by one these archaic stage directions were reconstructed and obeyed, so a kind of ethic came to be unearthed, charted by the modesty and passion of the work, and rescued finally from neglect by a company that recognized that neglect as having been their own, forced upon them by an inconstant profession. This job referred back to the day each had decided to become an actor, and for the time being it confirmed that the decision had had value. How often in their careers they had had reason to doubt it.

There seemed to be no bad performances; each actor contributed with the full strength of himself, and frequently shortcomings became virtues. When Don Petersen, playing the tiny part of the madman, revealed his crippling self-consciousness, Ivan persuaded him to incorporate his inhibition into his part. A stricken catatonic creature, moving in agonized jerks, turned up when they next rehearsed the scene, surprising everybody, not the least Don, who, though he had appeared on a stage before, had never up till now actually acted. Ivan watched the birth of this extraordinary and decidedly courageous performance with jubilation. Other actors began to take risks. With little choice in the matter a risk had been what Sam had taken at the beginning of rehearsals, and apparently this had won him Ivan's esteem.

One day after lunch Ivan said to Tom, "In that first scene when Sam, here, comes on as one of Ferdinand's courtiers, I think it might be better if he came on as the Doctor. Establish his identity early on. The play is full of references to disease and hospitals. It would be nice to have the court physician in attendance from the start. He could come on with a jar of leeches."

They tried the entrance with Sam as the Doctor. "Take the Duke's pulse," said Ivan, interrupting. "He's talking about going off to the wars. Give him a medical."

It was a suggestion which Sam was prepared to take further. "Would it be too much," he asked, "if I bled him?"

"How do you mean?"

"Well, we're bringing his armor on with us, which presumably he's just taken off or is about to put on. If his forearm was bare . . ."

Ivan gave a cautionary chuckle.

"No, look," insisted Sam, "there's a perfect place for it. In the pause when Ferdinand shuts up his flatterers, I strip four leeches off the inside of his forearm and pop them back in the jar."

"An outrageous suggestion. Try it."

They returned to their marks. "But listen," he added, "do nothing until the pause. Just very discreetly take his pulse. And keep the leeches out of sight."

They arrived at the pause, and Sam did his business. Ivan wheezed with glee. "Splendid! A kick in the bum for the pedants. But three leeches, not four. Four's too many." He smiled naughtily at the stage crew. "Props, write down three leeches."

Sam was now emboldened to make a further suggestion that had been on his mind all week. In the scene where the Duchess is confined with the eight madmen (the scene in which Don Petersen had recently surprised them) Sam was playing the part of a mad lawyer. There was, however, a mad doctor among the group, at present being played by Toby Burton, and it had occurred to Sam that if he and Toby were to exchange parts, then the mad doctor and the doctor he was to play a few scenes later might become the one person. There was no textual justification for this, but it might work, and if it did it would certainly save him from the anxiety of a quick change before his big scene. He waited for a chance to speak to Ivan and Tom together.

"It's a possibility," said Ivan.

"We can try it," said Tom. "Will it really make sense of your next scene, though?"

"Mm," agreed Ivan. "On the other hand it's quite a nice macabre idea that the court doctor spends his time in and out of insane asylums. But anyway, have a word to Toby, and if he doesn't object we might give it a try next time."

More than the fact that Sam's part had grown by two scenes, what pleased him was the knowledge that he now had but a single identity in the production, his Doctor. There would be no running upstairs for a frantic change of appearance, no hasty donning of beards to give character to nonexistent parts. He had his proper role to play, and all his energies could be focused upon it.

This morning, on his way to work with the first complete run-through of the play ahead of him, he reflected on his good luck and on the source of it, the veteran actor who had become not only his benefactor but that of the whole company. Why was Ivan being so beneficently spendthrift with his energies? He had responsibilities enough with his own enormous part. Was it simply that the play had released in him a store of vitality that it gave him pleasure to expend? Sometimes when his exuberant, crafty gaze played over the faces of the company, in itself sufficient to spark off a morning's work, this seemed to be the case. But at other times during the yawning afternoons when the work stumbled and he gave it his concentration only with an effort of will, then it was almost as if he were engaged in some act of penance, making reparations perhaps for the wasted opportunities of the past. Ivan had always been a star, but certainly over the last ten or fifteen years he had done little to suggest the present reach of his talent.

Even the weather seemed to be sharing in the spirit of un-explained bounty, and this morning summer was suddenly in the air. Sam approached a small greengrocer's shop and collided with the pungent smell of fresh oranges. All the scents of the town had come out to play in the new warmth. For the first time this year he was walking through streets in his shirt-sleeves, carrying his jacket, his body liberated from cloth after a long winter and feeling as it used to along the leafy suburban avenues of Sydney. Around him English trees were turning green, but he did not know their names. The names he remembered belonged for the moment to the wrong language: gum, wattle, jacaranda, bougainvillia and (at the bottom of their garden) the imported palms and the big magnolia tree. Even those trees he should have recognized grew differently here in their homeland, greener, denser, more certain of themselves. Though unable to name them he felt welcomed among them, himself transplanted to the original soil.

In the rehearsal room the preparations afoot and the air of nervous expectation suggested the imminence of a small battle. The company stood about occupying themselves with small urgent tasks such as donning some fragment of costume, a cloak, a skirt, a makeshift hat, or consulting a script for the accuracy of a line. The stage staff darted here and there slightly bent at the waist, setting properties and checking them on their lists, keen to show their willingness if not their ability to move in two directions at once. Deposited around the room was a lusterless collection of arms—swords in limp scabbards, rusting pikes and daggers bereft of their past jewels—together with papier-mâché goblets, battered lanterns, bags of money and dusty tomes, all of them the skeletal remains of past productions put to work again. As far as this show went they had a decidedly neutral look. Sam felt for the spectacles in his pocket, new and brash. Though he had practiced in his room with them, he had not rehearsed with them before, restrained by some instinct to hold his fire. They would have their debut today, but not until much later in the play, in his big scene.

The room became still, wound up like a piece of machinery for the run-through. A spindly arrangement of benches and soiled rostrums showed the levels of the set, and the waiting actors stood by the properties tables, themselves become properties till the play was over. "Are we all right?" whispered Tom to the stage manager, who conferred briefly with his assistants before nodding.

"Stand by, everyone!" said Terence to everyone standing by, with the exorbitant authority expected in his post. He glanced at the stopwatch gripped in his fist. "Curtain going *up!*"

The play was under way, and one by one the actors queued up for the perilous business of boarding her on the move. Each was on his own, on trial, bearing the burden of immediate proof. Ivan stood by himself down left waiting to make his entrance. It was clear that this morning he had but one concern, his own part. His strength had retreated inward, and his gaze as it flicked about the room was resolute and cold, almost at bay. Of all the people in the room he was the most obliged to prove himself, and no one was more aware of this than Ivan. His stillness was profoundly active. Sam guessed at a pumping heart, the merciless demands on physical resources made by this odd manufactured crisis, the putting on of a play. No actor was exempt from the private humiliation of nerves. It was the common denominator of the profession. But Ivan, Sam remembered, had survived on top for forty years, and needed no one's encouragement. He had heard his cue and had glided into the play with the precision of a motor starting: "I do haunt you still." His first speech was not much more than a whisper, and his small audience craned forward imperceptibly as if something were about to happen which they should on no account miss. He played the whole scene in this somewhat low-keyed manner, and the restraint only served to whet expectation. Whether nervous or not Ivan knew what he was about. The morning was just beginning and he had a long way to go.

Sam's first appearance went smoothly. His business with the leeches (though on reflection he had come to feel a little shame-faced about it) seemed to work all right. His next entrance was not for an hour and he settled down to watch. Throughout the second and third acts, the most difficult stretch of the play, Ivan continued to hold power. He seemed mainly concerned with keeping the production lucid and swift. The rewards of the early part of the morning were going to the other leads, Duke Ferdinand, the Duchess, the Cardinal, who were attacking their parts with verve and daring. Ivan, on the other hand, seemed to be waiting for something. His best moments were moments of listening. It seemed as if he were straining to catch the pitch of the play, waiting upon it with mediumistic patience. Then suddenly with the fourth act his performance began to smolder. One sensed it immediately in the intenser rhythms of his body and in the heightened conviction behind his lines. It was as if he had begun to move in an atmosphere more sustaining than air. In the first speech of the act the play was there supporting him:

FERDINAND: How doth our sister duchess bear herself
    In her imprisonment?
BOSOLA: Nobly: I'll describe her.
    She's sad as one long us'd to't, and she seems
    Rather to welcome the end of misery
    Than shun it: a behaviour so noble
    As gives a majesty to adversity.
    You may discern the shape of loveliness
    More perfect in her tears than in her smiles.

The other actors took fire. The dark harmonies of the play were in command.

BOSOLA: Yet, methinks,
    The manner of your death should much
        afflict you:
    This cord should terrify you.
DUCHESS: Not a whit:
    What would it pleasure me to have my throat cut
    With diamonds? Or be smothered
    With cassia? Or to be shot to death with pearls?
    I know death hath ten thousand several doors
    For men to take their exits; and 'tis found
    They go on such strange geometrical hinges,
    You may open them both ways; any way, for Heaven
        sake,
    So I were out of your whispering. Tell my brothers
    That I perceive death, now I am well awake,
    Best gift is they can give or I can take.

In perfect silence the company watched the dreadful events of the play take place: Bosola directing the murder of the woman he had come close to loving, his reward from the Duke ("I'll tell thee what I'll give thee. . . . I'll give thee a pardon for this murder"), his remorse; the anguish with which Ivan spoke the lines

> That we cannot be suffered
> To do good when we have a mind to it!
> This is manly sorrow!

numbed the room. Act IV came to an end, and in the hushed assembly nothing happened; the company sat quite still, partakers in a mystery. Tom rose with pale excited features. "Let's go on," he said quietly, and the play proceeded.

With a shock Sam realized that his Doctor was but one scene away. Abruptly the spell cast upon him as an audience was broken, and he began to prepare for the earnest business of casting spells himself. He joined Francis Roland at the back of the rehearsal room and felt for the spectacles in his pocket. He held them out of sight until the scene was almost on him, then as inconspicuously as possible slipped them on. They had made their entrance and Pescara had spoken to him. He had just begun to reply when something appalling happened. The spectacles had slipped half an inch down his nose, and for a moment he was convinced that they were going to fall to the floor and smash. His reflexes, now established by rehearsal, guided him through the rest of the speech, and he found that for some reason the spectacles had held. He wrinkled his nose vigorously to return them to their original position on the bridge, and for further safety tilted his face upward. Nonetheless, in spite of these precautions, again the spectacles slipped. This time, however, he was ready for them, and blocked their descent with a twitch of the nostrils. Whenever he spoke, his spectacles slipped and his nose twitched. Sam was making a wondrous discovery. The Doctor, of course, had an academic tic! Not only did the tic seem right but so did the new disdainful carriage of the head; he felt luxuriantly at ease in his character, and this new security lent a sheen of improvisation to the well-trod patterns of his part. As long as he could maintain that freshness, his small audience would be mesmerized and he had the keen pleasure of knowing it.

The run-through was over and the company was atingle with its success. As Tom said in his notes, there were a hundred details yet to be attended to, but no one doubted that the company had in its care the opportunity for a remarkable occasion. The responsibility of bringing this occasion to public view on a first night had acquired a precarious splendor, and the first night was now the common thought of the company, a point to which many lines were converging. Sam remembered the way rehearsals had begun, and his desperation then seemed an age away. The passion with which he had fought for his own interests now flowed through the play in harmony with the interests of the others, suggesting Utopian simplicities. How long would it last? The thought itself was a betrayal. Common sense he had properly abandoned. There was no thought now beyond the first night. The work they were engaged upon was the most important in the world, and it held the promise of such manifest perfection that its unveiling could hardly be less than an apocalypse. Anything might happen: a planet stopped in its course, or an audience redeemed.

After lunch they returned for further notes. "Ivan has something to say about the scene with the madmen," said Tom.

Ivan rose. "Sorry, Sam. This affects you. I don't think it's right bringing the Doctor into that scene. In fact I think the trouble is we're overdifferentiating these madmen. I've had a word with Tom and the designer about it; it's largely a matter of costume. There's a statue of two madmen they used to have outside the old Bedlam hospital; it's preserved in a museum down in the City of London somewhere. That's what we want. Shaven heads and issue rags, the monotony, the dreadful uniformity of misery. The performances are fine. It's just a question of having the same look. Get your heads shaved. If we bring the Doctor in, I'm sure he's going to enfeeble that first visual impression. I see your problem, Sam. You don't want a quick change before your scene. Well, unless you feel strongly about it, I suggest you give your madman to someone else to play—is that possible, Tom?—and save yourself for the Doctor."

Sam agreed. The Doctor had no right to that scene. It had been an idea of convenience and undoubtedly a bad one. Sam was quite happy to abandon it, especially in the interest of his subsequent appearance. "What about the leeches, then?" he asked.

"No, no! Keep that! I like it. It's irreverent and fun. Very good for the play."

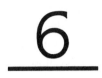

6

AMANDA's flat was situated beyond the theater on the far side of
the park. She had given him careful instructions on how to find it:
first locate the Drama School, a big Georgian building with a sign
up, then follow the road all the way round to the back of it, and
her flat was the old stables. During the week you could get to it
through the Drama School itself, but this was a Sunday. She had
drawn him a map with a note at the bottom in large confident
handwriting: "Don't forget the plaster of Paris!" He had been
surprised by her handwriting, unmistakably a woman's yet as bold
as a cricket bat. He was reminded of the hands of some women
(Valerie in the cosmetics shop for instance), where the resolution
of their natures appears momentarily to surface in the terminal
strength of their nails.

Sam had his plaster of Paris and also a bottle of Yugoslavian
white wine. Outside the Drama School he paused to examine a
poster advertising their season at the Playhouse. The two organiza-
tions were loosely associated, the school likewise having been
founded by Virgil Graves as complement to his theater. In the
middle of the poster Sam's own name saluted him, splendidly
haloed by his own fascination with it.

He stood in the courtyard behind the dark unlit bulk of the
Drama School, and listened to recorded harpsichord music. It
seemed to be coming from one small yellow window set high in
what had once been a hayloft. He followed the music into the
stables beneath, and traced it up the wooden flight of steps against
the far wall to a closed trapdoor. He knocked on it as he had been
told, and immediately overhead heard the rapid somewhat threatening approach of footsteps. The trapdoor swung open, held aloft

by Richard Wayland, who on one knee was smiling down at him. "Come on up," he said.

He ascended as far as his waist into the room, enjoying its light, its warmth, its Bach and its smell of onions cooking. "Don't dawdle," said Richard pleasantly, "you're letting the draft in." So stooping to avoid a beam, he stepped up into the room. It was timbered everywhere, the floor, the walls, the sloping roof. The furniture was old, perhaps valuable, but it had the sensible un-fussed-over look of long use. There were a big Flemish cupboard, a Chesterfield upholstered in worn leather, an upright piano and a number of unmatched ladderback armchairs. The present occu-pant's taste, impulsive and cheerful, was asserted here and there in objects of magpie hopefulness; a dishcloth printed with an old engraving of David Garrick was pinned to one wall, while a vivid Mexican blanket covered the chest on which stood her record player and a great stack of correspondence. Elsewhere there were magazines in French, books and (immediately recognizable) photographs of family. The room shouted information about Amanda. He had uncovered the second layer of the onion of her personality and for the moment found it absorbing.

Richard relieved him of his bottle of wine, and Sam was faintly put out; he felt more inclined to present it to her himself. "Amanda's busy in the kitchen," Richard explained and went to a doorway and called through, "Emma, Sam's brought you a bottle of white wine."

"How lovely!" she answered out of sight. "Emma," Sam de-cided, must be a family name. He wondered how Richard had gained access to it so quickly, and resolved never to use it himself. Then he remembered that Richard had been in a production with her mother a season or two back; he had either first met or heard about Amanda then, so perhaps he had some right to it.

She came into the room with a bowl of salad. "Hello, Sam. You caught me right in the middle of draining something. Thank you for the lovely wine." She picked up the bottle. "Yugoslavian! I've never had that! But, honestly, you needn't have bothered." This seemed probable. Two bottles of wine were already on the table.

She had taken over the social capability of some forceful parent as naturally as she had the color of her eyes, both as a matter of course and as little subject to stumbling questions.

"Let's have some now," she suggested, and Richard drew the cork. They sat with their glasses and talked. Sam was glad of Richard's presence, which provided a rivalry agreeable because largely unreal. Richard was already involved with a determined young actress who came up from London frequently and unexpectedly to visit him, and his own liking for Amanda was uncomplicated by any concealed sexual intent. Yet it was possible for the two men to engage in a gently competitive game, directing their talk turn by turn into a bid for her attention.

Amanda watched them, sipping her drink, secure in the enviable strength of her inexperience. Her eyes were bright with a general expectation so frank and unclouded that for a precious year or two she would have the gift of literally willing life to be good. Surely Sam was not the only one who wanted to thieve a little of that faith while it was going. Perhaps he and Richard were rivals after all. The photographs of her parents looked down assessing them both, and particularly in this environment it was impossible to dissociate her entirely from her privilege. She had thrown her head back to catch the last trickle of wine from her glass, and Sam shamed himself by remembering the tabloid rumor of her father's drinking. He felt impatient for the time when he would know her more variously than he knew of her parents' fame. Other sorts of renown—had she been the daughter of a duke or a murderer, for example—would hardly have touched him, but success in the theater was something against which no actor would be expected to have immunity. Richard, chatting away blandly about her mother's latest success, felt no such scruples, and this in Amanda's eyes, innocent of most things save the mischief of reputation, gave Sam the advantage with her.

They ate a casserole by the light of a practical oil lamp, mellow and agreeably smelly. She had cooked an excellent dinner.

"Isn't this super?" she said presently, and her guests agreed. Sam found himself smiling broadly; he was savoring the special pleasure of hospitality when there is no price to pay in the way of inhibiting social rectitude, a feeling of intense goodwill to those about him combined with the sly recognition of having got away with something for nothing. Amanda continued: "This is my first flat. I've never had a flat of my own before."

"That's not true, is it, Emma?" said Richard, as if the news contradicted a volume of family secrets. "What about New York?"

"I lived with Dad then. Of course I could do what I liked. He was hardly ever there. But it's not the same thing."

"I like this flat," contributed Sam.

"Isn't it *super*? I wouldn't mind living here forever." She was on her feet. "Let me show you round!"

The flat had two small bedrooms with the same sloping ceilings of unpainted timber, and a kitchen with an enormous Edwardian bath in it. "You see, I can lie in the bath in the mornings and lean over and make tea." While they were in the kitchen she prepared them coffee, and they perched on the edge of the bath drinking it. "Come on, then," she said when they put the cups down, "what about this nose? Where's the plaster of Paris?"

Sam waited stretched out on the sofa while they mixed the plaster. "First of all we have to take a mold of your nose," explained Amanda. "Then from that we make the cast." Using a fish knife, she began to smear the viscous white substance over the region of his nose. He closed his eyes, taking a barbershop comfort from the attentions of her careful fingers. He could feel her breath touching his face in little gasps of concentration.

"There!" she said. "Now we have to wait."

He opened his eyes and saw them grinning at him with playful malice. "What's the joke?" he inquired, heavily nasal.

"You," said Richard. "You look like a car smash."

"Oh, my God," said Amanda suddenly. "I forgot something. The vaseline!"

"What?" said Sam.

"The vaseline. Quick, take it off. We've got to put vaseline on first."

They scraped the hardening plaster from his face and he winced as it took with it some hairs from his nostrils. "That hurt!" he exclaimed.

"Better wash it all off quickly," said Amanda, unable not to laugh. "Then we'll try again."

"That really hurt," he insisted, returning from the kitchen.

"You're lucky it hadn't set," she said. "There was a girl at school who lost all her eyebrows that way." They all laughed so much at this they had to sit down.

"Come on," said Richard. "Suffer for your Art."

She soothed him by smearing his pink nose with vaseline, and despite her intermittent giggling, this time the procedure was successful. She played a record while the plaster set, then carefully removed the mold and he stared into the blind tunnel of his own nose.

From the mold Amanda made a cast, then another one for luck, and he went home that night with two noses in a box.

The following morning had been set aside for a costume parade. Sam read on the notice board that he would find his costume waiting for him in the dressing room on the second floor, which he was to share with three others. He climbed the stairs and was a little put out to discover that he was not the first to lay claim to the room. A canvas grip had been placed squarely on the best seat over by the window, and the next best place by the wall had also been reserved by someone who had unpacked his makeup things and left them neatly covered by a pink towel. The room was pervaded by the smell of the new costumes. He looked for his own among the laden hangers and two came tumbling down upon him. He hoisted their sumptuous weight back onto the rail and continued his search but was unable to find a label bearing his name. He checked through the hangers a second time, and it then occurred to him that he hadn't as yet had a fitting of any sort, which was odd. He felt some anxiety and set off downstairs for the rehearsal room, were Tom, his designer, David Beynon, and Eric from the wardrobe were conducting the costume parade. Actors stood here and there isolated by the insecurity and pleasure of wearing strange new clothes, like children whose fancy dress as yet inhibits play. One by one they took their turns on the rostrum, while Tom and his colleagues whispered in judgment.

Sam explained that he had no costume and Tom looked dubious and irritable. David spoke up, blushing. "I thought the Doctor's part was cut."

"No, it's back again," said Tom.

"It's still cut on my list," said Eric.

There was a silence while they wearily steeled themselves for another crisis. The morning had seen several.

"You haven't even started on the costume, then," said Tom.

"No," said Eric. "I understood it had been cut. It's cut on my list."

"Well, he's got to have a costume."

Eric fixed his eyes stubbornly on the list in his hand and said nothing.

"How soon could you get a costume ready?"

"The trouble is we just haven't allowed the time for it. The workroom is under tremendous pressure as it is."

"He's still got to have a costume! It's not a very complicated one, is it?"

David answered, "Just a black gown and gray breeches." Whereupon Eric sighed.

"Well!" said Tom.

"There's nothing very special about the costume," said David. "Just the ordinary black academic gown. We probably wouldn't have made that anyway. Maybe we could make him up a costume from stock."

"That's not very satisfactory."

"Let me try."

Tom snorted impatiently and eventually answered, "All right. But I'll want to have a look at it."

"Of course."

"And if it's no good you'll just *have* to make one."

At the end of the morning David preceded Sam up the steep wooden stairs that led from the flies to the big room where the costumes were stored. The stairway was now thick with undisturbed dust, but at one time or another the treads had been worn concave with use and the grain of the wooden handrail exposed in waxy corrugations. One was reminded again how old the building was. David was apologizing in gentle, Welsh, shocked tones at odds with his habitual bad language. "I'm really very sorry about this fuck-up. Bugger me, I did a design, you know, but then we were told the part had been cut. I'm very glad it's back, though. It's a nice little scene. I expect you enjoy it, don't you?" They had entered the storage room, a huge sinus in the dome of the theater, suspended over the drop of the auditorium and separated from it by worn floorboards and a lick of gilded plaster. It was no longer supposed to be very safe up there. Costumes hung in row upon row. "We might find something here," said David. "This lot go right back before the war. We never hire these buggers out. It's more like a museum."

It was hard to know where to begin. They waded in among the hanging garments, sending waves of muffled disturbance down their rows. "Look," said Sam, examining a label. "Godfrey Tearle wore that as Don Pedro in the thirties." They looked at the costume, a patchwork of the upholstery materials of its day, entirely deflated of life. It was hard to believe any diaphragm had ever heaved effectively within it.

They selected a heavy armful of jackets and doublets that might possibly serve, and Sam tried them on in front of the great speckled mirror with a splintered eagle crowning its frame. The mustiness of the costumes did not bother him. He had envisaged the Doctor in drab formal attire, and this chance to have some say in the way he would look delighted him. They decided finally on a worn black velvet jacket that needed only the addition of a ruff.

"I'll do a drawing and the wardrobe'll make you one of those black skullcaps, you know, very academic, maybe covering the ears," said David. "Are you going to wear a wig?"

"Yes, maybe just a little bit of dry hair poking out under the cap."

"There's wigs in all those cardboard boxes against the wall. You might find what you want there."

They searched among the boxes, but for the most part turned up wigs of a luxuriant and inappropriate auburn, a color as exceedingly rare in life as it was a common mutation in the close-bred environment under the lights. They had arrived at a set of wigs belonging to a production of *Richard III,* and prompted by an irrelevant curiosity, Sam sought out the principal's wig. Had there ever been a drama student, maimed by hopes without the skill to match them, who had not wanted to play that part? It was perhaps the first ambition of every unhappy child who had ever become an actor. Sam had little interest in the role now, but there had once been evenings when he, too, had hobbled to and fro before his gas fire simulating a withered arm and a hunchback. He lifted the shoulder-length of oiled hair from its box, smiling painfully at the funny shaming remembrance.

"There's another box here marked for Richard," said David. "He must have worn two of them." The second wig was similar to the first, but scraggier and touched with gray.

"I know, he wore this at the end," postulated Sam, "for the Battle of Bosworth. Here, I'm going to try it on."

The wig was an excellent color for the Doctor, though perhaps a little long. One ear had separated a thick gray lock, which ran like a whisker down the side of his face, and he quickly made a similar adjustment on the other side. The effect hinted at lugubrious Victorian scholarship and delighted him. He decided to try on the whole ensemble, black jacket, wig and spectacles. He stared at himself in the mirror, mouthed a line or two, and found himself laughing out loud with pleasure. Pending such odds and ends as cap, gown, shoes and breeches, it couldn't really have been better.

"What do you suppose the Doctor wore in that very first production?" asked Sam.

"The old *Malfi* costumes are around here somewhere. We can easily find out."

They discovered the remnants of the Virgil Graves production at the very end of the room, hanging limp and pathetically ugly beneath a fall of dust. The row commenced a gallows swinging as Sam hunted impatiently for all that remained of an earlier Doctor.

They found a torn maroon costume, quite useless. However, the black overgown hanging beside it had distinct possibilities. Sam tried it on, screwing up his face and holding his breath to avoid inhaling the dust. It proved to be exactly what they wanted, and both expatiated loudly over their find in the empty room.

They collected their precious rags together and, ridiculously excited, made their way back down the narrow flights of stairs.

As Sam left the stage door on his way to lunch, he saw approaching from a distance on strutting uncertain little legs the sugar-bag figure of Olive Delmer. At first he thought they would not meet, but it soon became apparent as they crossed the large car park in opposing diagonals that they were bound for the junction of the same street. Implacably like missile and target they were scheduled to collide, and even from a distance of fifty yards neither could conceal from the other the lack of relish felt for the prospect. To Sam, Olive was a pert flirtatious middle-aged woman to whom he went in terror of revealing by so much as a blink his complete sexual indifference. (He sensed that when he got to know her well she would expect a kiss on the cheek at almost every encounter.)

"Hello!" she crooned as they met.

"Hello, Miss Delmer."

"Call me Olive, dear!"

He nodded and didn't, already feeling himself lost beneath the sticky folds of concealment in which both were offering up their personalities.

"You going this way, ducky?" she asked.

"Yes."

"Oh good."

Sam stared up at the sky, a compromise way of alluding to the weather. It was a nice day; he hadn't noticed before.

"How's it all going, then, down at rehearsal?" asked Olive.

"Coming along fine, I think."

"I don't like the play much. Do you?"

"You don't like it?"

"No! I think it's a beastly depressing thing. *I* didn't want them to do it."

"Really."

"Pity about your part," she said, with an unexpected show of sympathy.

"How do you mean?"

"Having it cut and all that."

"It's actually back now. They've put it back."

"Oh!" she said, and the arc of her tone indicated that whatever previously she had felt on his behalf he had effectively destroyed by contradicting her.

They walked on in silence. "It's a nice day," said Sam.

"What about old Ivan? Has he started playing up yet?"

This interested him. "How do you mean?" he asked mildly.

"Interfering!" she whispered with a grimace. "Sticking his big nose in where it's not wanted."

"He's been rather helpful so far."

"Oh, he can be. Oh yes. When things are going well. But when things start going wrong! Then he can be a terror. A *terror!*"

What enraged him more than the impertinence of her judgment was the likelihood that there was some truth in it.

"You're too young to remember, of course, but when he did that season in London just after the war—the stories that were about! The tantrums and the scenes!"

He saw his chance for escape. "This is me, I'm afraid," he said, halting outside the cosmetics shop.

"Buying lipstick, dear?" she asked, and laughed so much he needn't have bothered with his mumbled reply about nose putty.

"Bye-bye, then," said Olive, "and don't forget what I said. You want to watch your step with that old one."

"Bye . . . Olive," he forced himself to say, and was glad he had when he saw the brightening effect it had had upon her. Then he fled into the shop.

Valerie was there and his eyes came to rest upon her with wonder. The injustice of her beauty was a marvelous and terrible thing. What failure of instinct prevented Olive from plucking the three corkscrew hairs that grew from a mole on her cheek? It turned the simple act of looking at her into a kind of treachery. Valerie smiled and he moved, aching, toward her.

"I've been wondering when you'd be back," she said. "I've got it all wrapped up for you." She produced a small box wrapped in the exotic paper of the shop.

"You're all by yourself today?" he said.

"Till two o'clock. Mrs. Willis's at lunch."

Whether she realized it or not, she had let slip a challenge, and for a moment the spell of her flesh took second place to it. He became nervous. This was an improvisation he hadn't really intended; Mrs. Willis was at lunch, he was alone with her in the shop (though another customer might come in the door), and if he wanted her, which at the moment seemed beyond any question, then now was the time to act. The opportunity might not come again.

He tried to steady himself with a smile. "Do you ever come and see us at the theater?" he asked.

"I went last year to see the *Midsummer's Night Dream*."

"Did you like it?"

"Oh yes."

"Would you like me to get you a ticket for the next show?"

She looked pleased and surprised. "Thank you very much. That would be lovely. Thank you very much."

So far it had been fairly easy. The procedure was one he had used before. He was not so confident about the next move, however.

"Look, um, I'm only rehearsing at the moment and I've got most evenings free. You wouldn't like to have dinner with me one night . . ."

Valerie looked down at the counter. "Well, I don't know . . ." she said, and his question fell into a pocket of silence. They both seemed to be watching it plummeting.

Someone had to speak. "The play will be on in about a week. After that I'll be busy every evening. It's just that, well, now I'm free. Look, I know this is a bit premature—" He immediately wondered whether the use of the word "premature" had been wise. He suspected it of having vague sexual associations, though he couldn't for the moment recall what they were.

"But I don't know your name or anything, do I?" She had looked up at him and smiled, and he took heart, remembering what it was that was premature: ejaculation, also birth. An unhappy conjunction.

"Yes, you do. You took my name when I ordered the nose putty. And I know yours: it's Valerie. Valerie Who?"

"Hilary," she answered.

Valerie Hilary. He pressed his advantage. "After all, I'm a stranger in the town. How else can I get to know people?"

"All right, then," she said.

"What, you'll have dinner with me?"

She nodded.

"That's wonderful," he said, and they both tried hard to smile. Valerie looked away.

There were now some practical details to be settled: a day, a time, a place to meet. He negotiated them as gracefully as he could, pulse quietly thudding, but something in the nature of their arrangements, rigid and final, discomforted them both, a barely perceptible foretaste perhaps of guilt and regret. It was like submitting to some primitive test of nerve without which they could not participate in the games involving men and women, and they hurried to conclude their arrangements in toneless voices, holding each other's eyes only by an effort of will. They had agreed to meet the following Wednesday. Valerie would be working late making cold cream for Mrs. Willis in the basement, and he would pick her up at the shop at eight o'clock. With this settled, there seemed no point in hanging around. Both wanted to be alone to think about what they had let themselves in for.

He said goodbye and left the shop, but had to return to collect his nose putty. Again he returned, this time to pay for it; and when he finally departed, Valerie was laughing, her even teeth displayed like stars.

7

THE FIRST dress rehearsal was scheduled to begin at eleven o'clock in the morning and would continue indefinitely, possibly late into the night. Sam arrived at a quarter to ten just as the cleaner was finishing in his dressing room. It was otherwise empty, which pleased him, and he hastily arranged his makeup things before his mirror, eager and anxious about making a start. He looked at himself and removed some sleep from the corner of one eye; this was a jarring hour to embark upon a makeup and his dry face would take to the paint unwillingly. Nevertheless he knew exactly what sort of effect he wanted and was determined to achieve it. He handled his sticks of makeup with gingerly care as if, like a schoolboy's pen, they threatened him constantly with blotting, and he held his tongue between his teeth as he plotted the contours of the Doctor's face with areas of color.

Toby Burton, the actor whose radio had claimed the best place in the room, made an excessively rowdy entrance, or so it seemed to Sam, who strove to disguise the hostility he felt toward this or any other interruption. Without looking he mumbled a return to Toby's greeting and craned over the bench to draw a fine outline beneath one eye. Toby stood behind him watching the work, his expression reflecting the rebuke implicit in the industry of another; then with a sigh and a cheerful blasphemy he set about his own face-painting. Soon they were joined by Paul Poulsen, a young actor whose knees were double-jointed and whose large drooping eyes seemed constantly to be dreaming upon his own inversion, and finally by Francis Roland, the senior of the dressing room with an expensive education left behind somewhere in the past of his forty-five-odd years. For a while the talk looped over and around

Sam, grudgingly respectful to his air of intense preoccupation, bu soon they were all absorbed in their own makeups and the tall became broken and finally ceased altogether.

"Got a brown eyebrow pencil, mate?" said Toby to Franci Roland after a silence of nearly five minutes, and Paul Poulser immediately found one among his perfectly organized stock and stretched out his arm with it. It was passed down the row. Sam had almost finished his makeup. He took the Richard wig out of its box and attentively crowned himself with it. He looked at himself a moment, exhilarated with the success of his makeup, then hurried into his costume. At last in the long mirror the complete, be spectacled Doctor returned his appraising stare. The others swiveled in their chairs to look at him, impressed.

"That's marvelous," said Paul. "Where did you get the idea from?"

"I don't really know," he answered truthfully. Where had the Doctor come from? He stood before him now dressed in the rags of the past. Sam had been merely a dealer in scrap, assiduously collecting suitable fragments: from the play, from himself, from the tradition in which he found himself working. Yet this was no the whole truth, for in a sense the Doctor had always existed locked within him in the company of perhaps a dozen other part: that had yet to find their play. Some aspect of his personality tha would otherwise have remained captive and mute was being granted its freedom. Perhaps in the last analysis it was the reason he was an actor.

Sam set off for the stage. From each dressing room he passed over the loudspeaker system came the sound of the orchestra rehearsing the introductory music. The passageways of the theater were suddenly possessed with this unfamiliar and thrilling addendum to their work, and he hastened downstairs with the good new: of a further tiny ingredient: his makeup.

The set was magnificent. He went to the back of the auditorium the better to appreciate it. David Beynon had designed an architectural complex, part colonnade, part steps, which embraced the stage in a huge crescent, and which, open to an expanse of somber

112

sky behind, could equally serve for interiors or exteriors. There was little color in the set, but against it the Caravaggio costumes, executed with a strict period sense that refused to permit of the least theatrical distortion, showed up with an immediate brilliance. Alone in the dark stalls, bent over an illuminated drawing board, Tom and a consultant were preparing the lighting plot. At their guttural whispers into a nearby microphone the set reared up in floods of light or sank swiftly into eclipse. From the pit, where the orchestra rehearsed unseen, came fragments of music, ceasing as abruptly as they had begun. The score had been commissioned from an Italian composer, famous for a recent film score, and was a fine pastiche of Monteverdi, in which nonetheless was preserved a murmur of the composer's own disturbing idiom, redolent of a more modern unease.

Sam felt a new sort of admiration for the man who had planned for and now at last convened the work of these talented people. Tom was providing as fine a frame to contain the play as the market would allow. It only remained for the play to come alive within it, and this was a responsibility that was now largely in other hands. Greatly excited, Sam stood and absorbed these new elements in the production. At the very center of this storm of changing lights and subterranean music an unperturbed Frank Butler hammered nails in his own time into the base of a marble pillar. He was the only figure onstage.

It was obvious that it would be some time before the rehearsal began, so Sam took himself up to the first floor to wait in the canteen. Most of the company were gathered there, parading their new identities in the coffee queue. He gave and received glances, enjoying his fellow actors in their new aspects much as he might the photographs in some striking magazine coverage; the captions were bold and easy to read. Toby Burton and Don Petersen, unlikely courtiers, were abandoned in their praise of his makeup, which seemed generally to please. Amanda was sitting in the corner with Richard Wayland and he took his coffee to join them.

"Success!" she said, smiling as she examined him. With a

fingernail she gently tapped the putty tip to his nose. "Let me touch. Is it a good fit?"

"Perfect, thanks to you. Look, I can twitch it and it still sticks." He demonstrated this and they laughed.

"I feel like Theda Bara," she said, but with some pleasure. She was lavishly dressed in green and gold, and wore a splendid copper-colored wig. Sam wondered if she might yet be good in her part. Her throat and shoulders were bare, and as they talked he took surreptitious account of them. She was a little too skinny to play the part of a great voluptuary, but the designer had made the very best of her small bosom and the shapeliness she derived from the slight muscularity of her young body. Her clear skin was checked along the top of her shoulders by a faint track of freckles, mark of idle days in the sun (like almost all Australian girls).

"Full company onstage please. Full company onstage." The announcement came over the loudspeaker, and the actors scraped and rustled to their feet. Downstairs they encountered the principals, who for the most part had waited for the call in their dressing rooms. Rachel Frost brushed past Sam, superbly costumed and looking Amanda's age, trailing after her the admiring stares of the company's young men, which she treated to a wry, amiable, slightly bitter disregard. From out of the shadows of the prompt corner Ivan strolled into view. For a couple of seconds he became once more the famous and remote star Sam remembered from the Saturday afternoon pictures of his boyhood. He looked years younger in a peaked black wig and a spare close-fitting costume of brown, and the whites of his eyes showed up vividly in his painted face. In a way it was an old-fashioned makeup, more highly colored and defined than the faces around him, yet the very anachronisms of his style, such was the honesty of his talent, were a source of excitement. Sam caught his eye and the two actors looked one another over. Ivan nodded his head and winked.

Tom had come up from the auditorium and was speaking. "All right, everybody. This is going to be a very long tiring day and I ask for your patience. I don't want any acting. This is a technical dress rehearsal and lots of things are sure to go wrong. So be prepared for a long wait. The canteen will stay open until ten tonight."

By four o'clock that afternoon they had not yet reached the end of the first scene. Sam had wandered about the theater, from the canteen, to his dressing room, to the auditorium, in flight from his own uneasy yawning. The stimulus of fancy dress had soon spent itself. He joined a line of actors slouched in the dark at the rear of the stalls. Onstage nothing was happening. The displayed actors sat wearily apart from each other, waiting for the lights to be adjusted and for the word that they should continue. Ivan had sprawled himself out full length on the floor and lay with his eyes shut. Nonetheless one sensed at once the tension behind their lassitude. These delays were taking a heavy toll of their confidence and vitality.

At midnight they were still at work, with the last third of the play untouched. Tom came on to the stage, pale and tired, to address the company: "We'll break for now. Tomorrow we'll begin where we left off and finish the play. Then after that we'll start the run-through that was scheduled for the morning. I'd like to begin at the same time tomorrow, please, so everyone in full costume and makeup first thing."

Eleven hours later they were boxed in their costumes again and waiting. Sam caught anxious sight of himself in the various mirrors dispersed about the theater; something was wrong with his makeup today but he couldn't decide what. It took six hours to finish the play, and they weren't ready to embark on the run-through until seven-thirty ʰhat night.

Tom addressed the company: "All right, everybody. The worst is over. Now let's have a straight run-through with lots of life and pace. We won't stop unless we absolutely have to."

The curtain rose in the empty theater and almost immediately something went astray in the lighting plot. "Sorry! Stop! Stop!" said Tom from the dark auditorium, but the actors, lost in the nervous momentum of the opening, carried on. *"Stop!"* he yelled, and they fell into an abashed silence. The lights were corrected and they continued, only to be interrupted a few minutes later when a movable component of the set jammed.

An hour and a half later they were still on the first scene. Each random hitch affected the actors as if they themselves were in some way culpable. A profound discouragement began to settle over the theater. Sam sat out front trying to catch a glimpse of the play they had known at rehearsals, but it had vanished, slipped through their fingers like water. They were left with a cumbersome, unworkable box of tricks, made of electric lights, wood and smelling canvas whose functions it would be impossible ever to synchronize. The weary actors were diminished by it, lost within it as in a maze, and every foot of the stage seemed fraught with hazard for them.

At eleven o'clock, barely halfway through the play, Ivan began to dry up on his lines. Up till then he had seemed, if rather low-spirited, admirably calm and detached. Now with some alarm the company had to watch him wading into difficulties. His fatigue turned to anger as he snapped his fingers for prompt after prompt. The text seemed to have vanished from his head. He stamped his foot and cursed savagely into the empty house.

"Don't worry, Ivan," said Tom out of the darkness. There was a tiny hint of panic in his voice.

Sam felt disinclined to watch further and left for the canteen but found it had just shut. He went to his dressing room and sat in the boring company of his own reflection, like a poor TV program to which one's attention nevertheless keeps returning. There was no position where he could entirely escape a mirror, so he reconciled himself to the fatuity of his own gaze and pulled a face or two. Over the loudspeaker he heard the play proceeding; it seemed to have settled down somewhat. They were approaching his scene, so he went downstairs again. Backstage in the semidark he saw Ivan slumped on a rickety upright chair looking dejected and exhausted. He heard him sigh, then mutter "Jesus Christ" to himself.

The final line of the play had at last been said by two-thirty that morning. Neither Sam's scene nor any part of the play had escaped the mockery of exhaustion that night, and the expressions on the faces of the gathered company were uniformly despondent. Their costumes hung on them like chains, and the makeup on their faces had become grime. Nothing seemed less likely than that the play would ever be in a state for presentation, and the optimism of previous rehearsals was seen to have been bred entirely of a remote ignorance. Only one stale comfort was available: all they were doing was putting on a play, and after all what could be less important?

Tom was addressing them. "Well, everybody, that was awful, absolutely awful. I can't tell you how bad it was. You've simply got to be better than that. And I know you can be. We've got four days to the final dress rehearsal and the first night, and there's a lot of work to do. I want to see a real change by the next time we dress-rehearse."

The company were too exhausted to react one way or another to the crude psychology of this exhortation, or to the undisguised peevishness of the tone. The assumption seemed to be that they had been bad on purpose. The ragged actors dispersed to their dressing rooms, unbuttoning their costumes as they went.

At the stage door Sam ran into Ivan, waiting there for his hire-car to arrive. He smelled of whisky. The sharp expression in his eyes might almost have been fear. "I've been worrying about the wrong things," he murmured, and shook his head. Sam bade him good night and, disquiet now added to his fatigue, set off for the Ozone.

Sam was still fretting about the play when he went to collect Valerie at eight o'clock the following evening. He had not anticipated so demoralizing a dress rehearsal and felt in no mood for the responsibility of dining a stranger. None of his scenes had been touched on that day and he had hung about the theater nervy and bored. He tapped on the glass door, and a sign reading CLOSED shuddered on the far side of the glass. It dangled from one small suction cup, pink in color and rather obscene.

Valerie's head appeared up the stairs from the basement and he prayed that he would still find her attractive. For a moment he doubted it. She had put her hair up, and he noticed the plump back of her neck, suggesting, he was not sure why, stupidity. She approached him soundlessly the other side of the door, smiling awkwardly. She was heavily made up and dressed in a two-piece suit of a soft lilac color, burdened with those accessories that Sam had not allowed for: bag, gloves, bracelets, high-heeled shoes and stockings pulled up tight over her surprisingly thin legs. (He realized with a shock that her legs were a detail he had never had the opportunity to account for.) He had somehow visualized taking her out to dinner dressed as he had first liked her, in her pink-nylon work coat. She fumbled with the lock on the door; then they faced each other, strangers. At once something reassured him: her smell, which she owed probably to some inexpensive but carefully chosen toilet water. In fact now that he was reconciling himself to the absence of her nylon work coat, he could see that she was dressed with a good deal of natural taste in colors that became her. This was something that evidently concerned her. He imagined her thoughts succeeding each other like the soft colors of a bunch of cloth patterns flopping silently beneath a thumb.

They discussed where they would eat and settled on a new Chinese restaurant in the market, practically the only place open in South Brad apart from the two expensive hotels, which Sam, still on rehearsal pay, had hoped to avoid. He suggested a drink somewhere first, and Valerie led him to her preference, the Orchid Bar of the Richmond Hotel. Here she asked for a Bitter Lemon. Some residuum of adolescence in him interpreted this as the first defeat of the evening. It took a long time to catch the attention of the waiter, who sensed perhaps the abstemiousness of the order. But eventually their drinks were paid for and within reach on the black glass tabletop, and he had no choice but to give her his entire attention.

"Well, here goes," said Sam.

"Skoal," said Valerie.

Her shyness was expressing itself as a kind of boredom. She sipped carefully at her drink and looked sidelong with neutral eyes at the goings-on around her, while Sam pondered on what to say next. She would answer him but invariably they would arrive back where they had started, at a pause, and her gaze would embark again on its indifferent roving. Sam ordered another round of drinks, wondering how long it would be before he started to sweat; some hours of this lay ahead of him. On the other hand he found her undeniably beautiful, though, if anything, this made it worse. Her bare forearms, as plump and delicate as doves, moved slowly here and there, answering the demands of her cigarette and drink. It was a great shame that they seemed to have so little to say to each other.

They set off for the Chinese restaurant, Sam anticipating a walk of awkward silence. Suddenly, on her own initiative, Valerie had slipped her arm through his, drawn herself close to him, and they were stepping along the Parade as harmoniously in step as ballroom dancers. This was one of the things she could do well, and she had taken charge. Apparently the discomfort between them had been his alone; Valerie's placid expression held no sign of it. It occurred to him, and his curiosity was aroused by the thought, that conversation was probably not something that she particularly expected from boyfriends. How many evenings had she spent in the Orchid Bar with partner, fingering her Bitter Lemon and keeping herself an impassive secret? She clung to him now, entirely candid in her acceptance of his protection, a puppy's assumption that amused and slightly embarrassed him.

There were only two other couples in the restaurant. A Chinese waiter disengaged himself from a group of his fellows at the far end of the room, and in a markedly surly manner handed each of them a menu. Valerie produced some coral-colored spectacles from her bag to study it. She was very shortsighted, he now discovered, which perhaps accounted for the lingering rather sensuous way her hands seemed to dwell on the things they touched. They read in silence while the sound of a Hong Kong pop song on record (like the waiter's civility, not intended for them) seeped into the room from the direction of the kitchen.

"Number twenty-seven. Is the pineapple tinned?" asked Sam, a superfluous question as he well knew.

"Twenty-seven," answered the waiter impatiently.

"But is the pineapple tinned?" he repeated.

"Twenty-seven. Twenty-seven," reiterated the waiter, nodding his head.

He gave up and ordered 27, 35, 36 and a dish which without explanation bore the code sign K53, and the waiter hurried off. These responsibilities over, Sam returned to Valerie, who smiled politely at him before allowing her gaze, a second later, to slide over his right shoulder at the beginning of its journey round the room. He decided to do something; he would *make* her talk, sting her into participation with a string of blunt personal questions.

"How old are you, Valerie?" he asked.

"Nineteen," she answered, alive to his change in tone.

In the next ten minutes he learned that she had lived in Braddington all her life, that her mother was dead and that she lived with her father in a house on the waterfront. She had a boyfriend whose name was Trevor, who had an MG and whose father owned a string of cafés in North Brad.

"Are you going to marry him?"

"I don't know."

"How long have you known him?"

"Twenty-one months."

"Why don't you marry him, then?"

"I'm not sure that he wants to."

"What about you?"

"How do you mean?"

"Do *you* want to?"

"Not unless he wants to."

"That's right."

"You ask a lot of questions, don't you?"

"Do you mind?"

She thought about this. "Yes," she said.

"It's just that I'd like to know all about you."

He liked her a little angry, but was glad his questions had stopped where they did. His next was to have been "Are you a virgin?" and he hadn't intended to offend her, simply to rouse her a little. He had, of course, acquired some useful information along the way. He might have expected that she would have had a boy-friend—what good-looking girl of her age didn't?—but it had still come as a surprise. One always assumed that the girls one met had somehow been born the day before, without history, delivered into one's life like a sealed package. He had much to learn about her, but in her time, not his. She was right to resent his impatience; it was a form of condescension.

They finished all the food put before them with appetites keener than they had realized. Sam ordered two cups of coffee essence fortified with condensed milk and hot water, and they sat pleas-antly becalmed by their digestions and at peace with the irregu-larity of the conversation. Valerie was still looking around the room, but from time to time and of her own accord her eyes returned to him to regard him with a look quizzical and un-expectedly realistic. He wasn't sure she liked him, but he interested her. They left the restaurant, Sam regretting he had not the strength of mind to refuse the waiter a tip.

Valerie lived a mile along the front from the Ozone at the end of a lonesome arc of lights. They walked along the promenade above the beach, passing in and out of the stalwart, civic illumination and in constant hearing of the mild wash of the sea coming out of the dark. Above their heads work had started on the erection of loops of fairy lights, which, like the small available joys of the holiday-makers, would soon be lit up for the few months of summer. In the shadow equidistant between two lamps Sam turned to kiss Valerie. She turned her head away, refusing him gently, so that their faces brushed.

"Why did you do that?" she asked simply.

"Because I wanted to."

They walked on and came to a flight of steps leading to the beach. He took her hand and led her silently down. In the dark she accepted his kiss with soft tentative lips, and his face sank to her neck; he was vertiginous with her scent. Nearby he could make out the shape of one of the wooden groins, clogged wreckage trailing down toward the black. The beach was moist and salty but Valerie's close presence overwhelmed it. He felt the subsistence in

E*

121

his loins and the pining warmth. The irrelevancies of the rest of the evening melted away. They clung together, time flying away, while they learned from each other procedures for their lovemaking. Her sensuality, like a second personality, became fluent. Above, a passerby gave them a sharp glance, just as he might have done the outline of any couple spied in a shadow. Sam knew how they must look, still and intent as spiders, their privacy established as forcefully as a threat. His hand had now discovered her, viscid and warm, her secret suddenly broached. Her face was lifted toward him, eyes closed and puffed mouth slightly open, and he watched her as with awesome precision she followed the path to her climax. She gave a little controlled moan and it was over.

"It's almost like a pain," she said presently.

"Mm."

"What about you?"

"I'll be all right."

He led her up the steps again and they looked at each other curiously under the streetlamp. They had been there, he realized with surprise, almost an hour. Using her handkerchief, she wiped the lip rouge off his mouth with intimate efficiency. She was completely at ease with him now.

"There," she said.

"All gone?"

"You'll do."

"Are you a virgin, Val?" he asked.

"Yes," she answered, lying with perfect composure and in the friendliest fashion. For some reason it delighted him. He smiled and slipped an arm around her and they continued on their way.

Valerie's house had a VACANCIES sign in the window. He spent some time kissing her at the front door.

"What about your boyfriend, Trevor?"

"He's away on business this week."

"You still like him, don't you?"

"Oh yes."

They said good night, and Sam watched the front door slowly close, click and lock, leaving him to himself in the quiet street. He set off at a vigorous pace for the Ozone. For a few yards he broke into a run and skipped along the cement edge of a flower bed, but whether this was in celebration of Valerie or in flight from her he was not sure. There was no doubt that it would be a wonderful thing to have her in bed with him; until it was over. Was he after the usual impossibility, something for nothing? And what about Trevor? Something was probably wrong between them, otherwise tonight wouldn't have happened. Nonetheless he was still her boyfriend and he had an MG and twenty-one months' constancy to lay at her feet, which was a good deal more than Sam was able or at least willing to consider. Not that he gave a damn for Trevor personally, whom he detested the sound of and whom in London it might have given him some pleasure to cuckold. But if he let it happen once it would happen twice, and if it happened a third time it would happen as often as it possibly could; and this was Braddington, a small town in which Valerie had to make her life. He felt suddenly cool and reasonable. It would probably be wiser not to see her again.

Mrs. Shrapnel intercepted him three steps up the staircase of the Ozone. She had darted out of her lounge with a glass of gin in her hand, eyes blazing with unrequited amicability. For an irrational moment he thought she was about to give him a full account of what he'd just been up to.

"Oh, Mr. Beresford, glad I caught you. I had a talk to the builders today, and your flatlet will be ready for you a week tomorrow."

"The builders," it had eventuated, was a single old-age pensioner called Mr. Moore, who worked on the sly in the afternoons.

"Oh, thanks very much, Mrs. Shrapnel. That's good news."

She looked up at him, smiling pointlessly, and he knew she was hungry for a chat, with him, with anybody, and that she had been waiting up for it. Any moment now she was going to ask him to have a drink. He hardened his heart. Tomorrow he would talk to her, but not tonight.

"Well, good night, Mrs. Shrapnel," he said.

"Good night, Mr. Beresford." Her eyes feigned a twinkle.

He continued up the two flights of stairs, undeterred by the scraps of conversation that sought to impede him.

"Got enough bedclothes up there?"

"Yes, thanks."

"That window all right now, is it?"

"Fine, thanks."

"Anyway, you'll be in the flatlet soon, won't you?"

"Yes." He yelled a terminal good-night from the landing, and closed the door of his room, successful in a second shamefaced escape from womankind. Soon he would be leaving this attic for a new retreat. If Valerie had been with him in the flatlet tonight, snug at the bottom of the garden, it would have happened. Without a doubt. And if it happens once it happens twice. It was easy to say now that it wouldn't happen, not even once. He slipped his sweater over his head and caught her scent embedded in the wool. Would he be as certain in a week's time? He knew the rueful answer to that one.

8

WHEN Ivan walked into the rehearsal room the following morning, the company knew that the worst was over. His eyes were as they had been, bright and sardonic, and he moved among them with an upright swinging gait more appropriate to a Savile Row suit or even a Sam Browne belt than to the old navy sweater with the polo neck that he had taken to wearing. He seemed quite remarkably younger, himself twenty years ago. Richard Wayland leaned over and whispered to Sam, "He spent all last night and the night before going over his lines with Hugh Beardmore. Hugh says he's really solid on them now." For such scraps of company gossip Richard had an infallible nose.

They covered much ground that morning. Tom worked his way through pages of notes, modifying clumsy entrances and exits or replotting moves that on the set had proved impractical. A couple of scenes were run in their entirety. Ivan had a word about the madmen's scene: "I think you chaps are being a bit too clever with the makeup. Why can't we see your own splendid pale faces just as they are? Maybe a bit dark under the eyes, a bit sunken; nothing else. And, look here, what about these haircuts? I must say you've all been a bit timid. Take the plunge. Get your heads shaved. I promise you the effect will be stunning." The madmen exchanged dubious smiles and Ivan laughed. That afternoon he turned up to rehearse with his own hair cut down to the shortest gray stubble. Immediately after rehearsal the madmen fled to the barber's. In other circumstances this simple gesture of solidarity might have earned a more circumspect reception, but this was the eve of battle, and for the next few days, at least until after the first night, sophistication would be very hard to come by.

The final dress rehearsal was to be as per performance, with the curtain rising promptly at seven forty-five and the only permitted interruptions the two ten-minute intervals. Sam heard the first line spoken over the tannoy and left his dressing room for the stage. He was nervous, but less on his own behalf than on that of the production generally. A smooth run before the opening was vital.

On the stairs he ran into Amanda. "Just think," she said as they stood listening to the rumble of the play coming up from the stage, "this time tomorrow night we'll be under way."

"Don't," he said. It was curious to think of the first night almost upon them after these months of expectation. The flight of time acquired something of the mystery he remembered from school when a day much desired (or perhaps dreaded like the last day of the holidays) was suddenly there, real and inescapable. "This time tomorrow night!" he repeated after her.

In the canteen actors sat quietly listening to the progress of the play coming over the tannoy. It was proceeding smoothly but with, as it were, its fingers crossed. So far there had been no hitches. After the second interval, nervous now with the approach of his own scene, Sam decided to distract himself by watching a little of the play from the auditorium. However, his fellow actors up there on the stage seemed at a distance so prodigiously assured that this only increased his own insecurity.

Just as he was wondering where he ever found the nerve to do it himself, something quite extraordinary occurred. A shaft of white light had cut into the dark stage and revealed the madmen wretchedly huddled together. They were quite still and it was difficult at first to tell them apart; then the group stirred into individual life and advanced brokenly. They dragged with them terrible associations. For a moment Sam had seen barbed wire and a hill of bodies come to dreadful life again under the thrust of a bulldozer. Probably not even Ivan could have guessed what the effect of his shaven heads and issue rags was to be. No conscious effort had been made to impose the twentieth century upon this old play, but their own time had had its say, nonetheless, in one shocking uncanny moment. People turned to whisper to one another in the auditorium, sharing their astonishment.

On the morning of the first night the company gathered in the

126

rehearsal room for Tom's final notes. Afterwards they had the day to themselves. Janet Bennett sat listening to these last words of encouragement and good luck, frowning with a zealot's attention. On her knee was a large packet of stationery, the greeting cards which she had bought that morning and which she would send, each appropriate, to every member of the company. She only sent cards when she approved of the production, but then there was no holding her. Small gifts and tokens would pass among the actors before evening like so many tender superstitious benedictions. More seemed at stake than a play. For just a little while the company had succeeded in creating a world where the relationship between ends and means was clear and honorable. Onstage tonight this faith, as well as the play, would be displayed and tested.

In the afternoon Sam went for a walk by himself along the beach. He had considered an hour in bed, but knew he was too tense for sleep.

It was a cold day for late spring. Disheveled white clouds sped low over his head, switching the weak sunshine on and off. He could see the great patches of shadow they cast gliding toward him from faraway down the beach. The tide was going out and the wet sand was channeled by innumerable tiny rivulets streaming toward the sea. He stepped to avoid them, dazzled by the complexity of the patterns they made, the same yet different with every tide. How irrelevant their hopes seemed to this endless slow tolling of the sea. He felt a familiar melancholy. It was a mood not invariable before first nights, but it had occurred just often enough to enable him to place a professional interpretation on it. It was a good sign, for it usually meant that the performance he was about to give had drawn on some hidden part of him, something previously undisclosed, and perhaps in the face of this indifferent beach it could not help but contain a small measure of sadness.

Before he made up, Sam did the rounds of the dressing rooms, wishing people good luck. Frederick Bell was already in full costume and makeup though otherwise quite naked with fright. In his splendid Jacobean costume he puffed anxiously at a cigarette. Perhaps because he was confident of just how good Freddie would be, Sam found his terror a little ludicrous. He thought of some encouraging things to say, but Freddie seemed lost even to the comforts of flattery, and he repaid each compliment superstitiously with one of his own. They might have been engaged in a last-minute exchange of confessions before battle.

Sam tapped on Ivan's door and found him sitting at his place, staring at the flyleaf of a small book.

"Hello, Sam."

"I've just come to wish you good luck."

"What do you suppose that means?" Ivan handed him the book. It was a very old pocket edition of *The Duchess of Malfi,* and on the flyleaf in pencil there was Ivan's name and some scattered notes.

"What, this?" said Sam, pointing to a note *"p.40* hat."

"No, farther on."

" 'Like diamonds. Don't forget!'?"

"That's it."

"That's easy, isn't it? It's from the play."

"What? Where?"

" 'Whether we fall by ambition, blood, or lust,
    Like diamonds we are cut with our own dust.' "

"Of course!" said Ivan, and his face creased with glee as he recalled something.

"Was this when you played the part before?" said Sam, returning the book.

"I never played the part before," said Ivan.

"I thought you were in that first production here."

"I was. But not as Bosola. I was meant to play it, but Virgil took the bloody part away from me. Do you know who played it? Jack Bellenger. He wasn't bad. Too young, though."

"What happened?" said Sam.

"It was my own fault. I'd been late a couple of mornings at rehearsal. You know, late nights; ambition, blood and lust. Virgil said he'd take the part away from me if I was late again. I didn't think he'd dare. We'd been rehearsing a week. Well, I *was* late again and he took the part away from me. Do you know what I played? Pescara. Pescara! Jesus, I was sour." He laughed. "A long time ago now."

"It was a good production, wasn't it?"

"Mm, it was. That made it somewhat worse. I'd *learned* the bloody thing, you know." He laughed again.

Sam was about to take his leave when Ivan called him back. "Incidentally," he said, "you're good as the Doctor. You're a good actor. Write home and tell your mother." Sam went to make up, warmed by the compliment and further unnerved by it.

His dressing room was silent. Paul Poulsen was organizing around his mirror an exotic display of cards and telegrams, as if upon their careful arrangement depended the success of the entire evening. Even Francis Roland's wry professionalism could admit the talisman of a large felt mouse, its potency after many years' service apparently unimpaired by the loss of one ear. There are no atheists in foxholes, thought Sam as he propped up his own cards. He had four telegrams: one from Australia, one from Sally, one from Sidney Cohen to whom he was subletting the flat, and, the most surprising, one from Frederick Bell. He decided to leave them undisplayed.

He was dressed and made up with ten minutes in hand. He stared at himself in the long mirror, drawing strength from the visible companionship of the Doctor. The crumbling assaults of nervousness abated. The part was all there, he assured himself; he had only to cling on to it.

In the shadows of the wings the actors waited, each alone with his nerves, isolated again by private hopes and fears. Beyond the curtain a sustained sound, which had something of the corporate vitality of massing insects, grew in intensity with each minute. There were actually people there! Hundreds of them. Ivan appeared, the whites of his eyes showing clear and hostile in the dark. If he was nervous, then he was stoically resigned to it.

There was a hush, and the National Anthem was upon them. The curtain was sucked up into the flies above their heads, and the theater was so quiet Sam could hear the clicking of queue-light switches in the prompt corner. It was like a wood at night silenced by some monstrous intrusion. In the auditorium some lone soul was betraying himself with a cough. The lights on the stage came up and the first line of the play was spoken, an act of amazing bravery.

Within minutes he had been swept onstage himself, an object of nine hundred pairs of eyes. At the blurred periphery of his vision he was aware of them, altering the physical aspect of the auditorium in a way that found him unprepared. This first brief wordless appearance was providing a useful reconnaissance.

He had been quite startled by the rumble of laughter that had greeted his business with the leeches. Now he came offstage to face a wait of an hour and a half before his important scene. He went up to the canteen and sat listening to the play coming over the tannoy like a news bulletin on the progress of some battle. It seemed to be going well, with a sharpness and definition to the performance that seemed new.

In the first interval he ran into Freddie Bell in the passage, a sweating but more relaxed actor than before. "How's it going?" he asked.

"Hard to tell. No one's actually throwing things. Old Ivan's on form."

"The applause seemed good."

"Yes, they're very attentive. Quiet as mice. Makes you wonder if you've done your fly up."

There was no part of the theater where he could escape the play. He sat at his place in the dressing room beneath the loudspeaker, fussing with his makeup. At last, though he realized it would increase his nervousness, he decided to go down to the stage and watch properly from the wings. In any case he never liked to miss the fourth act, and felt a superstitious need to be there. He stood in the dark and watched Ivan in a pool of light just a few steps distant. He knew at once the actor was on form. He had reached a part of the play he loved to do, and he was stalking it with ferocious attention. Sam watched him do familiar things as if for the first time, recognizing the alchemy that had changed nerves into a liberating exhilaration that was refurbishing every moment of his part. The silent house was riveted upon him. He looked the archetypal actor, crouched now, still and listening, against a pillar. Sam might have been watching an actor in Rome, or Burbage playing in the light of a winter afternoon. He was reminded of a photograph of Irving in *The Bells*. That suspending concentration, the mark of talent, could never be entirely concealed behind the vagaries of changing styles. There was Ivan, celebrating his playwright and celebrating himself in thrilling conjunction.

But his own scene was drawing near. The realization rippled outward from his stomach in a wave of nerves. His saliva dried up and he sank into a chair, possessed by a numbing indolence. The nervousness had left his body; now it danced maliciously in his mind, threatening his will. Ridiculous fears assaulted him: that he would not be able to open his mouth to speak, that he would slip and fall with the first step he took on stage, that one of the other actors would brush against him, dislodging his wig or smashing his spectacles. He threaded a path through such thoughts, like someone keeping a kind of mania at bay, clinging to that small part of him which he trusted to remain resolutely calm.

A few minutes later he was waiting with Francis Roland in the cramped dark beneath a flight of steps, from around the corner of which they were to make their entrance. He smelled the new timber of the set, as vivid and oppressive as the smell of his fear. The play, like a train approaching down the tracks, was rumbling toward them suddenly near. Familiar words flashed by. Would he recognize his cue when he heard it? His heart was thumping wildly.

He heard his cue when it came, and the sound of it was almost reassuring, a counsel to fatalism, and he felt a brief calm as he stepped forward into the lights. His companion was speaking to him, and Sam looked into the painted desperate face, eyes popping, and saw his own hazard and exhilaration reflected there. He replied, startled by the higher register of his voice and the power lent to it by crisis. The scene stretched taut before him like a tightrope, on all sides of which watching faces and brilliant lights sought fatally to distract him. He struggled to subjugate his furiously active mind to the practiced skills of his part. A line came out in a more interesting way than he had ever said it before, a slight but critical difference, and people laughed. He felt still in peril but now resolute. There was more laughter, and the skin down his back prickled, the power of the part playing upon him as it was upon his audience. He was their guide through a shared experience.

Then suddenly the short scene was over. He had walked off the stage, smiled at Toby Burton the sort of smile of someone who has taken an awful risk and survived it, when he was astonished to hear the noise of acclamation. He hadn't expected it. It seemed to go on for a long time, as if they were clapping not the actor, now smiling in the wings, but something he had left behind, his spectacles perhaps, spotlighted in the center of the stage. The play continued.

"Well done, mate," said Toby Burton, patting him on the shoulder as he walked past a line of actors all offering him their deprived but generous smiles. He glowed with the harmony of his small achievement. Catastrophe now seemed impossibly remote and he wondered why he had ever been so nervous. Instead he kept company with delightful certainties. He was an actor in this play, in this theater, at this moment, and it was where he wanted to be. He stood watching the finish of the play, participating in its somber conclusions, yet feeling beyond this a wild, tender benevolence abundant enough to encompass the play, its actors, the entire audience. It was as if he had found a way of doing something difficult and frequently rash: extending love.

The curtain slowly came down, and for a moment there was silence. Then as crisp as thunder the applause broke. The actors scrambled in the dark wings to get in position for the curtain call as the noise continued. They took their calls in groups and pairs while the ovation surged around them, until, the drill of their call having come to an end, they could do nothing but stand in ragged lines, their smiles growing ever more pleased and foolish as the curtain rose and fell in front of them. People had started cheering.

It was an astonishing reception. Ivan led the principals forward again, and the clapping rose in fervor. It seemed it would never stop. The actors exchanged bemused smiles, spectators now at the spectacle of their own reception. Few of them had seen anything like it, though Sam noted that nothing could altogether penetrate the sardonic professionalism with which Ivan invested his bowing. Perhaps he had seen it all before and was merely relieved that it could still happen.

From the wings Tom Chester in a dinner jacket, his naked face yellow under the lights, stepped onto the stage. He seemed genuinely abashed by the unfamiliarity of thus publicly displaying himself, and the audience roared their comfort. He raised a hand and there was silence. "I only want to thank you for being a marvelous audience. It's marvelously encouraging to have the work understood as you have tonight. I think we can promise you many exciting things in the future. All I can say is thank you again." He made a gesture of acknowledgment toward the company, who for the most part bowed with the prompt obedience of pleased children, and the curtain came down for the last time.

Stripped of its finery of bright lights, the stage was now a cramped drafty corridor. "Congratulations, everyone. It was marvelous. Really. And of course, see you all at the party," said Tom in a lively, matter-of-fact tone. The company began to drift, somewhat reluctantly, toward their dressing rooms, leaving Tom to whisper compliments to the principals, who were nodding and feigning surprise as they devoured his congratulations.

The dressing rooms were noisy and cheerful. Success had become the most natural thing in the world, the obvious consequence of putting on a play. Already visitors in evening dress were tiptoeing past the steam from the shower room, endeavoring to find attractive the brazen, corporate intimacy they had chosen to invade. Sam idled over the chore of removing his makeup and getting dressed, indulging a private rhythm after the disciplines of the evening, and he was the last to leave his dressing room.

The party was being held at the Royal Hotel. It was a fine night with a breeze coming in from the sea. As he walked, his lines kept coming back to him in a wash of restless pleasure; they circled in his head like obsessive thoughts. He found himself acting over again the bits that had particularly pleased him, enjoying once more in the safety of his mind the power he knew he had been able to lend them that night onstage. His small part now contained the germ of an entire repertoire of great roles, and tonight he felt the strength and ability to play almost any of them. He was hot with ambition. A wonderful future was suddenly in the perilous offing, and he was walking toward it undeterred by the silent needling of the stars.

Other people were at the hotel before him. The party was being held in two large rooms on the first floor, and he heard its drone from the lobby. His reveries hastily withdrew to safety. He paused in the doorway. The room was full of people, and their animated talk had about it the mechanical diligence of swimmers treading water. He felt a reluctance to dive in. Olive Delmer in a beaded green dress came toward him smiling rapturously at someone over his shoulder, and a tall figure slipped in front of him to embrace her. He saw her pouting lips reach up for a tanned cheek and cling there humming as unashamed as only poverty could make her.

"Marty! Darling!"

"Olive, my sweetheart. My lovely."

"How lovely to see you!"

"You too, my darling."

"Oo, we've got so much to talk about, we have. You and I."

"Put the office kettle on, then."

Olive shrieked with delight, then as quickly became impassive. "Well, what did you think of it?"

"Marvelous, Olive. Absolutely marvelous."

"Did you like Ivan?"

"I liked everyone, darling. Absolutely everyone. They were *all* so good."

"It's you I'm waiting to see, Marty. I saw the costume designs for *The Way of the World* today. Yours is bliss! Sheer heaven! I just can't wait to see your Fainall."

"Well, you'll just have to, won't you, old darling? Look, I must just go and say hello to Tom. But we'll get together soon for a real chat, a lovely long one. There's so much I want to hear."

"Oh yes, Marty. We must! Then you can tell me what you *really* think."

"Mm?"

"About *tonight!*" she said in an impatient smiling whisper, and received in reply a slow, departing wink. Olive stood alone, the thrill dying on her face. She noticed Sam nearby, but a conversation between them must have been a prospect for which she had as little stomach as he had himself, for presently she shot him a smile as huge as it was hollow and veered off to the left.

Sam had recognized her friend, and he was relieved that he should be an actor for whom he had some envy but no respect. He was Martin Dane, possessor of an Alfa Romeo sports car, a Park Lane flat and a list of lovers that might have constituted a new sex, so indifferent was it to the usual distinctions of male and female yet so constant to the abiding characteristic of fame. He chose them at the height of their celebrity and dropped them at the first sign of its decline. Ten years ago he had been a joke, ridiculed for his public conceit, his unabashed sexual opportunism, his dreadful acting; but now the very persistence with which he landed one remarkable job after another, in spite of bad notices and indifferent box office returns, was acknowledged to be if not talent then the next-best thing to it. He had acted in all the best theaters, and been the handicap to enough quality films to insure himself of participation in at least one great critical success with which his name was now linked. People offered him work because his insolence claimed it, and because they sensed as a kind of guarantee that for success he had the black courage to pay any price. None of this, however, could entirely justify his casting in the present season. He was joining the company for the last two productions to play Banquo and Fainall.

Sam made his way toward the bar. On every hand the play was under discussion, the experience of it being cocooned within weaving threads of busy opinion. He felt a sudden perverse distaste

135

for the room and everyone in it. It was like some lower form of existence to which he must perforce return, a betrayal in which he must take part and toward which his growing appetite for personal recognition was leading him. He poured himself a glass of champagne, and the man next to him asked for a refill.

"Thanks," said the man, and they faced each other. "Quite a night, eh?"

"You saw the play, then, did you?"

"Mm. Gloomy piece. But brilliantly done. You were there?"

"I was in it, actually."

"Oh!" said the man. Then his smile faded. Sam knew he had not yet been recognized. "What did you play?" the man asked carefully, after a pause.

"Just a little part. I was the Doctor."

The man's quick smile showed his surprise and relief. "But you were very good!" he exclaimed, meaning it.

"Oh, thank you," said Sam, nodding modestly. After this small climax there was really nothing further for them to discuss, and Sam wandered off.

Why did he need praise? he wondered. Not for his vanity; that was too proud and wily a creature to go begging. It was more a question of simple reassurance. He had passed through an evening of unnameable hazard, and like the survivor of an accident, still in a state of shock, he needed to discuss and dwell upon his narrow escape. Most of the actors in the room, those who had played that night, wore expressions that betrayed this solemn need, and it was a frame of mind not much helpful to the gaiety of a party. There was considerable noise in the room, but little joy. That had been used up.

Sam had some more to drink and felt a bit better. Across by the bar he noticed Martin Dane congratulate Ivan with an embrace, which the star returned with matching extravagance. He could not hear what they were saying, but their mouths were opening and shutting in an exchange of the baldest flatteries. The play seemed far away. He waved to Amanda, who was looking a little out of things in a corner of the room. Probably she was fretting about her performance. He knew she wanted him to join her, but he felt disinclined.

Jock MacLachlan came up with a bottle of champagne. "Sam, I really must congratulate you on your performance as the Doctor. A really delightful performance. Marvelously funny." Jock's able, untalented face, the more candid for champagne, came closer. "I never would have thought you had it in you," he said, thus robbing his praise of most of its pleasure. "And I'll tell you something. That performance has done you a lot of good. A great deal of good. Mark my words. There are plans, my boy, plans." And with this he pushed off toward the bar.

Sam drank his glass of champagne and perched on the wet end of a stained white tablecloth. "I'm getting pissed," he said aloud, but no one heard. He felt a sullen pleasure in being alone with himself in a crowded room, and screwed up his face to wring out its numbness. He found more to drink and went roving from group to group, occasionally joining in the chat with lurching animation, but more frequently simply falling into long swaying silences. An ugly sexual hunger was creeping up on him, and his eye began to scan the room. There were two women that appealed to him. He approached the first intent upon a graceful wooing but instead found himself becoming increasingly rude to her. She walked away. With the second, a dark girl intolerably complacent in her good looks, he had no better luck. She soon made it clear that she had arrived in the company of Marty Dane and would leave with him.

"Are you then, by any chance, a film director in drag?" asked Sam.

"Fuck off," said the girl.

"Don't talk like that to the Prince of Wales," he countered, and went off bowing to urinate, trying not to gnash his teeth.

Round the corner he ran into Amanda. She smiled, but clearly she was still miserable about her performance, which certainly hadn't been very good. Even as he felt sorry for her, his lust inventoried her. In that case it was time to go, he realized, momentarily sober.

"I'm off," he said.

"Oh, you're not, are you? What about getting some of the others and having coffee at my place? We could get Richard."

"No. No. I'm off. I'm too drunk. I'm off."

When he got home, the lines were running in his head again. He thought about Valerie and masturbated.

9

HE WOKE AT DAWN, still in the grip of the stale excitement of his lines, which not even a hangover could put to sleep. He lay there until one o'clock occasionally dozing, but felt no more rested when he got up than when he had gone to bed. His body felt as stiff and tired as if he'd been in a fight, and just reaching for his clothes became a sighing labor.

At the newsagent's he bought the London papers to read over lunch. It was hardly likely that his own small part would receive a mention, either favorable or ill; nonetheless he carried the crisp bundle into the restaurant with some trepidation, wondering what it held in store for their play. He swung each fresh crackling paper open and glanced swiftly down the notice to determine its general tone. One headline announced I DECLARE THIS SHOW A WINNER! and another review began "Hurrah! Hurrah! Hurrah!" It seemed they liked it.

He read paragraphs here and there. "Last night at the Braddington Playhouse Tom Chester moved effortlessly into that select company of directors to whom the word 'creative' can truly be applied. A creaking Jacobean melodrama has been transformed by his labour of love into a thing of such humanity, of such soaring imagination, of such sheer theatrical brio, that I can only beg you, humbly, to go see it. And soon. Never mind the distance. Up there in Yorkshire they are making theatrical history." Elsewhere he read "An indispensable production of our time" (whatever that may have meant), and "Most wondrous of all, he has coaxed from Ivan Spears the performance of his life."

Tom and Ivan shared most of the honors, though the more

intellectual critics showed a distinct bias in favor of the director, a figure with whom they readily identified themselves, and who they seemed determined to believe had presided over the play with the effortless command of a puppet master. To his surprise Sam found a reference to himself, though not by name. His business with the leeches was mentioned in a paragraph dealing with the production's "audacious invention." The notices were all favorable except for one that described the play as "tedious gloom" and found it of great significance that the previous year Ivan had appeared in a horror film.

Sam read them through more carefully a second time, enjoying most those that aspired to lively journalism rather than to the verities of Criticism, and where a perceptible levity of style seemed to concede that beyond a simple "I liked it" or "I didn't" all judgments must necessarily be hypothetical not to say presumptuous. But the press had approved of them, and in the circumstances he felt a certain kinship with these printed words, now so fresh and exciting, destined like the work of actors to a rapid protesting oblivion.

He arrived at the theater that night listless and yawning. He was not in the least nervous, which was quite irrational since a second night and a first both required of him the same performance. He seemed to have run out of nerves, and this brought with it another sort of disquiet. Sighing frequently, he applied makeup to a fatigued yellow face, elbows resting heavily on the bench. When he had finished, he sat looking into the mirror, but he saw not the Doctor, only himself painted.

"Does this look the same to you?" he asked Paul Poulsen, who proffered his reflection a momentary glance.

"Exactly the same," he answered flatly, continuing with his own makeup.

A stupid question, Sam thought. Already they were beginning to encroach on each other's patience. Francis Roland had gone to the door and yelled "Dresser!" down the corridor with raucous irritability. Jean, with frizzy gray hair, appeared almost immediately from the next-door dressing room, looking put out, "Oh, there you are, love. Button me up, will you?" said Francis in conciliatory tones.

It had become hot in the dressing room, and somebody's feet were smelling. Now that the first night was over, success was giving way to a more sober realization: that they would be doing this show not merely for one triumphant night but on and off for the next six months. Time had suddenly stumbled ahead, like the arm of a record player which some small collision displaces jarringly into the next groove. And the play was, as Olive put it, a gloomy piece.

Just before his scene the small, inner vacuum of nervousness descended on Sam, and it encouraged him that he still had the reserves to feel so. He went on, and to his surprise acted well, with ease and liveliness, and left the stage to applause. His faith came back with a rush, and he found himself wanting to watch the play. On the far side near the prompt corner he spied a favorable viewpoint, and set off down the circular iron staircase that led under the stage and up again. The play was overhead now, as remote and exciting as a row in an upstairs flat. It was dimly lit beneath the stage, and he made his way past dusty stage machinery that looked as if it hadn't been used for a century.

Just as he was about to ascend the twin staircase on the other side, he noticed the entrance to a small room. It had no door and appeared to be piled to the ceiling with junk. He hesitated, one foot on the stairs, then decided to have a look. The room was dark, and he felt for the metal light switch but it clicked to no purpose and he assumed the bulb had gone. The contents of the room were shrouded with neglect; he noticed broken furniture, discarded lighting equipment and old stage properties, damaged and rotting. At his feet were piles of unused handbills, and farther into the room, propped against an old sofa, was a collection of framed posters. He picked one up gingerly, backing into the light to read it, trying to avoid the velvety contagion of the dust. It was dated 1931. He picked up another, and a piece of glass fell to the floor and smashed. The poster was mapped into areas of white and

141

brown, where fragments of glass clinging to the frame had protected it from dirt and time. Sam read: "THE DUCHESS OF MALFI *from Friday, August 10th, 1928.*" Underneath there was a cast list, and his eye sped down toward his own part. The Doctor had been played by Ronald Dunne. Ronald Dunne: he had never heard of him. He recognized many of the other names: Ivan Spears as Pescara, John Bellenger as Bosola; in fact he had heard of almost everybody on the bill. But not Ronald Dunne. Who was this unknown actor, at work in a profession where a small measure of fame was the one indispensable qualification for employment? What had happened to him? He wondered what he had been like in the part, and made a mental note to ask Ivan. Then he put the poster back in the dark and wiped his fingers on his costume, a superstitious chill possessing him. Who could be more unknown than an unknown actor?

As Sam was crossing the car park after the show, some headlights a few yards in front of him snapped on and a horn hooted. He stood blinking in the light, wondering what next the car would do. Then he heard his name called. It was Ivan, sitting beside the driver in the car he hired to take him home every night.

"Come and have supper with me, Sam. Come on, you can keep me company."

His first instinct was to withdraw, to make an excuse. The professional relationship he had with the older man seemed too excellent and absolute a thing to tarnish with the inevitable trivialities of personal acquaintance. However, he quickly decided this was foolish. Besides, the flattery of the invitation was beginning to work upon him, and it would be an opportunity to ask about Ronald Dunne. "Thanks very much," he said.

"Get into the back. There's room." The car wheeled into the street. "What about the Royal? That suit you?"

"Fine," said Sam.

They drove through the town in silence, which Sam, in the back, was beginning to find uncomfortable. Was he expected to earn his meal with chat? He tried to think of something to say and remembered Ronald Dunne.

"What was the first Doctor you had like?"

"Mm?"

"In the first production."

"Of our play?"

"Yes."

"He was very good, I think. Yes. We've had good Doctors in both productions."

This was perhaps a compliment, but unreasonably he preferred to think that no one else could be good in what he had come to regard as *his* part.

"What happened to him?"

"Don't know."

"Ronald Dunne."

"That's right! Yes, he was good as the Doctor."

"Did he do anything afterwards?"

"Not that I know of."

"Nothing at all?"

"No." Ivan seemed unperturbed at the thought of his vanished contemporary, and again they fell into silence.

When they got out of the car, Ivan had a word with the driver. "You'll wait for us, will you?"

"Right, sir."

"Or you could go back to the garage and I'll ring."

"May as well wait, sir. There's nothing in it."

Ivan nodded and, apparently preoccupied with this exchange, led the way into the hotel.

Sam studied his menu and waited for the odd suggestion from his host that would assure him that he was free to choose from among the more expensive dishes. But no such help came. He relinquished the thought of smoked salmon and ordered instead a grapefruit and a veal escalope, with which Ivan seemed well pleased. The waiter stood nearby, not perceptibly impatient, though from the small sidelong glances Ivan gave him as he deliberated his own choice one might easily have thought so.

"It's a different waiter tonight. Usually it's Marco," he said.

There were only a few people in the restaurant. A party of four

143

over by the window had been to the play, and were now discussing in mesmerized whispers whether Ivan was who he was. Both actors were aware of this, though neither acknowledged it; instead they launched into a conversation of studied absorption. A man came over to their table.

"Excuse me, I'm sorry to bother you, but I wonder could I trouble you for your autograph. It's for my daughter actually. She collects them."

Ivan scribbled his signature on the front of the theater program, while a lady in the party beamed foolishly at them from across the room as though recognizing distant relatives.

"Thanks very much," said the man, and prepared to go. But a thought occurred to him, a way perhaps of reestablishing the opinion of himself which his own importunity had put in jeopardy. "I must say I didn't think much of your play. Just a horror film, really, isn't it? Though, mind you, I thought it was splendidly done. Splendidly. Well, anyway, thanks very much. My daughter will be delighted. Thanks very much." He walked away.

"We know what paper he reads," said Sam, and Ivan glanced at him coldly.

The old actor wagged his head. "You never know what the buggers are going to say when they come up like that. After I made those films in Hollywood, you'd never believe the things people said to me. Strangers in the street. Come up and ask you for money. Tell you about their sex lives. It's like waking up one morning and finding that half the world's insane. I got so fed up I went a whole fortnight once signing 'Edward G. Robinson.' "

Some food arrived, and Ivan sat very still while the waiter fussed about him. Outside the theater he behaved like a man under siege. The waiter, having made the initial mistake of not being Marco, elicited great suspicion. "The wine. What about the wine?" Ivan whispered urgently to his retreating back, and the waiter, impregnably amiable in the face of Ivan's celebrity, assured him that it was on its way.

Ivan began to poke among the shrimps in his shrimp cocktail, and Sam followed by eating the cherry off the top of his grapefruit.

"What's that like? Any good?" inquired Ivan.

"Lovely."

"Mm. I should have had that. Don't much like the look of these shrimps."

They ate in silence. From time to time Sam glanced up to see if anything was expected of him, but Ivan seemed lost in thought. The person now munching shrimps with a slow lack of relish opposite him still had a way of becoming at unexpected moments that same mythical figure who had held sway over those half-price afternoons in an Australian cinema.

"Do you know that *Cromwell* was one of the first films I ever saw," began Sam, but Ivan shot him a look so edged with suspicion—and, he almost believed, contempt—that he immediately regretted having embarked upon so sentimental an appeal. He must have looked quite put out, for presently the old man's face softened, as if wearily he had recognized behind Sam's lapse the stumbling goodwill of the young. He stirred the mangled lettuce at the bottom of his shrimp cocktail and muttered, "Bloody awful film. I saw it the other day on television. Rubbish, rubbish." And indeed it had been on the TV screen one Sunday afternoon four or five years ago; Sam remembered he had been disappointed to miss it.

They started talking about *The Duchess of Malfi*. Sam told Ivan the moments in his performance he particularly liked, and Ivan assumed a stern demeanor that could not entirely conceal his quickened interest. "You liked that bit?" he would say as though surprised, or "That works, does it?" Sam wondered if he should exonerate himself from the charge of flattery by alluding to the moments he felt didn't quite come off, but decided that this was a subject best left to the actor himself to introduce, and which in fact he soon did. "There's a moment in the first act which never seems quite right to me," he began, and thereafter shot Sam a series of brief questions which he answered as honestly as he could.

"Mmm," said Ivan eventually, looking at him much as he had at the waiter earlier on, and seemed to withdraw into himself a full minute. "Tell me," he said suddenly. "Do the young people in the

F

company send me up?" This was such an extraordinary question in the light of the play's success and Ivan's contribution to it that Sam could only laugh.

"I'll tell you a secret," said Ivan. "But I'd be obliged if you'd keep it to yourself. Tom's asked me to direct the last play, *The Way of the World.*"

"That's wonderful!"

"He was going to do it himself as you know, but with *Macbeth* to do next and a lot of new administration he finds he's got his hands full."

"But that would be wonderful!"

"I'm not too sure. It's a bugger of a play, you know. Some lovely parts, of course. I'm to let him know tomorrow."

The waiter came up and they ordered coffee. Sam's thoughts had become swift and furtive. He was as yet uncast in *The Way of the World;* if Ivan directed it, maybe he would get a good part. He was beginning to see the advantages of sitting in a restaurant with a star. However, even if Ivan was to help him to a part, this was no time to mention it. He decided to change the subject.

"The notices were good," he said, and once again that evening regretted opening his mouth. Ivan was glaring at him.

"Bloody fools," he replied eventually. "I wish I had the strength of mind not to read them, but I always do. They all think they're Hazlitt. As if the movie camera hadn't done them out of a job. I'm surprised the buggers don't go around wearing powdered wigs. Prigs and speculators mostly. They're so busy tipping tomorrow's winner they hardly report today's race. Staking claims in other people's talent. Christ!"

Ivan had gone off like a firecracker, and Sam, as it were, stepped back fascinated until the explosions ceased.

"The clever ones are the worst. Like Bernard Shaw, when he was a critic: playing John the Baptist to his own subsequent appearance as Christ. At least he did eventually haul his bum out of a stall seat and take a risk or two. People are always going on about Shaw's wonderful criticism. It tells you a damned sight more about his own ambition and malice than it does about the shows he saw. And he played dirty, really dirty. Have you ever seen that notice of Irving's Richard III? Apparently Irving used to get awful nerves on first nights, and on this occasion he did something we've all done when really nervous: he inverted some words. In his first speech. Something like 'Now is the discontent of our winter'; something like that. Shaw got hold of this and offered it as proof that Irving didn't know the meaning of the lines he was speaking. He savaged that man. All through his career. Then when Irving was dead and gone forever, he admitted he'd never seen an actor to touch him. Then there's a letter to Barrymore after the first night of his Hamlet at the Haymarket: cold, destructive and malicious; deliberately willing him out of business. He succeeded all right. Barrymore gave up after that. And it was an extraordinary performance. I took Jack Bellenger along to see it when we were kids. He'd just left drama school. I think we saw it four or five times; we couldn't keep away from the damn thing. The point is that kind of acting is really a sort of raw poetry; there's something inarguable about it, something that appeals direct to the hairs down your back. And this the moralists can't stand. They want to banish us from our own city and take over. Turn us all into obedient bassoons and flutes and fiddles. And bore the pants off everybody! Bugger them!"

Ivan thundered on, fired by old grievances and modern instances, growing increasingly more ribald and dismissive. Something of the fluency and conviction of his acting had taken hold of his talk, and Sam listened enthralled. Yet his words also possessed a discomforting quality of danger, a threat not so much to his enemies as to himself, as if at any moment he might lose hold of his humor and simplicity and tumble into a consuming rage. Then, abruptly, the mood had entirely changed and he was telling Sam about his meetings with Shaw in the early thirties. Apparently, they had taken a great liking to each other, and Shaw had written a part especially for him.

When the waiter brought the bill, they had sat some time over coffee and they were now the only customers in the restaurant. Ivan fell silent and picked up the bill suspiciously. He stared at it and began to do sums, his lips occasionally moving. He seemed quite oblivious to Sam and the waiter, and as the seconds passed, Sam at least began to feel faintly uncomfortable.

"What's twenty-seven and eight?" Ivan asked suddenly.

"Thirty-five," answered Sam.

"Mmm. Got a pencil?" he asked the waiter shortly.

"Certainly, sir."

Ivan carefully signed the bill, then fumbled in his pocket for a tip. He put three half crowns on the white saucer, looked at them, then replaced one with a two-shilling piece. The waiter bowed and departed. Ivan remained silent, still caught up in his mental arithmetic. Some of his ways were decidedly eccentric, the narrow preoccupations and enclosed rhythms of someone who lives too much alone brought into a public place. Sam had seen the same qualities carried to extremes in tramps. The weaknesses one might have expected in him and gladly indulged, some complacency, a little of the sentimentality of success, he was completely without. Instead he gave the impression of being a man hedged about with unknown dangers and mocked by achievements the value of which he had come to doubt. It was awesome and a little bit ridiculous.

They re-joined the driver, who had been reading last Sunday's *News of the World* in the front seat, and Ivan dropped Sam off on a corner half a mile from the Ozone. He asked Sam if it was all right for him, and Sam said it was.

10

Was this the sixth or the seventh performance of *The Duchess of Malfi?* Sam calculated and realized it was the seventh. Each of the first four performances he could remember distinctly and in order. Now one performance was beginning to run into another, and soon he would be remembering weeks, not days: the second, third, fourth week of the season. But being in the play still afforded him an exhilarating sense of privilege. He was beginning to know sections of it by heart, and to be able to forecast by small signs, as a fisherman might the weather, what the quality of the performance might be on any one night. If, for instance, in his first scene Ivan slightly altered the inflection of a line—discovered, by accident as it were, some tiny new detail to add to his performance—then Sam knew that this would be a night to watch him.

Now that the company were free from rehearsals, the nightly performance was the fulcrum of their day. It was a splendid thing to come to the theater each evening, to make one's ritual preparations in front of a mirror, and, thus accoutered, embark upon that small adventure on the stage, seemingly the same with each performance but for the actor at least always a voyage into the unknown of his own ability. The returns of acting were as mysterious, and beyond a certain point as little subject to an effort of will, as those of lovemaking.

They had a week of such luxury yet before the rehearsals of the revival of Tom's production of *Macbeth* began to occupy their daytimes. In other years the first two plays had been rehearsed simultaneously, opening within a fortnight of each other, but this year because of Sir John Bellenger's film commitments Tom had decided to delay rehearsals of the second production. It had been a gamble but one which the success of *The Duchess* had vindicated. For the actors in the company it meant cramming most of the performances of *The Duchess* into the first half of the season; by the time all three plays were in repertory they would be playing it perhaps once a fortnight.

On Sunday Sam rose late, to have Mrs. Shrapnel prepare a breakfast for him of a scope that made lunch superfluous. She was celebrating the completion of the flatlet, and she had laid a special place for him over by the new plate-glass window in the Oyster Bar. As he enjoyed her coffee, made from real grains to celebrate the occasion, he heard her going about the house singing "A Nightingale Sang in Berkeley Square." She was in excellent spirits, and had been ever since her first holidaymakers had arrived. She was busy all day long now, and in the evenings if Sam bumped into her after the play she no longer smelled of gin-and-tonic.

He lingered over breakfast for two hours, gorging himself on newsprint and coffee, and feeling at the end of it vaguely bilious. It was time for a brisk walk along the waterfront. As he proceeded through Mrs. Shrapnel's back garden, her two cats, Majesty and Philip, sunning themselves on the gravel path, leaped to safety behind a garbage can, and he kicked an apple core toward them: due punishment for their lack of trust. The front was busier than he had known it; despite the cold wind he could feel the pleasant sting of the sun on the back of his neck. He lingered awhile near a Salvation Army band, which hawked a plaintive redemption to the noncommittal faces of the middle-aged couples who passed by arm in arm. The breeze tossed their song about like so much litter, making it now loud, now soft. He set off along the promenade away from the harbor and people. Over by the railings he passed a stricken boy in a wheelchair, deserted for the time being by whoever it was who pushed him. He was wrapped in an old tobacco-colored plaid blanket and his skin had the livid transparency of chronic illness. As he walked on, he heard a last wispy appeal from the Salvation Army band carried suddenly on the wind. Ahead were some steps leading down to the beach. He had just decided to use them when he saw Amanda back up on the promenade.

"Go away!" he heard her call down the steps and then laugh.

"Me?" he said, approaching, and she turned, surprised.

"No, look!" Up the steps was trotting a young Alsatian dog. It was a huge creature, but its paws still flopped against the concrete as if the bones in its legs were made of black rubber and it couldn't have been more than a year or so old. "I made friends with him, and now he won't go away! He's followed me all the way down the beach. I'm frightened he'll get lost or something."

"Who does he belong to?"

"I don't know! I just found him on the beach." The dog was now circumspectly licking Sam's knuckles. "He hasn't got a collar on or anything," said Amanda.

"Let's take him for a walk, then."

"What if his owners can't find him?"

"He'll be all right. He knows what he's doing. Don't you, dog?"

They set off along the beach, and the dog, having assessed the new situation with a series of bright prick-eared looks, galloped on ahead in a show of partial independence. It stopped and looked back at them; then, as though pursuing some pressing and mysterious responsibility with which it had been entrusted, it commenced a self-important sniffing of everything in its path. Again it looked back, this time for approval.

"What will we call him?" asked Amanda.

"I don't know. What about Dog? *Dog!*" To their surprise the Alsatian came bounding back to them. "Or Al?" said Sam.

"No, Dog's better. I like Dog."

Sam picked up a length of black wood and hurled it along the beach, and the dog with frantic zeal retrieved it. But when Sam took hold of one end he refused to let it go, and they pulled at the wood, the dog looking sideways at Sam with a Tartar's cunning and growling softly from between clamped teeth. Then suddenly the rotten wood had snapped in its mouth, and Sam was in possession again. The dog delicately spat splinters onto the sand, in a good-humored way that implied that Sam had won that match by default, then crouched in readiness for the resumption of play. Sam hurled the wood out to sea, and the dog bolted after it. But at the water's edge it thought better of it, and instead tore off down the beach again in wild crazy circles, bent upon improvising the distraction of an alternative game. Presently it just sat and panted.

"Hey! Have you read the weeklies yet?" said Amanda.

"No."

"You got a super notice."

"Really?"

"Yes. I've got it here in my bag. I cut it out." She had some newspaper cuttings pressed inside *The Pelican History of Music.* "I brought the old raffia bag along in case I saw any nice shells. Wasn't that lucky? Here."

Sam's eyes scanned the notice. He wondered if he should exercise a measure of control and read it through from the beginning, but quickly decided that this was not only hypocritical but a waste of time. "Near the end there," said Amanda, helping him, and he read: "There is not a member of the cast who does not seem to share in the lucidity and passion of Ivan Spears's astonishing performance. If I single out Samuel Beresford's small part it is only to show what can be achieved onstage in the space of four or five minutes. His Doctor is a man who knows that science will always be an inferior accomplishment in this corrupt, courtly world, and his reaction is to become a raging intellectual snob. It is a performance of infinite subtlety, that also happens to be extremely funny."

Sam read it through a second time, astonished. There was his name in print and decked with flowers. He had had good notices before, but never one quite like this, and in a national paper, too. He read it through a third time, and it was as if something deeply primitive in him, as mindlessly committed to its own existence as an anemone clinging to the seabed, had been stroked and comforted. Simple decency, not to say policy, made it important that he minimize the pleasure he felt, at least publicly. "What an intelligent man," he said, and they both laughed.

"Not so good for me," said Amanda, bravely matter-of-fact and pointing. "Unfortunately," he read, and didn't want to read on, but made himself. "Unfortunately, the hockey-team zest that Amanda Maitland brings to her role is the one quality which the lady in question might be presumed to be without."

He gave her a kind look, wishing that there was no need, hating the treachery that lurks behind all shows of kindness.

"Ah well, it's all a load of rubbish," he said.

"I've always had good notices before. This takes a bit of getting used to," she said cheerfully. "I'm sending all these to Dad in America. He made me promise. I wish he hadn't."

They had walked clear of the promenade now, and the sand had given way to pebbles. Sometimes they walked across patches of flat rock, crisscrossed by cracks into squares and geometrical shapes that aggravated yet also soothed the mind by their slight, relentless imperfection. Inland, cliffs were building up from the decaying, chalky hill, but they would have no trouble scrambling up if the tide caught them. Sam glanced out to sea, eager to deploy some of his old coastal skills.

"We want to keep an eye on the tide," he said, aware that there was really no need.

"Yep," said Amanda.

The dog came galloping back with a bounty of foul-smelling seaweed. They shooed him away and he dropped the seaweed at their feet, then set off immediately on a new commission. On the sea near the horizon something white opened and shut like a slow silent blink.

"Look out there!" said Sam.

"What?"

"At the horizon."

"I can't see anything."

"Just keep looking. You will."

"Where?"

"There! Again! Did you see it!"

"What?"

"A wave breaking. Way out there."

"That white?"

F*

153

"Yes, that was a wave breaking."

"What does that mean?"

"It must be shallow out there. A sandbank or something."

"Couldn't it just be the wind?"

"No, it rolled! The wave rolled. In Australia you could paddle a surfboard out there, and maybe catch it."

"Really?" She looked out to sea again. "How wonderful!"

Sam began to tell her about the Australian surf. Suddenly he felt exceedingly talkative. He told her how he would trot down the beach in the morning with his board balanced on one shoulder, launch it against the cold, swaying water with a great slap, then scramble aboard and make for the open sea before a breaker caught him: slow, fervent paddling in an attitude of prayer.

"The best thing of all, though, was body-surfing, providing you had the right day."

"What's that?" Amanda's eyes were bright with a crisp, almost humorous pleasure. It wouldn't really have mattered if he'd been talking about butterfly catching or veteran cars, provided he did so with a similar passion. She had struck a gusher of vitality in him, and was watching it delighted.

"Body-surfing is when you just swim onto a wave, catch it to the beach without using any aid. But you've got to have the right conditions, otherwise it can get a bit boring."

"What are they?"

"Well, you need a nice high tide and an easterly wind."

The word "easterly" was still a magic word for him. "Northerly," meaning a sea as flat as a lake, had been a word as dull as too much sunshine. "Southerly," meaning clouds and a choppy sea, was a tarnished, depressing word. But an easterly! After the wind had blown all night, he had caught the tram down to the beach under a metal sky, catching glimpses between the houses of an ocean on which the restless play of light presaged enormous waves. Frequently rain would make the surface of the sea oil-smooth, and beneath this skin the superb waves, a glistening musculature, moved against the beach. He would watch them, mesmerized, then run to scramble into his swimming trunks, his heart thumping with excitement and dread.

"Why on earth did you leave it?" asked Amanda.

"God knows!" he answered glibly. Could he explain? Sometimes after he had spent an hour dozing in the sun, he would open his eyes, and by some trick of the vision the brightness would seem darkness, and for a moment the brilliant landscape of the beach would be as opaque as a photographic negative. The summers he had lain on the beach were the same winters that cattle trucks of human beings had trundled across Europe.

"You wanted to come to England and act?"

"Yes, I suppose so."

"You were convinced that there was something better elsewhere?"

"No, I wasn't. That's the point." But he wasn't explaining it well, or enjoying explaining it. "You lie in the sun. Nothing else matters," he said.

"I've got an idea!" said Amanda presently. "You can hire motorboats in the harbor. Why don't we get one one day—it's only about ten bob an hour—and sail out there and have a look at the waves."

"All the way out there?"

"Maybe you'll be able to do some surfing!"

"All right!" It was an excellent idea; he wondered why he hadn't thought of it himself.

They had come to the end of the beach now, their way barred by rock. They decided to follow some crude steps and go home along the cliffs. The dog scrambled on ahead, and sat at the top panting contentment down upon them, until suddenly a gull rocking on the wind caught his attention and he turned his head to survey it, mouth closed and expression stern. They walked along the cliff, looking down upon the way they had come, the dog trotting at an obedient distance ahead of them. They began to meet other people on the path, and soon, round a bend, came a woman leading a boxer dog. Both animals immediately tensed.

"Come here, Dog!" commanded Sam, and the Alsatian hesitated in his advance toward the other dog. "Come here," repeated Sam, and the dog looked back and forth between him and the boxer, ears and nose as sharp as triangles. "Come on," said Sam, and after a moment the dog shuffled toward him with its head down and its tail wagging slowly. "Sit," he said, and the dog sat. The boxer passed, straining and whimpering on its lead, and the woman gave Sam a Tea Shoppe smile which he returned.

"Isn't he marvelous?" said Amanda. "I'm going to give him some chocolate as a reward."

"It isn't him; it's me. I'm a born leader."

"I'll give you both some chocolate," she said, and fed them in turn, the dog first.

"Let's go somewhere and have a great pot of tea," suggested Sam.

"What time is it?"

"Twenty to five."

"I'm meeting Tom at five. Near the bandstand. He's picking me up and we're going to have drinks or something."

"Who?"

"Just some people in the company. Come along and wait with me. He might ask you, too."

The cliffs had petered away to a slope running down toward the promenade. Shortly they would be walking on concrete among people. As soon as they were in sight of home, the dog had run on ahead and was now some distance away. Sam called him. This time, however, he merely stopped for a moment, gave them one considering look, then continued on his way. They saw him run down a flight of steps onto the beach and purposefully set off along the sand. It seemed his walk with them was over. Far away up the beach he stopped once more and looked back, and it was like the end of a cowboy film; Sam almost expected him to rear against the setting sun and wave his hat. The dog pleased him. His social instincts were without fault, and he said goodbye without regret. "There he goes," said Amanda happily, with something of the same spirit in her own leavetaking. Sam had the feeling that this sort of undemanding encounter happened to her all the time.

They sat on the edge of the bandstand watching the parade of plain people and sluggish Sunday traffic. It seemed very noisy after their walk. Sam had bought them each an ice cream and they licked away, content not to speak. When he had finished his ice cream, Sam said, "I think I'd better go. Tom won't want me around."

"No, silly. Stay. He might ask you to the party, and if he doesn't, so what?"

"O.K."

An MG had pulled up at the traffic lights, and Valerie was in it. The slob sitting next to her in a tweed hat, his hands in driving gloves resting upon the wheel, was, presumably, Trevor. Valerie's forehead and bare arms were faintly sunburned. Sam watched the car to see if Valerie would catch sight of him, but it drove off without her having turned her head, and he felt in some sense relieved. It's a small town, he cautioned himself. Nevertheless, he was still obliged to get her a seat for the play. He had said he would, and he had no wish to disappoint her. He would call in at the cosmetics shop tomorrow (sometime when Mrs. Willis was there), find an evening that suited her, fix it with the box office, and with this friendly, disinterested gesture settle accounts.

On time Tom drew up to the bandstand in his Mercedes. He leaned over and opened the passenger door and stayed craned in his seat to smile at them. "Hello, Emma. Hello, Sam. What have you two been up to?"

"Sam and I've been for a walk up the beach. We met a wonderful dog."

"Lucky you."

"Yes," said Sam. He could think of nothing else to add, so stood there smiling while the other two chatted. Tom shot him an affable look from time to time, but did not ask him to the party. Amanda climbed in and Sam slammed the door for her. She turned and made a little private face for him through the window, indicating disappointment. They drove off, leaving him suddenly relieved that his begging had stopped where it did.

He had two things to do the following morning: go to the theater for his mail, and on the way call in at the cosmetics shop about the ticket. In the High Street Valerie anticipated one of these intentions by coming out of a cake shop and all but bumping into him. Sam discovered all over again how good she smelled. She was wearing her pink-nylon work coat, and in the V of her neck he saw how the sun had tinted her incredible skin.

"Hello," she said, looking at him without expression.

"Hello. I was just coming along to see you."

"Were you?" She blinked at him slowly in a way that was both shy and stubborn.

"Yes. About that seat I promised you. When would you like to come and see the play?"

The need to show some sort of formal gratitude slightly unsettled her, and she blushed. "Oh, thank you very much."

"But when would you like to come?"

"Any time."

"This week?"

"Yes."

"Tomorrow?"

"That would be lovely."

"Would Trevor like to come? I might be able to make that a couple of seats."

"Trevor's away again on business this week," she said. Sam looked at her. His resolves crumbled.

"Look—um—why don't we meet afterwards and have supper or something . . ."

"That'd be lovely."

"I've just moved into a new flat, as a matter of fact. We can go back there, and I'll cook you something."

"All right."

"I mean, there's nowhere much open late at night, is there?"

"No."

"I'm a pretty good cook. Look, I'll leave a ticket for you in my name at the box office, all right? And meet you after the show in the front-of-house bar. You can get a cup of coffee while you're waiting."

They parted, and Sam began to walk fast toward the theater. What am I *doing?* he said to himself, but already he felt a keen impatience for the following evening. The truth was he was pleased he had acted as he had; even yielding to temptation was a way of making up one's mind.

"There's one for you, sir!" said Alfred, the stage-doorman, jumping up from his stool. Sam found the old man's sprightliness oddly affecting. Age had left him with but one modest demand to make on life: that he continue in usefulness. In the letter rack under "B" he saw the blue edge of an Australian aerogram, and knew immediately that it was from his mother. "Here we are, sir," said Alfred, and Sam felt the touch of his dry, undemanding fingers. He tore the letter open and leaned against one wall reading it.

SAM DARLING,

Sue and Wallace Biddymead came to dinner last night and said they were in London when the reviews of "The Duchess of Malfi" came out and what a great success it was. I can't tell you how thrilled I was and simply can't wait for your next letter telling me all about it. How did your Doctor go? How I wish I'd been there! It was very disappointing having to cancel the trip, but I'm keeping my fingers crossed about next year. I feel so sure about this new job and that it will be the turning point for you. And about time, poor sweet, after so many years of hard work. Sue and Wallace were of course absolutely exhausted after their flight, but Wallace was on very good form and told us some very funny stories about the mad English. They are a madly active pair and seem to have seen a great deal. Your father is away in Melbourne staying with Monty Rossiter and his new wife. I think he's as pleased as I am about your new job (though of course he doesn't show it), and is slowly coming round, darling. I think you would find that age has mellowed him a lot. I had a very pleasant afternoon with Bid Nettleton (she was Bid

159

Smythe) yesterday. They've just built a gorgeous new house at P.B. above the Marlowes, and had a huge party last week to show it off. Some of the young were there apparently. Ros Peterson, Barbara's sister, who's grown up now, and her young man, Bill Penny, whom everyone seems to like. Also Peter Conville, who married Antonia Paul the other day. She wasn't there but I believe is charming. It's fantastic how well Convilles marry.

I'm keeping up your subscription to the R.S.G.C. I know you say you'll never need it, but an absentee membership is only a couple of quid, and you might want to use it one day.

Don't forget to send me all the cuttings. I'm longing for your next letter. Good night, darling,

Much love,
MUM

Sam smiled over the letter, his breathing slightly constrained by the worrying amusement and the great affection it had touched in him. He was glad that he had already written to her about the first night. In the nine years he had been in England, his mother had made two trips to visit him and had planned a third this year, but for reasons he was not quite clear about it had had to be postponed.

They corresponded regularly, Sam writing the letters that he hoped would please her, accumulating a partial record of his career for her custody. At first such censorship as he brought to bear on his letters, omitting humiliations and disappointments in which he could find no appeasing aspect, had been for his own benefit. (At twenty-one it had been necessary to take one's own legend very seriously.) Later it was for hers. She supported his cause because of her love for him; the cause itself remained something of a mystery. She had paid his fare to England, ceaselessly acted as peacemaker between him and his father, seen him through drama school, and sent him drafts of money so frequently during bad spells that it alarmed him to think about it. Yet the fact remained that there was so little in her own nature of the passion or indeed the presumption necessary to the undertaking of any artistic work that she had little understanding of the motives that really governed him. In her letters she had written "You have so much to bring to your profession," ascribing to him the professional virtues of perseverance and moderation, from which he knew himself to be as alien as he now was from his intended law studies. His mother would have tolerated any aberration in him, any lapse, just so long as he continued to wear a tie to meals. And yet he loved to see her and to receive her letters. She brought with her to England the calm and style of an identity that he might question, but which he was neither able nor willing entirely to jettison. He was rather proud of her.

"Seen the cast list for *Macbeth* yet, mate?" said Toby Burton, shuffling past.

"No! Where?"

"Up on the board. This morning."

Sam hurried to the notice board. There was the new, crisp sheet of white paper bearing the typewritten names, and altering the configuration of green beige and old notices that they had grown used to over the past few weeks as abruptly as a clap for attention. Sam's name was down twice. He looked around for someone with whom to share his rude laughter. He was playing Donalbain, which he expected, but also (could it be otherwise?) the Doctor in the last act. They had decided what he could do: play doctors. Were there any other doctors in Shakespeare? He could only think of the apothecary in *Romeo and Juliet,* and he obviously was no graduate. It wasn't the most promising field in which an actor could specialize. However, he hurried upstairs to his dressing room, where he knew Paul Poulsen kept a *Collected Works*, and read quickly through the Doctor's two scenes. It was really quite a good part, and a wonderful contrast to his other Doctor. He had a feeling already how it should be played: very simply, without frills, perhaps with no makeup. It needed straightforward acting with as much simple conviction as he could muster. In the turmoil of the end of the play the man stood for a kind of cautious, sorrowing good sense. He wondered who had proposed him for the part.

Sam listened to the buzz of the audience gathering beyond the curtain and thought, Valerie is sitting out there somewhere. That is, if she had collected her ticket. He imagined all the extra resolve of tonight's performance being proffered to a single, empty stall seat.

After the show he hurried to undress, trying not to draw attention to the fact that whereas he was usually the last to leave the dressing room, tonight he would be the first. Then he dashed downstairs, saluted Alfred good-night with a passing wave, went banging out the stage door, and, in the open air at last, slowed himself down to a walk so that he wouldn't arrive at the front-of-house bar panting in too unseemly a manner. Valerie was seated in a corner of the room demurely sipping Bitter Lemon. She was dressed up with preposterous care, her nails and lipstick were a matching lilac, and her hair was up again. He wondered if he would ever know her sufficiently well to tell her he preferred it down. She looked a little nervous as she smiled at him, and he recognized the brief but most potent advantage that an actor has in such a situation, stepping down from the stage, as it were, after a good performance. And he had been good tonight. Valerie's presence had seen to that.

"Look, it's rather late. I suggest we push on to the flat and have a drink there," he said.

Valerie rose obediently. "All right."

He bought a bottle of vin rosé from the bar, wishing he had attended to this detail in less transparent circumstances; then with the wine in one hand and Valerie's elbow in the other he guided her toward the exit. He wondered what the odds were against his getting her out of the building and away into the night before Amanda and her raffia bag came smiling round the double doors.

In the safety of the empty streets he began to feel more at ease. He asked her how she had enjoyed the play, and she replied that she had loved it, but beyond her prompt and dutiful superlatives, about the production, about himself, about anything he cared to mention, it was difficult to get her to discuss it. Sam had the feeling that she had really enjoyed it, but was nervous of risking the cheek of an opinion. However, the play had definitely made an impression on her because she kept returning to it. "It's very sad, really, isn't it? That man, that one that Ivan Spears plays—"

"Bosola," suggested Sam.

"Yes, him." She knew the name but was shy about pronouncing it. "Well, doing these awful things, knowing they're wrong, and not being able to help himself."

Sam encouraged her to enlarge on this, but she quickly withdrew to the compliance of unqualified praise and they discussed other things.

Sam had persuaded Mrs. Shrapnel to leave the garden approach to his flat unlocked, and she had agreed on the condition that he always remembered to bolt it after he got in. Now he led Valerie by the hand along the narrow paving path. In the dark she stumbled against an ash can and giggled. "Sshh. We don't want to wake the hotel," he said, expecting that at any moment the weak beam of Mrs. Shrapnel's torch would expose them to the entire town.

"Is this where you live?" announced Valerie loudly. "It looks like a garage."

"It was. It's been converted," he whispered, opening the door. His hand scuttled frantically up and down the wall for the light switch; then, having found it, he guided her through the door and closed it swiftly behind them. "That's better," he said with a cheerful sigh. "Let me take your coat."

Sam had stocked up with lamb chops, frozen peas and new potatoes. He poured a glass of wine for Valerie and left her sitting on the bed while he prepared the meal. She made little attempt at conversation while he cooked, which was something of a relief to him; this was the first entertaining he had done in the flat, and the cooking was demanding all his attention. He stood gazing at the scummy potato water, as though its bubbling could only be sustained by his continuing concentration upon it. Soon it was time for the frozen peas. He came into the middle of the room opening the packet.

Valerie was reading a magazine. "Won't be long now," he announced, and Valerie looked up and gave him a little dead smile. He came over to the bed and bent to kiss her. She allowed him a touch of cold, puckered lip, then turned her head immediately back to the magazine.

Slightly shaken, he returned to the cooking recess, where, however, experience soon offered him its sly reassurance. Girls couldn't help discouraging you sometimes. Nature made them, to test your nerve. He took the saucepan of potatoes round the corner to drain them in the washbasin. His eye fell upon the lavatory and he suddenly realized the full implications of having no door to the bathroom recess. Guests would be out of sight, but hardly out of hearing. Unless one was on familiar terms this could be embarrassing; he would have to wait outside, and it might be raining. He silently cursed Mrs. Shrapnel's lack of foresight, and his own. Perhaps she had arranged it thus on purpose, though with what infinitely corrupt motive he could not guess.

They ate their meal off a card table, Sam perched on the edge of the armchair, Valerie strategically positioned on the low bed. Mrs. Shrapnel had explained that there was more furniture to come, and had hinted at a brand-new contemporary suite, though Sam trusted that this was more dream than tangible threat. He was perfectly content with the present arrangements.

"What were you doing on Sunday, then?" said Valerie, putting her knife and fork together with the same genteel precision with which, upon sitting on the bed, she had earlier closed her knees.

"On Sunday?"

"Down at the bandstand, eating an ice cream."

"Oh, you saw me, then. I didn't think you had."

"That was Amanda Maitland with you, was it?"

"Yes. We'd been for a walk along the beach."

"Is she nice?"

"Yes, very nice. You should have waved."

"I didn't think she was very good in the play."

"No, she's miscast really."

"There was a picture of her in the Christmas number of *Vogue*."

"Oh."

164

Valerie suddenly giggled. "I liked the part you took," she said. "He's such a fool, isn't he? I wish you could have seen me. I couldn't stop laughing. I don't know what the people round me must have thought."

They were both better for a glass of wine. Valerie's large brown eyes were flecked with radiant needles of yellow. He marveled at her hairline, the way each hair suddenly leaped from her cream forehead as if acting in simultaneous obedience to some mysterious dictate of sexual desirability that had been blithely decreed without Valerie herself having even been consulted. The three feet of card table between them was a chasm. If it had been possible to touch and fondle her as naturally as he had handled the Alsatian dog on the beach, perhaps his resolves would have melted into something more generous and communicable. But until he had revealed himself by making a pass at her, he knew that he was all deceit and cunning.

Valerie helped him dry up, and they executed little constrained arcs around each other as they moved here and there with plates and glasses. Sam hung up the tea towel, steeled himself and kissed her. It was surprising how easy it turned out to be. They stayed silently embracing in the kitchen recess some minutes. He soon forgot about everything beyond how nice she tasted.

"What are you doing?" said Valerie.

"Let's lie on the bed."

"Why?"

"It's more comfortable."

He had her by the hand, and, resisting slightly, she allowed herself to be pulled toward the bed.

"You're wicked, Sam," she said.

He switched off the light and in the darkness lay down beside her, and sighed and breathed her odor in great, hungry draughts. Valerie, with a small, expert movement, tucked herself against him, and the bed creaked and their clothes rustled as they embraced. Sam held his breath in the dark as with the fingers of one hand he tried to negotiate the strange catch of her brassiere. After an interminable few seconds in which success and defeat seemed to hang in the balance, he heard it snap free. Valerie didn't protest. His hand glided beneath the slack nylon of her bra, and he realized with a swooning gratitude toward her that the thinking part of it was probably over. . . .

He lay on his back, his mind clear and cold, and felt the limits of the room come into hard focus again; the ceiling, the walls at right angles to it, the obstructing furniture, placed so. He was still a little astonished. That hadn't happened to him for years, since his teens. In a way it was a great compliment to Valerie; clearly she had a most potent effect upon him. When he had first realized it might happen, he had hardly believed it, and had let it continue out of curiosity and a kind of nostalgic wonder. Now all that had gone, and he had to decide what best to do about the sticky inside of his trousers. He had only picked them up from the cleaner's the day before.

He was oppressed by a sense of vague danger. He looked across at Valerie, lying with her eyes closed and her mouth slack, and felt the loneliness of such bleak, private thoughts. He kissed her, his goodwill a melancholy substitute for passion. But it had been extraordinary nonetheless. Despite layers of clothing, their bodies, like prisoners fervently tapping the walls of their cells, had discovered a communicating rhythm, and as if from a long way off they had reached a climax together in a kind of aching slow motion. Perhaps because it was unfamiliar he had found it very exciting, his hand working with her in the silky clamp of her thighs. Perhaps, too, it was for the best; technically, she remained inviolate. He wanted to get her home before this depressed clarity of mind clouded over with a return of desire.

They both bucked like shot rabbits and lay frozen. The concrete room was screaming with the noise of an electric bell. It pealed out hideously a foot above their heads, then stopped, leaving behind a vacuum of silence. For some seconds, neither spoke.

"What was that?" whispered Valerie.

Sam didn't answer. He had not the faintest idea. They stayed as they were, shocked into the primitive defense of stillness. Inevitably, the dreadful bell started again. Sam jumped to his feet.

"Is it the front door bell?" asked Valerie.

"I didn't even know I had a front door bell!" And he added with real hatred, "Bloody Mrs. Shrapnel." He had crept to the window and looked sidelong through his curtains, but there was no one to be seen on his doorstep. He wondered if some kind of awful joke was being played upon him.

Again the bell sounded. He knew the source of it now, a black plastic box screwed to the wall above his bed. He decided it must be ringing from the hotel.

"Who can it be?" asked Valerie.

"Could it be Trevor, do you think? Is it Trevor?" He was ashamed of, but could not prevent, the gathering panic in his voice. She didn't answer him. "But you told me he was away for the week!" Still she didn't speak, but stayed, propped up on one elbow, listening. One beautiful, calamitous breast swung out of her unbuttoned dress. "Does he know you're out with me? Could it be Trevor?"

"I don't know," she answered in a voice that expressed alarm but nevertheless passively accepted the situation. She was being no help at all. He pictured her delicately nibbling grass while he and Trevor locked antlers in mortal combat. Reason counseled him. How could it possibly be Trevor? It was much more likely to be Amanda. Yes, Amanda! That's who it must be.

"Listen!" said Valerie. Again they became perfectly still. Footsteps were approaching down the winding paved path from the hotel. They stopped outside the door. There was knocking, then a long pause and more knocking. After a further pause of what seemed at least five minutes they heard the same delicate steps retreat.

"They've gone away," said Valerie.

"Thank Christ!" he said, collapsing in a chair. A damp patch was beginning to show through the front of his trousers. He looked at Valerie, half naked on the bed, and the magnitude of his folly began to dawn on him. He visualized Trevor's great fists in driving gloves shaping up to him in a just cause. What on earth did he think he was doing? He had to get her home.

They began to arrange their dress. Sam, still whispering, apologized for not offering her coffee, but pointed out the inadvisability of turning on the light. In the half-dark he watched her dexterous fingers hook firm her brassiere and button away the secrets of her body. Desire stirred sadly in him. Even tonight he hated the part when the woman puts her clothes back on.

"Is there a toilet?" asked Valerie.

"There's only that one round the corner. It's not very private, I'm afraid."

He sat and listened to the strange, blatant noise of female water falling like an irregular blade in the dark. It made an awful din. The sound seemed part of Valerie with her hair up, the plump back of her neck threatening stupidity. He felt sad and confused.

They walked the mile home along the front, past the frosty, recurring lamps. For the last time, Sam insisted to himself. He stayed with her ten minutes at the front door, kissing her a mournful, unexpressed goodbye.

Next morning Sam met Mrs. Shrapnel as she was emptying some rubbish into the ash can.

"Oh, Mr. Beresford. Did you hear the bell last night?"

"What bell, Mrs. Shrapnel?"

"Didn't I tell you about the bell in your room?"

"No."

"I had a bell installed in your room so that if you're ever wanted on the telephone or something like that, I could call you from the hotel."

"Oh."

"Yes, last night—Mr. Boulsen, is it?—called in on his way home from the theater. Young man with drooping eyes."

"Oh, you mean Mr. Poulsen. Paul Poulsen."

"Boulsen, Poulsen, something like that. Anyway, he said you'd got dressed in such a rush last night you left your wristwatch behind. He called in with it. For safekeeping. Wasn't that nice of him?"

"Very nice."

"I knew you were in because I'd seen your light. But you can't have heard the bell."

"No, Mrs. Shrapnel. No, I expect I slept through it."

11

ON THE MORNING of the first *Macbeth* rehearsal two unfamiliar cars, a Daimler and an Alfa Romeo, were parked snugly side by side in the stage-door parking lot. Toby Burton, wearing his scooter helmet and beneath it an expression of frank, cheerful envy, was standing looking at the pair. "How would you like one of these for Christmas?" he said, as Sam approached. Not much interested in cars, Sam paused nonetheless. He had to concede that the Alfa Romeo, with its hood down and the sun glinting on the mysterious gadgetry of the dashboard, looked very seductive. "I'll have this one for weekdays," continued Toby, "and this one for picnics on Sunday." He kicked one of the new-looking tires, then looked at Sam with a grudging smile; the cars belonged to a world not his.

In the rehearsal room it was easy to identify the strangers who owned them. Martin Dane signaled his presence with a brilliant turquoise sports shirt; Sir John Bellenger sat in conversation with Tom. The company, chatting among themselves, appeared to be disregarding the new arrivals, but the focus of the room was undoubtedly theirs.

Martin Dane, being Sam's contemporary and in his opinion a decidedly untalented one, elicited a quick, skeptical look from him, but about Jack Bellenger he had to admit to an awed curiosity. In his early Hollywood films he had been an extraordinarily glamorous figure, blond and smooth, and it was rather peculiar now to discover that all the time he had been an entirely different physical type. His graying hair was red, and the backs of his hands were densely freckled. The year before, with Tom, he had triumphed as Macbeth, and it was this production they were now reviving. There were some cast changes, Martin Dane and Sam among them, but otherwise the show was to be as before. Sam had seen it and admired it for its great central virtuoso performance. The critics had found much favor with the way Tom had handled the supernatural in the play, deploying musique concrète and stylized acting. The witches in masks had chanted and danced their parts, and certainly they became less improbable figures than they frequently are on the simple plane of drama. The difficulty was that one hardly understood a word of what they said, a not insurmountable one perhaps to an audience already overfamiliar with the plot. Indeed these spectacular scenes created an agreeable diversion from listening. In other respects, and notwithstanding the claims for originality made on its behalf, the production was an oddly conventional one, set upon what looked like the top of a granite mountain, and dressed in the usual horned helmets, goatskins and draped tartan rugs. The final battle scene was magnificent, the stage engulfed in smoke and yelling extras running back and forth in frantic diagonals as if in flight from a volcano. Audiences had filed out of the theater, exhilarated and faintly wheezing, possessed of their money's worth.

The costume designs were pinned to the back wall of the rehearsal room, and Sam sought out his Doctor. He found him represented as a bent, white-bearded old man, and he tried to calm the feelings of revolt that this notion of the part immediately stirred in him. Francis Roland, now graduated to the part of Ross, had played it in the original production, and he began to remember that performance now, needlessly aged and tremulous. But perhaps he wouldn't be required to copy it.

The morning's rehearsal passed smoothly. Tom explained that they would spend the first week resurrecting as much of the original as they could remember, then build from there. He had no intention, he said, of rigidly adhering to the old prompt copy, but neither would they neglect it. His program seemed sensible, and he spoke with the confidence of the production's original success.

Not until the end of the morning, when he looked around to find Amanda for coffee, did he remember that three faces were absent:

hers, Ivan's and Frederick Bell's. All of them had this play out. He would miss her. After they had collected their mail in the mornings they had got into the habit of meeting in the canteen, where frequently Richard Wayland joined them at their table in the corner. Without particularly intending to, they had become the nucleus of one of those groups which temperament and common interests were loosely carving out of the company, groupings as yet uncorrupted by any sense of mutual advantage beyond ready laughter. Sam ordered his coffee and sat by himself, a little disconcerted to be deprived of the flattering mirrors of his friends. Don Petersen, who had rung a change in his sweaters for this new production and was now in thick yellow, joined him, and their solemn politeness with each other was a measure of an incompatibility which they had discovered in the last few weeks and which no effort of goodwill could hope to redress.

Toby Burton came into the canteen in impressive company. He was discussing cars with Martin Dane, and his round face was all attention and respectful friendliness. The idiom they had adopted (Toby called Martin by his Christian name and Martin called Toby "love") was splendidly egalitarian, except in the one respect that it existed only by Martin's permission, and this was reflected in the weary friendliness of his replies, broadcast more or less to the entire room, on such matters as mileage, revs and maximum speeds.

"Can we join you?" said Toby. He was proud of his catch but also a little nervous of it, and was glad to sight familiar faces.

"Sure!" and "Mmm!" said Sam and Don simultaneously, scraping their chairs together with a jerk and making more room than was strictly required.

"This is Sam Beresford and Don Petersen," said Toby, and Martin said "Hello, love" twice. They sat in silence awhile, then Toby said, "Are you looking forward to Banquo, then, Marty?"

"Well, love, you know how it is. It's a challenge. I hope I'm up to it. Not to play it. I mean anyone can just play it. I mean to play it with real meaning, you know?"

"Yes," said Toby with a serious nod.

"I mean these parts, all these Shakespeare parts, they've got to be done fresh, you know what I mean? It's no good doing them the old way. All that's got to be scrapped. I mean if you're a talented person, you've got to find a meaning for your own time. That's what talent is, for Christ sake."

"How do you see Banquo, then, Marty?"

"Well, love, it's not so much how I *see* him as how I *do* him. Without the old tricks, you know? I want him real. Look, I'm from the North myself. I know what it's about. I want him to be as real as that."

"Sounds interesting."

"Look, love, I know the risks. I could fail. All right, so I fail. But talent has got to demand the right to fail."

Sam listened, tonguetied in the face of such fatuities but doing his best to disguise the hostility that he felt resounded from his silence. Don's and Toby's serious, nodding faces seemed ample proof of the precept that people take you at your own value, and Martin presumably sensed this because it was to these two that he was addressing all his remarks. He hardly glanced at Sam.

"Have you seen *The Duchess* yet?" asked Don in a deferring voice.

"On the first night, love! I was there on the first night."

"What did you think of it?"

"Great. Great. Marvelous. A great evening in the theater. Tom's done a just incredible job on the production. I mean, let's face it, the play is crap. It's got to be *done,* you know what I mean?" Martin let the conversation hang there.

"What about the acting?" said Toby.

"Great. I liked nearly everyone. Freddie, Rachel. They were all good."

"Did you like Ivan?"

Martin smiled indulgently. "Look, love, we all know Ivan's marvelous. Really marvelous. There's no one like him. But *I just wish* he wouldn't *do* those things . . ."

"What things, Marty?" inquired Don.

"Those things he's been doing for thirty years. Look, don't get me wrong. Ivan's a great actor. There's no one like him. And, hell, he doesn't need those tricks. But the cunning old bastard just won't give them up."

"Why is the play crap?" Sam endeavored to ask casually.

Martin gave him his first sustained look, then laughed. "Come off it, love. You know as well as I do, it's crap. Melodrama. It's got to be produced. That's why old Ivan's so useful in it. He knows how to trick it up. And he can get away with it. It's right for his generation. But, look, when young actors use those tricks, I just don't want to know . . ."

Sam scrutinized Martin. Was this last remark intended for him? His manner had been impossibly condescending, but there was nothing actually hostile about it. It seemed too bald, too open an attack to be believed. Martin was smiling at him, waiting upon a reply. "Mmm," agreed Sam.

Martin's attention returned to Don and Toby; Sam watched him talking. The fact alone that he had control of the table and meant to keep it aroused Sam's resentment. Simple talk had become a win-or-lose business, and he felt himself forfeiting personality with every minute he remained with them. He wanted to get up and go but could think of no way of extricating himself that was not an open declaration of enmity. Martin's wrists were big-boned, white and hairless; he was reputed to have an enormous penis; what alarmed Sam, much more than Martin's vanity and malice, was his own immediate, blind dislike. It ruled out the comfort of moral superiority. He was beginning to realize something: he had encountered a natural enemy.

After rehearsal Sam met Martin again as he was crossing the car park. They smiled at each other. "Can I give you a lift, love?" said Martin, and Sam thanked him but explained he had some shopping to do. The silver car drove away, leaving him lumbered with an aspect of himself he disliked. How could he slough it off? He had an hour and a half before he returned to the theater for the evening performance. A visit to Amanda's might help.

He had become familiar with the shortcut to her flat through the Drama School. There were classes still in progress, and as he

173

walked along the passageway, he passed the noise, in one room, of the martinet commands of a ballet mistress rising above a thumping piano accompaniment; in another, of the strained, earnest voices of students rehearsing a play. He remembered the cheerful, bogus industry of his own drama school, and found himself smiling. The private discoveries he had made there and the fun he had had sufficiently justified the two-year course; as to the curriculum, it had been better obeyed than examined. Of the twelve young men who had been in his class nine years ago only two others to his knowledge were still acting. The rest had just faded away. Drama schools were the garish recruiting centers of the profession, and there would never be a shortage of volunteers to replace the ranks of those hundreds of actors who each year fell before the play of paper bullets. In the corridor now he passed some of the latest recruits: self-conscious young men and almost-pretty girls, all moody with wild, trite hope.

At the end of the passage was the door leading straight into Amanda's kitchen. He opened it and heard her piano. He walked softly through to the sitting room and stood watching her, unobserved, while she played. In a pause he tapped on the door frame, and she turned, startled.

"Hello. Don't stop. It's nice."

"I was just going to stop anyway."

"No, please. Play some more. I like it. What is it, Bach?"

"Yep. Goldberg Variations arranged for piano. Very tricky. Let's have some tea."

"Play a little bit for me first."

"Well, what part?"

"Anything."

He stood by the piano as she played. He had no musical skills himself, and watched with naïve approval as her hands shuttled nimbly over the keyboard, producing beautiful, detailed lengths of sound. Occasionally she would strike a wrong note, and stop to stare, biting her lip, at her music. "Damn," she would murmur, then as abruptly return to the attack and the music would ribbon forth once more.

"There!" she said at the conclusion of a passage, dropping her limp hands to her lap and looking up smiling. He thought he would kiss her. He did so, but it seemed a rather clumsy gesture, the wrong one in the circumstances. One state of mind had spilled over into another, and he regretted it. Amanda looked taken by surprise. She had flushed deeply, but this was quickly giving way to a look of pleased, curious embarrassment. "Was that a reward?" she said, and then appeared to change the subject with one of her long matter-of-fact sighs. "You should hear Kirkpatrick, though; on the harpsichord. He's just unbelievable. I'll play the record for you while I make tea."

She put on the record and vanished into the kitchen. Sam, unfamiliar with the music, made no effort to concentrate on it but let it accompany the rambling of his thoughts. He sprawled in the Chesterfield, looking around him and taking pleasure in the room.

"How did it go today? Tell me all about it," she said, turning the volume down and making herself comfortable on the floor. He knew she liked to hear him talk, and this made him talk well. He had the knack of making her laugh; or perhaps she had the knack of feeding his self-esteem. At all events, they did each other good. He didn't mention Martin Dane. Their enmity seemed far away now, and he didn't want to commit himself to it. Perhaps he was really mistaken about it.

"Have you heard about the party?" said Amanda.

"No. What party?"

"Sir John and Rachel are organizing a barbecue on the beach after the show on Saturday." He was amused by the way she carefully said "Sir John." It was a kind of tact, a form of self-effacement. Probably he had been "Jack" or "Uncle Jack" to her all her life.

"Who's going?"

"Everyone. It's a company party."

"Might be fun," he said, doubting it.

"Should be. I don't think I can make it, though."

"Why not?"

"I've got some relatives in York and I said I'd visit them this weekend. They're expecting me to catch the train after the show."

"That's too bad. Can't you put them off?"

"Maybe. It's a bit difficult, though. I've put them off once already."

They walked to the theater together across the park, a low yellow sun behind them, and in front their own shadows, two huge figures scouting ahead with long legs and ominous, small heads. The performance that night lacked a certain edge. *Macbeth* had made its first just demand on the company vitality.

The following morning there was a notice on the board about the party. It was to be held at Sandy Cove, three miles down the coast, and a bus was to be hired for those members of the company and staff without transport. Richard Wayland told Sam that the party had been Rachel Frost's idea, that she had first tried to enlist Ivan's cooperation some weeks before, but without success, and so had had to wait upon the arrival of Jack Bellenger and Martin Dane, both of whom immediately fell in with the idea and were helping to finance it.

"Bit sour of old Ivan," commented Richard.

"I expect he hates parties," said Sam.

At that moment Ivan himself came through the stage door. He asked about mail, then came over to the notice board to see what the fuss was about. The five or six actors gathered there made room for him, then watched him as, with raised head and narrowed eyes, he read about the party. He gave a friendly grunt, nodded to the people around him, and made for the stage door. Jack Bellenger had just entered and blocked his path. The two stars greeted each other warmly and a shade warily.

"Hello, Jack!"

"Hello, Ivan!"

"Going all right, is it?"

"I think so. Looking forward to seeing yours."

"You haven't seen it yet?"

"No, I'll get this thing on first, I think."

"Good idea."

"Had a letter from Virgil the other day. He may be coming up to see us."

"Really!"

Their small audience of young actors lent a tension to this simple exchange. The stars suggested the people they might have been at Sam's age young actors as yet unproven, as realistic about each other's ability as only contemporaries can be, friends who were first rivals. Over the years they had got to know each other, and each other's work, a little too well. Now, at Braddington, both were seeking colleagues among a younger generation, where their skills were not without mystery and where the threat of youth was so explicit as to be almost a truce.

By Saturday the prospect of the party had generated the excitement of a tribal event. Actors, stage staff, wardrobe, box office—everyone was to participate in it. The two performances that day suffered a little in consequence, and in the evening Rachel Frost almost missed an entrance when she became involved in some problem regarding the food. She had spent the day in a flurry of organization and command. The only detail over which she seemed to have no control was the weather, which looked decidedly treacherous. She had dispatched Jack Bellenger and Martin Dane ahead to the site to collect firewood and organize a bar, and she conscripted other members of the company according to their special abilities. Amanda was to play the piano, and Rachel was having one transported to the beach in the back of a truck. "I'm coming to the party, after all," Amanda had explained to Sam. "Tom's driving down to Birmingham for a TV interview afterwards, and he says he can give me a lift as far as York."

After the show Sam set about his allotted task of loading the hampers of food onto the bus. Richard Wayland, who on his own initiative had reserved the back seat for the three of them, grinned at him through the rear window. In the dark the illuminated inside of the bus looked sleek and exciting, and Sam felt chastened that he had originally regarded the prospect of the party with indifference. Rachel was presiding over the loading and boarding of the

177

bus with evident enjoyment. "You've all got your bathing costumes and french letters, I hope," she murmured in an audible aside.

Ivan emerged from the theater and made his way past the noisy bus toward his waiting car. "Night-night, Ivan darling. Sure you don't want to come?" Rachel crooned after him a shade maliciously. He waved and shook his head, and vanished into the black car park.

"What's happened to Emma?" said Richard as Sam sat down beside him.

"Don't know," he answered.

The driver, abashed by but enjoying the novelty of a busload of theatrical people, turned straight in his seat and started the motor. "Everyone aboard!" commanded Rachel, and at that moment Amanda came running out of the stage door. "Jump in!" yelled Richard through the window.

"No, look, I'll meet you there. Tom's expecting me to go with him, and I think I ought to. You know, because of the lift afterwards." The bus began to move and she cried, "Gosh, it looks fun on the bus. I wish I were on it."

"See you there," they shouted back, and they were on their way.

They swung and rattled through the streets, and soon they had left the lights of the town behind them, and the bright capsule of the bus's interior was the only light on the winding coastal road. Toby Burton produced his mouth organ, somewhat prematurely, Sam felt, and two of the company's guitar players joined in. They struck up "The Foggy, Foggy Dew," and in desultory fashion some voices took up the song. Rachel spurred them on, her own vigorous contralto singing the wrong words. The driver seemed to know the road well and drove at hazardous speed up and down the hills. Sam looked out at the passing darkness and saw his own face hanging a foot outside the window. The journey was giving him an agreeable feeling of peril, and he smiled at his jolting image.

The bus slowed down, turned hard left, then hard right, and stopped. It had arrived. They all sat a second, summoning up the will to move, then rose in ragged concert and shuffled toward the exit. Outside the air smelled fresh and salty. The sky had momentarily cleared and there were a few stars and a bright moon. Sam and Richard took an end each of one of the hampers and, their feet sinking to the ankle in the sand, made their way toward the fire suspended in the dark 150 yards down the beach. They made their way toward it with the odd confidence of night walkers, trusting their feet as horses do. It seemed a long walk. They heard voices and saw figures moving back and forth in front of the fire. Jack Bellenger, in butcher's apron and cook's hat, approached them.

"Are these the chops, lads?" he asked. He had evidently decided that the best way of fulfilling his social obligations at this party was by giving himself a great deal to do, and he had appointed himself chef. In this role he could be generally friendly without inviting any unwarranted intimacy. "Over there, and Martin will give you a drink," he said, taking the hamper from them.

Martin, too, was working hard on behalf of the party. He had made the bar his responsibility and was distributing drinks. "What'll you have, loves? Red, white, cider, beer?" His manner was simple and friendly, and Sam and Richard chatted with him awhile. It seemed the party was to be a brief time out from company antagonisms.

From the direction of the bus a straggle of figures continued to be drawn toward the light of the fire, now fueled and sparking with the fat from the cooking meat. Sam had a second glass of wine and joined the even circle of people who had gathered round the fire and were now staring into it with wondering, patient greed. In the distance new carloads of guests kept arriving, and he could hear thin, raised voices and the banging of car doors. Soon the area round the fire was thickly peopled. Someone gave him a buttered roll from a large cardboard box, and he queued up, holding the roll open like a second mouth to receive its quota of blistered chop. He wandered off into the dark with this succulent prize, biting into it, unseen, without the least mistrust. It was soon eaten and, hoping for more, he rejoined the circle of mesmerized, orange faces. They all stared at the fire. The corporate voice, the eddying of the party,

179

was beginning to quicken with a faint expectancy, untroubled and hinting at licentiousness. Time was changing gear. It was going to be a good party.

From a long way off came the diluted music of a piano. There was silence as everyone listened. "What's that?" somebody asked, and Rachel answered, "Amanda's piano. We couldn't get it off the truck in the dark. I sent her back to play it. She's got to pull her weight." Somebody laughed. The song was from *My Fair Lady,* and it reached them as an offering of the humblest and most forlorn gaiety.

Richard Wayland came up to Sam, trying to control a grin of relish. "Oh, it's not fair, poor love," he said. At the end of the song Toby Burton's group cheered and clapped. The pianist immediately embarked on another song.

"Come on, boys. Let's give her some help," said Toby, and they took up the chorus with raucous, ironic enthusiasm: "All—I—want—is—a—home—somewhere."

"They're sending her up," said Richard. "Rachel's a devil, isn't she?"

The noise of the chorus entirely drowned the pianist, who could only be heard now faintly reemerging in the linking passages. They kept her company with brutal community singing for a further five minutes.

"She must be feeling awful over there," said Richard.

"I don't think she knows," said Sam, who had been walking up and down alternately laughing and feeling bothered.

"Why don't you take her a drink? She deserves one."

Sam procured a tumbler of white wine and a blackened chop in a bread roll, and set off across the sand. Midway, piano and chorus proved to be quite out of synchronization and this sounded even funnier. Some latecomers approached him from the parking area, and passed him close by on his left. He had caught the scent of one of the women and wondered why it was so vivid to him. They were twenty yards away before he recognized it as Valerie's scent. He turned quickly to scrutinize the group, now picked out against the distant fire. There was a girl there who conceivably could be

180

Valerie, but he wasn't sure. He felt impatient to get back and find out.

Amanda and the piano were in the back of an open utility van. She was sitting on an upright box, playing a medley from *South Pacific* for all her worth, and it took a little while to get her attention. "Just a sec!" she yelled, and brought the number to its conclusion. In the distance they heard cheering and applause. "Well, they seem to be able to hear me, anyway," she said confidently, and Sam knew that she had misjudged the nature of her reception. There was no point in disabusing her.

"I've brought you some goodies," he said. "I think you've just about done enough." He stayed with her while she drank and ate.

"That was lovely," she said.

"Some of the others are talking about going swimming. Come on back, and we'll all go for a swim."

"No. I think I may as well play some more, now I'm here. But you go on if you want to."

He tried further to persuade her to leave the piano, but she was adamant. He was quite relieved; the hunt for Valerie was rapidly becoming his first priority.

"All right, then. We'll meet later."

"Oh yes, please. Let's meet later and have some more wine!" Her tone was unexpectedly plaintive. She remounted her box and was playing again as he set off toward the fire.

Valerie was nowhere to be found. First of all he checked up on the people near the fire, then he searched for her among the groups that had gathered here and there at the perimeter of the light, bending close to examine strange faces. Somebody yelled "Boo!" at him. Farther out in the darkness he perceived solitary couples, standing or lying together, and he wondered, suddenly jealous, whether Valerie and some strange buck might be among them. He returned discouraged to the bar and had another drink. In the distance he could hear the swimmers splashing and crying to each other, and realized that he had overlooked the sea. That's where she was! He could go for a swim himself, and find her. This

181

necessitated a long walk back to the bus to get his trunks and towel. While he was hurrying across the sand, Amanda suddenly stopped her playing, and he increased his speed, hoping that he would not meet her.

By the time he had reached the water the last two people were just coming out, Janet Bennett and Don Petersen. "In you go," shouted Don, seizing the opportunity to splash him. The water was shockingly cold and, he was convinced, filthy, and he realized what a rash tactic the swim had been. However, already half soaked by Don's ambiguous high spirits, he decided that he might as well go through with it.

He waded into the still water, feeling under his feet the unpleasant silkiness of the seabed and imagining the presence of floating orange peel, sump oil and, possibly, sewage. He stood some time with the water up to his nipples, his elbows and shoulders raised and shrinking from the wet, then pushed off and swam thirty yards out to sea. As his body adapted to it, the water became temperate and caressing, and he began to enjoy himself. The shore seemed a long way away and the fire as small as a lighted match. The noise of the party reached him feebly over the inky water, and he began to sing a song of his own above it, doing some backstroke and faintly smudging with phosphorescence the immaculate black of the sea.

He wasn't cold until he left the water, when he immediately began to shiver. He found his towel and set off to join the other swimmers by the fire. Suddenly he stopped. There, in front of the blaze, her arms bare in a summer dress, was Valerie; and right beside her, within touch, was Amanda. Valerie sat on a hamper, staring into the fire and looking a little neglected. Amanda, on the other hand, was on her feet and looking about her restlessly; she was obviously searching for somebody and he guessed who. He stood quite still, watching them both, as naked as an Apache intent on ambush. He willed Amanda to go away, and presently she did so, moving off in the direction of the bus. Sam crept closer and whispered "Valerie!" He called to her again, louder, and this time she looked into the darkness where he stood. "Over here! It's Sam!" he said. She walked toward him.

"What are you doing here?" he asked.

"You're shivering," she said.

"I know. I've been swimming. What are you doing here?"

"Why are you whispering?"

"I'm cold. I've been swimming. What are you doing here?"

"I've got some friends in the box office. I came with them."

"Is Trevor here?"

"No. He's away this weekend at a car rally."

"He neglects you a bit, doesn't he?"

"He does."

"He must be insane. Are you enjoying the party?"

"I was just thinking of going, actually. My friends want to leave."

"No, stay! Why go?"

"They're going to give me a lift."

"There's plenty of other cars. You can come home in the bus if you want to."

"I think I'd better go with them."

"No, don't be silly. That's no problem. I'll get you home all right." He was shivering now in great disjointed shakes. "Look, let me get dressed—my things are up at the bus—and then we'll have a drink or something."

"I think it's run out."

"Well, that doesn't matter. We'll have a cold chop instead. I'll be as quick as I can. Ten minutes at the most. You won't go away, will you?"

"No."

"Promise?"

"All right."

"Say it."

"I promise."

In the bus he hurried into his clothes, panting; he had run most of the way there. He turned the light on to find his sandals and combed his hair in the reflection of a windowpane. As he stepped from the bus, he heard a car door open and from its suddenly illuminated interior Amanda emerged. She ran toward him.

"Where have you been? I've been looking for you everywhere."

"I've been swimming."

"We haven't had that drink."

"No."

"And I've got to go now! Tom wants to go."

"Oh."

"What a pity! It's a super party, isn't it?"

"Yes."

"Oh, *damn!* Look, come to supper on Monday night. After the show. Would you like that?"

"Yes, I'd love to."

"Good. Lovely. Now I must go. The others are waiting." He hoped she wouldn't expect a Judas kiss from him, but she merely squeezed his hand and ran back to Tom's car. She slipped in beside the two people in the front seat, and they drove off.

He set off once more toward the fire, at liberty. It was going to happen tonight. He was certain of that. And he was glad. Unrepentantly joyous. Valerie was waiting for him, and it was a prospect for which suddenly he had not the least misgiving or doubt. It was going to happen because, obviously, it had to happen.

"They've found some more bottles of wine," said Valerie, as he joined her.

"Good. Let's have some."

"You're still shivering," she said, smiling.

"I know. I can't help it." He laughed, and this made him shake more. "Warm me," he said, and they slipped an arm around each other and walked toward the bar. They were given some white wine and Sam clinked glasses with her. Even so sentimental a contact was not to be despised. He wanted to touch her every way he could. Her arms were gold and smooth in the light from the fire, and swelled most beautifully where they joined her shoulders. She looked as if Sex itself had breathed into her and delicately puffed her up. There was a sudden gust of wind and they felt heavy drops of rain on their faces. The men cursed in loud delighted voices, some of the women screamed, and people began running to and fro hunting for nonexistent shelter. Sam and Valerie joined happily in the panic, but their feet took them not in the direction of the only possible cover, the bus; they ran along the beach, hand in hand, holding their free arms away from their bodies in an idle attempt not to spill their wine. They were soon wet with rain and panting. They stopped and he embraced her.

"You taste of salt," she said.

"You taste of Valerie."

"I've got wine all down the side of my dress. I'm sticky."

"It's stopped. It must have been just a shower."

They walked on, then again paused and embraced. The wet beach had narrowed and was covered with patches of dark, leathery seaweed. There was nowhere for them. They carried on and came to an upturned boat. The sky was clearing now as rapidly as it had clouded over. He kissed her standing by the boat, then gently laid her back against the damp wood. Her pliant thighs helped him to divide her clothing, and they found each other with perfect ease. It seemed amazing. As he went into her he heard the breath leave her body in something more rasping than a sigh, and he felt a drugged exultance. The irrelevant moon came out and shone upon their solemn, rocking pleasure, and he saw it broken in pieces on the disturbed sea. He felt himself served by everything. Valerie moaned, and her sex began a further slow contraction around him. His control tumbled down. He withdrew, and they both glanced downward to watch him, in spasm, spit upon the moonlit beach.

He was sober again, but didn't mind; spent but not robbed. He felt a brittle elation. It was extraordinary to come to himself again in these surroundings. He put his cheek against Valerie's gratefully. "That was marvelous."

"Mmm."

"Did you come?"

She gave him an almost raffish smile and pulled his ear. "Twice, almost."

Someone from the wardrobe gave them a lift home in a minicar. Halfway there Sam, in the back seat with her, said, "Would you like to come back and have coffee?" And she answered, "All right."

In the flatlet he made love to her twice more with protracted, fierce competence. She insisted on keeping her slip on in bed, but otherwise astonished him. She got up to dress just as a gray light was beginning to seep out of the walls and furniture. He continued to lie in bed, half hoping that his look of exhaustion might prompt her to excuse him from seeing her home, but no such exemption came. So he, too, put on his clothes, and they set off along the waterfront. At the front door she gave him a brisk, contented kiss, and vanished smiling. She wanted to get a few hours' sleep in her own bed, she had explained, because a friend of Trevor's was collecting her at ten to take her to the rally.

12

"IF ONLY he'd have a little patience!" Sam had to raise his voice because Amanda was in the kitchen cooking. After the show she'd gone ahead on her bicycle to get the meal under way, and he'd walked across the park by himself.

"Have you talked to him about it?" she answered after a silence which signified some preoccupation with the food.

"That wouldn't do any good. He doesn't want to talk." He sighed noisily. "I can understand his point of view. Francis played the part last year as a very old man and it was successful, and he can't understand why I won't play it the same way, too."

"What does he say?"

"He comes up after the scene looking sulky and says, 'Make it older.' Damn it, I don't think he should be older! It's too easy: a white beard and the shakes. It's boring!"

"After all, Sam, he *is* the director. He's got to say something."

"Well, I wish he'd start directing Martin Dane. There *is* a performance that needs it."

"Is he awful?"

"Honestly, I don't know what he thinks he's up to. It's a kind of 'Method' Banquo, all scratches and mumble. He's playing him as a Glasgow mercenary."

"Sounds awful, but he probably needs time same as you do."

Sam laughed. "Check!" he said. "I suppose I resent it because Tom listens to him and he won't to me. The time those two waste at rehearsals is just incredible. Whenever Martin makes a mistake, he stops and talks about it for ten minutes. If he dries up, he takes the prompt and then pretends he didn't really need it—he'd only stopped to think. And Tom takes him seriously! They talk about 'motivation' and so on for hours while the rest of us just stand around waiting. I can't watch. I have to go outside. The schedule is all to hell. People hang around the theater all day without ever being used!"

"What does Sir John think about it all?"

"Nobody knows. He never gives a thing away. You get the feeling that he's not going to let anything interfere with his own performance. He kind of husbands himself all day long. Sometimes he comes into the canteen for coffee and sits with the boys. He's very friendly. But remote. Ivan was, too, I suppose."

"Ivan was pretty remote about the party."

"Mmm. That's the trouble with the big stars. They've got so much to lose. The rewards and the penalties are a bit too much for anyone to take without going slightly crazy."

"I can't wait. Can you?"

"What?"

"To go slightly crazy."

"No."

The meal was excellent. Amanda had lit the oil lamp and given him a fresh glass for his wine. After a difficult day's rehearsal it was nice to be spoiled. She attended to what he said with just the right amount of solicitude, allowing herself to be impressed but selectively so. She was wearing a silk shirt of a cinnamon color, and he was aware, rather more than usual, that she had a lovely line to her jaw and throat.

"How exactly do you want to play the Doctor, then?" she said.

"That's the point. I haven't quite decided yet. But I don't want to 'characterize' him. I don't want him to draw attention to himself in an obvious, theatrical way."

"I don't quite see what you mean."

"Well, real doctors, for instance: they may be fat, they may be thin, young or old. But if they're any good, you sense it in them at once, a sort of unemphatic strength. And this thing, this professional competence, is really the most striking thing about them." He remembered the quiet-spoken, professional men he had grown up among.

"And you'd like to convey that?"

"Yes. If I can. There was a friend of my father's, a physician, Dr. Bradley. He'd be marvelous as the Doctor."

"Why don't you try playing him Australian?

"What, like this?" He recalled what he could of Dr. Bradley's mild drawl, and applied it to his part.

"I liked that. It sounded good."

Perhaps she was right. The familiar lines certainly acquired an ease played in his native accent. Possibly he could retain its rhythms while eliminating the accent. He would work on it.

He helped her with the washing up, and entertained her with a further malicious analysis of Martin Dane's character. He liked her in the kitchen; she was very thorough without being officiously tidy. While she hung up the tea towels and her apron, he took the coffee into the other room and poured them each a cup.

"There. That's done," she said. She came straight over to him on the sofa and kissed him lightly. "Thank you for helping me." Her gesture pleased and quite touched him. The spontaneity of her affection seemed to deliver him up momentarily from awkward male calculation. It might have been one of her own family she had just embraced. She had on an expensive, bitter perfume that he liked. Hadn't someone worn it in Australia? He couldn't remember who.

"Would you like some music?" she asked.

"Good idea."

"What?"

"You choose."

"How about some Dave Brubeck?"

"Fine."

She put on the record and sat away from him in the other corner of the Chesterfield, and they talked. He thought about gently embracing her again. She was being in no way provoking; to essay anything of the kind would have embarrassed them both. But he knew from the serious, rather dreamy way she heeded his words, following less the meaning he intended than the tracing of some feminine logic of her own, that she would have liked him to stretch out a hand and touch her. She was already allowing language that intimacy. It was a small and easy thing to do. Besides he wanted to. Rather.

He moved across to her part of the sofa and kissed her. He was aware of the music, an isolated sound in another part of the room, and that their talking had pointedly stopped. They continued to embrace, and his hands gently ran over her. He liked her body, with its small breasts and protuberant shoulder blades, suggestive of vigor. He felt desire, then it halted and marked time. He wondered quite what he was doing. After a while he raised his head and looked at her. They said nothing but exchanged oddly formal smiles.

"I think we'd better stop this or we'll finish up in the bedroom," he said.

"I know."

"And that's really not a very good idea, is it?"

"No, I suppose it's not."

"You 'suppose' . . . ?"

"Well, you know . . ." There was a pause.

"I'm glad, though," she said.

"What?"

"That we've done this."

"So am I."

"Do you think it's wrong?"

"What?"

"To make love."

"Like this?"

"Well, no. Properly."

"God, no."

"Neither do I."

A confirming silence followed, which he felt the need to qualify. "It can be complicated, though."

"How do you mean, complicated?"

"Well . . . just . . . complicated."

"You mean you and I could be complicated?"

"I suppose so. Yes."

"How?"

"How?"

"Yes, how?"

"Well, to begin with, I think I like you too much."

"That's not much of a complication."

"No, seriously. I like what I've got with you at the moment. I wouldn't like to risk losing it."

"How would you lose it?"

"All the fun and so on we have. The companionship, if you like. All that might go. Sex can be bloody solemn."

"I don't see why."

"Are you trying to seduce me?"

"Of course not. We're just talking."

"Theory?"

"Yes."

"Anyway, have you ever been to bed with anyone?"

"Of course I have!" She sounded positively affronted. "I'm fed up! People always think I'm a virgin."

He laughed and they were silent again.

"Tell me, Sam, and you can be honest: do you like me?"

"Of course I like you."

"No, I mean do you like me physically?"

"Yes, I think you're very attractive. I like your shoulder blades."

"Why would it be complicated?"

"I don't know. Maybe it wouldn't."

"I think it would be nice."

"I think it probably would, too."

"Yes."

"However."

"What?"

"There's something else."

"Another complication?"

"Yes, in a way. I already have a girl friend, sort of."

"Here?"

"Yes."

"Oh."

"I don't see her regularly. That's not possible."

"Are you in love with her?"

"I don't know. No, not really."

"Do you sleep with her?"

"I have done."

They were silent.

"Are you annoyed?" he asked.

"No, not at all. I'm glad you told me. It's honest. I like you for it."

He knew it was nothing of the kind. He had merely laid down a condition, half hoping that upon it she would reject him. But she had accepted it. He saw the way they were going and it filled him with a shadowy excitement. After all he did like her firm, young body. So why not? She was making it almost a breach of friendship not to. He did not know whether it was the component of pleasure or of power in the opportunity she gave him that was making his heart race. He spoke carefully. "Would you like to make love? . . . I mean properly?"

"Yes," she murmured.

"All right, then."

"Yes."

As she led the way to the bedroom, his thoughts took a proverbial turn: "To him that hath shall be given" and "It never rains but it pours." Much later he was to wonder if he had really worn that look of complacent amusement, as if loyally preparing a report to some grinning, all-male fraternity, or whether he had subsequently punished himself by imagining it.

At any rate fifteen minutes later such odious self-satisfaction was far from his mind. It had been a disaster, and he lay facing her, silently cursing his weakness, his vanity and his blind disregard of his own admonishing instincts. It had been brief and joyless, and they had both sweated horribly. His hand on her back felt her wet and cold, and it needed some resolve to keep it there. If he could not control the way he felt, at least he was determined to conceal it.

Amanda didn't seem particularly concerned, and he realized

that she probably didn't know the difference, and that her frank idiotic offering of herself could only have proceeded out of a total ignorance. The word "copulation" occurred to him. That's what they had been doing: something desperate out of a manual. She had been like a parody of herself, eyes closed, mouth set in prim determination and flailing body quite pointlessly active. He guessed her sensuality had hardly been touched. She probably didn't know what pleasure was. But she had been keen, God knows. Perhaps she would be able to sustain their friendship in the face of this experience; he wasn't at all sure he could. He felt that he had participated in an act of willful destruction, and he wanted to get as far away as he could, and forget about it.

She, on the other hand, was full of beans. "Are you satisfied?" she asked. She might have been a nurse asking cheerfully after a bowel movement.

"Yes."

"Let's go down to the beach and have a swim. Maybe we wouldn't have to wear suits!"

"Oh . . . it's a bit late, isn't it?"

"I forgot. You've got to rehearse in the morning."

"Yes. What time is it? Twelve? God, I must go! . . . In ten minutes."

He lay beside her the statutory period demanded by his conscience, then got up and dressed. On his feet he felt a little better.

"Would you like it if I made us a cup of Ovaltine?"

"Better not. I don't think I've got time."

He looked down at her. She was sitting up in bed as frankly naked as a child. He would have liked to sit beside her and tell her that it would be better next time, that there were things to learn; but he had already determined that there would be no next time.

"You're not sorry, are you, Sam?" she said.

"No. Of course not."

"Good. Neither am I."

He walked home as fast as he could. Had he not liked her, it might have been excruciatingly, grotesquely funny. As it was, he occasionally broke into snorts of rasping laughter and stamped his feet as he walked—before remembering again that they were supposed to be friends. The awful potency of their few minutes in bed seemed to show up friendship as a sadly sentimental concept, at least between a man and a woman. What on earth would they say to one another when they met in the canteen the following evening?

On this score, however, he was to be surprised.

After he had left the stage at the end of his first mute appearance, he set off for his usual visit to the canteen. He dreaded the prospect, but knew that to depart from custom tonight would be nothing less than cowardice. Amanda was there as he expected, she and Toby Burton seated at the corner table and about to resume a card game which the play had interrupted. "Hi!" she said. "Come and join us!" He got a coffee, took a deep breath and went and sat with them. He waited for her to give him some look, make some small, bruised claim to intimacy. It was the thing he feared, but when after some minutes it was not forthcoming, he realized it was also the thing he expected. Was she perhaps ignoring him in this amiable manner deliberately? He studied her but she seemed quite genuinely absorbed in her card game.

"You want a game, Sam?" asked Toby. He shook his head. "Your deal then, Mandy."

But she had turned to Sam. "Oh, I forgot to ask you! How did it go today?" she exclaimed, laying two hands artlessly on his arm.

"What?"

"The scene! Playing it in the new way."

"Oh, yes! It went much better, as a matter of fact."

"What's that?" intervened Toby.

"My Doctor in the last act," said Sam. "I'm playing him differently."

"That's right. I thought he seemed different. Better somehow. Sort of slower."

"Yes."

"Are you going to get another cup of coffee, Sam?" asked Amanda.

"Why?"

194

"You are! You know you are. You always have two."

"All right. What do you want?" He dramatized a sigh. It was one of their routines.

"Just a tiny packet of cigarettes."

He rose, clicking his tongue.

"And, Sam—"

"Yes?"

"Can you lend me the money? I left my purse upstairs."

"The coffin with the flip top," he murmured, collecting the cups. He went to the bar and ordered the coffee and cigarettes, mystified as much by his own lack of concern as by hers.

He rejoined them, and Toby Burton did a card trick, which didn't work either the first or the second time. They were laughing a lot. Sam had his misgivings when Toby rose to go up to the dressing room, but, alone together, they continued to talk with an unimpaired good humor. He began to wonder whether the night before had really happened. As she was leaving to go onstage, Amanda asked, without any particular stress, "You got home all right last night?" He nodded. "Good," she said, and pointed to her cigarettes. "Guard these, will you?" It seemed her temperamental optimism was more than the consequence of being young and lucky. She had been born wearing armor. He was feeling something new for her: admiration.

By the end of the week their lapse seemed far away. It had happened, was to be regretted, but clearly it was to make no difference. Or very little. Sometimes in company he thought he saw a faint look of conspiracy in her eyes, a suppressed excitement beckoning to him, but as to any new demands made upon him, there were none. It was true she had asked him what he was going to do over the weekend, but when he quickly explained that he had work to do and letters to write, she appeared quite happy with his excuses.

The following Monday morning Sam was watching Jack Bellenger and Rachel rehearse a scene together. It was going well, and the rehearsal room had that special attentive hush that descends when the work comes suddenly into focus. Alfred's red face appeared round the door at the back of the rehearsal room. The stage-doorman had some message to deliver, and he began to tiptoe in his heavy squeaking black boots behind the working actors and down one side of the room. Sam was uncomfortably surprised when Alfred's message proved to be for him.

"Miss Maitland on the phone for you, sir."

"For *me?*" whispered Sam. Alfred simply stared at him, florid and self-conscious, and Sam remembered that he was partly deaf.

"Shall I tell her you're busy rehearsing? I can take a message." Sam quickly decided that the easiest way to terminate their whispered public conversation was for them to leave the room together. They began the conspicuous tiptoe toward the door. Sam looked at Tom, hoping to make some sign of apology, but the director continued to stare straight ahead, his expression peeved. He felt rather peeved himself as he went to answer the phone in the stage-doorman's cubicle.

"Hello?"

"Sam? I haven't torn you away from rehearsals, have I?"

"You have, as a matter of fact. But it doesn't matter. I was only watching."

"Sam, have you been down on the front this morning?"

"No."

"Because there are waves, real waves! Breaking all along the beach."

"You're joking!"

"No, honestly! The tide's very high, and there's hardly any sand, but the waves are rolling in. I thought you'd like to know."

"You bet I would!"

"I suppose you're busy this morning?"

"No, actually, I could take the morning off. I'm not wanted until after lunch. Where are you ringing from?"

"I'm on the front now."

"Look, why don't I meet you near the Ozone. Then I can pick up my swimming trunks."

Sam approached the Ozone indirectly; he was too impatient to see the sea by any other route than the quickest, and made straight for the front. Waves indeed there were, admittedly small but rolling beautifully toward the beach, where the wooden groins sliced them into foaming sections. He became greatly excited. As he walked along the promenade toward the Ozone, he reasoned what must have happened: the very high tide had drowned the sandbank out at sea so that it no longer acted as a breakwater; the waves would last as long as the tide was up.

Amanda was waiting for him. "Are they the right sort?" she cried happily as he approached.

"A bit small. But they might do. I don't think they'll last long."

"Hurry, then, and get into your things!"

He left her leaning on the railings and went to the flatlet to change. As he pulled on his trunks, still damp and chilly from a previous swim, he felt some apprehension. His rhapsody on that Sunday walk was shortly to be challenged. In the sunshine he was conscious of how white and imperfect his skin was, and he carried his shoulders in a way that vainly sought to minimize his nakedness.

"Go on, then! Don't hang about," she ordered him when he showed signs of sinking onto a municipal bench. He went down the steps toward the few feet of beach, grinning back at her and miming his lack of resolution. The water washed around his ankles; it was icy. He went in up to the knees and stood awhile. A small unbroken wave was approaching, and he saw its hill-shape run along the side of a groin as lightly as flame. It tempted him. He waded in up to his waist and did a slow dive beneath some approaching foam. He felt the wave suck past overhead, and old reflexes began to assert themselves. He came to the surface blinking and feeling his wet hair smoothed flat over his forehead.

The largest of the waves were breaking in about five feet of water, and he went out to wait for one. It soon came, tiny but adequate, and as it reached him, he pulled himself onto it with a stroke, and it carried him twenty-five yards to the beach. He jumped to his feet and waved to her. He was beginning to feel marvelous, and hurried out to wait for another wave. He started doing familiar things, things he had never even put a name to, so entirely had they been a part of him waiting upon a wave. They consisted of slapping the surface of the sea with his open palms; of making bubbling noises with his mouth, which turned into snatches of toneless song; of pushing off the sandy bottom so that his head and shoulders bobbed up to periscope for waves. He caught half a dozen more small waves, showing off to Amanda as brazenly as a schoolboy. Some other swimmers had followed him into the water, and he saw with pleasure their impressed smiling faces; it was better than acting, a pastime to which there was absolutely no point save joy: nothing to win or lose. All you had to pay for was time.

He came out of the sea scrubbed and toned by his brush with the water, and Amanda handed him his towel. "It looks marvelous! Like a bird or something flying over the water."

"These waves aren't really big enough. I wish you could see it at home."

He trotted off, shivering, to dress. There was no time to take advantage of the sun; he had to have lunch and return to work. It had been a good summer so far, and there was still the rest of July and August to come. He looked forward to other days of gentle surf. However, during his stay at Braddington, though he was right to expect many more fine days, the waves never occurred again.

13

IT WAS eleven days now since the party on the beach. At the end of each day's rehearsal Sam went out to have tea before the show, and it was perhaps coincidence that his route usually took him past the cosmetics shop. If the MG was there, he walked on. Today it wasn't. He approached the door and peered in. The CLOSED sign was up, and what had been slight trepidation turned rapidly into disappointment; he rapped on the door for luck, and waited. Valerie's head came up from the basement. He was glad he had thought he had missed her; it made him genuinely pleased to see her.

She opened the door a few feet. "Actually we're closed, but you can come in for a while if you want to." He slipped inside, wondering if he was being observed from the first-floor windows across the street. "I'm staying late tidying stock," she explained. This was the first time they had been alone together since the party. It should have been easy enough to greet her with an embrace, but he felt as separated from her, and as desperate about it, as when they had first met. Perhaps it was because the inside of the shop was visible from the street.

"You're working downstairs?" he said.

"Yes."

"What happens down there, anyway?"

"You can come down and see, if you like."

"All right."

He followed her down the steep flight of stairs, and fell headlong into a trap. At the far end of the room near the sink and the gas burner Mrs. Willis in an apron was pouring something into green bottles. She turned and smiled at him, and he smiled back, furious with Valerie for not having warned him. "This is Sam. I've told you all about Sam," said Valerie.

"Yes, Valerie's told me all about you," said Mrs. Willis. She was a plump woman with thin ankles and wrists, and an aggressive bust which she carried lightly like some solid but perfectly balanced piece of machinery: a safe door perhaps. "Sit down, won't you, Sam?" she said, indicating a small wooden chair. "Haven't you a performance tonight, then?"

"Yes, but I don't have to be in for an hour or so," he answered politely.

"I used to go to all the plays once upon a time, but these days I just don't seem to get around to it. Let me see, it must be five years now since I've been to the Playhouse. *King Lear* I saw there. It was very good—"

"Good."

"—but rather long. Well, how do you like our little town? He's thinner than I'd visualized him, Val. I'd visualized you fatter. I don't know why."

"Oh."

"Well," she said, abruptly removing her apron, "I've finished for the day. I'd best be off." He had just begun to credit her with admirable tact when, to his amazement, Valerie interposed: "Won't you stay for a cuppa, Mrs. W.? I've put the kettle on." Mrs. Willis stood so long in the middle of the room making up her mind that he felt sure she would eventually decline. It was hard not to interpret her acceptance, when it came, as an act of willful provocation. "Well, if you insist, you young people. It might be nice." He rose to offer her the only chair in the room, inwardly preparing the glare that he would direct at Valerie at the first opportunity.

Tea was passed around, and he stood above the two women, the one seated on the chair, the other on a cardboard crate. "I like those shoes, Val. I've said that before, haven't I?" said Mrs. Willis. They started to discuss shoes. Sam was completely ignored. At first he was amused, then he became annoyed, then at last resigned. Valerie was listing the entire stock at the local Dolcis shop, and the pair she described with most love was in navy, made in Italy, with sling backs, open toes and little matching white bows. "I don't think I'd like those," said Mrs. Willis. "No, not quite my style, really."

Valerie clearly had the edge on Mrs. Willis, and Sam observed with growing interest her almost cruel relish in it. She was the older woman's lifeline to fashion and smartness, to what was going on, and she brought her discomforting news. Skirts would be shorter, busts were in or out, waists moved up and down; it was all as alarming as it was imperative to know. Sam pictured their days together in the shop, Valerie chatting on about Trevor's MG or her visit to the Playhouse, a tidy, bowdlerized serial in daily episodes, while Mrs. Willis listened, her mouth a little drawn to one side, forced to play the part of the wise, detached older woman, the only role in which her curiosity and envy could be indulged with dignity.

Mrs. Willis had finished her tea and was looking for somewhere to put the cup. Sam came to life. "Let me take that for you," he said, and she looked up at him, startled and girlish. At last she was on her feet. Again she stood in the center of the room an interminable time before actually making a move toward the stairs. Valerie followed her up to the shop, and he heard them above him talking about the morrow. Eventually the glass front door rattled shut, and there was only the sound of Valerie's returning footsteps.

"She's sweet, Mrs. Willis, don't you think?" were her first words.

"Very nice. What was all that about you've told her all about me?"

"I didn't say that, did I?"

"Yes, you did. When I first came in."

"I expect I've talked about you."

"Where's Trevor?"

"He's at a committee meeting at the Yacht Club."

"Oh."

"Don't, Sam. Mrs. Willis's car hasn't gone yet."

They both listened. "There," said Valerie, as a motor started in the street above the sink. "She's got a minicar," she explained.

"Has she gone now?"

She nodded, and his hand returned to her waist. Valerie gave him one of her direct looks, shrewd, measuring and forbiddingly realistic. It might have meant anything—it might have meant that she hated him—but it did not mean "no."

He hurried into his dressing room five minutes late for the half-hour call and did what was unusual for him, slipped straight into the trousers of his costume. He did not wish to appear too brazen about the smell of sex. (He had laid down brown paper on the basement floor while Valerie stood watching him. Then it had been his turn to watch as she stripped off her pants.)

His makeup wasn't going well. He hated to have to rush it, and tonight it looked smudged and uncertain. The performance ahead of him refused to take first place in his denuded, nervously alert mind. Other images prevailed: her expanse of belly with its neat arrowhead of shining, coarse hair, the spring of her uncorseted bosom. He had looked down upon her with an almost fearful vertigo. His pleasure had been of a keenness that anxiety and discomfort only served to accentuate.

Now he set off down to the stage, superstitiously concerned about the debilitating power of the orgasm, baffled by his nature and the consequences of his own impulses. Had he really gone in to see her with that intention?

He sat in the canteen drinking coffee among people, and occasionally consulting the odorous secret that still clung to his finger-tips. It was as vivid as some memory of recent violence.

When he went down to make his entrance, he was yawning and irritable. He slumped beside Francis Roland, sitting as usual on the bench underneath the fire hoses. "Couple of managements in front," said Francis casually.

"Who?" he asked, unpleasantly alerted.

Francis named them, and Sam became nervous, but the wrong kind of nerves, jumpy and irresolute. As soon as he was on stage and challenged by light, he knew it was going to be one of those nights that all actors must expect, however infrequently: a night when the courage fails. He carried his part like a pile of crockery that any minute might fall to the floor and smash. Memory and tongue were not quite synchronized, and he seemed to have only the most tenuous grasp of his lines. He struggled to anchor himself in the words that were being spoken to him, but, listen hard as he might, one thought was gradually overriding all his efforts at concentration: there were hundreds of people sitting silently in the dark looking at him. Their gaze reduced him to an object. How could they fail to notice his hesitancy and discomfort? His actor's bluff of assurance had failed, and now they waited with patient malignance for his complete undoing.

As it happened, no such catastrophe occurred, but when he came offstage he was visibly shaking.

"Christ, I was nervous tonight! Did I look nervous to you?" he asked Francis.

"No, not particularly."

Sam sank into a chair. "You got your laughs, didn't you?" said Francis. But he was not to be comforted. He had acted badly, and on a night when important people were in front. How many other such nights lay in wait for him in the course of his career? It seemed he would always come full circle to these key moments of frailty. And it was no good blaming it on sex. It would have happened anyway, if not tonight, then sometime—but invariably when someone important was out front.

He and Paul Poulsen, both slow dressers, were the last in the dressing room. In contrast with his own mood Paul seemed in excellent spirits. "I've got to tell someone or I'll burst!" he announced suddenly. "I've had a play accepted!"

"What play?" said Sam.

"I write plays. Didn't you know?"

"No."

"Yes, I write plays. This is my third."

"I didn't know that!"

"A new management. M. L. Productions, have taken an option on it. They want to do it in the new year."

"That's wonderful." He was astonished and genuinely pleased to learn that Paul had written a play, if, at the same time and for no good reason, he was also skeptical about its merit.

"Yes. It is exciting, isn't it?"

"What's it about?"

"It's about the Casement trial. You've heard of Roger Casement?"

"Of course. That sounds a very interesting subject."

"You can read it if you like."

"Really? I'd love to."

From his briefcase Paul produced a new-looking script bound in red, and handed it to Sam. He was quite touched that Paul should trust him with it.

"Thanks very much," he said, handling it in a way that demonstrated the care he would take of it.

"Just one thing," said Paul. "Don't show it to anyone else, will you? I don't want anyone else to know about it for the moment."

"Of course."

Sam read the play that night. It impressed him. The first act inclined toward the pedestrian conventions of historical plays, but the trial itself was excellently done, and there was a scene before the execution that was moving and powerful. As might have been expected, Paul was more interested in Casement as homosexual martyr than as Irish patriot, but the play nonetheless bore signs of careful and thorough research. Sam closed the script and smiled. Who would have thought Paul could have written it? As Jock MacLachlan might have said, "I never thought he had it in him." One of the humbler functions of the arts, he reflected, was to remind one that people are frequently more interesting than one thinks. And frequently less so.

July 20th, the first night of *Macbeth,* was a warm, still summer evening, almost too beautiful for the putting on of plays. But it was perfect weather for an occasion, as the packed car park testified. As Sam approached the stage door he saw his audience, many of them in evening dress, scattered elegantly about the grounds as irrelevantly lyrical as an advertisement for a quality cigarette. He was not particularly nervous, though later on he expected to be. In the last fortnight of rehearsal his Doctor had come to life in just the way he had hoped. Tom had not gone so far as to approve of his characterization, but there had come a point when he dropped his insistence on the old age and seemed content with what the actor was offering him.

Before the first interval it was clear that the evening was, as it should have been, Jack Bellenger's. Like a champion athlete excelling himself, he moved effortlessly to the front of the field and stayed there. At rehearsal there had been readings of lines, details of interpretation which Sam had questioned. Tonight such minor reservations were swept away by the heightened force of the actor's presence. His performance was sustained on a pitch of physical vitality which stayed all question. He could already see the sort of adjectives the critics would use: "magnificent," "soaring," "breathtaking," words which went struggling frantically after a quality which was meant to be seen, not described; words, too, which both would have to pay for when an audience arrived anticipating a spectacle no less explicit than a public execution. But he was making a marvelous sound. The theater rang with it, was lifted a few feet into the air by it. The curtain came down on the second great success of the season.

The party that night was to be held onstage. The first person Sam met as he walked down the corridor was Ivan, looking unfamiliar in a dinner jacket. He put a hand on his shoulder. "Well done, my boy. Very good. Very discreet. Just right."

"Thank you."

Ivan's expression turned glum and serious. "It's good, isn't it? The show. Eh? It's good."

"Mmm."

"Great night for Jack. We'll have to look to our laurels. By the way, I'm definitely doing *The Way of the World,* but keep it under your hat. Going back to town tomorrow to work on it. It's a bugger."

They parted. Ivan was not going to the party. He had paid his respects backstage, and was now on his way home.

As Sam came through the swing doors onto the stage, he was caught in the flash of a camera. But fortuitously. A little distance away Martin Dane and his equally celebrated wife posed for a gaggle of pressmen. She had stolen a few days off from filming in Spain, and tomorrow would fly away again. The couple were always news. For the photographers they smiled, kissed, embraced and laughed, their gestures embedded in frozen globes of flashlight. She was small and thin with a very pretty, ravaged face that suggested she was missing a layer of skin. It was impossible to say whether they were happy or not; or whether they smiled at the prospect of reunion or separation, so quickly did one follow upon another. With their two careers they were hardly ever together, but when they were, they were invariably photographed.

The stage was crowded and noisy, but Sam knew in advance that it wouldn't be much of an evening. These gatherings onstage rarely were. The empty auditorium was a rude yawn, reminding all that it was used to far more imperative sounds than the buzz of any party. Amanda had smiled to him and he went over to join her. He had never seen her so dressed up before; she looked lissome and elegant.

"It worked!" she greeted him. "The Doctor was super! Truly."

"Honestly?"

"Yes! I heard someone talking about it in the foyer afterwards."

He smiled with pleasure. "What about the show?"

"It's *marvelous!* Don't you think?"

He agreed with her; it seemed churlish to voice his few small reservations.

"Not a very promising party," she said, wrinkling her nose with attractive malice at the assembly.

"They never are."

"Why don't we go back to my place and have supper? I've got some steak." The idea appealed to him, but he hesitated. She noticed, and smiled. "Think about it, anyway. See how the party

206

goes." Without giving him time to answer she slipped away to re-join her group.

He had been granted his liberty, but was to find little pleasure in it. He wandered here and there and came to rest eventually against the bar beside a subdued Toby Burton. The noise other people were making left them nothing to say to each other, and both stared apathetically at the party, disappointed in it, and then in themselves for feeling such disappointment. Someone had put on a record and couples started to dance. The accomplished dancers pleased him the least. He detested their cool self-consciousness, their pretense of not being watched. Fifteen minutes later he approached Amanda.

"Yes?" she asked.

"Yes."

She collected her things. A single photographer was still focusing upon the Martin Danes, who were wearily obliging him with a long look into each other's eyes. As they passed them Sam heard her, from between lips drawn into a smile, whisper one terse word to her husband, and though he couldn't be sure, he thought the word was "cunt." In the corridor Amanda asked him why he was laughing. He explained, and for a while she was silent. Then she said, "She can't be very nice to live with," which made him laugh some more, because it would never have occurred to him to interpret the incident in Martin's favor, especially since his wife in her nervy, ambitious way was by far the better actor. He then explained this, and they both laughed.

"Wasn't he shocking as Banquo?" said Sam.

"Shocking. Still, in a way, I could see what he was getting at."

"Cut it out. He was just plain bad."

"No. I can't agree with that. Or at any rate I mustn't."

"Why not?"

"Well, for one thing, I've got to play opposite him in *The Way of the World*. So shut up."

At Amanda's they spent the whole of the meal discussing his career, a perfectly proper subject since he was the one to have just survived a first night. Sam allowed her freedom to say any number of agreeable things about him. "You've just had these two successes in character parts. Now you want something different to follow it up. What are you playing in *The Way of the World?*"

"Don't know. Everything decent's cast."

"That's bad."

"I did wonder about one of the understudies. Mirabell, even."

"Why not? Have you asked anyone about it?"

"No, I haven't actually."

"But you *must!* Of course you must. Ivan's producing, isn't he?"

"That's right. How did you know?"

"Tom told me. You must ask him. He likes your work. He's sure to let you have it."

"Too late. He's going back to London tomorrow. He'll be away for a fortnight."

"Well, write him a letter, silly!"

"What'll I say?"

"Just ask him if you can understudy Mirabell."

"Like that?"

"Yes! Of course. Look, there's paper and pen over there. Draft a letter while I wash up."

Sam brought his letter into the kitchen. "What about this?" Amanda wiped her fingers and took it from him. He watched her reading it. "Well?"

"Frankly, Sam, I think there are too many 'I was wondering ifs' and 'I hope you don't minds.' "

"What should I put, then?"

"Just put 'Any chance of understudying Mirabell?' No, 'May I understudy Mirabell?' "

"That's a bit bald, isn't it?"

"If you like, you can finish by saying you're looking forward to working with him again."

"That's a good idea."

"And the beginning here. Do you call Ivan 'Mr. Spears'?"

"I don't call him anything."

"All right, then. Begin 'Dear Ivan.' He'll love it, the silly old thing. Of course he will."

Sam went back to the sitting room and rewrote the letter. He had to admit it was much improved the new way, concise and, oddly enough, better-mannered. Amanda came and leaned over his shoulder reading it. "That's much better. I've got Ivan's address in my book. And a stamp. You can post it on the way home."

"Thanks," he said, smiling. It pleased him to defer to her judgment on this matter; he liked the way it equalized things between them.

They removed themselves to the Chesterfield and talked. She asked him more about his life in Australia, and he was in the mood to tell her. Her head was lifted and her lips slightly parted, and he recognized in the way she listened to him that she was attending again to that something else she had discovered in his words. He had no idea what that something was, or if beyond her gaze it even existed, but he knew that her expression, eyes dreaming and mouth drawn almost in pain, was one that stirred and quickened him. He stood up and stretched forward a hand, and they went silently into the bedroom.

As he made love to her, his thoughts had a certain brutal turn to them. She had offered him the pleasure of her, and he was availing himself of it; he was having her. And leaving her to fend for herself. For both of them it seemed better than before.

Afterwards he lay on his back and sighed and laughed, the fantasy over. The word "romp" occurred to him. "I liked that, that time," she said in a shy way that was new to her, and he answered with a rough friendliness which was also new. "Not too bad, was it?"

This time he accepted her offer of Ovaltine. She slipped into a faded blue toweling dressing gown, rather too big for her. "That's nice," he said, fingering it.

She sat on the edge of the bed. "I like it, too. It's Dad's. I pinched it."

He laid a hand on her upper arm. He was glad that her nakedness was still there beneath the folds of toweling.

H

She brought the Ovaltine in mugs with some shortcake biscuits still in the packet, then she got back into bed in her dressing gown and they sipped their drinks. Sam asked her about her past.

"There've been two others," she said. "Well, only one really. I don't count the first. It was after a party and it didn't mean a thing. The second was in New York last year."

"Tell me about it."

"It was when I was in the play. There was this actor. He didn't have a very big part but we had love scenes together and everything. We got very friendly. We had all sorts of interests in common. You know. We used to do things together."

"And you used to make love?"

"Not at first. Not for a long time."

"How did it happen?"

"Well, as I say, we were always doing things together. We were always being interviewed and photographed together. And I thought it was silly: being lovers in the play, and being together so much, and not being lovers in real life."

"Did you like him?"

"Yes, I was mad about him."

"Did he like you?"

"Yes, but not as much."

"So what happened?"

"Well, one night after the show I asked him back to the flat. Dad was away."

"Like us?"

"A bit. Yes."

He laughed. "Amanda, you mustn't do that! It's dangerous for you."

"How do you mean?"

"It doesn't matter. Go on."

"What?"

"What happened?"

"Oh, well, we went to bed."

"At your suggestion?"

"Yes."

"Oh Christ." He laughed again. "What was it like?"

"It was horrible."

"Did it happen again?"

"Yes. I thought it might get better. But he was always drunk when we did it. I hated it."

"But you were mad about him?"

"Yes, that part of it got worse."

"Are you still in touch with him?"

"Oh no. It's all over now. He's in America. He's an English actor, actually. We were thinking of bringing him over when we do the play in London in December. But I didn't think it was a very good idea. What do you think?"

"No, it's not a very good idea," said Sam, but he also thought of the poor, weak, bloody actor, persuaded into an affair with the star of the show, half hoping it might advance his career, instead of which it was putting him out of work. He leaned toward her. "Well, as long as you don't give the part to me. That would be too much."

She kissed him. "No. You're not right for it. He's got to be very tall."

They made love again. It seemed still better for her this time. "You're beginning to get the hang of it," he said, and she buried her face in the pillows, smothering a laugh and perhaps a blush. Life is getting complicated, thought Sam, but whether the accompanying emotion was concern or complacency he wasn't at all sure.

Later on he rose to dress. On top of her chest of drawers under a hairbrush was a script. She noticed him looking at it. "That's the play," she said.

"Your father's?"

"Yes."

"And you're doing it in December?"

"Yes."

"You must be looking forward to it."

"Sort of. But I've done it for two years already, don't forget."

"You're a bit fed up with it."

"Oh, no. It's not that. It's a super part. It's just that I'd rather be doing something new—you know—on my own."

"You mean something that your father hadn't written for you?"

"Well, yes, sort of."

Sam smiled. This was a refinement of ambition open to remarkably few actors, but he did not comment upon it. "Paul Poulsen writes plays, you know," he said.

"Are they any good?"

"The one I read seemed very good."

"Isn't that amazing!"

"It is a bit." He told her something about the play.

"You can read Dad's if you like."

"Can I? I'd love to. I've read so much about it. I remember the notice in *The New Yorker.*"

"Oh, *he* didn't understand what the play was trying to do! It's a *comedy!*"

"He liked you, I seem to remember."

"Mmm. But he was very unfair to Dad."

The Drama School was closed, so he had to leave through the trapdoor. She held it open for him. "What are you doing on Sunday?" she said.

"Nothing, I don't think."

"Why don't we go for a picnic? I've heard about this wonderful beach. You have to take a bus, but we could do that."

"Sure. Good idea. Why not?"

"And we could take our things and go swimming."

"Lovely. I'll build a fire, if you like, and we can cook chops and make tea in a billy."

"Good on you, cobber."

"What a shocking cockney accent!"

" 'Night."

" 'Night."

"And Sam . . ."

He looked up at her.

She touched his cheek with her fingers. "Thank you," she said. Where had she learned that, he wondered. She had done it

212

beautifully, and moreover had meant it. Nevertheless he wouldn't have been at all surprised to find that the girl in the play said "Thank you."

In the morning Sam had another good notice. One of the papers described him as "definitely a young actor to be watched." Admittedly it was not one of the prestige critics, nor one with whom he had often found himself in agreement in the past. But it was there, in black and white, for all to read. Life was taking a bounteous turn.. Two successes in a row, two women; he had a feeling that this time his luck might last. That night in the dressing room he found that success gives you something to hide: self-satisfaction.

Mrs. Shrapnel had a cake rack she was going to lend Sam to grill the chops on, and after breakfast on Sunday he went up to collect it. The Ozone throbbed with life. It had its full complement of guests—sleeping three and four to a room, he had discovered— and there was ample evidence of them in the scattered cornflakes and tea stains that decorated all the tablecloths in the dining room where Mrs. Shrapnel was now working. She had taken to wearing a white cotton housecoat, and presided over her bluffed guests like a cheerful school matron. She had just shooed the last of the breakfasters into the lounge.

"Oh, Mr. Beresford," she said, screwing back the top of a ketchup bottle, "I'm that exhausted I can't tell you!" But he had never seen her looking better. "My cook's let me down, and I'm doing all the cooking, three meals a day and afternoon tea as well!"

"I think it agrees with you, Mrs. Shrapnel."

"Never again. That's what I say every year. Never again! But here I am up to my eyebrows!" She gave a peal of laughter which diminished abruptly into a philosophic sigh. "Oh well, you've got to do something, haven't you?"

He carried a tray of dirty crockery into the kitchen for her, stepping carefully between the slices of a cut loaf which had been spilled all over the floor, then trodden on. The newness of the appliances, things like the elephantine white refrigerator and the Mixmaster, only served to underline the squalor.

"Now, where was I?" she said.

"Cake rack," said Sam.

She knelt down and opened a cupboard full of dull, greenish pots and pans. "What about this? Bit greasy, I'm afraid."

"Ideal. Thanks, Mrs. Shrapnel." Before he was out of the door she was singing "We'll Meet Again," Vera Lynn style.

The bus they were to catch passed right by the theater, and they had agreed to meet there at eleven-thirty. It was going to be a hot, fine day. Invaders from North Brad were abroad in the streets, come to have an apathetic look at the old buildings. Already two invalid cars had drawn up against the back wall of the theater. Sometimes in the afternoon the small, black-hooded vehicles were lined up there as thick and still as a colony of bats. No one seemed to know why they chose this sunny spot rather than another, why it had become a kind of meeting place for the ailing. As Sam climbed aboard the bus, he looked at them with the benevolence or the indifference that his own youth and good fortune secured for him. He wished them well; they did not touch him. The journey took twenty minutes; then they had a twenty-minute walk at the other end.

The bus let them off and they started down a humid path between two hedges. Immediately the air overhead was thick with a mass of whining insects, and they ran for the open country. Sam looked across the gently sloping fields to the bordering stream, beyond which the round trees in the hazy air looked like a series of green explosions. How close and lush the English summer was. It always surprised him. He thought of all the foreign landscapes he had seen, beautiful and wearying, for him as fractionally incomplete as a repeating decimal.

They approached the beach and from over the sand dunes they heard the shrill, percussive cries of small boys playing at battle. One of them, seven or eight years old, stood by himself on a rise of sand, holding a wooden cutlass in his fist, wrapped about with

214

pistols, and lost in some dream of perfect violence. They went swimming at once, then Sam built a fire and they drank beer from cans while they waited for the food to cook. They lay back in the July sun, replete, pleased with the day and with each other's squinting presence.

Going home, they just missed the last bus, and had to start along the road on foot. Someone gave them a lift part of the way, but it was still a three-hour walk back to Amanda's flat, and they arrived with red faces and stinging shoulders, weak and laughing from their exploit. They had something to eat, then in the small bedroom, timbered about them like the cabin of an old ship, they made a last journey of the day.

14

HER father's play deserved its success. Within a couple of pages Sam had capitulated to the grace and mockery of the writing. It was very funny. And he could well understand her own great success in it. Her part, concocted of much love but little reverence, was a dexterous exploitation of the full spectrum of her character. It was impossible to visualize anyone else saying the lines. The play itself had been considered audacious, because its subject had been a Communist witch-hunt in an American university. But actually (and this was the gist of *The New Yorker's* objections) it played an exceedingly safe game. The very amusing climax, in which the girl is brought before the investigating committee only to expose the frailties of their own pasts, could be comfortably relished by an audience already in the know that her political background was unstained. Moreover there were a couple of genuine subversives prowling around the campus who came to a sticky end. If the investigators were ridiculed it was mainly for their ineptitude; their function was more or less endorsed.

Sam handed the play back to her, told her he had enjoyed it and how right he thought she was for it. It seemed foolish to say more when the entire New York press had already offered her their approval. Amanda knew she was good in the part; in fact the knowledge now rather bored her. This time next year she would be a West End star. It was almost inevitable. He wished he didn't feel even as slightly bitter about it as he did.

"What about you, though? Have you heard about the understudy yet?"

"Oh yes! I haven't told you. I had a nice letter from Ivan. Quite a long one."

"There! What did I tell you?"

"He wants me to have supper with him the next time we do *Malfi*, and we can discuss it."

Ivan took Sam to the Royal as before. It was busier than on their previous visit, and across the room Sam noticed Tom and Martin supping together. Ivan gave them a cheerful wave as they made their way to their own table, and they waved back. Sam wished they hadn't been there. He felt in some sort compromised to be discovered in the role of protégé. However, Ivan, who did not share in such morbid sensitivity, was in the best of spirits, especially now that Marco was back on duty.

They disposed of their menus and Ivan came straight to the point. "You can certainly understudy Mirabell if you want to, Sam. Tom's quite agreeable and so am I. Though, frankly, I think understudying is a bugger of a job. I'd hoped to cast you in a decent part, but there's nothing left. All the good parts went with the contracts. Between you and me I'm not too happy about this myself. Some of the casting looks decidedly ropy. Young Amanda, for instance, as Marwood. All wrong. Though, mind you, a sweet little actress. There *is* a little part I want you to do: a footman in the first scene. One tiny scene but important. We might be able to build him up, have some fun with him." It was clear that Ivan was thriving on his new responsibilities.

Over coffee he reminisced about his beginnings as an actor. "I remember I broke the news to my father in his surgery. He was a G.P. in Bristol. It upset him; I could see that. But he was very dry about it. Not that he had much choice in the matter. I'd just come back from the war and knew my own mind. 'Everyone to his tastes,' he said. 'Frankly, I prefer to make a fool of myself in private.' The only other time he mentioned it was that night at dinner when he said out of the blue, 'I think I'd sooner have a daughter on the streets than a son on the stage; at least she'd make some money.' My poor mother was very upset."

"He must have been pleased when you made it, though."

"I suppose so. He grew all diffident and apologetic as he got older."

H*

Ivan was an excellent host that evening and Sam enjoyed his supper, though he never managed quite to forget about the table across the room. He made a mental note to tell Amanda that she had been supplanted as favorite.

The news that Ivan was to direct *The Way of the World* went up on the notice board the following morning. Expectancy grew as the day of the first rehearsal approached. Sam found himself on various occasions doing his best to promote it, sometimes excessively so, and in the dressing room it had become necessary for him to watch his tongue. Once, midway in some paean to Ivan's virtues, he had been checked by the skeptical, somewhat denied expressions growing on the faces around him. Regardless of the truth of what he had been saying, his listeners had been quick to recognize a vested interest. He felt oddly ashamed, and fell silent.

Now, however, the play had arrived to speak for itself. He went into the rehearsal room on the first morning, glancing rapidly through the mail that Alfred had handed to him. One was a postcard from his subtenant in London:

DEAR DONALD MEEK,

Read your notices, and can't resist coming up to Braddington to personally discredit them. Reserve posh seat for August 16, 17, also room for two nights in four-star digs (17/6 a night top). Great plans of my own afoot. Will tell you about them next week. Flat comfortable, but where is the lavatory? Makeshift arrangements breaking down. Also bedsprings sag a bit toward the middle, but only to be expected. More jokes next week.

Cheers.

EUGENE PALETTE

The letter was from his mother. He had only time to read the first few lines:

SAM DARLING,

"A young actor to be watched" indeed. I should think so! Congratulations, honey, I can't tell you how thrilled and proud I am. . . .

Tom Chester was calling for attention, and he put the letter away. His mother's excitement seemed to have affected her writing, which was more spidery than ever. When everyone was seated, Tom introduced their new director with a few pleasant words, then departed.

Ivan rose, and the company gave him an affectionate round of applause. He popped his eyes by way of ironic comment, but was clearly pleased.

"Promise to do that again in three weeks' time," he began, "if you're able. Well, let me start by making my excuses. This is a very tricky play indeed. Some of you may know that it was a dismal failure at its first performance. Congreve was so disappointed by its reception he gave up writing and instead became a gentleman. I've seen it done four times, and it only really worked once. And then because of a great solo performance. And when you read it, this is hard to understand. There are so many good parts and good scenes, so much superb language. But somehow the play is flawed by its own excellence, mothered out of existence by an oversolicitous author. The plot is so refined and complicated, so devious, that in performance the play seems to have no story at all. This is our central problem—to make the narrative clear and interesting. Certain parts of it can be carried by the acting—Lady Wishfort's scenes, for instance—but there's much that has to be most carefully sorted out. Spoon-fed to the audience. I'm thinking particularly of the first act, that opening scene between Mirabell and Fainall. If the audience can be made to understand this, if we can hold them for the first half hour, then we've succeeded. No audience has ever understood the plot of *The Way of the World*. Let us be the first to make them. I don't think we'll bother with a reading. It discourages those with big parts and bores those with little ones. We'll get straight down to placing it. But, first, let me explain the set."

He turned to David Beynon's model on the table behind him, and the designer rose from his chair to assist him. "Gather round, everyone," said Ivan, "so that you can get a better look."

But in fact the hunched crowd around the model precluded the vision of at least half the company. Sam stood on a chair at the back, and by craning could just see what was going on. Ivan seemed absorbed in his toy, and it took him the best part of half an hour to explain his way through the various changes. Sam had heard from Richard Wayland that David had been in favor of a simpler design but that he had been persuaded into this extravagance by Ivan. Most of the stage machinery was to be employed, including the revolve. Undoubtedly the sets were going to be spectacular and ingenious, but at this stage it was difficult to take a sustained interest in them. He saw Toby Burton conceal a yawn behind his script, and stifled one himself.

That afternoon the company saw a little more of the Ivan they were expecting. His production was to begin with a prelude of mime, which would serve to introduce the leading characters, to illustrate to some extent the direction of the plot and generally to soften up the audience with a stylish musical promenade. The revolving stage would show first the women on their way to St. James's Park, allow a glimpse of Lady Wishfort's apartment, and complete its circuit to reveal the coffeehouse and the card game taking place inside.

After an hour's work Ivan's small appendage had blossomed considerably, as he invented additional flourishes or built on the suggestions of his willing cast.

There followed the placing of the first scene of the play itself, and perforce the temperature of the rehearsals dropped. Frederick Bell was playing Mirabell, Martin Dane was Fainall, and with their faces buried in their books, neither could be expected to give anything approaching a performance, especially since Ivan was already stopping them with quite detailed direction. He had clearly prepared his script with the utmost care, and perhaps could be forgiven for showing at times (and then very slightly) some impatience with his stumbling cast. Nevertheless, it was the first time he had ever shown anything of the kind. Watching him, Sam felt a certain uneasiness.

Working in as much detail as he was, Ivan took until the beginning of the following week to get once through the play. At first the company had remained in the rehearsal room, expecting from their director the diversion of some gratuitous entertainment.

As they realized that this would not be forthcoming until perhaps later in rehearsals, they dropped away one by one and were soon to be found, when not actually required, lounging upstairs in the canteen. Sam stayed to watch until he felt that to remain any longer in attendance was a shade ostentatious. Then he, too, left for the canteen.

Toby Burton, sitting with Paul Poulsen, hailed him. "Hey, Sam! Have you heard the news?"

"What?"

"Go on. You tell him, Paul."

Paul was trying to contain his pleasure behind a girlish listlessness. "It's all a mystery to me. I don't know any more than you do."

"What's it about?" asked Sam.

"It's about my play. Tom's got the option."

"Your play? But I thought this other management owned it. The new one."

"They did own it. M. L. Productions. Now Tom's bought it off them. Don't ask me why or how. I don't know. I didn't think he even knew I'd written a play."

"What's going to happen?"

"No idea, darling. All I know is he wants to see me this afternoon. I presume about the play."

In the dressing room that evening they were all waiting for Paul's news, and he made the best of it by arriving slightly late.

"All right, all right! Don't rush me," he said, then made himself comfortable at his place. "We just talked, that's all." There was an outbreak of questions from the others.

"Well—!" said Paul, pausing to relish this windfall of attention. "He was charming. Absolutely charming. He'd heard about the play from Amanda, though I don't know how she knew. And naturally, he said, he was interested in new plays now. And if he does do a new play, then mine will be very seriously considered."

"That's fair enough," said Toby. "Hey, I can see it now! 'A new play by Paul Poulsen.' Up there on the bills. I suppose you'll be coming back to act in it?"

"You'll *all* be coming back to play *marvelous* parts in it!"

"Is that so? Are there a lot of good parts in it?"

"Yes, there are. There really are!"

"Roll on, next season!"

"First time this year," said Francis Roland, and they all looked at him. He was the least talkative in the dressing room; the others supposed it was because he was some fifteen years their senior.

"What?"

"That's the first time I've heard next season mentioned. It usually begins about now. Wait till *The Way of the World* is on. You'll hear nothing else."

"You mean about being asked back?"

"What else?"

Sam kept quiet. That morning outside the box office, where he had just been booking seats for Sidney Cohen's visit, he had encountered Jock MacLachlan. "Well, Sam, you're full of surprises, aren't you?" Jock had said. "Your Doctor in *Macbeth* is a little gem. I saw it again the other night. I never thought you had it in you. I think you can take it from me, my boy, you don't have to worry overmuch about next season."

Sidney was to arrive on the Friday afternoon train, and Sam went down to the station to meet him. His friend and subtenant came through the ticket barrier peering about him through black library frames, his demeanor the usual one of a man arriving slightly late for the theater. His thin Jewish face relaxed as he caught sight of Sam. He was wearing his deerstalker; one of his Shylock Holmes days, apparently. (Sidney's joke, or so he claimed.)

"Douglas Dumbrill!" exclaimed Sidney.

"Lionel Stander!" countered Sam.

"Frank McHugh!"

"Alan Hale!"

"Edna May Oliver!"

"Marie Dressler!"

"No good!" crowed Sidney. "Disqualified! I win."

"Why not?"

"She was a star. Stars don't count. I win."

The rule of the game was you had to name a character actor working in Hollywood films between 1932 and 1942. Stars and Englishmen were not allowed. The discovery that both were the possessors of a great load of useless information about the early talkies was the thing that had first brought them together.

Sidney's knowledge was quite extraordinary. He could remember lists of cameramen, directors and makeup artists twenty-five years forgotten. He could recall the way certain films had been advertised: what stills had been used and what slogans. He could still hum the principal themes from a dozen ripe Warner Brothers' scores. Sam had been better on supporting actors, and "Douglas Dumbrill" had originally been his. As they picked over the films they had seen as children, their game provided a whole host of small-part players with a fleeting comeback. From different countries and different backgrounds, both were nevertheless marked as the beneficiaries and victims of the world's first, tin-pot, homogeneous culture, and they held it in affectionate dismay.

They had first met as members of a repertory company. Except in certain bizarre comic roles Sidney had been a pretty awful actor. Onstage he invariably gave the impression of thinking furiously about something else, which he was. His ambition was to direct, and in the seven years Sam had known him, with tenaciousness, courage and no loss of good humor, he had scrambled after a legend which read "Written, Produced and Directed by————"— a legend which each year receded a little farther into the distance.

He was not yet a new young Orson Welles, nor was it certain he would ever be a new middle-aged Orson Welles, but he had still done some remarkable things. He had run his own repertory company for eighteen months until a row with the town council had deprived him of the subsidy of a nominal rent. He had made a film in his spare time about drug addiction and youth, which a TV company had bought but not used. He had done satirical cabaret a year or two before it was the vogue. Most recently he had been working as company manager for a West End musical, a job which he disliked but which kept him going while he laid new plans.

They had become very good friends. Sam knew and liked Sidney too well to precisely admire him, but his qualities of resilience and guts were ones he never ceased to envy. What really cemented their friendship, however, and made it proof against any number of minor disillusions, was the fact that they were, each to the other, the funniest people they knew. This was a comfort neither would lightly sacrifice.

"Everything's fixed, Sid. Seats for the plays, a camp bed at my place, and tonight Amanda Maitland's giving a small dinner party in your honor."

"Great. Where are the Redcoats?"

Sam took Sidney to the Old Town's only coffee bar, a tired affair of bamboo and plastic plants, rich in dust. "Horrible. Really horrible," said Sidney, looking about him with smiling satisfaction. They were experts on the tawdry decor of such places, having spent so many hours in them in London between appointments.

"Feel the seats, though," said Sam. "Grade-A discomfort factor."

"And the coffee?"

"Not merely piss. Frequently *cold* piss."

"My God, what a find! How do you class it?"

"Early '55 Tahitian Gothic, Unventilated."

Sidney nodded his head sagely. He had once had a project for a Bad Food Guide of London, and he had taken it very seriously: a best seller with tourists, he had insisted, for whom it would be invaluable.

"Well, what are these great plans of yours?" Sam volunteered. He would sooner now than later have Sidney talk about his schemes. It would get them out of the way and leave the field clear for levity. Sam liked everything about Sidney's ambition except the one thing that made it a reality: his obsession with it. He well knew that moment when the jokes stopped and Sidney's eyes got that fretful, talking-to-himself look that presaged half an hour in

224

the stony company of his dreams. Equally Sidney had learned to reconcile himself to the fact that the jokes would be few and halfhearted if the coffee bar they were in happened to contain a few good-looking girls. They did their best to indulge each other's frailty.

"London's for the birds, Sam. I realized it suddenly one night when I was doing this bilious musical. I've got to get out, I said. I'm going insane! It's a brick wall, and who's got two heads?"

"What are your plans, then?"

"Back to the provinces, my boy! It's the only thing! But none of your rep tat. A new sort of theater. A living theater! A really new approach. Listen, I've got a list of five towns that haven't had a professional company near them for fifteen years. Next week I start exploring them. As soon as I find the right building—maybe it'll be a warehouse, maybe a disused restaurant, maybe just a big room—then I move in. I don't want a lot of space—250, 350 capacity, something like that. A new sort of provincial theater for a provincial elite. No compromises. No censorship. A club theater, my boy, with a bar and sandwiches!"

"What about the money?"

Sidney looked as pleased as a fox. This was the bit that was always a mystery to Sam. "I've got a backer," he crooned.

Sidney was mad about the show. He came into the dressing room afterwards, and went straight into his imitation of the scene in the prewar film of *Beethoven,* where Ivan Spears as the composer goes deaf and breaks the strings of his piano composing the Ninth Symphony. Words were not enough to express his frantic approval. Sam had expected him to like Ivan; not only was he a marvelous actor but he possessed those haloed associations with the Golden Age, the time before adolescence had cursed them both with judgment. Sidney's demands on a show were simple: he asked to be stagestruck all over again; and it was a demand, after all, not in excess of what most people ask of life, that they be confirmed now and then in the folly of their choice. Alas, experience and such ravishment were at odds, but when it did still happen, as tonight, his joy and gratitude were unbounded. The others in the dressing room were delighted by him, and Sam felt a degree of pride in his companion. Another thing he liked about Sidney was that he never permitted himself to be shy.

Walking across the park on the way to Amanda's flat, Sidney said, "I saw Sally the other night at Hector's—one of his usual crummy bottle parties."

Sam had wondered when he would mention her. "How was she?"

"She was beautiful, really beautiful. She's a great girl, Sam." Sidney was inclined to be sentimental about women because he wasn't really interested in them. He needed them, however, and there was always one, a little sulky with neglect, somewhere in the rear of the trail he blazed.

"I know she is," said Sam.

"I hope you know what you're doing there."

Not even Sam had expected quite such a lavish dinner party. Eight people sat down to four courses. He had supplied the wine and left the food to Amanda. Sidney watched her stage-manage the meal with that slightly startled attention that was a sure sign he was being impressed. He frequently jumped up to help. Once he missed the step up from the kitchen and upset a bowl of baked potatoes all over the floor. The guests observed them rolling to a standstill, and Sidney on his knees adjusting his spectacles. He solemnly returned the potatoes to their bowl, rose and said, "For my next trick," and the incident passed with laughter. He and Richard Wayland struck up an antagonism rich in entertainment. Over coffee the rest of the table yielded to them as they warmed to an argument about Bertold Brecht, one of Sidney's heroes if he happened to be in that sort of mood. Richard brought out his pipe and proceeded to emphasize a point he was making by stuffing it full of tobacco.

"What are you smoking?" asked Sidney.

"St. Bruno's Flake," said Richard.

"Sounds like a medieval disease," said Sidney, and was conceded the winner of the argument.

The room was happy with the artless self-congratulation of a successful dinner party, a sense of privilege doubly agreeable because it came hand in hand with the conviction that it was entirely deserved. Sam looked down the table at Amanda, admiring the balance she kept between her enjoyment of the party and her responsibilities to it. She deserved a page to herself in the *Evening Standard:* "Amanda Maitland's discreet dinner parties after the show." Amanda Maitland's discreet coupling after the dinner party. Who there knew they were lovers? No one. The thought gratified and excited him.

It was time to go. Sam took Sidney to one side, gave him the key to the flatlet and explained he was staying awhile to help clear up. He had not intended to remain behind, but had decided on impulse toward the end of the evening. Sidney gave him a slight smile, questioning and a fraction bitter, and said "Uh-huh." Sam held the trapdoor for him while he followed the others down the ladder. He closed it, and they were alone together.

"What about Sidney? Will he be all right?" she asked.

"Yes, he's got the key." They could hear voices below in the lane. "Richard will probably give him a lift home. Do you like Sid?"

"Yes, I do. He's nice."

But he was a little disappointed she hadn't enthused more. "It was a marvelous dinner. Really." He collected some dirty glasses and a half-empty bowl of nuts.

"No. Don't do that. Leave it. I'm not wanted all morning. I'll do it then."

They embraced gently.

"Oh, Sam, I'm worried."

"Why?"

"I don't think I'm going to be good in my part. I thought I was right for Marwood. I'm not sure now."

"How did it go today?"

"Awful."

"Would it help if I did some work on it with you?"

"Would you? I'd love it if you would!"

"Of course. Anyway—let's forget about it for tonight."

They went into the bedroom. "Rehearsals are a bit . . . disappointing, aren't they?" she said.

"Mmm," he said, but he was glad he had better things to think about.

"Do you think Ivan's doing a good job on the production?"

"I dunno." He didn't want to talk about it. "I think maybe he's done a bit too much work on it. You know, overprepared it. It's all a bit rigid."

"How do you mean?"

"I don't know."

He drew her to him. Amanda, who was already good at so many things, was becoming good at this, too. He hadn't taught her. She had learned from him. Now when she made love she smiled, but tremulously, strangely like someone smiling in her sleep. When he had told her about it she hadn't known.

Sidney was asleep when he got in, but he was soon completely awake. His camp bed and extra bedclothes had been supplied by Mrs. Shrapnel with a roguish disbelief—expressed in pink sheets—in what Sam maintained was Sidney's sex.

"She's a great girl, Amanda," said Sidney. "Fantastic."

They talked about the play, and Sidney did some more Ivan Spears imitations, accurate and very funny, to which Sam rejoined with his merciless line in Martin Dane. Sidney was avid for theater gossip, and Sam gave him his own highly colored and biased account of the season. They talked for an hour, then decided it was time for sleep. But five minutes later they were talking again. There was so much to say and relish. Five vows of silence were broken.

It was almost a year, Sam reflected, since he had felt this splendid, wanton, flattering exhilaration, and on that occasion, too, it had been with Sidney, after a party. Ten years ago it had been a commonplace of friendship, and ten years before that his only language. It was something you could never force; he wondered when it would happen again. In a way he was glad Sidney was leaving after the matinee tomorrow. That they ran the risk of fatiguing each other was a danger of which both had grown more aware in the last year or so. Tonight, however, they were safe. The room was growing light when Sidney started on his Charles Laughton speech from *Les Misérables*. At the age of seven Sam had thought it was someone's name, Leslie Miserables. At last, chastened by dawn, they fell asleep.

15

THE *Reader's Digest* is wrong, thought Sam. The best part isn't afterwards; the best part is when you're doing it. "The shared peace of mutual satisfaction" was a much overrated state of mind.

Valerie lay beside him, and all the beautiful lengths and protuberances of her body seemed only to encase blind tunnels which had led him nowhere. Perhaps he might have felt differently if they could both have looked forward to sleep, but ahead of him was the climb out of bed, the dressing, the walk there and back under the counting lights. But tonight at least he would desist from the vain resolve not to see her again. He had already broken it four—or was it five?—times. It wasn't that he didn't like Valerie. Each time they met he found something new to surprise or delight him. It was simply that he knew he wasn't good for her, and it was humiliating to find this discovery always waiting for him at the end of an evening of two or three bouts of love. The better the lovemaking the more depressing was the discovery.

She was Trevor's girl; he was the one who offered her a future, who regarded her with some sort of responsibility. And it had little to do with it that Sam didn't like him. Valerie did, quite. He had some money, a good job, and according to Valerie was quite capable in bed. "He's a bit lazy," she had said. "Sometimes he doesn't feel like it, and I have to prompt him." And Sam had had a vivid idea of just how expertly she must have set about that. "I find him very sexually attractive," she had confided, and after his initial surprise Sam could see that is his Rugger way, with his black hair and large handsome hands, he was quite a desirable male. "Where do you do it?" he had asked, and she had replied, "In the open on a rug. When it's winter, in the car. Trevor lives at home with his

230

parents, you see." Valerie frequently amazed him. Her infidelity to Trevor was really quite courageous, and perhaps justified. He neglected her, took her for granted. Very well. Coolly, and with complete presence of mind, she was insuring that she would not be denied what was due to her youth, beauty and undoubted sexual talent.

Their meetings were falling into a pattern. First he would decide not to see her again; within a few days he would start thinking about her, in bed at night or before he got up in the morning; by the end of the week he had made up his mind to see her again. He would call in at the cosmetics shop to arrange an evening, usually to find that Trevor, who seemed to have an instinct about his visits, was already in attendance; whereupon it became absolutely imperative that he see her again. He would ring in the lunch hour when Mrs. Willis was out. What with Trevor's sense of property and Valerie's own playful contrariness, it was usually another week before they met. Trevor virtually arranged it for them by going out on a night's drinking or driving away to some motor event where Valerie was superfluous.

So they were meeting about once a fortnight. And in between times he was seeing Amanda. There were times when he felt anxiety or guilt about the arrangement, but there were also times when the thought of it filled him with crowing exuberance. He never asked himself which of the two women he preferred; it was an absurd question because he liked them in such different ways. It was a contradiction to say so, but in the arms of either he felt completely committed. And the arrangement seemed so lacking in deceit. Or rather the convenient interlocking of a variety of deceits gave it a kind of honest stability. Amanda knew about Valerie (though not by name), and apparently didn't mind. Valerie had guessed about Amanda, and apparently didn't mind. Sam knew about Trevor, and didn't mind. Only Trevor was in the dark, and it served him right; or so Sam strove to convince himself.

What usually happened was that Sam picked up Valerie at her house after the show and took her back to the flatlet for a meal. He tried to be imaginative about the cooking, and bought various wines to match his dishes. Valerie's favorite was sparkling Burgundy, but she also liked Hungarian Bull's Blood, though mainly on account of the name. Once he had been so impatient for her he had insisted that she get straight into bed and let him serve the food to her there. "I feel like an invalid," she had said, propped up with pillows, naked, in an ecstasy of good health. Sometimes she said things that left him smiling and abashed. "I like to see you cooking. I like to watch your hands moving, touching things."

Her conversation as they ate was mainly prattle, about her clothes or about some minuscule wrong that Mrs. Willis had done her, but he never minded. He knew that her other personality, the one that gasped and made those beautiful concluding sounds, would soon be speaking a better language. She always undressed slowly, putting things like earrings or hairpins neatly in a row on the window ledge. The day Sam finally persuaded her to divest herself of her slip was as triumphant as the taking of any conventional virginity. "Why did you always want to wear it?" he had asked, and she had replied, "I'm two inches too big around the hips." He had smacked her for her foolishness.

Notwithstanding his postcoital glooms it was afterwards that they had their best talks. She would display that crystal realism that he loved, talking about Trevor and about herself with a candor in which there was also a level of sadness, as if she was recognizing the weakness of men, and the weakness of women for allowing their lives to depend upon them. If they talked long enough he made love to her again.

As he was walking her home along the waterfront, she said, "Trev and I are going on our holiday soon."

This was news to him. "When?"

"In September. We're taking the MG to France and we're going to follow the course of the Monte Carlo rally."

"Christ. . . . How long will you be away for?"

"Three weeks. Mrs. Willis is letting me have an extra week off."

"Do you think you'll enjoy it?"

"Not the driving part."

He felt an odd relief. He would probably miss her, but three weeks wasn't long. It would give him time to think, though about what he had no precise idea.

His call the next day was not until eleven-thirty, and he arrived at the theater with half an hour to spare. By the notice board he came upon Tom and Martin, laughing together about something, and they greeted him with unexpected warmth. A little surprised, he stopped and had only just exchanged a few words with them when the harried face of one of the stage crew appeared round the corner and whispered urgently, "You're on, Martin, love!"

"Thanks, love. Oops, Old Father Spears won't like this."

"You'd better hurry," said Tom, grinning, and Martin left them.

Sam was now alone with his employer. There was a moment of silence which bothered Sam because it clearly did not bother Tom. An awkward pride suddenly claimed him and he spoke on impulse. "I've been wanting to see you, as a matter of fact, Tom. I was wondering if we could have a chat sometime."

"Oh, good. Certainly. What about?"

"About next season, actually." What had he just said? Earlier in the week Richard Wayland had divulged that approaches were beginning to be made to certain actors in the company, but this was hardly a reason for Sam now to initiate an approach of his own.

But Tom proved indulgent. "Yes, I'd like to talk about that, too. Well, are you free at the moment? We could go up to the office now."

"Fine," said Sam. He followed Tom up the stairs and along the corridors, feeling increasingly unsure of the wisdom of doing so. He knew his chances of being asked back were better than most. Months ago in London Jock MacLachlan had assured him over the telephone, "We're engaging you very much with a second season in mind," and he had dropped a variety of hints since. It would have been better to keep his mouth shut and bide his time.

They talked for fifteen minutes. Tom explained that until he knew what plays they were doing it was impossible to discuss parts, but he described Sam as one of the most interesting young actors of the season. He went further and said that he was a quite brilliant interpreter of character cameos, and that he was very curious indeed to see what he could do with a leading part. Sam had little to say because he was kept so busy making the right modest, self-effacing noises.

Yet as he closed the door of Tom's office behind him and walked down the empty corridor, it was hard to feel pleased with the interview. For one thing, he was certain now he had misjudged the time to speak, and for reasons which it would never be given to him completely to understand, this error in timing was a significant one to Tom. Moreover if Tom had been really interested in him, as a talent, or more simply as a person, would he have risked such naked flattery? His praise had been as fluent as Sam's reactions had been predictable. He had a choice. Either to acknowledge that in a small way he had blundered, or to take the interview at its face value and be comforted by it. He chose the latter. But his want of a sense of the politic still depressed him. In the theater it was a necessary and just part of one's equipment.

Downstairs he met the one person whom at this particular moment he would have preferred to avoid, Richard Wayland, who asked, "What's the matter with you?"

"Nothing. Fed up."

"Well, this'll cheer you up. You know what old Ivan said about you the other night?"

"No. What?"

"He said, 'I smell talent on that boy.' "

He gobbled up this ludicrous crumb of comfort. "Where was this?"

"In the pub the other night."

"Who was there?"

"Me, Tom, Marty, a couple of others."

He felt a little better. "What are they doing in there?" he asked, looking in the direction of the rehearsal room.

"Still hammering away on that first scene. They'll be on the first act all day by the look of things."

Sam tiptoed down one side of the rehearsal room. Martin and Frederick Bell were running the opening of the play, and he could tell without looking that it wasn't going well. It sounded forced and unnecessarily loud. Martin, in particular, was needlessly bellowing his lines, and doing so in a very affected manner as if determined to convey not their meaning so much as some extravagant notion of style. Freddie was occupied simply remembering what he had to say. There was little contact between the two actors, and it was very hard to give them one's attention.

Ivan was scowling. Presently he clapped his hands and came forward, his expression now transformed into an agreeable smile. "Marty, you're giving us very strongly the Restoration flavor, and that's quite right: it must be there. But I'm not sure that at this stage we shouldn't be attacking the scene in a simpler way. Go back to the beginning and try just saying the lines to each other, very simply; forget about the style for the moment. Just speak and listen."

The two actors nodded and began again. Except that they spoke more quietly, the performances were little altered. Martin's mannerisms were cemented to his part, wedded to his lines by muscular memory, and he was not a sufficiently good actor to break or vary the pattern of something he had already learned. Moreover, he was growing uncomfortable in a way that could turn swiftly into hostility.

Ivan clapped his hands again. "Good. Good. Much better," he lied. "Just a point, though, Marty. You're inclined to run over that pause I gave Freddie—"

"Where do you mean?"

"After 'my virtue forbade me'; there's a big change of thought there, and I gave Freddie a pause. I think it's justified. You're coming in too soon before he's finished his speech."

"Am I?"

"Yes, you've done it twice. Look, do it for me just once more, eh? Then we'll leave it. Keep it light. It's just a conversation between two men, remember. Not too much volume, and above all listen!"

They began again. The only perceptible improvement was that Freddie was becoming surer of his lines.

Behind the dialogue Sam became aware of a peculiar sound, a kind of moaning. It was coming from the passageway outside.

"What's that bloody noise!" Ivan suddenly cried out. All his irritability with the scene he now vented on the interruption. "Sorry, boys," he said quietly to the two actors, who were looking at him startled and speechless.

Terence, the stage manager, rose from his seat and stood listening to the sound, but made no move to investigate it. It was beginning to dawn on everyone in the room that outside in the passageway someone was weeping. It was an ugly, strange sound, discordant evidence of real emotion which seemed to show up their make-believe for the false and tawdry thing it was.

Ivan looked about him perplexed and miserable. "Sam, go and see what the trouble is, will you?" he said.

By the time Sam had reached the door the sound had stopped. At first he thought the passageway was empty, then he heard a movement behind him. He turned and confronted Richard Wayland, his face frowning, a finger to his lips. In the crook of Richard's arm a small figure leaned a head against his chest. It was Olive. Sam watched them, uncertain what to say. "That's better, Olly." Richard patted her gently on the back. "She wants to see Marty," he said to Sam.

Olive turned. Her face was ravaged with weeping. Her cheeks were wet, her features red and puffed, and in spite of the tentative control she now had of herself, her mouth trembled and shook. "Is Marty there? I want to see Marty," she whispered between small catches of breath.

Mystified, Sam looked at Richard, who gestured vigorously with his head. "I'll go and see," he said.

In the rehearsal room they were waiting for news. He walked over to Ivan. "It's Olive. She wants to see Martin," he said.

"Marty, it's Olive. She wants to see you," said Ivan.

"What about?"

"I don't know," said Sam.

"Well, I can't see her now, love. I'm rehearsing!"

"She seemed a bit upset."

"I can't help that. Work comes first, doesn't it? I'll see her later."

Sam returned to the passageway. "Martin's a bit busy at the moment, I'm afraid, Olive," he said, and she burst out in fresh weeping. He stared at her horribly contorted face in some fascination, uncertain what to do. Then he returned to the rehearsal room, where her crying was quite audible. "I think it's pretty important," he said.

"Oh, for Christ's sake, I've told you, I'm working!" exclaimed Martin. "What's the matter with the bloody woman? Look, tell her I'll see her later on, the stupid cow."

In the passageway Olive had stopped crying. With her mouth open and expression frozen she looked as if she had just been slapped. "He's busy, Olive," said Sam. Richard led her away down the corridor, and he went back to the rehearsal room. The faces there seemed to expect some explanation from him, but all he could think of to say was "She's gone."

"Well, come on, let's get back to work," said Ivan, but he followed this up with silence. Eventually he spoke. "I think we'll leave this scene for the moment. And press ahead. But let's have another shot at it after lunch when we're all a bit fresher."

For the rest of the morning, though there were times when he was not wanted, Martin did not budge from the rehearsal room.

When they broke for lunch, Sam knew where to find Richard, in the pub, and he went straight there. But Richard was sitting out in the garden with a group of people, and there was no spare seat. Sam bought drinks for Don Petersen and himself, and waited indoors. He managed to apprehend Richard when he came in to buy cigarettes. "Hey, Richard, what was going on this morning? What was the matter with Olive?"

"Haven't you heard?"

"No, what? What happened?"

"Olive's been sacked." He collected his cigarettes and made a move toward the garden.

"Sacked? How do you mean?"

"Just that. Tom's sacked her."

237

"When?"

"This morning."

The sacking must have been next on Tom's schedule after Sam's own interview with him. Had Tom been thinking about it while they talked? Maybe seeing him had just been a way of postponing it.

Richard was impatient to return to the garden. "But why did she want to see Martin?" Sam asked.

"*I* don't know, love. Sympathy, I expect. You know, for old time's sake?" With this ambiguity Richard left him.

That afternoon in the canteen while they were waiting for rehearsals to begin, he heard a fuller account from Richard, now encouraged to enlarge perhaps by the fact that he had the additional audience of Frederick Bell. "I was just standing by the notice board, and suddenly I heard this wailing coming from up the stairs. It sounded like nothing on earth. Then Olive appeared looking ghastly and wanting to talk to Marty."

"But why Marty?" asked Sam.

Richard sighed and smiled as if dealing with an innocent. "Once upon a time they were very close," he said.

"How do you mean?"

"Look, Martin did a season here in 1950 when he was just beginning. Right?"

"Yes."

"And Olive was the big casting director then. Right?"

"Yes."

"Then."

"What? Marty and Olive? You're joking!"

"That's the story, love. At one time Olive was a very powerful woman. Martin arrived here practically walking on and finished up with a juve lead."

Olive was thought to have already left town, gone home and packed her bags that very morning. The rehearsal room was agitated and restless with scandal, which, however, was forbidden expression because of the presence of Martin himself. He sat alone to one side, reading a newspaper in nonchalant disregard of the

238

curious or hostile speculation all around him. Sam could not help rather admiring his studied lack of concern. It was almost as if he derived a kind of bitter vitality from the situation, enjoyed the way it seemed to condense life around him. Whatever else, he was undoubtedly the center of attention.

Ivan arrived ten minutes late, wearied and preoccupied by other and more mundane concerns. "Sorry, everyone. Been having some trouble about this damned revolving stage. Now, where are we?" As he passed, Sam had caught the yeasty smell of digesting liquor.

"You said you wanted to do that opening scene again," said Terence.

"Yes, that's right! Let's begin."

The stage managers issued Martin and Freddie their props, and they took their seats on either side of the gaming table. Ivan nodded and the scene commenced. It played with a new smoothness. Freddie had apparently consulted his lines during the lunch hour, and even Martin's performance had acquired a new definition. In detail it was unchanged, but now he was setting about it with a certain defiance, which, though it in no way illuminated the part, was in itself peculiarly arresting.

"That was a bit better, I thought. How did it feel?" said Ivan.

"Got a better grip on the words now," murmured Freddie. Martin said nothing.

"I think we can now afford to examine the text in more detail," continued Ivan. "Take these two long speeches here." He went carefully through a page of text, drawing attention to some shade of meaning that possibly they had overlooked and suggesting the change in stress which would convey it. "Now try all that again for me."

They did so. Freddie incorporated Ivan's direction. Martin did not.

Ivan hummed, then spoke. "Marty, don't you think in that last sentence of yours the word to hit is the verb? Try it for me."

Martin said the line for him.

"No, no. The verb! 'Continued' is the key word. Try it again."

Martin said it as before. In exasperation Ivan spoke the line for him. Martin looked at him and laughed. "You aren't by chance giving me *inflections,* are you, Ivan, love?"

They stared at each other a few seconds, then Ivan smiled. "No, no, not inflections; just suggestions. Come on. Let's go back to the top and run straight through. But before we do, Freddie, just a couple of points here." Martin waited while Ivan whispered to the other actor.

They began again. Freddie had gained in confidence, and in this quality, at least, Martin was determined to match him. His performance remained unaltered.

Suddenly Ivan was clapping his hands. "Marty! Marty! You must wait for that pause! You're not letting Freddie finish his speech. It doesn't make sense. You did it the time before, too."

Martin had gone quite pale. "I'm sorry, Ivan, love. I don't feel it."

"What? What don't you feel?"

"That pause. I don't agree with it. I don't feel it."

"But it's not your pause! It's Freddie's."

"Still, I don't like it. It feels wrong."

"Well, whether it's wrong or not, if you come in too soon it makes complete nonsense of the dialogue. For Christ's sake, your speech is meant to be in answer to the bit you keep cutting! If you listened to what the other actor was saying you'd realize that."

"I'm sorry. I don't feel it."

"The pause is in, whether you feel it or not. I'm the director, or I'm meant to be."

"That's right, love. You're meant to be."

For a moment it seemed that Ivan was going to explode with rage. That Martin should choose to defy him on this of all points, that he should so willfully abandon any reasonable basis for their difference, flabbergasted him. He stared at Martin, trying to grasp and assess the fact of his open malice. Freddie, embarrassed and unhappy, looked down at the floor, while those in the room less directly concerned waited tensely for the tirade which must surely come. Ivan's lips moved silently as if preparing to speak. His antagonist looked almost calm, a slight set smile around his mouth. Then suddenly the outrage had gone from Ivan's expression. He looked terribly tired. He walked back to his chair, sat down, and said very quietly, "Let's take it from the top, shall we?"

The room was silent as the stage crew moved about resetting the furniture and the properties. The scene commenced, and at once everyone present was aware that it was moving toward its arbitrary crisis point. One by one, the lines, now ugly with familiarity, brought the disputed pause a little closer: the derailment of the scene. Freddie made the pause and there was a moment of silence in which the room seemed to catch its breath. He was a second too late in completing his speech; Martin had already spoken. Ivan looked gray and brutally hurt. The scene came to an end. "Carry on," he said in a flat voice.

Uncertain what was required of them, the actors went on to the next scene. Ivan struggled to give them his attention, but his face wore a look of miserable preoccupation, and one could see his thoughts returning again and again to the injury that had been done him. Once or twice he stopped the rehearsal to make a suggestion, but all the life and buoyancy had gone out of him. He looked old and sick. Soon he did no more than sit and have the play unroll before him as mechanically as a film. The sympathy the room felt for him was qualified by a sense of bafflement and disappointment. Why had he allowed himself to be defeated without a fight? However grudgingly, Martin was being conceded the inevitable prestige of the victor. Without interruption scene followed scene in lugubrious succession as the actors performed before their silent director. In a sense it was their first run-through.

The rehearsal was scheduled to finish early that day, because of the performance in the evening of *The Duchess of Malfi*. They had not done it for an entire fortnight, the longest it had ever been out of the repertory. Sam had planned to call in on Valerie, but so disturbed was he by the events of the afternoon, and apprehensive, too, about returning to a play after this lapse of time, that he decided to walk a different way and have tea by himself.

Just as he was crossing the High Street, he saw the revolving

I

door of the Royal Hotel brush into its depths a man with close-cropped white hair, a stocky frame and a brisk, almost military carriage. He was instantly familiar and he tried to place him. It was not someone he knew but someone whose photograph he had seen often, not an actor but someone celebrated in a similar way. It was not until he had ordered his tea and opened his paperback that it dawned on him who the man was. It was Virgil Graves, the theater's founder, in his seventies but still one of the legends of the profession. The last Sam had read of him was that he had produced a black *Macbeth* in one of the new African states, and that for his pains he had been nearly arrested.

"You've heard who's in front?" exclaimed Paul Poulsen as Sam came into the dressing room. Both were in earlier than was their custom.

"Yes, I saw him in the High Street."

"Who?"

"Virgil Graves."

"You haven't heard the half of it, darling. Do you know who's coming with him?"

"Who?"

"Sir John Bellenger, *and*—"

"Oh, hell. Who else?"

"Tom's bringing a great party along."

"Who?"

"Some of the nobs on the theater council, and Martin's coming, too, I think. It's going to be another first night."

Ordinarily, a celebrity or two in front acted as a stimulant, but not tonight. Even about his own few lines he began to feel some insecurity, and as he made up he ran them in his head. Nervousness was expressing itself as a kind of irritability, and he felt a wave of sudden annoyance if anyone in the dressing room tried to engage him in talk. He needed two shots to get his nose properly affixed, and even then was not entirely happy about it. This, of course, would be the one night in the run when the bloody thing fell off. With this pessimistic reflection his nerves gave way to a certain combative sullenness, the right feeling of professional fatalism, and he set off downstairs reasonably assured.

The buzz of the audience sounded louder tonight, though perhaps this was because it was the first time for some weeks that he had actually heeded it. It hovered and vibrated beyond the curtain, waiting for them. What a mercilessly expectant sound it was.

Ivan was seated by himself in the dark on one of the upright rickety chairs against the wall. It was hard to tell how he felt because his usual demeanor in the wings before a show was one of grumpy withdrawal: his way of conserving himself. Sam greeted him and the old actor looked up and nodded. Neither spoke for a while, then Ivan gave a sigh like a curse and said, "Why tonight?" His breath was stale. Sam sensed the weariness that the wig, the paint, the costume now papered over. "Party clothes" was how Ivan usually referred to it all. There were nights when to have to put them on was an obscure humiliation. However, as soon as Ivan had made his first entrance it was clear that the stage offered him greater safety than the wings. At once he put his insecurity to work sharpening his performance, and Sam left for the canteen reassured.

Here he had expected to find the troubles of the day busily under discussion, but apparently talk of them was being avoided. He was glad. Unreasonably, he felt in some sense responsible for what had happened, and he knew that the rest of the company, too, shared in this vague culpability. It was not anything that Martin had done so much as their own disappointment in Ivan that now in some way shamed them.

"What's that!" said Richard Wayland suddenly, and the talk at their table stopped.

Sam listened and heard nothing. "What?" he asked.

"Listen. The tannoy. It's stopped."

"Must have bust," said Toby Burton.

"No, you can hear coughing. Something's gone wrong."

They rose in a group and went to stare at the small loudspeaker over the door. The play had come to a standstill.

"Somebody's forgotten an entrance," said Richard.

243

They waited, mystified, for something to happen. Presently an urgent but inaudible whisper rasped over the speaker; then they heard Ivan's voice, and the play was suddenly moving again.

"Must have been a dry-up," said Richard. The familiar text rolled on comfortably, but no sooner had they turned away from the loudspeaker than there was another startling silence. The whisper cut in more promptly this time, and once more they heard Ivan pick up a speech.

"Something's gone wrong. Come on!" said Richard. In the passage they ran into Frederick Bell. "What's happened?" they asked.

"Don't know. Sounded as if somebody'd dried up."

In the wings they could hear the play continuing normally. Sam looked around for someone who could explain what had happened, but met expressions as ignorant as his own. In the prompt corner there was some agitated whispering. Terence, the stage manager, looking both harassed and officious, strode past them on tiptoe, ignoring their queries. Someone said, "It was Ivan. Look! He's just going off." And Sam glanced out at the lighted stage just as Ivan was disappearing into the opposite wings. That was where Terence was bound, and he decided to follow his steps round behind the set. But when he arrived, neither Ivan nor Terence was to be seen. Only Rachel Frost was there sitting sheltered in the dark from the remorseless progress of the play. He asked her what had happened.

"Poor old Ivan dried up, and that bloody girl on the book was asleep. She gave the prompt about a minute late." They were interrupted by the sound of a muffled argument coming from the corridor beyond the stage. "Listen. That's Ivan now. He's in a towering rage. It threw him badly, poor old thing. He was drying up all over the place."

Sam approached the swing door. The noise was such now that he wondered whether the audience might not hear it. He allowed himself one glance through the glass panel and in that moment saw Ivan, his painted face abandoned to anger, and fists clenched and raised above his head, beside a desperately apologetic Terence, trying to calm him. Then he walked hurriedly away; the argument was no concern of his.

But if anyone in the company preferred to mind his own business, it was very difficult to do so. In the interval the row continued its public course. Ivan had sent for the prompter, and was now bellowing at her and Terence in the passageway outside his dressing room. Sam joined a group of actors listening down the top-floor stairs. The cement corridors reverberated with Ivan's raging, which would die down only to flare up suddenly again. Later Sam caught sight of the girl weeping her heart out in the prompt corner. "There's no point in yelling at the kid," he heard Rachel say. "Just fire her."

When the curtain rose after the interval, dressing rooms and canteen were deserted of actors, who instead now swarmed in the wings. Ivan came onto the stage to confront two audiences, and he appeared to run this gauntlet with composure. But anger had seriously depleted his energies, and the suggestion of withheld power, which normally made his playing so arresting, had gone. There was some coughing in the house and he struggled with his fatigue to quell it. The actors in the wings watched him with no cruel intent; on the contrary they were there to encourage him, but cruelty was present nonetheless in their simple curiosity. They were expecting a show. Presently they got one.

Ivan was ascending the flight of steps that swept up on the right of the set. He used this climb to bring a particular speech to its climax, marking the lines with each successive upward step, and ordinarily it was a thrilling technical feat to watch. Tonight it was clear that the vocal power, which usually was his so effortlessly, eluded him. The veins in his neck stood out with strain, but his mark was wide. Almost at the top of the steps he appeared to trip and stumble, and suddenly, in mid-sentence, he had stopped speaking. For a few seconds a disconcerted house sat in a completely silent theater.

The prompter's whisper was thrown across the stage toward him as clumsy and apparent as a life buoy, but still he did not speak. She repeated the line in a panicky tremolo, then said it a third time, prefacing it with an absurd, frightened appeal, "Mr. Spears! Mr. Spears!" The audience had heard her, and a surreptitious whispering began in the theater.

Ivan stood swaying very slightly but otherwise frozen. Then he raised one foot and felt for the next step up, carefully, like someone proceeding in the dark. Having found it, he lifted himself to the top of the rostrum and at the same time began to speak. The right foot followed the left, but an incredulous public saw him step not onto the further support of the high rostrum but straight out over the edge of it. Within the frame of the proscenium arch something alien and dreadful was about to intrude. They could do nothing but watch as, still saying his lines, Ivan stepped out into the air. When Sam remembered it afterwards, it seemed, as do all such catastrophes, to have happened in slow motion. There had been the moment when he had realized the absolute inevitability of Ivan's fall. Then the few protracted seconds in which he slowly toppled, the moment in midair when he turned his shoulder against the drop, and the final leaden plummet eight feet onto the stage.

At the thud of the collision, much louder and sharper than anyone would have imagined, first body, then head, a gasp of horror and bewilderment went up from the audience. Then there was silence. The other actors onstage stood where they were, staring dumbly at Ivan, who lay on his back as still and ill-arranged as a dead bird. For what seemed ages nothing disturbed this awful tableau, until from the crumpled figure itself they presently heard, like a parody of sleep, a slow, loud snoring. From the auditorium someone shouted, "Do something, somebody!" One of the actors took a step toward Ivan, and at the same time the curtain began a hesitant descent.

The moment auditorium and stage were sealed off from each other, consternation broke out in both places. Sam joined the press of shocked excited people swarming onto the stage. "Don't touch him, anyone," he heard Terence shout, "until we get a doctor." He pushed forward and caught a momentary glance of Ivan, lying with his mouth open and bottom lip sucked in. A little blood was seeping beneath the gauze of his wig.

With the sudden arrival of authority everyone was still. Two doctors knelt by Ivan, and over by the prompt corner Tom, Jock MacLachlan and Terence were in urgent conference. Soon Terence was dispatched to make an announcement to the audience. They saw the heavy cloth of the curtain yield sluggishly as he burrowed his way between the deep overlap, and then as from a distance heard his unpracticed voice raised to address the house: "Ladies and gentlemen, I know that you'll all be very pleased to know that Mr. Spears has not been seriously injured. He's in the hands of the doctors now, and receiving medical attention. There will be an interval of twenty minutes, then the play will resume in twenty minutes' time. The part of Bosola will be played by Francis Roland. Thank you."

Onstage Jock MacLachlan was now speaking: "I think you all heard that. We'll go up again in twenty minutes. In the meantime it'd really be a great help if you all went back to your dressing rooms and waited there quietly for an announcement. I promise you we'll keep you all informed over the tannoy. I know you all want to help, but I don't honestly think there's anything anyone can do. Mr. Spears is going to be all right. So please, everyone, back to your dressing rooms and wait for an announcement."

A makeshift stretcher (in fact a bier used in the play) had arrived, and Ivan was carried away into the wings. The actors began to scatter.

On the canvas floorcloth there was one small stain of blood the size of a shilling. Sam stared at it, feeling he had never properly observed blood before. All around him the floorcloth was stained with the spatterings of the red liquid supplied by the property department and liberally put to use at each performance. He felt utterly dismayed. What had they been playing at? Himself, the play, the piled scenery—all were ridiculed by this single smudge of real blood.

He fled from the stage and approached the corridor at the end of which was Ivan's dressing room. People were gathered outside the open door. Freddie and Rachel were there, also Martin, Tom and some of the theater council. Their expressions were serious but full of suppressed animation, as if they were waiting to partake in something: some grim, intent ritual not yet wholly explained. Jack Bellenger and Virgil Graves brushed past Sam and joined the group at the door. Ivan was evidently conscious, because from time to time his voice rose above the general murmur, slurred but loud. One of the doctors came out into the corridor and talked to the group in a solemn, assured undertone. Sam moved forward to hear but was stopped by Jock MacLachlan, who spoke to him with an air of aggrieved patience: "Go back to your dressing room, Sam, there's a good chap. I've already asked you once."

16

FRANCIS ROLAND steadied his trembling right hand with his left as he carefully underlined his right eye. He had run up from the stage, wiped off his Pescara makeup with a few vigorous rubs of his soiled towel, and was now almost at the end of his Bosola makeup. In six minutes he would be on. The others in the dressing room stood behind his chair, solicitously watching his progress in the mirror.

"Mouth's gone dry," said Francis.

"Don't worry, mate. You're going to be all right," said Toby. Francis probably would be. Weeks ago when he had first heard that Ivan would be directing as well as acting, he had readied himself for some such emergency and at the understudy rehearsal only three days before he had been pretty well word-perfect. In his work he always went as far as thoroughness would take him, which was frequently quite a long way.

There was a knock on the door, and Paul opened it to admit Ivan's dresser, his arms laden with the costume, the boots, the sword and the wig in a box which Francis would now wear. The costume was laid over the back of the armchair, damp patches of sweat still showing in the armpits.

"I brought along the wig," said the dresser. "It might fit you. You can try it on." He removed it from its box. "I got it as clean as I could. Look, the gauze is quite clean. Just a little stain inside."

"How's Ivan?" asked Sam as he was leaving. For answer the dresser shook his head.

Paul delayed him. "Has he come to yet?"

"Oh, yes. He's come to," he answered, and left.

The costume fitted and so did the wig. They congratulated Francis on his appearance, though all felt a sense of usurpation to see him thus attired. In another dressing room Don Petersen would also be climbing into strange warm clothes, preparing to take over the role of Pescara. Sam reflected privately on what this change of cast would do to his scene. Over the tannoy beginners were called, and this was followed by an announcement that there would be a full company meeting onstage after the performance.

When the curtain rose there were a number of empty seats, but those who remained proved an attentive and encouraging audience, and the play moved swiftly through its last hour. Francis had done admirably, and at the end received a long ovation when he stepped forward to take a call by himself. In the lesser understudy of Pescara, Don Petersen had not done so well, in fact Sam's one scene had been botched, but in the circumstances nobody could be expected to be very concerned about that. He tried to forget that Jack Bellenger had been in front; he was one actor he would very much like to have impressed. As soon as the curtain had come down for the last time, the actors milled around Francis offering him congratulations. He pulled himself free of the black wig, and mopped a white, wet hairline with his sleeve: a diver come up from the deep.

Tom came onto the stage from the wings and Terence clapped for attention. Tom spoke: "First of all I want to thank you all, every one of you, thank you with absolute sincerity, for the way you carried the play tonight. It was a magnificent effort. Truly. I've always thought I had the makings of a great permanent company here this season. Now I'm convinced. And Francis. A magnificent effort. Truly. You heard the applause. Magnificent.

"Now, the most important thing, I know you all want to hear news of Ivan. Well, I can tell you he's going to be all right. He was knocked unconscious by the fall, but he's now recovered consciousness and is going to be all right. The doctors aren't quite sure yet what happened, but they seem to think he might have had a slight stroke and that's why he fell. However, he's in hospital now, and it's obvious he won't be able to continue directing *The Way of the World*. So I'll be taking over for the last week or two. We've decided *not* to make a statement to the press about Ivan's accident, and I'd like to ask you all not to talk about it too much outside the theater. I think we've got the makings of a marvelous show from what little I've seen of it. And of course Ivan's name will stay on the program as director." Tom paused, and the company, led by Francis, applauded.

"Now then, I need hardly tell you that we've got a great deal of hard work ahead of us. But I know I can depend upon you all. In the next few weeks you may hear rumors about our plans for next season. There are things happening which at the moment I can't yet talk to you about. But whatever you hear, I want you to feel, all of you, that you all have a share in those plans. That's all for the moment. Full company call for tomorrow morning at ten. Once again, thank you."

Francis' succession to the part of Bosola called for some sort of recognition, a celebration of a necessarily somber order. The dressing room decided to stand him a couple of bottles of wine which they would all drink back at Paul's flat. Dismay at what had happened was confused and to an extent changed by contrary emotions of tribal solidarity, and all of them felt the need to talk. They bought the wine at the front-of-house bar, then set off to the flat ahead of Francis, who was having a drink first with Tom and his party. He arrived an hour later, flushed and a little drunk, and he needed no prompting to tell them the news.

"Well! What busy little boys and girls *we're* going to be for the next ten days," he announced.

They urged him to explain.

"Working all day and all bloody night, by the look of things. Where's my drink?" They settled him in the most comfortable chair. "We'll be working all day as usual, then after the show up till one o'clock in the morning. And not only that: *during* the show anyone who's off for the odd half hour will be upstairs rehearsing."

"Bit early for panic stations, isn't it, darling?" inquired Paul mildly.

"The Powers That Be don't seem to think so. They were drawing up great timetables and rosters when I left."

"Who?"

"Oh, Tom and Terence and Martin."

"Martin?" said Sam.

"Yes, he's helping Tom with organizing it all."

"What about Ivan? How is he?" asked Toby.

Francis' expression was unmistakably that of the man with inside information. They stared at him. "Not too good" was all he volunteered.

"A stroke, is it? A stroke's pretty serious," said Toby.

"He's not paralyzed, is he?" said Paul.

"No, nothing like that."

"What, then?"

"Well . . . I shouldn't really tell you this . . ."

"Go on."

"I'm not supposed to say anything about it. Ivan did have a stroke—of a kind. It didn't affect his brain, though. I don't understand it. Something about the optic nerve—a chiasmal lesion or something. He was onstage and suddenly he couldn't see. Then when he fell he got concussed."

"How is he now?"

"Well, the concussion wasn't as bad as it looked—"

"Yes?"

"But he's still blind."

They looked at him in silence. "The poor old bugger," said Toby.

Next morning at ten the company waited for Tom Chester to begin the day's work. Sam saw Amanda come in and crossed to speak to her. The night before he had sought her out, but she had already left her dressing room when he knocked on the door; gone, as he was to gather from Francis, to join the people in Tom's office. This morning she had on her determined expression, one which at other times had amused him. Today it was surely superfluous and it irritated him. "This is pretty awful, isn't it?" he said, and she answered, "Gosh, yes. Awful. But if we're all

252

prepared to work, I know it's going to be all right." Which hadn't been quite what he meant. He opened his mouth to reply but she cautioned him with a "Shh"; Tom was about to speak.

"Well, everybody, I'm afraid we've all got a great deal of work ahead of us. We'll begin by doing a straight run-through of the play, without interruptions, just to see what we've already got. Then we'll begin again working through it scene by scene. At lunchtime Terence will put up on the board a full breakdown of the rehearsal time left to us. I'd like you all to study it very carefully. And I'm afraid I'd better warn you"—he paused and smiled around the room—"any private plans you may have made, at night after the show for instance, well, it might be a good idea if you postponed them until we've got through the next ten days." Sam tried to catch Amanda's eye—they had planned to have supper together the following evening—but she was giving her whole attention to Tom.

They started the run-through. Ivan's prelude of mime went well, and the audience of actors looked to Tom to see if he liked it. He appeared to and the rehearsal took heart. In the first scene Martin was ostentatiously careful to honor Ivan's pause, and with this gesture buried the controversy, which, though in fact only a day old, now seemed remote and wearisome. The company positively desired his exoneration; there was too much else to worry about.

After the coffee break the performance began to tire and it ended in a decidedly lame fashion, but it was nonetheless a relief to discover just how much work Ivan had managed to pack into the play in the few weeks he'd been on it. It was still very much a production in the rough, but the signposts to Ivan's intentions for were clear for anyone who cared to follow them.

For the rest of the week Sam was on call at the theater from ten in the morning until midnight, but for at least three quarters of that time he was idle. He had soon read all the back copies of *Time* magazine in the canteen and had developed a sullen distaste for the way Hilda behind the bar stewed the coffee, a distaste which, however, in no way diminished his consumption of it. There was nothing else to do but drink cups of the stuff, develop a coated tongue and wait to be called.

Amanda was always rushing off to some corner of the building for a private rehearsal of her own, and he saw practically nothing of her. She seemed to have worked herself up into a state of mixed anxiety and zeal, where even to spend ten minutes over a cup of Hilda's coffee was a fall from grace. However, before the show one evening he managed to persuade her to go out somewhere and have tea with him. She looked tired and preoccupied, and rather perversely he said, "I think it's rather silly keeping everyone hanging about the theater all day and all night. It's not as if we hadn't rehearsed it for over two weeks already."

"I don't agree" was her toneless reply. She looked very depressed, and he knew it was about her part.

He tried to make amends. "I haven't been much help, have I? I said I'd do some work with you on Marwood and I haven't done a thing."

She smiled but he sensed that in some way he had disturbed her. "How could you, silly? There's been no time."

"If there's anything I can do—"

"No, it'll be all right. We're rehearsing all we can now. Tom's being marvelous."

"Good. But look. When are we going to see each other?" What had prevailed upon him to inflect the question in that loaded manner? He saw it jar upon Amanda, disturb the single track of her concerns.

"I don't really know," she said wearily. "The weekend, I suppose. No, that's no good. This Sunday I've promised to go over to York and see those relatives again. And next Sunday is the Sunday before the show; we're sure to be working then—"

Sam considered. "Well, let's get the show on first, shall we?" he said. "That's the main thing."

She looked absurdly relieved. "Please let's!"

"Maybe after the first night. We can have a celebration on our own. How about that?"

"That'll be lovely. After the first night. Oh, I'll look forward to that." She touched his cheek. "Sam, you're a dear." She had lost her preoccupied look and he felt very pleased. She leaned across and kissed him lightly, and the waitress bestowed a simplifying smile upon them.

On the way back to the theater Tom and Martin drove past them in Martin's open sports car. They exchanged waves.

"I wonder if those two are having it off together," ruminated Sam.

He had never seen Amanda quite as angry. Perhaps he had shocked her. "That's a dreadful thing to say!" she said.

"Why? I don't give a damn what they do."

"That's not the point," she said.

"What is the point?"

They parted unsatisfactorily and went to their respective dressing rooms on opposite sides of the theater.

Sam was no longer watching rehearsals. He had done so for the first few days of the crisis because he felt his duties as understudy required it, but now that he had learned Mirabell's lines he preferred to remain in the canteen keeping company with his own boredom and restlessness.

He had observed a pattern emerging in the way Tom rehearsed each scene, and it disturbed him. First the scene would be run a couple of times just as it was. Then for often as long as an hour everyone would sit down and discuss it. Its deficiencies decided upon, Tom would now endeavor to remedy them by altering the moves. At once they would run into difficulties. Whether or not one agreed with Ivan's scrupulous and rather old-fashioned methods of production, some ingenious thought had gone into his placing of the actors, and often a change in a single move was enough to upset an entire scene. Relationships lost meaning, and bits of business became unworkable. However, rather than return to the original move, Tom would now scrap the business. The production, in fact, was slowly being stripped of all its detail. There was nothing deliberate about this; Tom appeared to be doing his best. All day long and most of the night he frowned and concentrated upon the actors, altering things.

Something began to dawn on Sam, something which had been in front of his nose all season but which he had been reluctant or unwilling to admit. And this was that for all Tom's brilliance as a convenor of spectacular talent, as a policy maker, as a man of some taste, in that area which the layman might reasonably assume to be central to his job, namely, the ability to make something happen at rehearsal, he was, quite simply, without talent. He had nothing to give, a fact which the monotonous absence of delight in his work amply confirmed. Was it naïve of Sam that this discovery about Tom should so astonish him? He was shocked by it. He wanted to tell someone, explain that he had anatomized Caesar and found sawdust. But there was no one to tell. Certainly not Amanda. In any case loyalty forbade it. The production might have been a sinking ship, but they were all on board.

Sam's misgivings were confirmed when on the fifth day they had another run-through. Practically the only effective thing left was Ivan's prelude, and this was not even part of the play proper. Tom was additionally handicapped because in spite of the excellence of his cast there was no great self-sufficient talent present—a Jack Bellenger or someone like Ivan himself—to give the production a center, to go his own splendid way and take them all with him. Frederick Bell was a fine actor, but he was too impressionable and insecure to be the leader of a company.

In any case this was a role which Martin had now assumed, and it had to be admitted that he was doing it rather well. He worked hard and obediently, encouraged faith in Tom and the production, and went out of his way to be friendly to everyone in the company, including, to his surprise, Sam. He had even organized a Ping-Pong tournament for those actors kept waiting about with not enough to do, and once during one of the late night rehearsals he had treated the company to sandwiches and wine.

After this second run-through the company retired to the canteen understandably depressed. Only Martin appeared undaunted, and Sam heard him talking to the group at his table: "No wonder Ivan couldn't help, poor old love. All those weeks he was a sick man. If only we'd known that; if only Tom could have got to the production sooner. Now it's this question of time; he's got no time."

"Thank God we've got him now, anyway," said Don Petersen. He and Sam had had an unhappy exchange the night before about the way he was playing Pescara. Sam regretted it, but now that Don was botching up his scene it had become impossible to conceal his impatience with him. The result was that Don was now conspicuously enlisted in the enemy camp. Sam picked up an old *Time* magazine with a grinning Nixon on the front, and struggled to interest himself in the Business section, the only page he hadn't read. But Martin intended to be heard.

"I *knew* something was wrong. I *felt* it, you know? But of course I had no idea what. It's tragic. In his day Ivan was a bloody marvelous actor, you know that?"

Martin's listeners murmured their agreement. Ivan was rarely talked about now; mention of him was almost superstitiously avoided. Even Sam lacked the heart to speak of him. He had written him a letter: to his London address, as no one seemed to know the name of his hospital and he didn't feel inclined to ask Tom. And the curious thing was that though every rehearsal amply demonstrated how badly they needed him, in a sense they didn't need him at all. One day followed another and they were getting on without him. Not even excellence was indispensable; perhaps excellence least of all. It was all a question of taking turns.

Spirits rose a degree at the first dress rehearsal. The sets were elaborate and lovely, and only the designer himself seemed displeased with them; he had always wanted a much simpler presentation of the play, and had argued in vain about this with Ivan, who, on this point at least, was getting his way. There it was, however, a huge mechanical toy, and very pretty it looked. The revolving stage came into play at once for the prelude, and it had hardly concluded its first circuit before centrifugal force sent two Corinthian pillars toppling into the wings. They tried altering the position of the pillars only to find when the set moved again that the pillars were catching on the overhead drapes. To the accompaniment of cries of protest from the auditorium and the sound of an irreparable splintering and ripping onstage, the mechanism ground to a belated halt. But no real damage appeared to have been done, and after a further hour and a half they had devised a way of keeping all the set firmly in place during its spin. At last they were ready to run the prelude. The curtain rose and the set began its elegant revolving course, the actors stepping on and off as was required of them. Not until the very end of the prelude did they run into difficulties. The coffee shop had swung into view, and the first words of the play should properly have been spoken; but they were an actor short. Only Frederick Bell was in position, sitting alone at the gaming table holding his hand of cards. A moment later Martin came on from the wings. He stood and squinted into the general dark of the auditorium. "Sorry, Tom," he said.

"What's the trouble, Marty?" inquired Tom evenly.

"My cloak. I've got to get rid of my cloak."

"Yes?"

"Well, I've got this promenade bit to do. That takes me round on the revolve to the back of the stage; then I've got to get off into the wings, lose the cloak, and be back and sitting in the chair before the revolve stops. There's no time."

There was a long pause. Martin stood, Freddie sat and Tom thought. Then Tom spoke. "Try it all again then, and let's see just how many seconds we can knock off. I'm sure it can be done."

They tried it again, and again Martin arrived onstage too late. They tried it a third time, and the same thing happened.

"It's absolutely essential to lose your cloak, is it, Marty?"

"I'm afraid it is, love. Definitely. I can't play the whole scene in a *cloak,* can I? It's indoors."

"What about the first bit, then? Could you play that without the cloak?"

"That's outdoors." They had reached an impasse.

"Do it just once more. And, Marty, have your dresser standing by in the wings to take the cloak from you. Be as quick as you can, Marty." As before, the prelude went like clockwork until the last ten seconds. The company stood about on stage, disconsolately waiting for a solution and trying to remain uncontaminated by the growing tension. They had been in attendance for three hours and the play hadn't even begun.

"Well, I'm afraid there's only one thing," said Tom at last. "We'll have to cut the prelude completely. I've never been mad about it. It's not really anything to do with the play."

"Fair enough," said Martin. "And save the cloak for the second act."

"But that's *ridiculous!*" Sam had spoken before he had thought. Now everyone was looking at him.

"What's ridiculous?" said Tom.

"Cutting the prelude. He can easily bring the cloak on with him."

"And wear it all through the scene?" said Martin.

"You don't have to *wear* the bloody thing, for Christ's sake! You can hang it up." Sam was wading into danger, knew it and didn't care.

"Show me the hook on this set."

"All right, then. Hang it over the back of the chair."

"No, love. That's quite out of character. I can't possibly play the scene sitting there cluttered up with a cloak."

Tom interposed. "No, I'm sorry. The prelude's cut and that's that."

Sam felt himself slide fast into the black satisfactions of rage. "It's feeble! You're both feeble!" he shouted with the ineloquence of a lost temper. The set was shuddering where one hand had shot out violently to connect with it.

But they had disregarded him. "Carry on then, Tom?"

"Yes, we've got no time to waste."

"I'll save the cloak up for the St. James's Park scene."

"Excellent idea, Marty. Much more effective."

The actors around Sam looked at him with embarrassment and some pity. He didn't care about them, but at the same time he knew he had to go somewhere and be by himself. In the wings he noticed the iron banister of the steps that wound beneath the stage, and he remembered the small junk room with the playbills in broken frames. He sat there in the dark on the edge of the gutted sofa, trembling with anger and the beginnings of remorse. Beneath his makeup he could feel the blood draining from his face and into muscles that readied themselves for a conflict which would not come. He knew very well that he had been in the wrong. Losing his temper had been unprofessional, not to say unpolitic. Yet there had been pleasure in the explosion, however costly. He wondered if something of this sort had happened to Ronald Dunne, and if he, too, hadn't cared but had sat here trembling, grinning with incredulity at the force of his own unexpected passions.

Before the first night, Sam sought an opportunity to apologize to Tom, not for the opinion, as he explained, but for the temper. Tom looked a martyr to fatigue but there was no malice in his expression. "That's all right. These things happen," he said with an easy smile, and Sam realized too late that his apology had been superfluous. He was not someone whose opinions (or indeed tempers) concerned him.

The company advanced toward the first night like soldiers unwilling to forgo the comfort of ignorance. The play was going to fail, but not one of the actors, in his heart, was able to abandon hope entirely in the powers of miraculous deliverance inherent in a first night—at least as far as his own particular bit went. However, an outsider like Jock MacLachlan knew as soon as he had seen the final dress rehearsal, and Sam knew, too, when he saw Jock's face in the corridor afterwards. Even so as he made up for the ordeal, he felt the return of obstinate hope. Perhaps they would be all right after all. There were some bad omens, however, which he could not disregard. For one, he wasn't nervous; he felt a vague apprehension but otherwise was as removed from the play as if someone else was about to climb into his costume and do his acting for him.

In the first scene Freddie Bell's nerve went and they had to dispatch a second prompter to the far side of the stage to keep him on the lines. Martin, his face sheeted in sweat and his eyes gleaming with furious resolve, kept his head, and they managed to get to the end of the scene without the play's actually stopping. The evening picked up somewhat with the appearance of the principal women, and for the first time the performance was interrupted by the bark of an audience's laughter. After that, and imperceptibly at first, the play began its long decline. Though Freddie had made a splendid recovery and the company as a whole were much more relaxed, nothing in their fluent, grinding endeavor could prevent the gradual withdrawal of the audience's sympathy and attention. The evening simply leaked away. About halfway through the play the coughing started and soon became a ceaseless accompaniment. During the last act someone in the audience yawned audibly and a titter of fellow feeling went round the house.

They took their curtain calls to polite, apathetic applause, watching with surprising detachment the departure of those people who could not wait for the lights but were already stooping speedily down the dark aisles toward the exits. Usually this was the prerogative of critics, hurrying away to make the early editions. Tonight they were all critics.

The first-night party was to be held in the rehearsal room, but Amanda said she didn't want to go to it; not even look in for five minutes.

"I don't know what I've got to eat," she said as they set off across the park. The prospect of their supper together sounded hardly more attractive to her than the party. He had been looking forward to it, and he felt himself to be somewhat implicated by the wrapped-up bottle of wine now cradled in his arm. It was a still clear night, but cold for early September.

"God, I was awful tonight," she said with brittle distaste.

"So was everyone. You weren't alone."

They were silent for most of the way there.

"An omelet all right for you?" she called from the kitchen, and he said, "Fine," sensing trouble.

Over the meal he tried to deflect her attention away from the play, the only thing she seemed prepared to talk about. He mistrusted the aggressive way she continually broached the subject. It was over now and best forgotten, something well beyond the remedy of talk.

"I wonder if Tom is going to keep on rehearsing us till we get it right," she said, returning to the topic.

"Christ, I hope not."

"Why? You don't think we don't need it, do you?"

"What else can Tom do?"

"What do you mean?"

"What I said."

"No, what do you mean?"

"It doesn't matter."

"No, tell me. What do you mean?"

"Well, he hasn't really been much help to the show so far, has he?"

"Of course he has!"

"Let's talk about something else, shall we?"

"No, I want to talk about this. What do you mean?"

"Well, I just don't think Tom's been much help, that's all."

"But he's worked terribly hard!"

"I didn't say he hadn't."

"He hasn't been able to sleep, he's been so worried."

"I'm sure he has."

"I hate to think where we all would have been without him."

He sighed. He was getting angry. "Oh, cut it out."

"He's done wonders in the last ten days."

"You've been talking to Martin."

"I haven't, Sam! I haven't! That's a beastly thing to say!"

" 'Poor Tom's had no time.' "

"And neither he has."

"Listen, you know as well as I do the production was in a bloody sight better shape that first run-through than it was tonight."

"If you like that sort of production."

"That sort of production?"

"Tell me, do you think, honestly, really honestly, that Ivan's production was a good one, was going to be a good one?"

He made considerable effort to remain reasonable and answer the question truthfully. "No. No. I think there were a lot of things wrong with it. I think it was too elaborate. Too carefully prepared. Not enough elbow room, somehow, which was the last thing you'd expect from Ivan."

"It was old-fashioned."

"Yes. Yes, it was. I don't deny that."

"Well, then?"

"But at least it was *something*. Somebody had thought, and selected, and decided. And there were some wonderful things in it, some wonderful moments. Weren't there? Weren't there?"

She nodded.

"Well, they were entitled to respect. Ivan's name is still on the program, after all."

Amanda didn't reply, and he thought with relief that the subject might now be closed. Why were they arguing, anyway? It didn't make sense. However, he had underrated her persistence, for presently she said, "But Tom didn't *like* Ivan's work. He told me. He said he thought it was, well, stale. What else could he do?"

"I see. What else did he tell you?"

"He said there'd only been time to cut away the dead wood. There'd been no time for anything else."

"When did he tell you this?"

"Before we went up tonight."

This rather shocked him. "You must have found that encouraging. Well, all I can say is he seemed quite happy with the 'dead wood' that first run-through."

"He didn't want to demoralize us."

"Oh, for Christ's sake! Do you know how many laughs—how many ordinary robust laughs—the production's lost since that first run-through? Hundreds! It's meant to be a comedy! It's meant to keep people awake!"

"You want to watch that temper of yours, Sam."

"I'm sorry. . . . But you keep talking about it! *I* don't want to talk about it."

"Well, perhaps Tom would have done a little better if he'd had the whole company solidly behind him."

He looked at her and felt the small surprise of recognizing the obvious. "You mean me?"

"If you like," she said.

"You didn't like my outburst at the dress rehearsal."

"No, I didn't. I didn't like it at all."

"And that's what we've really been talking about?"

"Yes. Yes, I suppose it is! I think it was wrong of you, Sam. Absolutely wrong! There we were at the dress rehearsal. Everyone doing their best. And suddenly this voice! It was nothing to do with you! You weren't the director. You weren't even involved in it as an actor. And to lose your temper like that and shout! It was dreadful."

She was right, of course. But he tried to defend himself. "But didn't *you* like the prelude?"

"Yes, I liked it. It was good. Though I don't think a good play really needs that sort of embellishment."

She was right about this, too. He drank some more wine, but it was working the wrong way now. "All right, I was stupid," he said. "Anyway, I expect I'll have to pay for it one way or another."

"Of course you won't!" she said, changing her tone now that she had had her say. "Tom doesn't bear grudges." (And even about this she was probably right.) "He just thinks you were silly, that's all." This made him feel more desolate and foolish than anything she had already said. A trapdoor into depression had been sprung beneath him. It had been a bad idea for them both, this supper.

He helped her with the washing up and then sat alone at one end of the Chesterfield finishing his coffee. He was now thoroughly miserable. "Well, I suppose I may as well go home," he said, putting the cup down.

"Why?" she said. Her tone was crisp, almost academic.

"Well . . . we're not much use to each other tonight, are we?"

She said nothing, and after a while he got up to go. She rose, too, and in silence they stood looking at each other. Then she walked over to him and with gentle deliberation kissed him. "You don't have to go," she said, her matter-of-fact manner curiously at odds with the look of appraisal she was giving him. A lugubrious swell of desire caught him up. Her body offered marvelously firm comfort, and his mouth slackened at her touch. For a long time they embraced standing up, as if they were in the street at night and had nowhere to go.

"Take off your things," she said eventually. He undressed and waited for her on the Chesterfield. Naked, she turned off all the lamps except one, and came gazing toward him, delicate in her intention to use him. Her beauty almost alarmed him, some wonderful lost thing precariously regained. Afterwards it grew cold for them on the Chesterfield, and they went into the bedroom where they waited beneath the bedclothes to make love again. She had put on clean sheets and he found this preparation of hers not ordinary but strange and inciting. They slept and coupled and strove through a dozen slow chimings of some clock across the town. He had made love to her to the limits of depletion, welcoming loss.

Around four o'clock the telephone rang, and Amanda slipped quickly out of bed. "It's Mum," she explained. "She's going to read me the notices."

As far away as the bedroom Sam could catch the guttural response on the other end of the line, the assertive, confident, slightly weary tones of a successful actress. The press was evidently frightful, because Amanda was interrupting her mother with expressions like "Oh, no!" and "How awful!" and "Oh, dear!" He could just see her at the telephone, and she gave no indication to this parent that she stood speaking into the receiver naked and still warm from a lover's bed. He found himself, absurdly, regarding this concealment with admiration, as though it were something else to be classified among her gifts. Mother and daughter were laughing now—some long-standing family defense against professional dismay—and he became suddenly jealous of this intimacy from which he must necessarily be excluded. He tiptoed into the sitting room and embraced her slyly from behind. She made frantic smiling faces at him over her shoulder while her mother talked on. Then he went back into the bedroom and waited for them to finish. He looked around him, loving the small timbered room that had enclosed their pleasure. He began to think over the nights he had spent there. How often had it been? How often would it be? The bed smelled of her, of them.

"No, I won't worry. Promise. 'Night . . . Bye." He heard her conclude and hang up. She came into the bedroom, slipped on the toweling dressing gown, and sat on the edge of the bed.

"Bad, eh?" he said.

"Awful. Really awful!" She laughed. "They hate *me*. They absolutely *hate* me."

"What about everyone else?"

"They hate them, too."

"What do they say?"

"Oh, everything. That we're boring, dull, dreary, monotonous. One of them says the costumes are nice . . ."

"The production?"

She looked a little shamefaced. "There's an absolutely beastly headline in one of the papers. It says STICK TO ACTING, IVAN. They both thought about this and then began to laugh. He kissed her. "To hell with them." But there was always something shocking about a bad press, no matter how poor you knew the show to be. It was the critics' relish of the abuse that was so disconcerting. It didn't relate.

Amanda made them Ovaltine, then he dressed. "If it was the weekend, I'd suggest you stay," she said, "but the place is crawling with students in the morning." In any case it was better to go. Her single bed didn't encourage sleep, which she, in particular, needed for the matinee that afternoon.

She closed the trapdoor over him, and he went out into the street. She had said "Thank you" to him again. The stars had melted, and dawn was already ringing in the vacuum jar of the sky: silent tumult. He walked fast over the park in a state of vibrant fatigue. He had been steeped in her. Now he was by himself. Just past the theater he hesitated. They had forgotten to arrange when they would next meet. He looked back across the park, wondering if he should retrace his steps and remedy this insecurity. But she would already be asleep. He had never concerned himself about this before; why now? They would be seeing each other at the theater in a few hours' time. He walked on.

17

THE MATINEE proved a decidedly wilted offering. The notices had damped what little spirit and vitality the company still possessed, so that whereas on the first night they had extended to the public merely a bad show, today it was an appalling one. Amanda was in the canteen in the first interval, fretfully smoking a cigarette, a thing she rarely did, and absorbed all over again in worries about her work. She smiled unhappily at Sam, and he sensed that she was asking him to leave her in peace, at least until she'd got through the performance. Between the shows he went to visit her in her dressing room, but there was a notice pinned to her door written in eyebrow pencil: PLEASE DON'T DISTURB. SLEEPING. He obeyed it, and returned to his own dressing room, where he walked in upon some excitement.

"Just listen to this, Sam," called Toby.

"What?"

"Francis knows something—"

"About next season," added Paul.

Francis' information had been gleaned at a lunch party given by Jock MacLachlan. He was in considerable demand socially these days, a somewhat astonished response, after three seasons of neglect, to the fact that he had some ability. He was thriving on this new attention that his successful understudy had brought him; his complexion was quite definitely pinker, his carriage more upright. He was on the inside now.

"How would you like to work in America, Sam?" he asked.

"Why? What's this?"

"You've heard of the Braddington in the States, haven't you?"

"Yes."

"Well, there's talk—only talk, mind you—about building a new theater there, a kind of sister theater to this one. Tom's been approached by a couple of millionaires, oil men or something, who say they're prepared to put up the money. Tom apparently is excited about it because he says it would be a marvelous way of cross-pollinating the talent in both countries. The English company could play there sometimes, the American company here; or maybe they could be mixed up together."

"Sounds marvelous. When's it to be?" said Sam.

"If the plans go through, *if* the plans go through, the new theater could be functioning next summer."

"I wouldn't mind a year's work in the States, would you, Sam?" said Toby.

"No."

"Be all right, wouldn't it? Well, boys, looks like we joined the company at the right time."

Sam just missed Amanda after the show. He came out of the stage door in time to catch sight of her bicycling away beneath the streetlamps toward the park. He was about to call after her, but thought about it until it was too late and she was out of sight. There's tomorrow, he thought, then realized with a slight shock that tomorrow was a *Macbeth* day. Hadn't she said something the night before about going over to York? (Her visit during rehearsals had been postponed because of a working Sunday.) She would probably be out of town for the whole weekend and he wouldn't see her till Monday.

Back at the flatlet he wondered whether to go up to the Ozone and ring her from Mrs. Shrapnel's hall telephone. He stood in the middle of his room jingling four pennies in his hand, debating the issue. Mrs. Shrapnel, of course, would be listening to every word he said, but it was not only this that made him hesitate; he was remembering that Valerie would soon be going on holiday.

The next few days were quiet ones at the theater, a period of recuperation. There was an interlude of mild drama when the company disputed among themselves Martin's right to be excused the curtain call of *Macbeth*. Some argued that Banquo was far too important a part for the actor to absent himself from the lineup, but Terence, who as stage manager had authorized Martin's release, insisted that an actor not seen in the last half of the play was traditionally in his rights to ask to leave early. The top floor heard Martin splashing under the shower as they set off downstairs for the beginning of the last act. "Lucky bastard," said Toby, expressing the general opinion. Otherwise life at the theater had been markedly uneventful.

Yet the mood of the place was unmistakably changed. In the canteen during the performance the same actors in the same makeups, disguises that had become as familiar as stale anecdotes, sat drinking coffee or playing cards at certain times, their lives regulated by the clock of the play whose cuckoos they were. But there was a difference now. All three plays had joined the repertory; there would be no more first nights to look forward to or dread. Quite suddenly the season had come to the end of its possibilities. Tom was away in London now, laying plans for the following year. Sam remembered that in June at nine o'clock it had been light outside in the park; now the dark windowpanes showed him merely his own reflection. He had looked forward to the time when only the performance in the evening would impinge on the freedom of his days. Such leisure now upon him, it signified mainly the dying of the season.

Two more months of the Braddington engagement remained, but already the company were beginning to live in the time beyond, the time of their next jobs. Most hoped for another season at the Playhouse, and actors would now be watching for the re-appearance of Tom's car in the car park, for the opportunity to seek him out for a "chat."

The new secretary, the tall girl with the pleasant cool manner from a local county family, Clarissa Something-Something, with whom somewhat surprisingly Tom had replaced Olive, would soon be scribbling appointments in Tom's book. Toby Burton planned to have a word with her any day now. Francis, in a more favored position, had had the advances made to him; Clarissa had sent him a note saying that Tom was very keen to see him just as soon as he got back. Both Paul and Sam had already had what amounted to a preliminary interview, and now it was a question of waiting—for a second interview, or even possibly an offer. This was the time when actors must start fostering private hopes and advancing private interests. They would be broken up as a company long before the season ended, and perhaps it was this sense of dissolution before time that produced beneath the routines and amiable exchanges of theater life those undertones of weariness and impatience.

He met Amanda on Monday afternoon by chance in the High Street, and he felt as if he hadn't seen her for weeks. With idleness the days had lengthened, and for the first time since he'd arrived in Braddington he found himself wondering what to do. That Sunday he had felt quite at a loss without one of their expeditions together: to the beach (although it was getting a little chilly for that), or into the New Town to play the pinball machines in an amusement parlor. She was loaded down with groceries and parcels and a new LP in a paper carrier, and he hastened to relieve her of her bulging string bag. "Come and have coffee," he suggested.

"Oh, Sam, I'd love to but I *can't*. My agent's come up to see the play, and he's waiting for me at the theater. He wants to discuss Dad's play. Rehearsals start in six weeks, you know."

"So soon?"

"Yep. I'll be going back and forth to London while you're all doing *Macbeth*."

"You've got time for coffee! Come on."

"All right. But it'll have to be a quick one. Really."

The Tea Shoppe was stuffy and crowded, and they were directed to share a small table with two elderly and inquisitive women. There was nowhere for her parcels, so they had to keep them on their laps. He began to regret having had his way about coffee; he felt constrained with her, and found himself thinking ahead to what he was going to say, as if she were an acquaintance it was desirable to impress.

"I suppose you're busy after the show, then?"

"Yes. My agent's staying at the Royal and I know he'll want to have supper with me. He can't stand eating by himself."

"What about tomorrow night?"

"Oh dear, I've got myself in an awful muddle this week. I'm going to Rachel's on Tuesday night, and Martin's having some sort of a do on Wednesday night. Everything's happening all at once, now that all the plays are on."

Small parties for the upper third of the company had been going on all season. One usually heard about them afterwards from Richard Wayland, who always seemed to be able to get himself invited. Sam had even attended one himself, given by Freddie Bell shortly after *The Duchess* opened, when his stock had been high.

"Can't we meet during the day?" she asked, but he explained that starting tomorrow and for the rest of the week there were understudy rehearsals. Besides he wasn't sure he wanted this; not as an alternative. "What about Thursday night, then?" she suggested. He hesitated. He had arranged to see Valerie on Thursday. On Friday she was off with Trevor on her extended holiday.

"Actually Thursday's not very good for me," he murmured.

"Oh well," she answered brightly, "we'll have to make it next week, then. How about Monday?"

"But what about the weekend?"

"They're *Macbeth* days. I thought I might go away this week-end."

"Oh. York?"

"Mm. Probably."

"Oh. Well then, Monday, I suppose." But Monday was a whole week away.

"Lovely!"

Toby and Francis had had their interviews, and in the dressing room as they made up they told what they knew about the coming season. As usual three productions were to be mounted, a new play with a large cast which Tom would not name but which sounded as if it might conceivably be Paul's, a revival of *Three Sisters*, and, to open the season, a Shakespeare, either *The Mer chant of Venice* or *A Midsummer-Night's Dream.*

Francis had had a definite offer to play the old doctor in the Chekhov. Tom had also promised him a good part in the new play, as well as Theseus if they did the *Dream*. He was obviously pleased about the offer, as far as anyone knew the first concrete one of the season, but he seemed disinclined to discuss it beyond the bare details.

Toby, on less secure ground, gave them a full account of his interview. "It was marvelous! He sat me in the big chair, and Clarissa brought us a cup of tea. He told me he'd had his eye on me all season and how much he liked my work, and how he wanted to develop me, slowly build me up into a leading character actor. He said one day he'd like to see me playing parts like Bob Acres in *The Rivals* and even maybe Caliban."

"Yes, but what about next season?" said Paul.

"Well, he said just at the moment he couldn't say much about that—"

"Ah!" they all chorused with exuberant skepticism.

"No, hold on!" said Toby. "We did talk about parts, but he said it was difficult to make a firm offer until they knew definitely what the plays were. No, listen! That makes sense. First of all there's the new play. Well, that hasn't been announced yet. Then there's the Chekhov, and that's going to be pretty starry throughout—" Francis acknowledged the unintended compliment with a nod of the head, and Paul countered with shrill and rather spiteful laughter. "That leaves only the Shakespeare, and we *did* talk about that."

"What did he say?" asked Sam.

"He asked if I felt I could play Gratiano."

"In *The Merchant?* But that's a marvelous part!"

"I know it is, mate. That's what I said."

"And what did he say?"

"He said, well, yes, it was, and that it might have to go to a name, but that he was quite sincere when he said I would be very seriously considered for it. And that in any case he could absolutely promise me something in *The Merchant*. Maybe something

K

273

like Old Gobbo, but anyway nothing less than that."

"That'd be worth coming back for, wouldn't it?"

"You bet it would."

Tom was in Braddington only two days before he drove away to attend to his mounting responsibilities in London. But to the audiences who turned up each night to fill the theater, and to the actors (at least for the time they were onstage), the current productions remained the first consideration. Sam stood in the dark beside the new Pescara, Don Petersen, and thought how often he had stood precisely thus, waiting to make his entrance, smelling the naked timber of the set, and feeling well up, with his nervousness, the resolution that tonight he would be especially good, that once again an entire career was balanced precariously upon a single performance. So much tension, so much fervor, for ten minutes onstage; there was a wistfulness about it. *The Duchess of Malfi* was turning up in repertory only about once a week now. And when it did, some odd things were seen to be happening to it. Most of them had to do with Francis' growing security in the role he had taken over. Excellent though he was, so much of the ambiguity—the sense of a man divided against himself, that Ivan had discovered in the part—had gone, and instead a grinning Renaissance villain took the stage. The audience responded to this new presence, but it fostered in them an indulgent attitude toward the play, which with each performance was drifting more and more in the direction of improbable melodrama.

The Way of the World, too, was undergoing some changes, and again the bias of the acting was responsible. But here the changes were entirely for the good. Simple familiarity with what they had to do had bred a lively confidence in the cast, and in particular Frederick Bell's performance had improved unrecognizably upon the one he had given on the first night a few weeks before. The actors were letting their audiences—and the concealed impulses within the play itself—tutor them. Moves were fractionally altered as the instincts of the actors suggested them; much of Ivan's business crept back, often improved upon. To everyone's surprise it was turning into an amusing and stylish show.

On Monday as Sam was leaving the theater on his way to lunch, Alfred, the stage-doorman, checked him: "Just arrived for you, sir," he said, leaning out of his cubicle with a postcard. It was from Amanda, dated Sunday, postmarked York.

DEAREST SAM,

I know it's awful of me but I've got to put off our supper on Monday. I didn't know it but these relatives of mine are coming to the show on Monday night, and of course they want to see me afterwards. What about Tuesday or is this no good for you? Anyway, we can talk about it tonight, but thought I'd let you know in advance. Don't be angry.

Love,

A.

He stood holding the postcard and feeling something which at first he thought was disappointment. But it was sharper than that; in fact, rather like fear. He looked around for a means of evading such a ridiculous admission, and met Alfred's alert if watery gaze which had long ago forsworn the luxury of judgment. The old man offered him the simple distraction of an exchange of words, and he found himself welcoming it.

"Still lovely weather, sir."

"Yes. No more swimming, though, I'm afraid."

"Still, it's been a good summer. We can't complain."

"Yes, it has."

"I like September. Best month in the year, in my opinion. Not too hot. Not too cold."

"Yes."

He left the theater and began walking automatically in the direction of his lunch. On the way he passed the cosmetics shop, without Valerie just another plate-glass window. She was probably eight hundred miles away by now, bumping down some monotonous Continental road beside a silent Trevor. At the door of the restaurant he was stopped by the realization that he had no appetite whatsoever. He carried on through the town until he had reached the waterfront, then found a bench and sat on it with his

275

legs crossed and his face squinting in the sun. He was awkwardly aware of his isolation on the bench, as if it would have been a slight embarrassment for him to be discovered by others in the company sitting here by himself.

He took out the postcard and read it a second, then a third and fourth time, examining it for some concealed meaning or accidental admission. But her handwriting was a perfect mask of certainty, leaning and bold; he had always rather admired it. It occurred to him that he hadn't yet looked at the picture on the other side. It was a black-and-white photograph of York Minster. He studied it, then turned the postcard over and read about it in a line of tiny printing overwritten by her hand. Then he turned the postcard sideways and read the name of the printer and publisher. The warmth of the sun was beginning to permeate his clothing. He closed his eyes and lifted his face, suddenly anxious to make the best of its rays. It would be October soon. This afternoon, no matter how chilly the wind, he would get into his trunks and lie in the sun for an hour and try to get a little brown. He wondered if he might not be in love with her.

18

SAM sat in one corner of the Chesterfield and leaned back hard to prevent himself from shaking. It was not from cold or fear that he shook, though he felt a little of both, but from the state of absolute attention that Amanda's words had induced in him. He put each question to her with dreadful care, solicitous for the exact extent of his future unhappiness, and stared at her unblinking while she answered him.

From the start he had known that something was wrong. He had gone into the kitchen to see if he could help, but she had said in a friendly enough fashion but with impatience, "No, I can manage. You go inside and play a record." He had put on the Goldberg Variations, and had sat absorbed in it, wondering how he could have failed to comprehend its precise yet limpid beauty that first afternoon Amanda had played it for him. Soon, wanting to share with her this pleasure that he owed to her, he returned to the kitchen.

"Isn't it marvelous? Just listen."

"Marvelous," she said automatically, and he knew she had not been listening. He felt a little angry with her, as if he had been unjustly rebuked. He watched her turn up the raw side of the lamb chops.

"Anything I can do?"

"Nope." This was not one of her depressed moods. On the contrary there was an air of self-confidence about her, a steely equability that he had never seen before. He approached and bent to kiss her, but she turned her head fractionally to avoid him, eyes still on her work, and said in a pleasant voice, "I'm busy, Sam."

Over the meal he found her by turns argumentative and withdrawn. She would challenge him abruptly on a succession of minor points, but most of the time she sat in silence listening to him, her expression one of detachment and faint surprise, almost as if she were seeing him properly for the very first time. He fought to involve her in his talk, but his efforts were resisted. Finally, on the Chesterfield he had said, "You seem in a funny mood tonight," a heavily casual remark for which he had anticipated first a denial, then perhaps a discussion of whatever was on her mind. Instead she had answered promptly, "Yes, I know I am," and he was suddenly on the alert. She had been waiting for him to make this observation. There was something she wanted to talk about but was not prepared to initiate: something for which he must provide the cue and so invite his own distress.

"Why? Is anything the matter?"

She turned her head away. "No, not really."

"Yes, there is. What is it?" She did not answer, not this question or the ones that followed, but left him to catch up by himself. He looked at her lowered profile and ruefully advanced: "You're worried about something? . . . Have you had bad news? . . . Are you still worried about your part? . . . Is it anything to do with your father's play?" He had come to the question he had thought of first: "Is it something to do with us?"

"Well, yes, it is, sort of."

"What is it? Are you getting fed up or something?"

"No, not really that."

"Well, what, then?"

She was silent.

"Is there someone else?"

Eventually she nodded. "You mean another man?" She nodded. "But have you slept with him?" She nodded again.

His first reaction was stupid male amazement, his second anger that he had been blind to whatever had been happening. His third reaction, the sober and abiding one, was that a pain, as constant as the toothache, had come into his life.

"Well—who is he?" he asked quietly, his heart now thudding.

"He's nobody you know." The word "he" had suddenly become

extraordinarily charged, as potent and spare as the symbol for the male in biology.

"Is he in the company?"

"No, no! Gosh, no! He's nothing to do with the theater."

"He's not an actor?"

"No, no."

"Well, then, who is he?"

"Look, why don't I make us some coffee before we talk?"

"Coffee will keep me awake," he said miserably.

"All right, then, Ovaltine." But this was worse.

He leaned his head against hers and took a couple of slow recovering breaths; in a moment or two he was going to start shivering. She let him kiss her, then gently disengaged herself and went into the kitchen. He sat and listened to the distinct sounds of milk being poured from a bottle, of a match being struck, of the pop of the gas. Then she returned with two mugs and some biscuits on a tray, and cautiously submitted to his questioning.

It seemed the man was an American and that they were distant cousins. Amanda had met him briefly a couple of years ago in New York, but had not got to know him well (well!) until this summer, when he had come to York to stay with her relatives. That was a month ago. He was on the staff of Princeton University, something to do with archeology, and was in York to study the Roman remains. He was two years older than Sam, taller, and wore glasses.

"I'll bet he smokes a pipe."

"He does, as a matter of fact."

"How often have you slept with him?" The dialogue of jealousy, in the separate dialects of the sexes, had begun. He recognized its banality but could not prevent it.

"Only four times."

"But you've only been over to York once or twice!" he protested.

"He's driven over to Braddington a couple of times. . . . On *Macbeth* nights."

"It happened here?"

279

"No! Never here. You're the only one here. We went for drives."

He thought of Valerie and Trevor. "How long has it been going on?"

"Only recently."

"Had you already made love to him the last time we made love, after the first night?"

"No, no. I hadn't. It happened just after."

"Is he any good?" For the really disturbing questions his voice dropped to an impassive mutter.

She thought about this. "It's better with you," she murmured.

"Well, then, what is it?"

"Oh, Sam." She sighed like a child having trouble with its spelling. "It's just that I like him; and it's, well, a kind of little adventure for me, that's all . . . I can't explain."

"A little bit of life," he said dourly, but she disregarded his tone and took him at his word.

"Yes, yes. That's it. I know it sounds silly, but I think it's sort of good for me."

There were other details that he wanted from her, but for the time being he managed to contain his questions. They were both silent.

"Well," he said, "what do you want us to do, then?"

"I don't know."

"Do you want us to break up?"

"No, no. I don't think I want that."

"What, then?"

She did not answer, and he leaned over her sighing, and kissed and handled her. Her mouth did not avoid him, but it was quite cold. That way there was nowhere to go.

"I know it's hard for you to understand, Sam, but that's just what it is for me, a little adventure. I feel I'm entitled to it." He might have justified Valerie in similar terms. She knew about Valerie. Was this, then, something that perhaps he had taught her, one of his dismal lessons? If he was entitled to his adventure, then why not she? His feelings, which might otherwise have found

280

expression in anger or in some rough ultimatum, were grounded upon this awful reasonableness. Whether or not she expected the justice of friendship from him, he felt a sickly obligation to give it.

"For God's sake, Amanda, I hope you know what you're doing!" He sighed.

She buried her face in her hands, and laughed with a kind of unhappy excitement. "So do I," she said. He kept seeing her now in flashes of pained astonished admiration.

He left two hours later. They had lain on the bed in their clothes and talked and talked, and had at last struck a bargain. Her bargain. As he walked across the park he knew very well that he had been bettered. The American (whose name he realized he still did not know) would be in York three more weeks; after that he returned to the States. Amanda had asked Sam to give her those three weeks. In that time her movements would be her own and Sam would be denied her bed. At the end of those three weeks (if Sam still wanted to, of course) they would maybe start again. Would she be happier finishing it completely? No, no, she didn't want that—unless he did. Would they see one another at all during those three weeks? Of course they would, if he wanted to, for coffee, for walks or whatever; better not suppers, though. In any case they couldn't help seeing one another at the theater in the evenings, so it would be silly to avoid each other, wouldn't it?

He got into bed at the flatlet, turned out the light and lay with his hands behind his head. As his eyes accustomed themselves to the dark, the blotches of illumination cast by the street lighting clarified on his ceiling. He felt as strange and unbelieving in these surroundings as in a hospital bed on the eve of an operation. Something lay ahead of him; he had to go through with it, passively submit to a passage of time in the uncertain hope that it would lead to something better. Three weeks was not long, he told himself. By the present count of his thoughts, it seemed an eternity. He was in love with her. That secret had at last found a confessor: himself. There was no one else to tell now, least of all her. He struggled with the dawning realization that something had gone horribly, horribly wrong.

K*

He snapped awake with the first of morning, and at once his thoughts picked up where they had left off. When would he next see her? This morning, perhaps, by the letter rack collecting mail from Alfred, or later in the day, a chance meeting in the High Street; or would he have to wait all those hours until the play drew them together in the evening?

It suddenly occurred to him that the performance might not be, as he thought, *The Way of the World* but another Macbeth, and he leaped from his bed and fumbled for reassurance in the diary in his trousers pocket. Granted this small relief, he wanted to see her at once: get dressed and stride across the park and perhaps cook a breakfast for them both. But this was clearly impossible; it would be a tactical disaster. She was divided from him now not only by her new lover but by all the deceptions involved in his own agonized, necessary restraint. He wondered if it would ever again be possible to behave spontaneously with her. Somehow or other, over the next three weeks, he had to stop thinking about her. Vain hope. That morning as he walked to the theater beneath the already molting trees, he found he inhabited an altered world. He might have gone beneath the ocean. The thought of her was not inside his head; it was the glass window beyond whose distorting separation lay the rest of existence.

And now as one excruciating day followed another, he moved deeper into this new world. Like a virus that invades a cell, usurping the nucleus it so closely resembles, she had deposed him at his own center. He thought about her ceaselessly, picking over the past they had shared and systematically hoarding memories of her like the fragments of a wantonly broken treasure. He saw himself in these events as a figure of complacency and boundless foolishness, appalled that he had once taken her for granted. He had credited himself with eliciting her laughter and her desire, and realized too late that on the contrary they were things she had granted him.

He began to make secret pilgrimages to the places they had visited together: journeying in an empty bus miles down the coast, or spending half an afternoon in an amusement parlor sharing the neglected machines with one or two late holidaymakers. All these places seemed beautiful and drenched in regret, and he tried to find assuagement in the look, the sound and the smell of them. The most familiar things would strike volumes of feeling in him: the silent tumble of a leaf, or the plight of the old man who all season had sold matches outside the post office. One afternoon he sat by himself in a deserted cinema, choking with emotion, aware of the film's banality yet moved to tears by it. This was his condition exactly: he despised the mechanics of his love, one sprung on jealousy, yet the love itself was an exaltation of loss.

But even at the theater no one seemed to so much as guess at his condition. He sat among them trying to involve himself in the foreign language of their talk, now almost exclusively concerned with theater politics, about next season, about parts, about the chances of coming back. It all seemed impossibly remote. The only thing he wanted to talk about was Amanda, and he hesitated to open his mouth because he knew that it would only be to direct the conversation deviously toward her. He became extraordinarily skillful at this, and understood the obsessive masquerades of the spy. He could catch her name above the murmur of the canteen, and made do with any excuse for joining the table across the room where he had heard it pronounced.

Once he visited the haberdasher's where they had first met. He found the same assistant, bought a handkerchief from him, then beguiled him into recalling the morning he had purchased the jeans and whom he had been with. ("Oh yes. I remember. You were with Miss Maitland. Are you down at the theater, too, then?")

He began to feel a secret pride in the ways he had discovered for putting his unhappiness to use. His acting benefited; he could take it onto the stage with him and effortlessly feed it into his part. No longer nervous because his whole day was lived on a plane of nerves, he drifted onto the stage as heedless of danger as a somnambulist.

And yet at their meetings, these encounters of a few minutes that were the very heart of his day, he doubted if she guessed the true extent of what she had become for him. Vestiges of cunning and pride rose up to conceal it, advising caution. Mostly they met during the show, in the canteen, or in the wings before an entrance. Only on *Macbeth* nights when she wasn't there did he make no attempt to contain his feelings but roamed the theater in a trance of misery. He found a retreat in the little junk room below the stage, where he could grieve in solitude without the possibility of anyone's discovering him.

To begin with, he had called in daily at her flat, but he soon learned the necessity of depriving himself of what he longed for most. The more he saw of her the more his cause suffered. He realized he was losing all perspective of her. Even the odd physical detail, at which the idiosyncrasies of his taste had once balked, her skinniness for example, came to embody a kind of perfection. He had gained her in the first place because she perceived the sharp but just understanding he had of her. Now, with love, he had lost it, and, helpless, he watched her attitude toward him changing.

At first she had been a little frightened of him but she was quick to sense that the person she now had to deal with had been shorn of his male danger. She became casual toward him, then by degrees almost indifferent. Sometimes in small ways, and not to hurt him so much as to assure herself of the reality of her new power, she was cruel to him. She would fail to interrupt some trivial task when he arrived, or she would leave him over tea to make a string of unimportant telephone calls from her bedroom. He vowed to deny himself all meetings with her except those granted by chance.

Now he visited her flat only when he was certain she would not be there. He would arrive with a book in his hand, one of hers which he was ostensibly returning, find the flat empty, stay there an hour by himself, then go away again taking the book with him. He wandered from room to room as careful to examine all evidence of her as he was to leave no trace of himself. He played her records, read her magazines and lay on her bed, his face buried in the odor of her pillows. One afternoon, finding the bed unmade, he took off his shoes and with beating heart slipped between the sheets. That same day he had found one of her letters beside the record player and had sat staring at it for ten minutes before his fingers had found the courage to take it from its envelope. It was from her mother.

So he was seeing her now, and then never for very long, only at the theater; but his mind, like defective radar, wheeled and groped for her constantly. Two or three times a day he thought he saw her in the street, only to learn that the figure who bicycled toward him or whom he had pursued into a grocer's shop had been transmogrified into someone else. The discovery was almost a relief; too often when they did meet it brought him fresh pain. Bumping into her by accident at the stage door after she had been out of town for three days, he knew at once by her surprised formal smile that she hadn't given him a thought since the last time they had seen each other. She, literally, had never been out of his mind. She was there during the day, and she was there most of all when he went to bed at night. He lay reading magazines, frightened to turn off the light. Waiting in the dark, luminous, was her slim body; but waiting not for him. He saw the soft underside of arms fallen limply beside her hair, the raised embracing knees, and above all the smiling mouth, *his* smile which he had discovered, and which was now offered to the possession of a stranger. His heart thumping, he would reach for the switch of the lamp and blink desperately into the neutral room.

But the three weeks passed. With unbelief he saw the hour of his release approaching: four days, three days, two days away. He began to feel a little abashed at how extreme his feelings had been and to listen to the soft laughter of common sense. He knocked on Amanda's dressing-room door to ask her to go out to supper with him the following night, and she thanked him politely. In his own dressing room with Paul he felt talkative for the first time in weeks. Much appeared to have been happening at the theater, and with a shock he realized the necessity of catching up on it. Most of the company had had their first interviews, and hopes were high about the prospect of a second season. One or two had had firm offers, but it was difficult to find out who because a firm offer seemed to go hand in hand with an injunction to secrecy. Paul had managed to worm from Richard Wayland the details of the contract which his agent was at this moment negotiating. He was coming back to play Solyeni in *Three Sisters,* probably Lysander in the *Dream,* and another part as yet unnamed in the new play. This information stung Sam into the recognition that he had been neglecting his own interests. He and Paul determined to petition for a second interview. They would go and see Clarissa first thing in the morning.

"Together?"

"Why not?"

The evening Sam was to take Amanda to supper, Tom returned to Braddington on one of his short visits, and a full company meeting was called onstage after the show. "I just want you all to know that I saw the show tonight and it's improved enormously. Marvelous tonight, Freddie. And Rachel. Really. However—and I'm going to be absolutely frank with you because I believe in being frank—I *have* heard from the stage manager that on other nights the standard has been slipping. Giggling and so on. Now, I know we're getting toward the end of the season and that we're all a bit tired—I know I am—but we must keep the standard up! At all costs. Really. The company owes it to itself as a family. Because that's how I think of you all. As a family of actors. This theater has a magnificent future, and I like to think that all of you, every single one of you, has a stake in it. There're some very exciting things happening next season; you've probably heard by now about the American venture. Well, let's all earn them when they come by giving nothing but our very best now. That's all." The company listened solemnly to this exhortation, uncertain beneath their makeups whether to assume expressions suitable to congratulations or admonishment. Either way the carrot of next season had been dangled squarely before them.

Sam took Amanda to the Royal, and by a coincidence they were directed to a table he had shared with Ivan. Surely he could have bettered this bleakly respectable place to b gin a second wooing. However, it had come about: what a fortnight ago he had despaired of. They were sitting down to a meal, alone together again. They unfolded their heavy table napkins and turned their attention to their menus. Over dinner Amanda did her best, but she seemed tired and withdrawn. It hadn't occurred to Sam, so wrapped up had he been in his own misery, that she, too, probably had her reasons for unhappiness. He might have felt sorry for her if he hadn't suspected that he was to be excluded also from her distress. Not till coffee did he feel secure enough to broach the matter that he supposed to be on both their minds.

"Is it all over, then?"

"Yes," she murmured.

"He's gone, has he? He's gone back to America?"

"Yes, that's right."

There seemed nothing else to say. Later on he asked her, "Do you want to talk about it?" But she answered, "No. Not at the moment. Please, Sam. Maybe later." As they were walking back through the park, she said, "You'll have to be gentle with me, Sam. I'm a bit fragile." He had taken her arm but they were having difficulty keeping step.

In the flat they did the usual things, played a record, made a hot drink, sat and talked, but there was little joy or liberty to be found in them. What alarmed Sam was that unlike himself she seemed passively to accept this change in their situation. His need to embrace her was acquiring an element of desperation, quite alien to the drowsy impulses that had once guided them effortlessly toward the end of an evening. He stooped over and put his empty mug on the floor beside the Chesterfield, upsetting it on the edge of the carpet, and then, awkward with necessity, he embraced her. She made no protest and at first he felt nothing but a glad astonishment to be touching her again. However, her compliance could not disguise her lack of response; her flesh felt curiously soft and unresilient, and her mouth was damp. Sighing, he recognized the need for patience. But he was determined at least to see the inside of her bedroom again. "Let's go and lie on your bed, just as we are, and just talk," he suggested.

"All right," she said. "Actually, this is not a very good time for me. I'm just at the end of my thing."

Lying side by side in the dark it was easier to talk, and he left an hour later to some extent reassured. However, he had only to be by himself for the old anxieties to return. He tried to quiet them with reason. After all, they were meeting tomorrow, and the day after as well, and he knew from experience, surely, that in sexual matters propinquity was nine tenths of the law. He was in Braddington while his rival had flown to America; it would soon be all right again. But he was still unable to sleep when he got home.

The following afternoon Paul and Sam were to have their interviews with Tom, the one at three, the other at four o'clock. They had arranged to meet afterwards at Paul's place and swap accounts. Sam had never visited his flat before, and its ingenious chic, compounded of things like the brass birdcage and the marble-topped washstand painted mauve, took him by surprise. "I had no idea you lived in such elegance," he said, amused and impressed. And indeed it was something of an achievement on Paul's modest salary.

"Camp as Chloe, darling, but we can't help that. Tea or coffee?"

Sam asked for tea, and Paul disappeared to bustle about in his kitchen. He reappeared with a tray lavishly spread with cake, sandwiches and a large pot of China tea. He was in a state of some excitement. "Well! *How* did you get on?" he said, his eyes popping.

"You first. You saw him first."

"Well, honestly, darling, I don't really know. He said the usual lovely things, of course. I was there half an hour. But I've no more idea now where I really stand than when I went in."

"Did you talk parts?"

"Oh yes, endlessly. But he still doesn't know what the plays are going to be. Did he tell you that, too?"

"Yes."

"First of all there's the Chekhov and he admitted that's fully cast. Mostly with names. Then there's the Shakespeare, and that's not settled yet. Then there's the new play—"

"Your play?"

"Well, I don't know. He didn't actually say so. We didn't really talk about it."

"Why ever not?"

"Well, when I first went in, he said to me, he said, 'You've come to see me as an actor, have you, Paul? About next season?' And I said, 'Yes,' and he said, 'Good, good. I'm glad you have. Let's stick to that.' And after that I didn't really feel I ought to bring up the play."

"But he must have mentioned it."

"No, no. Never. He just kept saying, 'And then there's the new play. That's not quite settled yet.' I wanted to ask him, of course, but it didn't seem to be the right time."

"What did you talk about then?"

"Parts, darling! All the lovely parts I ought to be playing five years from now."

"What about next year?"

"Well, there was only the Shakespeare to talk about, wasn't there? He suggested I'd be a very good Arragon in *The Merchant*. It's quite an idea, isn't it?"

"Marvelous idea. You'd be a wonderful Arragon." Sam was remembering something, but like a name on the tip of his tongue it just eluded recall.

"What about you, then?" said Paul.

"Same story. A nice long chat with nothing definite at the end of it. He told me, candidly, that the Chekhov was fully cast, the new play not quite decided, and that left only the Shakespeare. Same as you."

"Did he suggest a definite part?"

"No, not really. We just talked possibilities. That sort of thing." What, in fact, had happened was that Tom had asked Sam to propose himself for a part, and Sam had suggested Gratiano, which he had done with some success in a good rep production a couple of years before; but Tom had cut in with "No, no. Let's talk about the *Dream*. What would you like to play in the *Dream*? They never mentioned *The Merchant of Venice* again, and this struck Sam as peculiar. As at the first interview, Tom was extremely friendly, but there was something perceptibly different in his manner, a quality of "understanding," which Sam was hard put to account for. Was it forgiveness for his behavior at the dress

289

rehearsal? Or had Tom heard something about Amanda? Had he spied Sam wandering forlornly into the theater from behind the office venetians? This seemed unlikely. In any event the solicitude was unwelcome.

Just as he was leaving Paul's flat, the memory that had been teasing him came out of hiding. It gave him quite a shock. He didn't tell Paul, not only because he preferred to check on his information before giving him cause for alarm, but also because he wanted time to think through any possible implications it might have for himself. Sam had remembered just over a fortnight ago (at a time when it was surprising that he had been able to take it in) Don Petersen telling him in the wings that Tom was very keen on having him back next season and that the part he had in mind for him was Arragon in *The Merchant of Venice*. Had not a confidence from Don Petersen been the last thing he expected, he would rapidly have forgotten it.

VALERIE in a green silk-knit dress she had bought in Cannes sat opposite him as crisp as fresh lettuce. She had never looked better; she was a deep, delicate brown all over, her abundant hair glinted auburn where the sun had caught it, and her eyes and teeth were the work of a jeweler. Nevertheless, and perhaps for the first time, it was as a friend that he had been glad to see her. They had met by chance outside the post office, and he had whisked her off to have tea in the lounge of the Royal Hotel.

"Well, how was it? Tell me about it."

"It was lovely. Once we stopped driving. I got brown."

"So I see." He desired her, but with much less aggression than before. Perhaps her beauty was another of the things that unhappiness had altered. He wanted to hear her talk; then he wanted to talk about himself.

Valerie told him how the car had broken down ascending the French Alps, how furious Trevor was when the Frog mechanic told him it would take ten days to repair, and how she had then set about persuading Trevor to leave the car behind and press on to the Mediterranean by bus. On arrival he had sulked for three days, after which it had all been lovely. Trevor's father had granted him an extra week off on account of the car; Mrs. Willis, too, gave her blessing to the extended holiday, and they had had two and a half weeks of swimming, sunshine and expensive night life.

"Trevor had to send for more money," said Valerie with deadpan satisfaction.

"Did you meet some nice people?"

"We met another English couple our age and went around with

them mostly. They had a car and could take us places. What about you? What have you been up to?"

"Well, I've missed you." This was a lie, but he was so pleased to see her again that he felt it a justifiable one. "A lot's been happening. Not much of it nice."

"What?"

He looked at her, wondering if it might be possible to tell her. She was about the only person he could tell. But there was a glint in her eye which cautioned him against it. "Oh, down at the theater. All the intriguing about next season: who's coming back and who isn't. It's boring."

They talked of other things; then suddenly Valerie said, "Have you been seeing Amanda?"

"Yes," he said, and held her look while privately he argued with the temptation to expatiate. He wanted to talk; more than that, he needed to, and he made the mistake of assuming that this was sufficient justification for doing so. He hurried the last part of the account, realizing that he had overstepped his rights with her. Valerie had been an attentive listener, but he knew he had abused something between them. Outside the Royal they smiled and parted, neither having suggested a time when they would next meet.

Over the next week he seemed to catch sight of her as often as a couple of times a day, but it was always from a distance. Once he turned a corner to see her stooping into Mrs. Willis's minicar, one brown, unstockinged leg abandoned momentarily on the footpath. Another time she was sitting beside Trevor as he drove her in a slow circle round the fountain at the end of the High Street. They both gave him a wave: she beautified and sedated by the new foreign clothes that graced her body and occupied her thoughts, he complacent under a suntan which despite its Riviera origins still had the look of makeup applied without instinct. (His bleached eyebrows were the trouble.) Another time, at the end of a lunch hour, he saw her framed behind the glass door of the cosmetics shop in the act of reversing the CLOSED sign to OPEN. The pale underside of her bare arm showed like a cat's belly, and he would have crossed the road to her had not another figure moved in the shadowed recess of the shop: Mrs. Willis. He waved, but she had not seen him and he carried on almost relieved to be delivered from coping with his compromised desire.

As to Amanda, as often as he saw her so his cause suffered, but he continued to seek her out every day. They lunched together or had coffee, and they had been twice to the pictures in the afternoon (she always insisting on paying for her seat). He approached each of these encounters with hope, but always in the time spent with her hope seemed to leak away, leaving him with the cracked vessel of a worsening discouragement. Tiny things would shatter an afternoon: a small, suppressed yawn, a flicker of impatience in one of her looks, a pocket of silence in their talk. Yet she accepted his company, even welcomed it, but always on a makeshift basis as a way of passing the time or as a rather listless alternative to solitude. She no longer took much trouble with her appearance in his company, and a whole range of expressions with which she had once appareled her face were also denied him. He felt the misery and the rage of someone locked out and evicted from his own premises. He despaired of making love to her. Her marble compliance when he had once tried to kiss her had so alarmed him that afterwards he always tried to keep some distance between them, and would start if, over some ordinary task like setting the table, they happened to touch. His thoughts on how to beguile or amuse her became ever more frantic. At a better time they had done everything. They had been to the town's two museums, they had done the trip to Rockdale Hall and walked with their ice creams through the aviary (in any case it was closed now), and the indoor swimming pool where they had once romped away half a dozen afternoons was now reputed to be rotten with athlete's foot.

One day, however, he made a marvelous discovery. All these months they had never been to the Aquarium in the New Town; they had completely overlooked it, and it was open all the year round! When he arrived at her flat, he found her lying on the floor with a magazine listening to some self-important modern jazz. He was with her an hour before the moment seemed right to suggest this new excursion.

"If you like," she answered without interrupting her indolent thumbing through *Elle* magazine. "When?"

"What about Sunday?"

She seemed not to have heard him but buried herself in the horoscope. (In French, he reflected with lugubrious admiration.) At last she said, "All right."

"Sunday, then. Don't forget."

A faint tightening of irritation showed around her mouth. "I've said all right."

But he refused to let it depress him. He had devised something for them to share. For the first time in weeks he felt he had taken a step toward regaining parity.

It was raining on Sunday, a fine drizzle that, had not the sea been entirely flat, might almost have been mistaken for spume. Sam wore his plastic mac, purchased for twenty-five shillings when the weather broke at the beginning of the week, and which he declared made him feel like a suburban sex offender. "It makes you look so forlorn," Amanda had said, and even this small attention pleased him.

They stood now on the front, arms linked beneath her umbrella, their backs to the sea. BRADDINGTON MARINE WONDERLAND, they read in dead neon above the entrance, and again in larger painted letters on the side of the building where beneath the streaking whitewash an earlier and more modest claim, AQUARIUM, could just be picked out. The place seemed deserted, but they found a sullen woman knitting a red scarf in the ticket office, and she let them through the rusty creaking turnstile at the exorbitant cost to Sam of eight shillings. They descended two flights of concrete steps and came to one large oblong room. Along two adjacent sides weakly illuminated fish swam behind panels of plate glass. There was no one else there, all other trade having rightly fled before the damp and oppressive smell of the place. In the corners of the room were wet patches, suggestive of the delinquent pissing of small boys. It was a very unattractive place.

They set about studying the tanks of fish in order, like paintings in a gallery. The water in all of them was filthy, or seemed so in the yellow illumination which picked up a precipitate of decay like dust seen in a beam of sunlight. First they observed a turtle, the shell on his back shaggy with parasitic vegetation. Later on they came upon an octopus stuck fast against the back wall of his tank, his livid torso hanging down and pulsing desperately like some malevolent disembodied scrotum. Then there was a great colony of tiny sea horses hooked by their tails along a piece of wire or, in groups of three or four, obscenely to each other, a community whose limblessness and scorched staring faces suggested the aftermath of some appalling disaster. The last and biggest tank was devoted to a medley of sea creatures; there was an enormous lobster, another turtle, another octopus, all keeping company with a variety of fish. Round and round the fish swam, their course determined precisely by their proximity to other life dangerous enough to remain still.

"Talk about the Life Force," said Sam. It was a joke, really, and in the summer Amanda would have laughed; she would have looked up at him, startled for a moment by a point of view different from her own, and then she would have laughed, delighted, almost grateful, as if it was lucky to be with him. But she was busy reading the card of information framed beside the tank and did not respond. She might not even have heard him. They left the Aquarium and went back to the flat for tea.

"I'm sorry, Sam," she said later that evening. "Honestly, I am. I wish I could, but I can't. I just don't want to. And there's no point unless you want to, is there?"

"No. Do you think you'll ever want to?"

"Maybe. I don't know. But not just now. I don't want to be involved, in any way, not with anyone, just now."

"What about the day after tomorrow? Will you be seeing him then?"

"How do you mean?"

"When you go to London."

She looked annoyed and unhappy. "I've told you, Sam. It's over! He's gone back to America. There's no one at the moment and there hasn't been for weeks. I don't want there to be. I'm going to London about the play, I've told you, a sort of first reading."

A lover or her West End job; he was as hopelessly jealous of one as of the other. She seemed to be drawing away from him, like a ship seen over churned water, and there was nothing he could do but watch.

He worked it out: if she left after the show on Monday night (Tom or someone might give her a lift down), and came back in time for the Thursday matinee, she would be away sixty-three hours. On Monday night he didn't sleep but thought of her racing through the night toward London and perhaps a lover's bed. Her honesty was less in question than his complete inability to assess it. (Later he was to discover that she had in fact spent the night in Braddington and had caught the early train in the morning.) Tuesday seemed interminable and he went to the theater that evening desperate for the distraction of work. On Wednesday morning he tried to read and failed, tried to write a letter and failed, and finished up simply pacing around the flat, his mind untethered and gone baying after her. The prospect of having to get through another twenty-four hours in his condition began to frighten him. He went up to the Ozone to telephone.

Wednesday was a half day in Braddington, and he caught Valerie just as she was shutting up the shop. She said, yes, she was doing nothing, and yes, she would come around after lunch, at about two-thirty. He returned to his room, ate two fried eggs without appetite, and waited for her, darkly becalmed.

She arrived wearing a yellow raincoat he hadn't seen before, and when he took it off her and unveiled her sunburned arms, his mind flooded with sweet despairing lust. But he sat her down in one chair, himself in another, and began to talk to her. He became very animated, and started promising her things: how he would buy her a copy of a novel he had just read (tried to read) and which he declared was superb; how, if she came to London next year as she had said she might, he would take her to all the theaters. Then he invited her to a small party that Paul Poulsen was giving after the show that same night, disregarding the fact that he had already told Paul that he doubted if he could make it. In the rather cold room her bare skin began to pucker into goose pimples and darken, like a child's after swimming. He stopped speaking and stared at her; then he slid from his chair, padded across the room on his knees and embraced her. She gave him one of her forbiddingly neutral looks, then spoke without expression: "I told myself I wasn't going to come here any more." For answer he fumbled with the two buttons at her throat, slipped her sleeveless pullover over her head, and stared with sad wonder at her fresh underclothes: the woolen vest with a lace edging and the complex of slender satin straps that tenderly indented her young shoulders. Perhaps if he looked at her flesh long and closely enough, he would exorcise it of its beauty. He tried it and failed. He locked the door, drew the flimsy curtains and they undressed and got into bed.

That afternoon it seemed she had never given him more pleasure; and yet an hour or two later when the last of his desire had been wrung from him, with a jolt that made his feet arch and seemed to bruise his entire nervous system, he knew none of it to have been of any avail. Thoughts of Amanda had been biding their time for just this state of exhaustion, and, horrified, he watched them marshaling afresh. He looked down over Valerie's caramel thighs, now quite still, and searched in vain for a meaning beyond an hour's oblivion in what he had just done. She was asleep beside him and he wished he could have joined her, but his fatigue was of the wrong sort. She would wake soon, and he liked her too much to avoid the obligation of disguising his weariness. He sighed, only to wake her. "What shall I wear tonight?" were her first words, and he remembered he had asked her to go to the party. Damn. Damn. Damn.

"I don't know; something informal. It isn't a big party, or a posh party, or anything like that."

"Sort of casual?"

"That's the idea." He slipped out of bed to busy himself with making a pot of tea. He was aware of her eyes, watching his movements and his nakedness. He glanced down at his penis and it seemed to him as withered and disposable as an old apple core.

But, surprisingly, when he picked up Valerie in the front-of-house bar after the show, he found himself glad to see her again and so soon. She looked very pretty in her knitted-silk dress, and there was a flush to her cheek and a pleased, sly look in her eye for which he felt he could, not unreasonably, hold himself responsible. Paul accepted their bottle with mock surprise and welcomed them effusively into his sitting room. They were among the first to arrive. Sitting on the divan a cluster of the company's homosexuals were enjoying that ambience among themselves of a gently contemptuous understanding (representing perhaps a kind of wisdom) at war with an inclination for shrill mischief (folly). Valerie was introduced to them all and a silence followed.

"They're new, aren't they? Those blue curtains?" improvised Sam.

"Peacock," corrected Valerie, and the gathering laughed, approving of her.

"Exactly, dear!" cried Paul. "Sixteen and six a yard. Look, I lined them with the old ones. I haven't quite finished yet."

Valerie immediately consolidated her popularity by asking for a needle and thread to finish the job. A place was made for her on the divan and Paul brought her a glass of sweet white wine which she drank down like cordial. Half an hour later, with many more people arrived, she was still sewing, if with some decline in efficiency. "She's a honey, your Valerie. I'm *mad* about her," said Paul, and they both looked across to where she sat with her work on her lap, trying to contend with her stitching and at the same time the efforts of someone from the wardrobe who was forcibly feeding her with sips of drink from his own glass. She shook her head but swallowed nonetheless. Sam wondered whether he should gently intervene but instead obeyed a cowardly impulse to talk to a group at the far end of the room.

298

Around twelve o'clock there was an influx of latecomers and gate-crashers, and every room of the small flat became uniformly pressed and noisy. When Valerie appeared at Sam's elbow, he was engaged in noisily contradicting Don Petersen on some point relating to the art of acting. "I'm a bit woozy" was all she said. He introduced her to Don, but she made no effort to join in their conversation but simply stood there looking up at him. His pleasure in acquainting Don with his own stupidity began to diminish, as, he suspected, did Don's pleasure in fostering what was already a flourishing dislike, and eventually Don excused himself.

"Anything the matter? Do you want to go home?" he asked her.

"No."

"Are you enjoying yourself?"

"Mm."

They joined other groups, but Valerie had given up speaking for the evening. Her silent presence beside him wherever he moved began to exasperate him, and it soon became imperative to escape her for a while. Toby Burton bumped into them, and he quickly introduced her, then sent himself on the false errand of getting them all drinks.

"I'll go," volunteered Toby.

"No, I'll go," said Sam.

However, he went not to the bar but to the kitchen from where he had smelled coffee being made. He would enjoy a cup by himself in the comparative quiet there, before taking Valerie a cup, strong and black. Five minutes later he peeked around the door, and was content to see Valerie and Toby both absorbed in Toby's talk. Someone had already given them coffee from a tray. He set off to find new people to talk to.

Suddenly the party was thinning out. Don Petersen, shuffling into his overcoat, approached Sam. "You'd better have a look at your girl. She's not very well," he said. Only five minutes before, Sam had seen her helping Paul with a fresh supply of food.

"What do you mean?" he asked.

"Have a look yourself. She's in the toilet."

The bathroom was minute. Valerie was sitting on the edge of the tub when Sam came in, her eyes hooded with nausea. She had kicked off her shoes and rose in her stockinged feet to meet him.

"What's wrong?" he asked superfluously.

She swayed, stumbled and sat with an awful jolt on the lavatory seat, then looked at him with a gaze of spaniel humility. "I'm sorry, Sam," she said.

"Don't be silly. There's nothing to be sorry about. Do you think you're going to be sick?"

"Mm," she said, staring apathetically in front of her. He bolted the door and waited with her while her nausea came painfully into focus. They had a couple of false alarms, then suddenly it was happening.

"Not the bath. Quick!" he said, wheeling her off the lavatory seat and around to face it. He held her head while she vomited twice. When it was over she straightened up, blinking, swallowing and taking gasps of breath. "I'm sorry, Sam," she said.

"You'll be all right now." He didn't want to smile but couldn't help it.

"I've never done that before," she said.

"Been sick?"

"Had too much to drink."

"Wash your mouth out and put on some more lipstick and you'll be all right."

She swayed past him to collect her handbag. Without her shoes and still quite drunk, she manifested a peculiar feminine clumsiness as if her center of gravity had subsided into her hips and firmly lodged there, and he hated the way this alarmed him. But he was pleased to see that she was making a swift recovery; her reflection was now laughing at him in the mirror over the basin. Her amusement didn't seem to have much point, but he endeavored to share it with her. "Hurry up," he said in a friendly tone.

"Look, Sam." She had taken the cap off her lipstick and was screwing the red cartridge in and out in a suggestive manner, laughing immoderately at her boldness. "Isn't it funny!" It was to begin with, but she kept on doing it.

"It'll fall out if you're not careful," he said.

She turned around, her expression suddenly solemn, and looked up at him. "I love you, Sam," she said.

They swayed together for a moment in her precarious embrace. He looked back at her, feeling shame, complacence, excruciating goodwill, unable to speak.

"I do, Sam. I do. I do love you."

"Oh, Val. Maybe . . . maybe you've just had a little bit too much to . . ." He felt too ashamed to finish the sentence.

"No, I haven't. I do, Sam. But, look, I don't expect anything. Don't worry. I just want you to know."

He sank onto the edge of the bath, wanting to answer her but unable to. "Don't worry, Sam," she said in a voice that was now firm and gentle. "I just wanted you to know. Look, you go back to the party and I'll join you. I won't be long." He didn't move. "Go on." They embraced, and she stumbled again, this time almost tipping them both into the bath. She had resumed her giggling as he undid the lock and let himself out.

Almost everyone had gone. Paul came up to him. "Is she all right? I've got someone here who can give you a lift home."

It was fifteen minutes before Valerie emerged from the bathroom, blithe and meticulously made up. In the presence of the few remaining guests she was somewhat on her dignity but gave Sam a wink when he brought her her coat. They were dropped off at her house and he kissed her good night, then stood under the streetlight wiping himself free of all her fresh makeup. He was about to set off for the Ozone when he remembered he had left his plastic mac back at Paul's. It was a black night with a clear threat of rain for tomorrow. He would have to go back for it.

Paul's expression when he came to the door was surprisingly hostile, but it changed when he saw who it was. The flat seemed empty, but Sam sensed another presence out of sight in the bedroom. He collected his mac and was about to leave when Paul said, "Like to see something?"

"What?"

"Follow me," said Paul mysteriously.

He led Sam into the bathroom. On the mirror over the basin, on the side of the bath, on the lavatory lid, on one tiled wall, the words "I do" were written in lipstick. For a moment he did not comprehend. Then, having comprehended, he turned to Paul with the camouflage of a joke. Paul's expression told him that any such evasion would be not merely discreditable but a waste of time.

Next day Sam received a letter which warmed him considerably. It was typewritten on expensive paper:

DEAR SAM,

Thanks very much for your letter which has at last caught up with me, or which anyway I am at last answering. (Actually dictating—to a charming secretary whom I believe to be a great beauty. The human race has gained immeasurably in comeliness now that I can barely see them.) Things are not as bad as they might seem. A nuisance mainly. Being born deficient in so many faculties the loss of an extra one is really neither here no there. I am being very well looked after, spoiled some say, and there are some quite interesting things about being confined in the dark. The doctors mutter about an operation next year to make me whole again but I think that's just talk. Meanwhile, thank God and rather to my surprise, work is pouring in. I've gone into the recording game and am doing an LP of "The Odyssey." The promoters have had the marvelously vulgar idea of having a picture of me on the sleeve dressed up as the blind Homer. I now have grown the beard for it, anyway. All this keeps me busy. Hope the season goes well for you.

> Kindest regards,
> Yours ever,
> IVAN

He read the letter a couple of times, then wondered who he could show it to. He needed to be circumspect about the choice. Ordinarily it would have been Amanda, but that wouldn't do. What about Paul?

But Paul was not well. He came late into the dressing room and slumped into his chair, loudly complaining of a terrible hangover.

The following evening the hangover revealed itself to have been the beginnings of a bad cold, about which he was equally voluble, and the evening after that it was clear that he had the flu. The others in the dressing room knew he was really sick, not only because he was running a temperature but because he had fallen completely silent, and they all agreed he should be home in bed, fear of contagion now adding conviction to their solicitude. Even made up, complete with the blue eyelids for which he had a weakness in almost any role, he still looked awful.

By the end of the week it was clear that Paul's condition was part of a small epidemic. The rain and the cold had brought the germs with them, and now they were multiplying through the company with little respect for billing. Frederick Bell was reputed to be in dreadful shape, and Sam was not surprised when at the end of one performance Terence advised him to have a look at his understudy. *The Way of the World* would soon be turning up in repertoire again, and there was a strong possibility that Freddie would be off.

Sam was glad of this new challenge and he felt unexpectedly strengthened by it. He canceled the visit to the pub that he had suggested to Amanda, and went straight back to the flatlet to consult his script. He would study his lines while the supper cooked. Suddenly it seemed possible that work was about to resume its rightful priority in his life; rather timorously he tried thinking of Amanda in the old way: loved but adjunct. Mouthing his lines, he set about peeling some potatoes. They had been wrapped in an old page of the *Daily Express,* into which he now deposited the peelings. He had just cut away the rotten end of one of the potatoes when his eye was taken by a photograph in the crumpled sheet of newsprint, somewhat obliterated by dirt. A familiar young woman in dark glasses, her face cleaved across by a huge white smile, waved an airport greeting. He dusted away the fragments of earth and read that Martin Dane's wife had returned from filming in Greece.

The newspaper was three weeks old.

SAM sat up in bed and stared into the darkness of his room. He could almost hear the purr and rattle of the machinery of his mind as the items of information that had been fed into it over the past months clicked effortlessly and remorselessly toward a tally. It was suddenly so entirely obvious, beyond dispute. Shocked, horrified, yet in some bitter way elated that his intuition had managed to find her out, he began to check back over the facts.

He astonished himself by the host of small details that were emerging from the recesses of his memory: a car parked at a certain angle on a certain day, two teacups on top of her piano, a look of hers across the canteen which he had observed but at the time attached little significance to. These were the small things, the corroborating minutiae. There remained the facts. Three weeks ago on the thirteenth of October Martin Dane's wife returned to England, and on that very day, a Monday, her supposed American had flown out of her life. And when had the affair with the American begun? Almost to the day that Martin's wife had left to film in Greece. And there were so many other things. For instance, Amanda had never allowed Sam to see her on Macbeth nights, the nights Martin left the theater early. And the weekends she spent in York were weekends when Martin, too, had been out of town. And what of those private rehearsals during *The Way of the World*, love scenes together in an upstairs dressing room for hours on end! A dozen times he had seen them driving through Braddington together, often in Tom's company, the three of them absorbed in some mysterious, exclusive smiling. As long ago as the party on the beach he remembered that when she had got out of Tom's car to say good night to him there had been a third person sitting in the front seat. Who could it have been but Martin? But most conclusive of all was the memory of her whenever he had tried to discuss Martin: how she would evade the subject, or sometimes in very careful terms defend him; or she would simply remain silent until his spleen had exhausted itself. He had interpreted this as some kind of reprimand to his malice, as evidence of her superior good nature.

But what did it really mean? With growing apprehension he realized he had blundered into a mined field. The conjecture was touching off a whole sequence of brutal, cumulative explosions. For what sort of person did it make of her? How could she have lied to him, on such a scale and with such extravagant invention? She had built a great edifice of untruth upon her American. How could she have countenanced the betrayal of giving herself to the one person she knew to be his enemy? No! It simply couldn't be true. And yet as soon as he had rested his head on the pillow, trying to calm himself, he knew that beyond any doubt it was true. His heart would start to thump again as he waited in the dark with staring eyes for the confirmation of some further recollection. And the worst of it was that at this very moment Amanda was in London again. He could not go to her flat in the morning, seize her by the shoulders and demand the truth. That would have to wait until she got back on Monday. Martin Dane. *Martin Dane!* How could it be true?

The turbulence of his mind had overtaken his body; he was certain the bed shook with each pump of his heart. Sleep was impossible. He rose and with trembling hands buttered a slice of bread and warmed some milk for chocolate. But the liquid went straight through him; his metabolism had become as overactive as his mind, and every half hour he had to climb out of bed and watch his urine as clear as water rattle away into the lavatory.

He watched the meticulous progress of daylight dissecting the contents of his room. It was nine o'clock in the morning and he had not had a minute's sleep. He got out of bed and pulled the curtains. It was a sunny day. All at once he felt foolish. Betrayal had diminished from a certainty to the merest possibility. Martin

L

Dane? How could it be! He looked back at those hours in the dark almost with embarrassment.

The day passed, and except for a burning feeling in the eyes he felt none the worse for having had no sleep. At times he felt almost proud of the fact, as if he harbored a testing secret. His performance that night did not seem to suffer; on the contrary fatigue had relaxed him, and he was rather good. He approached his bed that night feeling that he had earned his rest. But a mode of existence was waiting for him that had nothing to do with the day. Again he was awake all night at the mercy of a frantic, ungovernable mind. In the morning he felt limp and frightened, and wondered with a hypochondriac's nervousness just how long this could go on. But he was seeing her that afternoon before the show, so perhaps relief was on the way.

As soon as he set eyes on her he knew that it could not possibly be true. She had run up to him and kissed him as he entered the flat as exhilarated and pleased as a child. "Oh, I've had a wonderful weekend!" she said with perfect artlessness.

"Why, what's happened?"

"The play! It's going so well! Joel's such a marvelous director. I'd forgotten. We're getting all sorts of new things out of it. And the company are so nice; they really are. They're so understanding about my being there for only a day or two then rushing away. I'd be furious if I was them."

"Are the rest of them rehearsing full time?"

"No, no. We're only meeting at odd weekends at the moment. We don't start full time till next month when the season's over." She paused and smiled. "Oh, Sam, I can't tell you how lovely it is: being *good* again. I was beginning to wonder if I'd ever be good again."

He wanted to kiss her. It was the moment to do it certainly. But she had turned and gone into the kitchen to put the kettle on, and he had missed it.

"But what have *you* been doing?" she shouted. "I'm so self-centered! Always talking about myself. You must stop me!"

"Nothing much," he said, then added as a leaden afterthought, "missed you a bit." She was in a wonderful mood, just as she used to be, and he had an awful feeling that he was somehow going to spoil it. They had their tea on the Chesterfield, and he encouraged her to chatter, looking at her rather than listening to her, taking in the tricks of her expressions and the jerky, hopeful gestures of her shoulders and arms. The couch they were sitting on seemed practically to buck with her vitality. His insomnia and its reasons were all foolishness now. He doubted if he dared even mention them.

"No, but what have you been doing?" she insisted at last. Reluctantly he gave her a selective account of his weekend and it sounded very dull. His voice was trailing away. He saw an expression come into her face which he had learned to dread, an impassive expression intended to mask her thoughts but which on the contrary proclaimed them. That expression had so often been the point of decline in their times together. Today, possibly because of his fatigue, it depressed him less than it annoyed him, and as answer he reached out, pulled her toward him and peremptorily kissed her. She lay passive against him, and they looked at each other a long time in silence. The imperturbability of her gaze began to anger him. He wanted to shake her confidence, her complacency with him, and he decided on a reckless course. It was a long shot that would probably do more harm than good. He didn't care.

He spoke quietly and carefully. "I think I know who it is."
"Who?"
"You know, your 'American.' " His inflection was just sufficiently ironic to be understood. Something extraordinary began to happen. He could feel another person's heart thudding through two layers of clothing against his own ribs. She had hidden her face against his chest. He was amazed. So it really was true!
"Shall I tell you?" She didn't answer. "Shall I?"
"No."
"Why not?"
She was still not looking at him. "Because it will be the end of everything if you do. You'll hate me."

"Would that matter?"

She did not answer.

"It's Martin Dane, isn't it?" She was silent. "Isn't it?" He took her head in his hands and forced her to look at him. She was very frightened and her heart was beating wildly. Then he let her go, and she averted her head again. "Isn't it?"

"Yes," she whispered, low and barely audible.

He leaped to his feet and paced up and down the room blaspheming. He was like an animal that tries vainly to shake off some physical injury as if it were something apart, a bramble or a thorn. And yet at this moment he also experienced a kind of jubilation; he had beaten her. Once again he had her in the net of his mind, and the huge rent through which effortlessly she had been able to come and go without his so much as guessing was mended.

"How could you have lied to me like that, Amanda! How could you have been so bloody dishonest!" he shouted at her.

"I didn't want to lose you, I suppose," she murmured. "It was only for a month—with Martin."

"While his wife was away?"

"Yes. He was so lonely."

He snorted contemptuously. "But why Martin? Of all the people in the world! Christ! You know what I think of him!"

But there was no time to talk. They were both due at the theater in ten minutes. What about after the show? he insisted. But she was going out to supper with friends, up from London to see the play. He demanded that she give him a quarter of an hour before she joined them.

As soon as the curtain came down, he went up to her dressing room. "Better shut the door," she said. Then in hushed voices, his urgent, hers dragging, the inquisition was resumed. Occasionally an actor on his way home rapped her door in passing and shouted good night, and she broke free from his gaze for a moment to answer with a buoyant greeting. He wondered how he could possibly have failed to credit this woman with the reserve of deception that was the natural weapon of her sex.

"But when did it all start?"

"Well—from his point of view, almost as soon as he joined the company."

"What did he say to you, for God's sake?"

"He didn't say anything."

"What do you mean?"

"He hardly talked to me. I would never have known from him."

"How did you find out, then?"

"Tom told me."

"Tom?"

"Yes. You know what good friends they are. Martin used to tell him everything. How he was mad about me and everything."

"And Tom passed this on to you?"

"Yes. It was very muddling, really. Tom would tell me how desperate Martin was. Then when I saw Martin he'd almost cut me dead. It was sort of contradictory."

"So what did you do?"

"Well, I wasn't interested to begin with. There was you, and then, well, Martin was married and his wife was still here."

"So—?"

"But Tom kept on and on about Martin . . ."

"Yes?"

"He said he thought it was a good idea. He used to say—" She hesitated and glanced modestly at the floor. Everything she did now seemed "acted," but alas, this did not enable him to love her any less. On the contrary it made her the more extraordinarily able, himself the more inadequate.

"Go on."

"I can't."

"Go on, damn it!"

"Well, he used to say I had . . . star quality . . ."

"On the strength of this season?" He could not resist it; he knew it would hurt her and it did.

"He saw Dad's play in New York," she murmured.

"Well?"

"Well . . . he used to say that people who had this thing had to organize their lives very carefully. They owed it to their talent. They had to choose their parts carefully and their friends and everything . . ."

"And their lovers?"

"He said he thought Martin and I would be very good for each other. Anyway that Martin would be very good for me."

"And did he know about us?"

"Who?"

"Tom."

"Yes."

"And what did he think?"

"He likes you, Sam. He thinks you're very nice."

Nice. It had become the most dismissive word in the language. "But he didn't think you and I were a good idea?" She didn't answer. "Whereas you and Martin were?"

"Yes."

"And when did he convince you?"

"How do you mean?"

"When did it start?"

"I've told you. Martin's wife went away to film and Martin was so lonely. I felt sorry for him. But I told him quite definitely that it would only be for a month. While his wife was away. And it was. She's so beautiful, isn't she? I wish I were like her. I think they're still very much in love."

He commented bitterly and obscenely. There was a knock at the door. It was Terence. "You've got some friends waiting for you downstairs, Mandy."

"I know. I must hurry."

"And, Sam"—Terence turned to him—"I'm glad I caught you. Freddie isn't getting any better. We've had the doctor in tonight. I'm pretty certain you'll be playing on Thursday."

Somewhere in his mind he found a pigeonhole for this information; it seemed of little consequence. But Amanda turned a keen smiling face to him, the last ten minutes apparently forgotten, and said, "Sam! Isn't that exciting! This could be your chance."

For a third night he did not sleep, but lay awake patiently

suffering instruction in the varieties of insomnia. There was a list of questions it was imperative to ask her, and drawing them up was a night's labor.

They met again the following afternoon, a Tuesday.

"And was it any good with him?"

"I've told you, Sam. It was better with you." Her expression became genuinely puzzled. "It hurt a bit with him." She was adjusting to the change in their situation, his knowing, and she was no longer frightened of him, which he regretted. She answered his questions mechanically as if their inconvenience was just another part of a woman's lot. Of these questions there were some he felt he had a right to ask, others not, but it was precisely those questions that threatened him most that he felt impelled to ask.

"Was he bigger than me?"

"How do you mean?"

He gestured.

"Oh, Sam—" she turned away with an annoyed sigh.

He tried to recover ground. "So you used to have weekends in York by yourselves?"

"Not always."

"What do you mean?"

"By ourselves. Tom used to come."

"Tom?"

"Yes. He used to come, too. He knew all about us. It was sort of friendly."

"And you'd all book into a hotel together?"

She hesitated. "Yes."

He stared at her, framing the next question. "And did you do it . . . all together?"

She didn't answer and he gripped her by the shoulders. "Tell me!"

"No, we didn't. They wanted to, but I wouldn't."

"Are you sure?"

" 'Course I'm sure. They used to say there was no harm in it. I don't suppose there was really. They used to laugh about it, but I didn't like it."

For a moment it became possible to see her unobscured by the rubble of his own emotions. He struggled to retrieve some fragment of understanding or good sense to help them both. "Look, Amanda"—he sought for words—"before we were lovers we were friends." Wasn't that the lyric of a cheap song? But how else could he express it? "Let's never lie to each other again. Promise?"

"Oh, yes! Promise," she said fervently.

"Let's try and salvage the friendship part of it at least."

"I want that, too, Sam," she said miserably.

Seeing her sitting there repentant, and yet for all that rather admirably stubborn in her right to lead her own life as she wished, he felt oddly reasonable about her. He sighed. "Well, what about us? Do you want us to stop seeing each other?"

"No, no. I don't want that."

"You want to see me—what?—just as a friend."

"I don't know, Sam. I don't know."

"Do you not want us to sleep together any more?"

She gave him a look of pleading. "I *can't* just at the moment. Couldn't we wait until the season's over and see then? Maybe back in London? All I can think about at the moment is the play. I don't *want* to get involved again at the moment. I just want to get the play on."

"You're not still seeing Martin?"

"No! No! No!"

But his reasonableness had passed. He had thought again about the lying: the humiliation and insult of having been excluded from her trust. He burst out: "Martin! Christ, you really chose well, didn't you? Honestly, that nothing! I just can't understand how you could have done it! How could you?"

He had angered her. He saw her withdraw from him and compose her reply. She didn't look at him, but spoke in short isolated phrases as if carefully thinking her way. It was a trick of expression she had picked up from him. "Well, it's like this . . . if Martin were free . . . if he weren't married . . . I think he's a man it would be possible for me . . . to love . . . to live my

312

life with and work with . . . but he's not free, is he? So that's that."

There was nothing he could say to this. It wasn't that he believed for one moment that she loved Martin; nor did he give her the least credit for her unctuous respects to the institution of marriage, the young person's usual way of insuring her own expectations of it. What she had told him, in so many words, was that he, Sam, would not do for her, and never would do for her. He finished his tea and left.

That night he lay in bed with his hands crossed behind his head, thinking. His thoughts, for all their rancor, seemed more ordered and under control than they had been for months. He knew the worst now, and to his surprise he had discovered in it an ominous kind of liberation. She did not want him in her future. She did not care to sleep with him now. He thought about these things for a while. "Very well. Fuck her." He spoke the words aloud and briskly into the empty room, and it worked like an incantation to remove a spell.

He knew suddenly that there was an alternative way of looking at this girl. He had been wearing blinkers so long he had forgotten how bright and sharp the world was without them. An alternative way of looking at her meant an alternative way of treating her. He laughed, impatient to put these new intuitions into practice. But they would be meeting tomorrow morning. Terence had called a special rehearsal of *The Way of the World* to ease Sam into the part he would probably be taking over on Thursday. In the meantime he needed as much sleep as he could get. He turned over on one side and went off almost at once.

They met first thing in the morning by the letter rack. There was nothing for her; for him a postcard from Sidney which Alfred stretched past her to deliver. "Hello," he said with a quick smile, then turned away and gave all his attention to the postcard. She paused beside him a moment, but he neither interrupted his reading nor acknowledged her presence in any way. Then just as he sensed she was about to speak, he walked away and left her.

L*   *313*

He enjoyed the morning's work. He was surer on his lines than he had expected and found a certain physical pleasure in the exercise of a leading part. He liked, too, the feeling of coming to the rescue of the play and the way the other actors encouraged and at least temporarily deferred to him in this capacity. He had occasion to meet with Amanda often during the morning, onstage and off, and he was as careful to be pleasant to her as he was to show her not the least tittle of real concern. He noticed and relished her growing bewilderment. At the end of the morning Terence came up and congratulated him on the work he had done, and several actors assured him that when he came to play the part the following evening he would have nothing to worry about. Even Martin found something pleasant to say, and he had no trouble accepting his assurances.

Lunch provided him with a lucky tactical advantage. He had gone off with Paul to his usual restaurant when halfway through their meal Amanda came in from the street and stood by the cash desk frowning and looking about her. He recognized that expression from the night of the barbecue; had she come looking for him again? He redoubled his interest in Paul's conversation. She came up to their table and he looked up feigning surprise. He would make her say it.

"Can I join you?"

"Certainly. Please do." He cleared some books and his newspaper off the free chair.

She sat down and he passed her the menu. "The chicken's good," he said, mechanically polite, then left her to make up her mind on her own. Paul was in a talkative mood, and today Sam was happy to let his camp friend have his head. He was discussing his party, an excellent subject since Amanda, away in London, had not been there; maybe she had not even been asked. Paul went through the entire evening, incident by incident, concluding with some arch references to the lipstick inscriptions on the bathroom wall. Sam smiled faintly and allowed him to say what he liked. On his left he could feel Amanda's unease like a draft. By the time they had finished their coffee her chicken had still not arrived and they begged to be excused. From outside in the street through the steamed-up window they saw her smile bravely at the waitress as a plate of food was put in front of her.

He met her again that afternoon. They caught sight of each other at opposite ends of the car park, and he observed with satisfaction the difficulty she had in sustaining her smile throughout the distance that separated them. He had an intuition as they drew close that she was about to ask him to tea.

"I'm just on my way to have a haircut," he volunteered.

"Oh. . . . How long will that take?"

"Not long . . . but then I've got to go to the library, then collect my laundry and things."

"Oh . . . I'd better not keep you, then."

It was really rather horrible how deft he found himself at the game of malice. Perhaps he would have had a more absolute distaste for it if he had not been so fascinated by its effect on Amanda. The girl was crumbling before his eyes. And he had done nothing, literally nothing, about which she could specifically complain. But there was no need to actually *do* her harm. It was enough to wish it. And be patient. After all, the drift of life was on one's side. He smiled at her, with the confidence of insincerity, and turned to go. He had walked thirty yards before he heard her call after him. He stood still while she approached, resisting the impulse to go halfway toward meeting her.

"Sam," she said, trying to express her bewilderment in naked appeal, "would you like to come to supper tonight?"

He looked at her steadily for some moments before answering. "All right. Thanks." Then he walked away.

In the canteen during the performance that night Amanda brought her coffee to his table. He smiled, then disregarded her. His conversation with Richard Wayland became charged with subdued, cold glee, and he found it very easy to laugh. He wished he had realized a long time ago that she respected cruelty.

After the show they walked together across the park. He left to her the responsibility of a conversation, keeping his own peculiar high spirits to himself, now whistling, now kicking a pebble along the gravel path. While she did the cooking, he stayed in the sitting room reading one of her magazines and tapping his foot to some undisclosed tune. She asked him to set the table and he jumped to his feet with insolent cheerfulness. She stood in the doorway watching him, willing him to speak; he steeled himself not to.

"You're in a funny mood tonight, aren't you?" she said.

"Am I?"

"Yes. What's the matter? Are you depressed or something?"

He laughed loudly at her audacity. *"I'm* not depressed. I'm fine!"

The meal went wrong that night. The potato water boiled away, ruining both vegetable and container, and the meat turned out to be undercooked, tough and inedible. They ate some cold ham and a little limp salad instead.

Later on she said, in tones of complaint rather than refusal, "No, Sam, I've told you. I don't really want to." But she did nothing to resist the bald advance of his hand between her thighs. He began to undress her, and she winced or grimaced as each article of clothing was taken from her and tossed aside. He took her into the bedroom and lay where he thought he was never to lie again. He enjoyed her once, then turned her round and had her as a boy. Afterwards her face was darkly flushed and she was trembling. She put her arms around him and pulled herself close. Then, after a time, she got up unbidden, slipped into her toweling dressing gown and went to make them both a drink.

He lay waiting for her, trying to digest the fact that he possessed her again. Yet the possession of her seemed to have less substance than the principle he had unloosed in bringing it about. He didn't like the principle much, nor himself particularly for putting it to use, but he could not help being impressed by its svelte, speedy workings.

She returned with a tray, which she put on the table beside the bed, and looking at her he found he was unable to prevent himself from relenting toward goodwill. He gazed at her until she, too, very grudgingly, returned his smile. But only for a moment. All at once her jaw went forward in a complete change of expression, her fists clenched, and she was attacking him: swiping him hard, hitting him on the side of the head, the shoulders, the back, anywhere she could see an opening. He shook with laughter, weakly fending off her blows, until eventually he had no choice but to retreat off the bed, dragging with him the slender protection of the eiderdown to cushion her blows and shield his nakedness. It seemed to go on for minutes, her blows and his laughter. It stopped only with her complete exhaustion.

21

IN THE MORNING when he woke he was nervous. It took him a moment or two to understand why: that night he would be playing Mirabell in *The Way of the World*. It was as if the significance of this fact had only just dawned on him. The rehearsal the day before seemed dreamlike in its inconsequentiality. He got out of bed to a miserably cold morning, another abrupt stage in the decline of the weather, and shivered his way through washing and dressing. Over a pot of tea he studied his lines for a couple of hours and found that he knew them all right, though he was beset by a stubborn anxiety that somehow he ought to have done a little more work on them. However, it was too late now. He closed his script, slipped it in his pocket, and set off to collect what mail there might be for him.

Even as he approached the theater across the car park he sensed the disturbance in the warren. Jock MacLachlan had passed him in some sort of unusual hurry, smiling and distributing a "Good morning" to him with scrupulous civility, whereas a knot of actors standing just outside the stage door were so absorbed in something they were reading in the newspaper that they did not even look up as he passed.

"What's happening?" he asked Alfred.

"The plays for next season, sir," answered Alfred cheerfully. "They were announced in the paper this morning."

"What are they?" Sam realized he had practically barked at the old man.

"I don't rightly know, to tell you the truth," said Alfred, leaning confidentially through his window. In that case Sam wanted to set off at once and speak to someone who did. However, he found

318

himself detained by Alfred in an expansive mood. "Hold on a minute, though. I was told. Now what were they? There's a new play, a modern play, I do know that. Then there's a Shakespeare. Well, there would be a Shakespeare, wouldn't there?" The old man's plodding guileless manner was exasperating him. "And wait a moment, I remember now: there's a play by that Russian chappie. *Three Brothers,* is it?"

"*Three Sisters.*"

"That's right. I knew it was something to do with brothers and sisters, one or the other. *Three Sisters,* that's it."

"Thanks very much," said Sam, backing toward the stage door. Outside he looked for the group who had been reading the newspaper, but they had already dispersed. He ran past Alfred again on his way to the canteen, where he encountered someone sure to have all the news: Richard Wayland.

"Don't you know yet? I thought everyone knew. Opening with *Three Sisters,* then the *Dream*—"

"Not *The Merchant?*" Sam interrupted.

Richard's expression was one of amused derision. He shook his head. "Wake up," he seemed to be saying.

"But I thought they'd practically cast *The Merchant,*" insisted Sam.

"Well, maybe, love. But if you can find the actor who's been approached to play Shylock, you're cleverer than I am. And you don't do *The Merchant* without finding your Shylock first, do you?"

"You mean they were never going to do it?"

"Work it out for yourself, love."

"What about the new play, then?"

"Oh yes. That's the one about Roger Casement. Here, it's in the paper. Keep it. I've read it."

"That's marvelous news for Paul," said Sam, but Richard looked uncomprehending. He left Sam to the study of the newspaper, already folded open at the Arts page. NEXT SEASON AT BRADDINGTON, read the heading. His eye skimmed quickly over the two paragraphs. But that was odd: ". . . and a new play, *The*

319

Black Diaries, by Bernard Loss, about the Casement trial." Was Paul writing under a pseudonym? And hadn't his play originally been called something else? He remembered the word "Patriot" in the title. Something seemed to be wrong, and ten minutes later when he went up to his dressing room to check on his makeup things for the evening, he found out what. Paul was sitting alone at his place, very pale and still, and at once Sam had a sense of having walked in on some private distress. "What's all this in the paper about your play?" he asked, aware as he said it of the blunder of such a question.

Paul struggled to compose his features into some kind of social front. "Haven't you heard of Bernard Loss, darling? He's a very clever playwright. Nó, really; he is. Very clever. First-class. Didn't you see *The Pitchfork* at the Arts?"

"He wrote that, did he?"

"Oh, yes. No, he's good. I have to admit it."

"Then . . . this isn't your play?"

"Was mine called *The Black Diaries,* darling?" he demanded with a sudden display of waspish offense.

"No, I realize that, Paul. That's why I asked." There was a silence. "Well, what's happened, then?"

"It's perfectly simple. In fact I'm sure it happens all the time. Bernard Loss and I have written plays on the same subject. His, I daresay, is better. I'm sure it is. He's a good playwright . . ."

"But what happened!?"

"I suppose Tom owned his play, Bernard Loss's, and planned to do it next season. Then he heard about mine . . ."

"When this other management had hold of it?"

"I suppose so. You remember they were going to put it on after Christmas. Look, that's what they *told* me, darling. Maybe they had no intention to. But that's what they told me . . ."

"So—?"

"So Tom bought the option off them. Now he owns both plays and nobody can spoil the market for Bernard Loss."

"I'm sorry, Paul," said Sam. He didn't know what to think or say "What about the acting? Have you heard any more about that?"

320

Paul turned a stricken, angry face on him "Are you joking? You don't think he'll want me hanging around next year after this little lot. No, he'll want me out of the way at the Labour Exchange where he won't have to think about me."

"Have you heard from him?"

"I don't need to hear from him! What did he offer me? Arragon in *The Merchant.* And they're not even doing the bloody *Merchant!*" His rejection as an actor seemed to wound him even more than as a playwright. His lips were trembling, and for a moment Sam thought he might cry. However, he turned back to his place and speedily composed himself by making camp, rather courageous little faces at himself in the mirror. When he next spoke he was quite calm. "Well, he's done what he wanted to. He's kept us all happy until the last fortnight. We've all worked hard for him, and now it doesn't really matter what we think, does it?"

By the time the company had gathered in the late afternoon for Sam's final rehearsal, the sheep had been separated from the goats, and, moreover, knew it. There were those who had been promised parts in *The Merchant,* and those with whom other plays had been discussed. No one had as yet been actually informed that he would not be wanted for the next season, but that would follow doubtless within days. The condemned group were muted, grotesquely hurt, yet withal clinging to hope. Those more fortunate were equally reserved, but with the wary complacence of privilege, like people tactfully evading mention of private means.

Sam was too preoccupied with other troubles to concern himself with where he fitted into this picture. He was looking at himself in Frederick Bell's long mirror, and he was not assured by what he saw. The day before he had mentioned to Terence that Freddie's costume might need some alterations, but nothing had been done about it. Now, at the last minute, the wardrobe mistress on her knees with a mouthful of pins was busy tightening the waistline of the breeches. However, no makeshift stitching could alter the fact that the costume hardly flattered him. Freddie, broader in the shoulders and deeper in the chest, had looked splendid in it, but on Sam it drooped inelegantly. Worst of all the periwig simply did not suit his sort of face. He looked like a basset hound. "Give me the breeches, then, dear, and you can have the rest of the costume to rehearse in," said the wardrobe mistress with the brisk cheerfulness of a nurse preparing a patient for the knife.

Sam set off downstairs, dressed below in his own trousers, above in full costume and wig. In two hours he would be doing it. He wished he felt angry about the costume; that would at least be better than his present mood of dismal withdrawal. The company in their ordinary clothes were waiting for him, and he moved among them feeling himself a somewhat ludicrous figure. Toby Burton looked him over. "Yes . . . yes . . . that's good. 'Course, you need the right trousers," he said with no great conviction. Sam caught Amanda's eye and she smiled nervous encouragement at him. He tried to be fatalistic about it; maybe it would be all right with some makeup on.

They began to run his scenes. It was oppressively hot onstage, and he started perspiring. With the arrival of the first really cold day someone had overstoked the boilers, and the theater was a hothouse. He forgot his lines only once, but that was enough to send a chill of fear running up his back. The tighter grew the knot of tension in his mind, the more flaccid and devitalized became his physical apparatus. All his energy seemed to have dried up. Though his fellow actors gave every sign of wishing him well, their way with their lines, an almost ostentatious ease, became, as scene followed scene, a kind of mockery. Sam's troubles had become a respite from their own, and they were prepared to indulge their cruelty just as far as the point of having to recognize it. At the end of the rehearsal his costume was soaked in sweat.

He went upstairs to make up. Forlornly he picked up the sticks of color; their magic was his last hope. Why wasn't he nervous? Did he lack energy even for that? He felt only the gnawing apprehension of the waiting room. What he really wanted was for the evening to be over and behind him. He was made up and dressed with fifteen minutes in hand, so he went down to the canteen to see if a cup of black coffee would restore him.

He sat in full costume analyzing his exhaustion and reached the conclusion that it had been brought on by sweat loss. Salt, he had read somewhere, was the remedy, so he picked up the saltcellar on the table, poured a little hill of it, about two teaspoonfuls, into his palm, and willed himself to lick it down. A minute later he realized that the salt had been effective only in producing prompt nausea. He was going to be sick.

He ran down the stairs and along the corridor to the lavatory on stage level, but was appalled to find it occupied. He heard the flush and hung on, unable to risk speech, one hand rapping on the door, the other clasped over his mouth. At last the bolt clicked and the ENGAGED sign snapped to OPEN; whereupon Martin, in full costume, expressionless, his face an orange mask with a large black beauty spot below one eye, brushed past him. Their glances met, then immediately ricocheted away. Sam bowed over the lavatory and retched. He watched his own vomit mingle with the fragments of excrement slowly circling in the water below.

Five minutes later Martin and Sam sat on either side of the gaming table waiting for the curtain to rise. It was their stillness that belied their apparent equity, as if the detonating of their hatred waited only upon a look or a gesture. Sam studied the speckles of vomit on the elaborate lacework at his wrist as he tried to generate a little saliva in his dry mouth. Martin stared straight ahead, looking bored. Beneath them they could hear the orchestra tuning up. Amanda ran out from the wings and wrapped Sam in her arms. "Good luck, Sam," she said. "You're going to be marvelous!" Martin disregarded them, and in a few seconds she was gone. Her good wishes, the desire to do well for her, had had the effect of making him suddenly nervous, and once again he was experiencing what had become a commonplace to him, the drumming of his heart. The costume felt very heavy on his shoulders.

The stage darkened and the introductory music pealed forth into the auditorium; Sam listened hard to it, trying to steal some of its gaiety for himself. Then with a sound like an intake of breath the curtain went up and they were bathed in light.

"You are a fortunate man, Mr. Fainall!" said Sam, and at once felt a little encouraged. His voice surprised him by its power and incisiveness, and before long he was tripping along the tightrope of the Restoration prose without too great a sense of vertigo. He had to resist the temptation to gabble, a temptation much encouraged by Martin's automatic and unconsidered delivery of his lines. The other actor was not listening. During Sam's longer speeches his eyes would either glaze over with irrelevant thoughts or go wandering over Sam's shoulder to feed on some distraction in the wings.

But they were approaching that moment in the text where Ivan had decreed a pause. Sam determined to use it to collect his dissipating concentration. He paused, but was unable to resume his speech. Martin had cut in, meaninglessly replying to what had yet to be addressed to him. Sam's lines rattled from him automatically while his split mind furiously debated the question of Martin's deliberate malice. Incredulity yielded to anger, and he felt all his energies go up in a blaze of rage.

By the beginning of the next scene, playing with other people in a different set, he was no longer angry; nor for that matter nervous, nor frightened, nor anxious. He was not anything; he had burned himself out. He felt nothing at all beyond a dull longing to have the evening over. He seemed to have run out of fuel. It was all he could do to dredge his lines from memory and get them spoken. The part was not working for him, and now it was just a question of summoning up enough courage or pride or desperation to see it through to the curtain.

His long break came in the middle of the play, and he returned to the dressing room to wait an hour for the scene with Millamant. How could he make a recovery? He fiddled with his makeup, ate some chocolate, lay down flat on the floor, read a newspaper, but nothing helped. The play was coming loudly over the tannoy, and it sounded rather the better for his absence.

When at last he returned to the stage, his fatigue was gone, but in its place was an excruciating insecurity. It was like the first entrance of another play. Where relish and enjoyment were demanded, he contributed only inhibition and self-consciousness. And he was suddenly so unsure of his text! At any moment he knew his lines would slip from the grasp of his mind. He was sweating with suppressed panic. The audience coughed. He might have been playing to them from behind glass.

At the curtain Sam took a bow by himself and received polite applause. To his audience, as to his fellow actors, his performance had not seemed bad; merely dull. He had not forgotten his words or shown his fear; but neither had he brought personality or fresh meaning to his part. "Well done," a couple of actors said to him in a friendly and perfunctory fashion, while Amanda, a determined smile on her face, stayed behind to congratulate him. But he knew that for her as for them his having failed, or at any rate having been merely adequate, grievously diminished his small supply of mystery. It was true for all of the company that after six months together they were now defining each other in terms of limitations. Perhaps the limitations of others were what each of them had always hungered to discover. At any rate that night Sam had presented himself to them surveyed and charted, and they would not forget it. He went upstairs too tired even to feel discouragement. He was to have another go at the part the following night; maybe he would do better then.

He hung his heavy costume on its hangers, then put on his dressing gown and went down the corridor to the shower room where there was a urinal. The room was full of steam. Without directly looking, he knew that the person under the shower was Martin. It seemed he could not escape him. He mounted the porcelain step and stood, wanting to pass water, suddenly unable to. He waited, staring at the tiled wall in front of him. At the edge of his vision a naked body moved to hold another pose under the noisy shower. Through a veil of steam and splashing water he was aware of a white, white skin covering a bony frame, all the lines of which seemed to converge toward the seaweed darkening at the groin and the copious spill of sexual parts. There was the thing that had explored her. He continued to stand, humiliated by his own arrested function but determined to enforce it. Eventually he dispatched a trickle of water, shook himself and left.

The following evening he set off to work resolved to make the best of his second chance. He had slept satisfactorily, and had gone through his part twice, once in the morning, once in the afternoon. But the theater he returned to was a dog kennel. Small crimes like small glories: in the enclosed world of a theatrical company both cried out for justice. The place seemed to be silently howling. In the letter rack most of the company had found waiting for them written confirmation that their services would not be required for the coming season. Jock MacLachlan's signature was at the bottom of the letters, writing on Tom's behalf. Their tone was friendly, their import inarguable. There was no letter for Sam (was he to construe from this that he was among the elect?), yet he could not help feeling disgust at an impatience and lack of curiosity that could dispose with such carelessness of so much human material. The season had been a success. Did this prove nothing?

He played the part a second time, and again had to recognize his failure with it. And he could no longer solace himself with the excuses of the previous night. His lack of rehearsal, his fatigue, Martin, Amanda, all these he might have blamed and certainly they had not been much help, but the simple truth was that he was no good in the part. He did not fit it. In some odd way it elicited only the negative aspect of his personality. Every actor now and then ran the risk of such a part. It was not something you could prepare against at rehearsal, because you didn't know about it until an audience told you. Then their polite indifference to your presence was unmistakable. And how horrible it was to be bad! In a couple of nights he seemed to have wiped the slate clear of every good performance he had ever given. Even his work in the other two plays seemed to be canceled out by this inept display.

When it was over, he asked Amanda to go out to coffee with him. That night she had not hovered in the wings watching over him as she had during his first performance; probably she could no longer bear to watch. But he needed someone to whom he could confess that he knew better than anyone how poor he had been. Perhaps he would win her assurances about those remote times when he had actually been good. Her expression, however, warned him that this evening's display was too fresh in her mind for him to expect her to recall much of that. It was best to shut up.

"I'm exhausted," he said to break a silence.

"You must be."

"Thank God for the weekend. Are you going to London again?"

"I'm not sure yet. I think so."

"I wouldn't mind going away myself."

"Why don't you, Sam?"

"With you?"

"That would be nice, but you've got to be back for Monday night, haven't you?"

"Yes."

"Why not make a trip by yourself? On Sunday. There are some lovely little bays and things farther down the coast. You can get a bus."

"I might do that."

"Do. It'll do you the world of good. A change like that."

In the morning he was not really surprised to find that he, too, was the recipient of a white envelope, stampless and, beyond his typewritten name, unaddressed. Respectfully and a little sadly Alfred handed it to him. He opened it and read:

DEAR SAM,

The way the casting for next season is turning out, I'm afraid we have not been able to find a really suitable line of parts to offer you. We very much regret this because Tom is very conscious of all the hard work you have put in this season and thinks highly of your work. Please come and see me any time.

Yours sincerely,
JOCK MACLACHLAN

He read the letter twice, then carefully, as if it were evidence of something, put it away in his pocket. He decided to take Jock MacLachlan at his word. He would go and see him at once, without a moment's delay. He had no clear idea of what he would say to him or what he would gain by such an interview; he even

had the feeling that such action might prove foolish and destructive, but he no longer cared. He was heartily sick of the place. He
wanted simply to thrust himself, physically, into the orbit of Jock's
attention. Then he would do the same to Tom. He would sit in
their offices as tangible and perhaps as dumb as a piece of
furniture, and for five minutes they would have to recognize his
existence.

Jock MacLachlan was very busy, his secretary said, but would
be pleased to see Sam if he could come back later in the morning.
He returned at twelve o'clock and sat a further thirty-five minutes
before the door opened and Jock, affable and weary, ushered him
into his office. He sighed over a huge pile of correspondence on his
desk. "Sorry to keep you, Sam, but it's this American thing. We're
right in the middle of it at the moment. Now, what can I do for
you?"

"I got your letter this morning. I thought I'd just come and talk
about it."

"Yes. Yes," said Jock, nodding his head sagely. "Our trouble,
you see, is not just to find a part, I mean there are plenty of good
parts you could play, but a line of parts in all three productions,
and in the case of someone like yourself a line of parts that's an
advance on what you've already done for us."

Jock's manner was bland and steely. Someone else had decided
against Sam, and his job was to support and effect that decision.
Sam realized he was seeing the wrong man. Jock would not
remember, even though Sam could recall every word of them, the
promises he had made over the telephone when he had first
offered him the job. But what good would it do to remind him
now? Yet there was something he expected from Jock, something
foolish he felt he had a right to: just a word from him that in his
mind at least Sam was still the good actor he had so frequently told
him he was, and that there had truly been times in the season when
he had been impressed, surprised even, by his ability. This was all
he really wanted from him. What was that expression he had used?
"I never thought you had it in you."

328

"Quite frankly, Sam," Jock was continuing, "we were a little disappointed in your understudy . . ."

Sam hastened to defend himself, suddenly wounded. "I admit I was bad in that. I know I was! But that was just two nights. What about my other work all through the season?" The appeal was naked now.

Jock raised his eyebrows and smiled. "They're much smaller parts, Sam." He said this as if it were a brutal truth which must be broken gently. He was conceding nothing. Sam knew he had been a fool to come and see him, and that moreover Jock considered him a fool to have done so. It was a tactical error in the handling of his career, and in Jock's mind this was eventually the area that separated the men from the boys. What happened onstage (that is, when it wasn't actually happening) was in a sense almost secondary. At any rate it was more impermanent than a contract. Jock had a great deal to do that morning.

"I'd like to see Tom, though," said Sam.

"I'm sure he'd like to see you, too. I don't know quite when, though. He's away at the moment. As you know yourself, he's very busy."

But there was no problem about seeing Tom. Clarissa made an appointment for him after the show that night. "He's coming up again this afternoon and I know he'll be working late. I'm sure that will be all right, Sam, but in any case I'll leave a note downstairs for you to confirm it."

The days when Clarissa had called everybody "Mr." and had rather expected a "Miss" herself were over, and she had adapted smoothly to the theater's surface egalitarianism. She scribbled Sam's appointment on a memo pad, and he wondered if those capable elegant fingers had helped to type out all the dismissals. She was definitely on the inside now, and not really such a bad person to be there. Better than Olive. She was a pleasant girl who worked hard without the handicap of caring deeply, and in the environment in which she found herself this was almost a distinction. She might go far with it.

Except for the night watchman, Alfred's nightly usurper, who sat scowling over a pink evening newspaper, the theater was deserted by the time Sam had dressed and was on his way to see Tom. He deposited the key of his dressing room with the night watchman, then set off across the darkened stage toward the pass door which led up behind the boxes and beyond to the corridor of administrative offices. There was a bar of light beneath the door of Tom's office, the only room in the building which still seemed to be occupied. The prince was alone in his palace. He knocked, and Tom called "Come in!" in a high, loud voice.

It was some time since they had seen each other. At once Sam was taken aback by the look of great fatigue on the other's face. Nor had he prepared himself for the curious inversions of a confrontation such as this, whether with enemy or lover, when one is faced suddenly with the opposite of what one has been expecting. Seeing Tom standing behind his desk with a hand extended, he was aware only of his forgotten virtues. Here was a man, he realized, who might intrigue but would never bully, who might drive and exploit others but no more than he did himself. He did not envy him, but it was difficult not to admire him. Twenty-eight years old, and sitting on top of the heap. And after all they were contemporaries; the same wave was washing each toward his own kind of bleak recognition. Tom had changed in the last year quite as much as Sam.

Tom offered him a drink and chatted amiably about a number of things unconnected with the theater while he busied himself finding clean glasses, pouring Scotch and squirting soda. They sat opposite each other maintaining the stream of pleasantries, Sam, as much as Tom, yielding to a pattern of behavior as prescribed as it was involuntarily deceitful. Why should one sit smiling before a man one had good reasons for detesting? But for the moment there seemed no alternative way of behaving. The truth would have been far too abrupt and shameful.

Eventually they came to the point, sensing the moment more or less simultaneously. Tom slipped in and beat him to it. "Yes, Sam, we were very disappointed not to be able to find a line of parts for you, but I think you'll agree there would have been no point in offering you just a single play with nothing to do but carry a spear in the others."

"No."

"That's our problem, you see, Sam, to do justice to an actor with a *variety* of parts." It was the same line he had heard that morning from Jock, somewhat elaborated and more flatteringly expressed but essentially the same, and as with Jock he nodded his way through it. He wondered if he should suddenly cry a halt to the performance, smack the desk with his open hand, and scream "Amanda!" into Tom's smiling face. In a play he would have been able to act it beautifully. But the conversation seemed to run on steel rails, predetermined, and he could only mark its passage with his reasonable nodding. But surely there was something he could challenge! "Who have you got in the company, then?" What he had meant to be a blunt interruption emerged as the mildest of queries.

"Oh, I'll show you. It'll be in the papers on Monday. Here, you can have the news in advance." He smiled confidentially at Sam and handed him a typewritten list of names. Sam studied it. At the top were a couple of big stars; then followed the names of the few survivors from the present season intermixed with a number of young actors who had all made reputations quickly, one in a TV series, another in a first West End appearance, another in a repertory production which had transferred to London. As a gathering of talent it put Sam in mind of the latest designs in kitchenware at an Ideal Home exhibition. He knew he did not really care much about not being among them. He looked up and realized Tom was actually expecting him to offer some sort of reassuring comment. It was becoming absurd.

"Looks very interesting," he murmured.

"I think so," said Tom.

Sam shifted in his chair as if to rise, but Tom checked him. "Sam . . ." he said. His head was on one side, and he wore a magnanimous expression as if he were about to do Sam a favor. "Would you like me to be completely candid with you?"

"Of course." He resettled in his chair.

"I've already told you—haven't I?—that I think your two little Doctors are brilliant. Quite brilliant. That was never in question. But do you know what I look for most of all in my actors?"

"What?"

"Well, it's difficult to describe. But at the moment, and I say at the moment because people do change, and there's no reason why you shouldn't change—I mean people in my position must never forget, actors change—it seems to me you haven't got this thing."

"What is this thing?" said Sam, and added steadily, "star quality?"

Tom laughed. "That's a bit old hat, isn't it? The old star system, all it did was reflect the prevailing social system. Take away one, you take away the other. You probably would have done very well in the thirties. No, I don't mean that."

"What, then?"

"Look, take Martin for example." Sam was flabbergasted. Did Tom realize what that name signified for him? Or did his complacency extend to assuming Sam's ignorance? The latter, apparently, for he went on to misinterpret the look of incredulity on Sam's face. "Yes, I agree that at the moment he has something to learn as an actor. But he has this thing, you see, and everyone recognizes it. After all, acting is really quite a simple thing—not easy, mind you, but simple. In ten years' time Martin will have learned most of what there is to learn. And I'll guarantee you one thing; I'll stake my reputation on it: in those ten years he'll never be out of interesting work. And, of course, he has this fantastic sex appeal. He'll get star parts and be paid well for them. And eventually he'll become what at the moment some might say he only presumes to be. That's the point, Sam. Talent's important, of course. Of primary importance. But talent's nothing without— well—ferocity. That's what makes it interesting. Class has gone. Race is going. You can't be above the battle any more. Which I sometimes think you try to be? It's a small pond with too many big fish in it. That's what I look for first in an actor. Determination is the polite word. Your trouble is you're a bit too nice. You know what old Ivan said about you?"

"No. What?"

"We were talking one night in the pub. He said, 'I smell talent on that boy. I wish I could smell success.' "

Sam had heard only the first part of this remark in Richard's tactfully emended version. "Oh, yes. Richard Wayland told me."

"Richard. Now, he has it."

"Yes. Well, apparently I must acquire it." His attempt at irony passed unnoticed.

"That's right. If you really want it, you'll get it." Tom had risen and was standing over by the window. "Look down there." He pointed to the car park where Martin's white Alfa Romeo sat with its nose in a pool of light. "That's what I call success," said Tom.

"I hate cars."

"That's not really the point, is it? Prove you can grub for one of those and you'll get all the work you want."

It was time to go. Why should he expect Tom to argue with the ways of a world which had so swiftly and entirely vindicated his existence? In any case Tom was doing no more than any of them did—Sam, Martin, Amanda—striving to create the sort of world in which each operated best. Tom was luckier than most in that the world he wanted was already there; more or less. "Well, thanks for seeing me," said Sam.

"A pleasure. And I'm pretty sure that one day we'll work together again."

Sam walked across the office, step by step, wanting only to be gone, to be out of it and away. But at the door, once again, Tom checked him. "Of course, Sam," he said, smiling, "if only there were a few more Doctors in the classics you'd never be out of a job, would you?"

22

Sam had made inquiries at the terminal about Sunday bus trips, but he awoke to a day so overcast and cold he decided to abandon any idea of a journey along the coast and instead spend his time locally. He would go for a long walk outside town and pay a last visit to familiar places. All the months of the season had now diminished to one last week. This time next Sunday he would be waiting on the platform amid his luggage for the London train. He dressed, then sat down for a preliminary browse through the Sunday papers, but no matter to what part of the room he moved his chair he could not escape a draft, so, after a bout of sneezing, he got up, put on his warmest things and set out at once on his walk.

He began along the beach until he was clear of the town, then cut inland along a wooded gully. This led upward to an old village well known for its church. He walked through the curving street, approving the constancy and scale of the old buildings; past a blatantly new petrol pump outside a hardware shop, then on to the church.

In the churchyard a man had spread his mackintosh on an overturned tombstone and was sitting there busily sketching. It was David Beynon, the designer, and he seemed quite indifferent to the cold and discomfort. Sitting there alone fervently at work, he looked a little ridiculous, and more than that, provoking, as if his complete absorption in what he was doing constituted a slight upon the ordinary concerns of other people, and Sam could imagine giggling children hurling pebbles at him from behind the protection of the wall. He approached, and the artist looked up from his pad, gave him a curt and rather suspicious greeting, then returned immediately to his work. Sam did not go away, as he thought perhaps he was expected to, but watched from a discreet distance the progress of the sketch. It was a detail of the church entrance. After a while David seemed to accept Sam's company, and they settled down to their respective roles, the one working, the other watching.

Five minutes later Sam went off to continue his walk. He followed a path toward the distant woods, and on the way passed a dead bird, as still and lusterless as old rags. The trees, with their dark tracery of leafless branches stretching up into the mist, were like nerve endings embedded in the transparent substance of winter, stoically waiting upon a message from it. Soon the ground had become carpeted with sodden leaves, already half earth. Thinking of the bird, he looked around for other dead creatures, but the woods maintained the closest discretion about their casualties. Anonymity partnered failure.

His route had brought him to the park, and far away on the other side he could see the Drama School set in the middle of a terrace of houses. Behind that building Amanda lived. She would not be there now, having gone to London to rehearse her play, but he decided nevertheless to walk to her place and pass by her window. If the trapdoor was open, he might even trespass and play the Bach record.

As he approached the Drama School, its aspect seemed altered somehow, but it was not until he had recognized Tom's Mercedes that he realized it was because of the number of cars parked in front of it. When he noticed as well the white Alfa Romeo and Richard Wayland's secondhand Austin, he concluded that a conference of some sort must be going on inside, and he became suddenly embarrassed lest he be discovered prowling around uninvited. He hurried to take the side streets which would lead him to Amanda's. In the narrow lane behind the Drama School and practically blocking it he came upon Freddie Bell's Jaguar, the only car he had ever seen parked there. Then he began to hear the unmistakable sound of a gathering of people, the single note of their collective voice, and he looked up to discover from which window of the building it emanated. Not until he had reached her gate did he realize that the sound was coming from Amanda's flat.

He looked up shocked at the windows of her loft. He had an impulse to panic and run, but suppressed it and proceeded cautiously, a step at a time, into the stable. Here the noise reverberated as within a drum. Above his head he could hear the passage of feet on the wooden floor and occasionally distinguish laughter and individual voices raised in exclamation. It was a party. She was having a party! But perhaps she had lent her flat to someone else while she was in London. Perhaps it was Freddie Bell's party. But why, when he had a flat of his own? He stood minutes mesmerized and stricken by the noise, before realizing with alarm how dangerously exposed he was should the trapdoor suddenly open. He fled to safety behind the parked Jaguar in the lane.

From here he had a good view of one small window of her sitting room. He would wait and watch. But he saw nothing except now and then the shadowy passage of a guest. Then in not very much more time than it takes to blink, an arm appeared at the window and ashes from an ashtray fluttered wispily down the side of the building. Sam dived for cover behind the boot of the car, slipping so that one knee grazed hard against the muddy gravel. The arm had been hers. He scrambled to his feet and began to run. He ran to the end of the lane, along the next continuing street, then off to the left toward the park and across the turf to the distant shelter of the wooded fringe.

When at last he had stopped and his panting had eased a little, he discovered that the knee of his trousers was torn and that he was bleeding. He tended it carefully with his handkerchief, almost grateful to have some distraction while his frantic breath returned to normal. He watched for half an hour, concealed among trees. Eventually one of the parked cars nosed slowly forward and drove away. A little later another did the same. He set off again across the park, keeping a constant distance from the Drama School, sufficient to observe without being recognized. During the next hour all the cars one by one disappeared. Now he dared to venture out of the park into the streets and to look down the distant perspective that ended in Amanda's lane. Freddie's Jaguar had gone, too. The party was over. He waited a further half hour before going to see her.

He did not knock on the trapdoor but raised it unbidden, dreading, hoping for, some unthinkable discovery. But the room was empty. He noticed and smelled dirty glasses, full ashtrays and the untidy remains of plates of onions and gherkins. Right in front of him on the seat of a chair was a saucer of peanuts into which someone had stubbed a cigarette. From the kitchen he heard the clinking of washing up; it stopped when he slammed the trapdoor shut behind him.

Amanda appeared wearing an apron and with her hands in yellow plastic gloves. She looked frightened when she saw him, but then she averted her gaze and her features took on a stubborn look. Clearly she would not be the first to speak. He began in a low, unsteady voice: "What's the matter, do you think I'm stupid or something? If I hadn't found out today, do you think I wouldn't have heard about it at the theater tomorrow—or the next day?" She did not answer him. "I thought we weren't going to tell any more lies. Wasn't that the idea?"

"I didn't tell you a lie," she murmured.

"You told me you were going to London to rehearse."

"I said I might be."

"I see. Then you changed your mind and threw a party instead."

"It wasn't me. It was my agent."

"What do you mean?"

"My agent said I should have a party. It was his idea."

"For all your old friends?" She did not answer him, and he walked up and down the room, then threw himself onto the Chesterfield. "Look, Amanda, if you want to have a party for professional reasons—it was a top-billing party, is that right?"

"Yes."

"—it's no business of mine. I don't necessarily expect to be asked." His words were reasonable only because he knew that

M

nothing he could say would succeed in hurting her. And he wanted to hurt her more than anything—as she was hurting him. He seemed to be a hairsbreadth away from striking her, twisting her arm, mutilating her, which made his present display of virtuous reason all the more absurd. But what weapon other than virtue did he possess? "But why didn't you *tell* me? Why did you leave me to find out like this?"

"How did you find out?"

"Accident. Sheer bloody accident. I happened to be walking by."

"I know I'm selfish. I'm terribly selfish."

"Everyone's selfish."

"It was just that my agent said I ought to do some entertaining before the end of the season—"

"For top people."

"Is that so wrong?"

"No . . . and I suppose if I'd been invited it could only have been for a private reason, not a professional one?"

"Yes."

"And you didn't want that private reason advertised?" She did not answer. "Because that private reason no longer exists?" He waited for her to say yes. "And letting me find out about the party—was that your way of telling me that the private reason no longer exists?"

"I suppose so."

"So it's over?"

"Yes."

"Well, that's that, then."

"I'm sorry, Sam," she said simply but with no repentance. "The season's become such a mess. I don't know. I want to make a fresh start." It was the most final thing she had said.

"With the play in London and everything."

"Yes."

She was on her way, and she intended to travel light. He understood the feeling very well. She had entirely withdrawn from him, and the expression on her face was sullen and ugly, and yet her youth and her certainties had never seemed more persuasive. A rapturous future beckoned to her. No matter that her convictions were shared by every tremulous insect ever hatched into daylight. Well, perhaps she was to be the moth for whom the candle flame really was the moon. His mind protested, but his heart told him it was true and he longed to go there with her.

He rose to go.

"You'll find someone new soon," she said.

"Yes."

He turned at the trapdoor. "Maybe see you at the theater, then."

"Yes. What happened to your knee?"

"Oh, I stumbled when I was walking."

Her face had softened, and without its particularly being her intention, she allowed him to see again an aspect of her that had nothing to do with being young or beautiful or lucky, the thing perhaps that in the days when his detachment was assured had first drawn him to her. A temporary excess of youth could account for her present cruelty and mendacity, a sort of innocence. He suffered now; her turn would come later. He wondered if she was feeling at all as he was, an astonishment that the person before him of all the people he knew or had ever known should turn out to be the one to inflict the punishments of love.

He prepared carefully for bed that night. He was not unhappy so much as nervously concerned with himself, like someone after an accident for whom the absence of pain obscures deeper injuries. For some time he sat with the light on, propped up with pillows, thinking. Something had happened to him, a change in him, and it had come about abruptly like a break in the weather. He turned out the light. He knew he would not sleep, but he knew, too, that this was to be the last sleepless night she would ever inflict upon him. He would think about her all night long, and in the morning that would be the end of it.

Around four o'clock he recognized the beginnings of a sore throat and climbed out of bed to dose himself with aspirin. By daybreak he had diagnosed signs of fever. The company germ, probably picked up from Freddie Bell's costume the nights he had

339

played for him, had at last claimed him. He stayed in bed all morning, escaping from time to time into a light dozing, and when he rose it was only to accommodate the habit of lunch. But dressed and on his feet, he found that he was a good deal sicker than he had realized.

That night at the theater he had a temperature and sat at his place, as Paul had done some days ago, silent and enfeebled. He performed without mishap but felt much worse the moment the curtain came down and released him from the brace of the play. He hoped Toby Burton would offer him a lift home on his scooter, but Toby, in robust health, appeared to be hurrying toward some engagement and he felt too weak to importune him. The walk home would do him no harm.

As soon as he set off, he knew that the journey was going to seem interminable. Behind him, felt but unseen, the dark bulk of the theater towered up in front of the park. It was a presence he wished to escape, but as in a dream his steps seemed unable appreciably to increase his distance from it. He stopped, panting, and looked back. Seen through a glass of illness, it was like a black palace. He knew too much about that building now. No wonder the drama abounded in stories of the rise and fall of tyrants, of the suffocations of court life, of the jockeying of favorites. The dramatists had found it all in their own disgusting world. Indeed as a field for politicians the theater could not be bettered: this jostling, frightened, overcrowded world where all were vulnerable because all were expendable. And were the actors any better than those who manipulated them, living undismayed with their colossal assumptions: that someone else would write words for them, build a stage for them, pay money simply so that they could play their public games under the lights? Actors were like some ragged infantry of the arts, going over the top in wave after futile wave to face the artillery of their own crippled vanity. This was the theater: inescapably second-rate and fake, dependent on rhetoric and display and all the tawdry language of power.

He arrived home, struggled out of his clothes and fell into bed. In defiance of Mrs. Shrapnel's strict instructions he would leave the small electric fire burning all night. He awoke several times, once to be sick into the wastepaper basket beside his bed, at other times merely to open his eyes on the red terrain of his fever revealed by the glowing bar in the corner.

In the morning he decided he needed a doctor, and at eleven o'clock he put on his overcoat and shoes and went up to the Ozone. He discovered Mrs. Shrapnel sitting among the stacked chairs in the empty dining room. She rose immediately, flew to the duster she had left on the sideboard and hectically busied herself with it. Sam's gray face and the fact that he had never appeared in his pajamas before seemed to make little impression on her. "Good morning, Mr. Beresford," she crooned unsteadily, and he realized she had been drinking.

"I'm not very well, I'm afraid, Mrs. Shrapnel. Could you get me a doctor?"

Mrs. Shrapnel's devices fell from her and she was immediately all solicitude. "No, you're not very well, are you? I can see that just by looking at you. What is it? Not this beastly flu that's going around?"

"I think so."

"Sure to be. As a matter of fact I've felt a bit funny myself this morning. Think I may be getting it, too, the beastly thing."

Mrs. Shrapnel telephoned and the doctor arrived, a gentlemanly old man with slow, patient ways, unable altogether to conceal his lack of confidence in his ability to absorb the vast number of pharmaceutical choices with which chemists had cursed his last years of practice. There was sureness, however, in the movements of his dry hands as they tapped and prodded Sam, and in his insistence that his patient remain in bed for at least three days. Mrs. Shrapnel was instructed to telephone the theater and tell them that Sam would not be performing for three nights. Lying there, he wondered why he felt admonished as well as comforted by the old doctor's plain exercise of his profession. "We'll soon have you on the boards again," he said, and Sam felt inexplicably shamed.

They left him in bed to reflect that this would be the first time in his career he had ever missed a performance. It did not bother him. Nor was he concerned that one of the nights he would miss would be the last performance of *The Duchess of Malfi.* Don Petersen would be substituting for him, but not even this disastrous fact was able to engage his feelings.

All his thoughts, like all the objects in the room that his eye fell upon—the glass of water, the limp, flimsy curtains—seemed to have had their corruption revealed by illness, and they repelled and wearied him. He wondered where he had ever found the impulse to be an actor, and what was the joy he had once imagined he would find in it. It had become the most incomprehensible and foolish of activities. Meaningless. How could he ever have *wanted* to do it? He tried to recall his enthusiasm and his zeal at the beginning of the season, but it was like raking over ashes. Where did it come from, this ridiculous desire to strut and bellow? He thought of all the young people who year after year volunteer for the stage, among whose ranks he, too, had once clamored for attention. Flu was not the disease, but health and youth, and vanity was the invariable symptom.

All day his thoughts ran parallel with his fever, until it seemed that the theater had bred and nourished his illness, that his job was the fever. He felt a total revulsion from it.

That night he had a nightmare about the theater in which he came onto the stage to confront a full house naked except for an Elizabethan ruff. He was about to launch into a soliloquy when he became aware of a woman, one of the front-of-house cleaners, furiously mopping the forestage between him and his audience. She upset her bucket of water. It was Amanda.

In the morning his temperature was gone. He lay in bed with a clear, cold mind. Something was becoming plain to him. If he hated the theater, then why not give it up? He wondered why it had taken him two days to think of it. There was really no decision to make. It had already happened. He was no longer an actor because the things that had made him one, the faith and the ambition, were no longer there.

The realization did not worry or disturb him; on the contrary it was a somber freedom, like an ache relieved. He spent most of the morning staring at the ceiling with his hands behind his head, carefully picking over the events of the season. Where had he gone wrong? (Or right, as his present frame of mind should have instructed.) Where had he lost that vital ignorance that made it possible for others to persevere? The trouble was, he decided, and it was an unemotional reflection, it wasn't so much the theater he disliked as life. He didn't really like life. No, that wasn't quite true. He liked life well enough when it came in the form of Valerie's scented shoulders, or a swim in the blue seas, or even the sterner tonic of concluding difficult work. The thing about life was . . . that he didn't *approve* of it. That was it! He didn't approve of it. This notion so appealed to him that he decided to say it out loud. He found so much satisfaction in doing so that he began to laugh.

On Thursday Sam had two visitors. In the morning Toby Burton called in and sat in a subdued fashion on the end of the bed, cradling his scooter helmet between his hands like a great egg. "How was Don?" Sam asked him.

"How do you mean?"

"In the understudy."

Toby showed the slight surprise of someone who adjusts to a question that doesn't really interest him. "He was fine. He was all right." (It was true; anyone could do it. Learn the lines and say them out loud; that was all there was to it.) Toby seemed more inclined to talk about the two big parties that Sam had missed by being sick. Tom had thrown one for the whole company in the rehearsal room, at which Francis had got very drunk and done a dance on top of a trestle table, and then the following evening after the show Jack Bellenger and Freddie Bell had organized something up at the Royal Hotel. The morale at the theater was apparently much improved by these events. In any case London was beckoning now, where anything could happen.

Toby had brought Sam some magazines, filched from the canteen and which consequently he had read, and also his copy of *The Way of the World*. "I found your script underneath the stage, lying about on the stairs. I thought you might want to keep it."

"Oh, yes, thanks. I must have left it behind when I played for

Freddie. I sometimes use that little room there if I want somewhere quiet to check my lines or something."

"What, that little room under the stairs?"

"Yes."

"You don't want to do that, mate! You don't want to go in there."

"What?"

"That room! It's haunted! Didn't you know? You wouldn't catch me sitting in there."

"What do you mean?"

"Honest. It's the truth. I'm telling you. That room's haunted. You ask Frank, the night watchman. He'll tell you."

"Who's it haunted by, for Christ's sake?"

"Listen, that's where Sarah Siddons' lover hanged himself. I thought everyone knew that."

Sam had the second good laugh of his convalescence.

At lunchtime, and as unexpected, his second visitor arrived. It was Valerie. She had heard about his illness from Paul Poulsen whom she had met in the street, and now she appeared on his doorstep smiling and blooming and carrying a string bag heavy with groceries. "Could you eat something? I've brought some food." And in fact this was the first day he felt any real appetite. He dispatched Valerie to the Ozone to intercept Mrs. Shrapnel, before she embarked on one of her soups, and in her absence struggled to the bathroom recess to tidy himself up. Pale and unwashed and with a three-day growth of beard, he looked dreadful. However, there was only time to give his hair a token comb before she returned.

That afternoon he was full of admiration for her. She cooked them both a crisp lunch of the sort she had learned he preferred: lamb chops, salad and a few potatoes, with fresh fruit to follow (the Cox's orange pippins were exactly what he felt like); then after lunch, having washed up, she set to work tidying the room. She made him sit in the chair wrapped in a blanket while she remade his bed with clean sheets; then she swept and dusted the room meticulously, even to scrubbing clean with no distaste whatever the speckles of dry vomit on the floor by his bed. Then, her blood up, she gave the bath a scrub and smothered the lavatory in Mrs. Plank's perfumed disinfectant. She had brought her transistor to amuse Sam, but most of the time they disregarded the comings and goings of a remote German pop program and talked above it. Finally, her face flushed and happy with her fulfilled labors, she sat on the edge of the bed and allowed him to fondle her. "You're getting that expression on your face," she said. Then, having given him a long look assessing his health, she crossed to the door which she locked, pulled the curtains, took off her clothes, and, notwithstanding Sam's conviction that he had never appeared less desirable, slipped into the fresh bed beside him.

On Friday just before lunch Sam took his gray secret down to the theater: that he was no longer one of them, no longer an actor. He had only three more performances to give, all of *The Way of the World,* which didn't really count. It was overcast and wet. Not far from the stage door, stacked there in the open and gently pelted by rain, the set of *The Duchess of Malfi* waited to be carted away. Exposed to daylight with its damp canvas sagging, it looked extraordinarily unconvincing, as tawdry as a float from last year's parade. Sam stopped and looked at it, then went through the stage door. Alfred had a letter for him. "There's one for you, sir. Special airmail from Australia. Arrived only an hour ago."

Sam recognized his father's handwriting. He wondered idly what the letter could be about. It was usual to hear from him at Christmas and on his birthday (two letters within a month of each other), but this was neither. He opened it and read:

MY DEAR SAM,

I'm afraid I have some bad news for you. Peggy died last night. She had been seriously ill for some time now, but we kept the news from you because it was her wish that we should do so. She was very pleased about the progress you've made in your career this year (as we all are) and was insistent that your work at this important stage should not be interrupted. Her plan was for you to fly home at the end of the season to see her, but this was not to be. She died quite peacefully. Please ring me at home any evening (reversing charges). You may like to come out to Australia for a while.

Yours,
DAD

Sam took the letter outside. Don Petersen was standing with his umbrella up, looking at the dismantled set of *The Duchess*. Every so often he gave part of the exposed softwood frame a gentle exploratory kick with his foot. It looked brash and flimsy, and almost invited it. Sam joined him, and Don offered him some umbrella.

"What do you expect they do with it?" said Sam.

"Burn it, I expect," said Don.

They stared at it in silence.

"My mother's died."

Don blushed. "Oh, I'm sorry to hear that," he said.

Sam left him and walked back to the Ozone.

On Sunday he decided to leave by the late afternoon train. It didn't arrive in London until around midnight, but it was a shade faster than the morning train, involving only one change (at York). Also most of the company would be traveling on the earlier train, and he preferred to be by himself. He packed in the morning, then went up to the Ozone to accept Mrs. Shrapnel's invitation of a last lunch together. She was roasting an Aylesbury duck in his honor. They sat in the Oyster Bar having a gin and feeling solicitous about one another, the one overtly, the other secretly. "Now, you're quite sure you're warm enough, Mr. Beresford? I'm not sure you should be traveling at all, you know," said Mrs. Shrapnel. Sam looked at her, dressed in one of her tailored outfits, similar to the one she had worn when they had first met, a trim cut intended perhaps to disguise or at least shore up her inner ruin, and wondered just how she would get through the next few months before a houseful of summer guests came to her rescue.

"Are you going to do any more building this winter, Mrs. Shrapnel?"

"I don't know, Mr. Beresford. I don't know. It's such a fag."

"I would. Why not build onto the flatlet and make a proper flat? You'd get a much better rent for it."

It was then that Mrs. Shrapnel divulged that she didn't really need the extra money. Apart from the Ozone, her husband had left her forty thousand pounds, nicely invested. The duck and the roast vegetables were excellent, marred only by pale lumpish gravy.

In the afternoon Sam put on his plastic mac and went for a walk on the beach. It was a ritual visit rather than a sentimental one; he would not be seeing the sea for some time so it was as well to pay his respects to it. A fine rain was still falling and the sand was sodden. The element of water seemed to have subdued the whole environment, so that the limits defining land, sea and air were all blurred and softened. Where water finally condensed into the gray expanse of the North Sea, it looked very cold and alien. Summer had never existed. Or if it had, it was scant consolation now. He looked toward the horizon, but it was obliterated by mist and he wondered if out of sight the waves were breaking today on the sandbank. That was something they had never done: gone out there in a motorboat to have a look.

He stared across the water and remembered his farewells to another beach. He had stood on the rise to the north of Bondi and looked out over the bay where the brilliant turquoise of morning was already yielding to the metal tones of the afternoon. There had been a big sea running, and he had watched the swell of yet unbroken waves rocking the heads of the swimmers farthest out with their slow giant's motion. Even then he had not regretted leaving it, though he knew he would miss it. But he had had the best of it, and it had been time to go.

Mrs. Shrapnel saw him into his taxi. "You might just find a little someone waiting to see you off when you get down to the station," she said with a wink. The door slammed. "Goodbye, Mr. Beresford. Look after yourself now. Goodbye."

Valerie was waiting for him at the ticket office: "I rang Mrs. Shrapnel to find out what train you were catching but I didn't want to leave any message because I wasn't sure I'd be able to get here.

Then Trevor went off with some friends to a rugger match and it was all right." They had fifteen minutes before the train, so he took her in to the refreshment room.

"How is Trevor?"

"He's all right. He wants me to marry him."

"Do you want to?"

"I don't know. Probably."

He knew she would marry him, dressed in white and making the best of a church wedding, accepting this as she accepted everything else that came her way, good and bad. It was simply not in her to complain or gnash her teeth over failed expectations. She would have children and be one of those plump middle-aged women with clear foreheads who resented nothing.

They said little while they sipped their coffee. He noticed that she had made up with special artfulness that afternoon; she was staring at him now from the center of some soft, private thought. Presently she reached out her hand and gently but deliberately rested it on the fly of his trousers. His first thought, ribald and alarmed, was that the waitress would see, but the table was masking them. Her expression was quite unchanged; there was no salacity in it, no daring or affectation. All she asked of him was the reassurance that he still desired her, and it was all too easy to provide. Her gesture seemed one of the simplest, nicest things he had ever had from a woman.

It was getting dark as the train pulled out. The compartment had the comfortable, sweaty smell of steam heating and old upholstery, and the feeble lights were on. He leaned in the corner and cleared a patch on the misted window with a brown paper bag someone else had left behind. Braddington was passing by, a town of a few watery lights. A distance away, hardly moving with the passage of the train, some kind of flame flapped over the darkening town. What could it be? Some industrial process perhaps, or a rubbish dump alight? Then he wondered if they were burning the set of *The Duchess of Malfi*.

Play-out

HE STOOD on the corner of the Strand and Trafalgar Square waiting for the lights to change. Since his return, the traffic seemed to have become more noisy, clogged and noxious than ever; it almost frightened him. So much for six months in a country town. He watched the vehicles stream past, unable to resist the feeling that something dreadful was happening to this city, something which all the people in it had agreed to overlook, and for no better reason than that each of them owned or aspired to own what collectively was the cause of it: the motorcar.

But now the lights had changed, and he crossed with the other pedestrians. On the other side of the road he stopped and debated whether he would walk or catch a bus the rest of the way to the Labour Exchange. He would walk; he had plenty of time. He passed the window of an agency selling theater tickets, and his eye went straight to it—the bill advertising Amanda's play. He knew the layout by heart. At the top in inverted commas it proclaimed "SMASH HIT!" and beneath there was a sketch of her, the one that had been used in New York, showing her holding a hammer in one hand and a sickle in the other and looking splendidly single-minded.

That was the trouble with concluding an affair with an actress, particularly a successful one; there was small chance of ever being allowed to forget her. She was constantly in the papers these days, praised, photographed, written about. The *Daily Express* had practically adopted her. He had predicted her success, of course, months ago in Braddington. This had not prevented him, as her first night approached, from wishing some vague calamity upon her, acute laryngitis or some irremedial short circuit in the lighting system. However, believing that one can be justly called to account only for one's actions, not for one's thoughts, he had sent her a first-night present, a warmly inscribed paperback of the poems of Gerard Manley Hopkins, a writer for whom he remembered she had once expressed a great liking (though at the time and for no clear reason he hadn't been able quite to believe her), and she had written at length thanking him. He was glad to get her letter, impulsive, funny and strangely unsure of itself, agreeably at odds with the immaculate image that haunted him on billboards and in newspapers.

In Victoria Street he saw approaching him the last person he had ever expected to see in the environs of the Labour Exchange: his agent, Kelly. He was in the company of an old man wearing new ill-fitting clothes, and they made an oddly assorted pair. Sam had not yet told his agents that he was no longer an actor. (They had never yet found him a job over Christmas so there was no danger of putting them to any inconvenience). In fact, except for Sally, he had told nobody. He was waiting, he assured himself, until he had decided what his new job would be. He had made some inquiries about teaching, and it seemed an obvious if listless alternative. Kelly greeted him in a friendly, surprisingly subdued manner, and introduced him to his father. The old man was over on a holiday from Belfast, his first trip to London, and Kelly was spending the day with him showing him the sights. They were just on their way to Westminster Abbey.

"Have you time for a cup of coffee, Sam?" said Kelly, and Sam said, "Sure." Ironically, now that he was no longer dependent on Kelly, he was getting on well with him. The two times he had called in at the office, they had chatted easily and at length. Now his agent was offering the astonishing proof that he had been generated as other men, by parents. They went into an ABC café and joined the queue. Kelly's father tried to pay for it, but Kelly chided him with a gentle, discomforted good humor which Sam would never have guessed him to possess. They took their cups to one of the plastic-topped tables and pulled up a third chair. Kelly's father had a lined face and a dim, apologetic gaze, which for the most part he kept fixed upon the mystery of his successful son, as if time had reversed their roles.

"C'mon, Dad," said Kelly. "By the way, Sam, how's Sally these days?"

"Well. Very well," said Sam.

"Give her my love."

Should he tell Kelly they were no longer seeing each other? No, it would take too much explaining. "Will do," he said cheerfully, and they parted.

The last time he had seen Sally, for the last time, had been nine days ago. When he first arrived back in London she had been away on holiday in Austria, but there had been a letter from her waiting for him at the flat. He had wondered how she had known the date of his return, but apparently she had heard from Sidney, to whom Sam had written about his subtenancy (he would not be able to let Sidney have the flat the following year, after all). Sally's letter was tonic and practical:

Sorry not to be there to welcome you, but stocked you up with supplies before I left. Tea, coffee, sugar, cream crackers in the usual place. Also some things in tins in the cupboard under the sink. There's a new milk machine outside the Express Dairy if you want some in the middle of the night. I've put clean sheets on the bed. Hope it hasn't got damp in the meantime. Austria is just great. You get a bit fed up being just another unit in a production belt of tourists, but the village and the whiteness and everything are so lovely it doesn't really matter. Incidentally, it's incredibly cheap at this time of the year. I'll never learn to ski. I'm hopeless. But falling down is quite fun and marvelous exercise. Our instructor is called Fritz. He's short and fat and thinks he's irresistible. I'll be back four days after you, in time for your *birthday* (30!!?!) unless you're forgetting about it. So much to tell you. And hear.

Much love,
S

It ought to have been nice to have a letter waiting for him, and it was, once he had read it. Why had her handwriting on the envelope at first so pained him? If the foreign stamp had not made him curious, he might not even have opened it.

When they met over a pub lunch the following week, his immediate thought was: she gets on much better without me. Her holiday had left her clear-eyed and sunburned, vibrant with the suppressed good news that something nice had just happened to her, and he was not unaware of the interest shown in her by the pale, November faces of the other men in the dining room. He was struck all over again by the handsome planes of her face.

She began to relate her holiday in an excited jumble of facts and impressions, and he listened to her as he had listened on so many similar occasions, suddenly remembering them again, touched and exasperated to have thrust upon him the role of paternal auditor, yet at the same time envying her the pleasure she derived from the simple telling of her experience. "I felt so guilty not being here to welcome you back," she said, and he was now pretty certain she had gone away for her skiing holiday with a man, as yet unmentioned. He felt a smart of jealousy, and was quick to recognize the use he could make of it in whipping up fresh desire and feeling for her; but the compromise of it wearied him. Later she volunteered the information he had been tempted to go hunting after: "So I said what the hell, why not? I mean I wasn't crazy about him or anything, he knew that, but I liked him and I'd never done any winter sports. It seemed sort of a chance. Silly not to, really. I've told him about you. He knew you were coming back."

The man in question was called Peter; he was twenty-eight and worked as an architect for a firm which dealt in office blocks. ("He hates it. Do you know what he wants to do most of all one day? Design a theater. Isn't that interesting?") He had been the most persistent of the three men who had been asking her out while he'd been away. In the end it had seemed sheer bloody-mindedness to go on saying no.

"Does he like you a lot?" asked Sam.

"I suppose he does. I don't know. One day he talked about getting married, but it was all a kind of joke. He was saying he wanted to get married in church, and I was saying I couldn't understand how anyone could be so hypocritical. I'm terribly rude to him sometimes."

They were to spend the weekend together. On Friday it started snowing in London, and snow was still falling on Saturday morning when she arrived at his flat with provisions. Her hair was matted white with it.

"Enough is enough," she said, brushing the melting flakes off her. "Listen, I've bought some salami and cheese and stuff, and if the weather's not too awful tomorrow, I'll make us an Austrian packed lunch and we'll go touring on the Heath."

"Big deal," he mocked affectionately.

"Oh, Sam, you are awful. You never want to do anything except go to the pictures. The Heath must be looking lovely at the moment! There might even be people skiing."

They idled the rest of the morning away drinking tea and reading the weeklies. In the kitchen, adding more hot water to the pot, Sam wondered when he would find the right moment to speak, and yawned unhappily at the thought of it. After the pictures, perhaps. Later in the day they were going to the National Film Theatre to see *Scarface*. It was, he reflected, the last of that handful of old films he had always been obsessed to see. At the age of eleven he would have given his little finger, quite literally, to see the original *Frankenstein,* at fifteen *Scarface,* at twenty-one *Greed.* Now approaching thirty, and with a full complement of digits, he would soon have caught up with them all. He wasn't sure whether this was an occasion to rejoice or mourn. He thought of Sidney, stranded up north on some enterprise, and how furious he would be to miss it.

They lunched late at the Chinese restaurant, where the plump Indian waiter solicitously welcomed them back. Afterwards, walking home, he began to tell her about Braddington. He tried to tell her about Amanda, but it was very hard telling the truth without in some way disparaging Sally. He knew he was causing her pain, and was loath to revive that small, persistent element of humiliation, up till now asleep, that had always played a part in their relationship, the pattern that they had long ago established and now seemed bound by: that he cared but never quite enough.

In the flat he told her his decision to give up the theater, and she looked at him, forgetting about herself in her deep concern for him. "Oh, Sam," she said, and started softly to cry. All the years they had known each other had been lived in the light of his hopes in the theater. He felt wretched and guilty; his faith had gone and taken hers with it.

She had stopped crying, and waited now for him to speak. He guessed she knew what he was about to say: that they must finish. He explained as best he could that they couldn't live with such disappointments, that they would only remind each other of failure, that it would be best for both of them to make a fresh start elsewhere. "If you think it's best, Sam," she said in a small, resigned, hopeless voice, and her submissiveness suddenly filled him with a kind of mournful rage, not directed at her, not at himself, but at the pair they made, this flawed, tangled closeness.

Why had she always left him to make the big decisions unopposed? He wanted her to fight him, even if only through perversity or pride, force him at least to look a little closer at his own motives and rationalizations. But the decisions had always been his, and they made a miserable, improvident catalogue: at first the postponed marriage, later an abortion, then the trial separations and the calculated infidelities. Worst of all, and in the very beginning, it had been on his advice that she had abandoned her job as a set designer in the rep theater where they had met and come to join him in London. He had genuinely believed that the work was too hard for her and that her health was suffering. Job had followed job for her, in advertising, in TV office work, once as a window dresser. She designed no more sets, but she still caught dreadful colds in winter. And she had been talented. His career had had to serve for them both, and that was now over. They were over.

Neither said it, but it became understood between them that this weekend would be the last they would see of each other. It was three o'clock on Saturday afternoon, and all that remained was to make the very best use of their time together. In a day and a half they had a great deal to remember and forget. An enormous concern grew up between them, a need to ask for and extend forgiveness. Their mood was gay and gentle. The poignancy, which both of them felt and restrained, seemed to stem less from their parting than from the neglect of just this quality of concern which it had taken their parting to rediscover in them. Perhaps it was just one of the tricks of farewell; they recognized this, but it seemed nonetheless as if they had been delivered from a sad and willful blindness to each other.

In the tube on their way to the film they held hands and laughed together as if they had found each other only the day before. A Negro student smiled at them, surmising generously and wrongly. At the beginning of the film Sam thought it was going to be awful, but it turned out to be most diverting, full of strange, archetypal violence. Even Sally enjoyed it, though she thought it absurd.

Afterwards they walked across Waterloo Bridge through a bleak wind, Sam chattering about the film, pitching the frail excitement he had found in it against the alien grandeur of the city and the river. In the Strand they passed another cinema crowd filing out into the night: blinking, dosed faces concealing the shame of the familiar discovery that the world they had just left and the one they were returning to were connected but tenuously, if at all.

It was inevitable that they should start talking about the past, and later on in bed they talked about it for half the night. There was little sentimental or nostalgic about their recollection; it was more a desire to take a last opportunity to get the record straight. Sam found himself obsessively concerned with correct detail. "Yes, but what was the *number* of the house, do you remember?" Each had a special set of memories about the experiences that had been common to them, and as they unraveled the past it became extraordinary to Sam that someone else existed curator to so much of the lost detail of his life. "But, Sam, you *must* remember; you

355

were wearing your new cord trousers and Terry spilled yellow scene paint all over them. You were furious."

"I don't remember that at all!" He felt almost indignant to be cheated thus of his own life.

"Oh, you must!"

He researched through her better memory as urgently as someone allowed a few hours' access to some unique private library.

They woke late, after ten o'clock, but rose almost at once. They might have made love again as on past spendthrift Sunday mornings, but some instinct was guiding them toward the most precise and tender use of their remaining time together. Sally pulled the curtains, and winter sunlight spilled into the room, as fresh as butter.

"Sam, it's a gorgeous morning!" she exclaimed.

They pulled chairs into the soft engulfing yellow patches and drank tea there. Then they prepared their packed lunch, and made a pile of such things as might be useful on the outing: an old rug, two scarves and Sam's plastic mac (to sit on). Sally insisted on making the bed and thoroughly tidying up the room before they left.

Going downstairs, both laden, she said, "I don't think I want to come back here after the picnic, Sam. I think I'll just get the Twenty-four bus and go home."

"All right," he answered.

Up Heath Street all the roofs were white-thatched, and the footpath was obscured by shoveled heaps of gray snow. In buoyant Swiss disguise the familiar environment demanded fresh consideration, and they were happy to give it. The Heath itself, when they got to the top, was even more surprising, all undulating whiteness, intricate trees and the small, urgent activity of distant people in bright clothing. There were some skiers, and some children tobogganing.

"It's fantastic! Like a Brueghel," said Sam.

"Was I or was I not right to get you up here," said Sally.

"Like a Brueghel," he repeated; the business of defining the day was too important to countenance considerations of who had initiated it. Then he murmured, "Quite right," and pinched her. The footpath from which they looked down upon the Heath was crowded with people who like themselves had come out to enjoy the novelty of the day, and the atmosphere was jolly and collusive. "Just like wartime," he commented dryly.

They left the crowd and went down a slushy path toward the Vale of Health, then up the slope beyond it to find a place facing the sun. There were no clouds, and only the pale gold liquefaction of the sun emblazoned the sky. Sunlight evaporated upon the snow, splashed and melted on the crusts of ice on the ponds, and condensed as bright mists among the distant trees: beauty as exact as geometry. They saw a bench thirty-odd yards off the main path, and made tracks through the snow to reach it. They swept it clean of snow, spread the unread Sunday papers upon the frosty, dry wood, then sat down and raised their faces to gauge the tiny sting of the sun's warmth. It was delicious. Every so often the faintest breath of wind would lower the temperature on their faces like a gentle caution. They could hear birds singing in the bare trees, which surprised Sam. "I thought they all went away in the winter."

"Not all of them, silly."

After that he noticed a robin, a blackbird and a fat old pigeon, the flap of whose wings as he passed above them made a sound halfway between a squeak and a wheeze.

The lunch consisted of small quantities of a great many different foods separately wrapped. In one paper bag Sam found four dehydrated apricots. While they were eating, a gray squirrel tripped fastidiously along the top of a nearby picket fence. Sam approached him and he made an astonishing leap to safety onto a flimsy branch overhead, which bent like a fishing rod to receive his scrambling retreat. Then he saw three more squirrels and realized they were in the midst of a colony. They laid bread out, and eventually one of the creatures hopped cautiously forward to sample it. They let him eat for a while, then advanced a step at a time until they were so close they could hear the delicate chop of his teeth and see the exclamation of frantic survival in his merciless button eyes.

A few clouds appeared. For a moment a mere wisp had obscured the sun, and a chill seemed to come up from the earth under their feet. They watched for the next patch of sunshine, but it was evident that the best of the day was over. Cloud was thickening to the west, and presently one half of the sky had gone the dark even color of slate. Low pink clouds sped past overhead.

They collected their things and set out upon a walk. Which part of the Heath were they to share and record? Whatever they did today would be remembered. They followed many paths, then walked over the lawns to Kenwood and went inside to see again the Rembrandt self-portrait. They had a trippers' tea in the café nearby while it darkened outside. Then they set off for the bottom of the Heath and the bus stop.

It was very cold now. In the distance high above them one bird flew on a slow straight course toward the blackening perimeter of the day. The way he took seemed extraordinarily brave and lonely. Sally walked ahead of Sam, and he stretched out his hand and rested it on the back of her neck. He saw her shoulders rise in pain at his touch. "Don't, Sam. I don't think I could bear it," she said, and he let his hand fall. He put her on to her bus, and when it pulled away it was as if something physically had been torn in him.

He walked up the hill through a terrain overtaken by catastrophe, as if the winter landscape like an old plate had cracked and shattered all about him. In his room he paced about, bewildered by pain, muttering to the four walls his need of forgiveness. His face began to contort into the unfamiliar grimace of weeping, but it was something he did so rarely now, cry, that he had no facility for it, and the sounds he made were as rasping and broken as those of a dog being sick.

That had been about a week ago. Now he was on his way to the Labour Exchange: Square One, and the same as ever. Or so he thought as he approached the building whose architecture always reminded him of air-raid wardens and food rationing. But when he went upstairs to sign on in the special room set aside for actors, musicians and performers, he found that some official had disallowed this small privilege of his tribe, and that in future they would have to queue up with everyone else in the big room on the ground floor. He went downstairs again, in a mood of rebellion until he realized that of course downstairs was where he now belonged. He joined the end of a queue so long that it could only be accommodated in the room in a series of sluggish loops. There were only a handful of actors there (none fortunately that he knew personally), the rest being the genuinely unemployed, men for the most part as dispirited as stopped clocks.

At the head of the queue the clerk was trying to explain to an old man in a filthy mackintosh why he was not eligible for benefit. The old man replied with some obscene abuse, and Sam saw the tobacco-colored ringlets on the back of his gray head trembling with agitation. He had the look of some grievously impoverished maestro. Sam took a paperback out of his pocket, a rather sententious work on the Montessori method of educating infants, and withdrew into it.

At last he received his money and went out into the street. He was thinking idly about Amanda, wondering how long it would be before he could read about her in a newspaper with comparative indifference. She would always be successful, he supposed. She would turn into one of those splendid old actresses, still blessed with a full set of teeth, prone to making public pronouncements that there was "always room at the top." Maybe she would write her autobiography, in which she would state unequivocally that she had resolved, had she not made it by thirty, to give the game away. He sighed, suddenly bored and exasperated by his own sourness, and tried to think of something else.

Ahead of him, sheltering in a doorway, stood the old man who had made the fuss inside. He was still furiously talking to himself. Sam passed within a few yards of him and stared directly into the red, decayed face, but the old man was too absorbed in his hatred to bother about anyone else; he poured forth his lewd imprecations for the world to hear, or not to hear, as it pleased. What he was doing, of course, was soliloquizing. Literally. A Hamlet of the pavements. Sam found this notion so pleasing that he stopped and

359

looked back to study him further. Yes, he was talking out loud to himself, as unconcerned as any actor on the stage, having somewhere lost the necessary trick of disguising from others the ugliness of his thoughts. But what suddenly interested Sam was the pattern in which those thoughts were cast: the old man was really engaged in a dialogue. Somewhere in his mind he had created an antagonist upon whom he was free to pour down the full spate of his wrath. Perhaps it was true of all thinking, that it was really a dialogue.

Sam walked on. How different from the stage convention of thought: as dreamlike and measured as a dance. He pictured the faces of various Hamlets, eyes raised nobly to heaven. The old man's eyes had been fixed on the pavement. As indeed were his own eyes now, ruthlessly tracking the scent of his thoughts. Thought *was* ruthless. And swift. Hadn't Shakespeare said something of the sort somewhere? It might have been a stage direction. He had never heard the Hamlet soliloquies done with that kind of urgency and speed. Perhaps that was the key.

> *O! that this too too solid flesh would melt,*
> *Thaw, and resolve itself into a dew. . . .*

The lines rang in his head at the pace of his own mind, and he was surprised by their freshness. They meant something new, something curtly dismissive, laden with abrupt self-disgust.

> *O God! O God! How weary, stale, flat, and unprofitable*
> *Seem to me all the uses of this world. . . .*

There it was, of course. The dialogue. And what better interlocutor to choose than the Creator himself? None of your dreamy, reverent, murmured O Gods, as automatic and mild as a modern sigh. Instead a direct challenge, a confrontation with Established Belief: *"O God!"* You up there! But the most interesting thing, he quickly realized, was what this did to the next sentence: "How weary, stale, flat, and unprofitable seem to me all the uses of this world." No longer was it merely fluent despair, attractive self-pity. It became a precise, calculated blasphemy. "You, God, made the world, and I do not care for it!" Sam became immensely excited. He ran the entire speech in his head, and it was as if he had never really understood it until this moment, as if the text had slowly ripened on the page, and now, this very morning, it was for reaping.

Down Whitehall and in the tube from the Strand to Hampstead he went systematically through as much of the part as he could remember. It had never made more sense. Suddenly he knew for an absolute certainty that he could play the bloody thing, that if a stage were to materialize at that very moment he could step on to it and astonish any audience, anywhere. He hadn't felt as good as this since he'd had the flu.

He looked at his watch; it was twenty past twelve on a Friday, an hour of miraculous deliverance. A feeling of wayward joy, as cunning as appetite, possessed him. He had rejoined the criminal classes. He was an actor again, and there was not the remotest possibility of his ever giving it up. Whom had he been fooling? Himself probably; providing a truce and a rest in which to regroup his forces and prepare for the next assault. How could he possibly give it up? And why should he—moments in his life like the present which were his privilege and his only message.

At the flat there was a letter waiting for him, postmarked Darlington.

DEAR DONALD CRISP,

Well, I've found the place and made the deal. It's down by the railway, used to be a big fish restaurant and still smells of cods' heads and last year's dripping. Now it's mine, all mine! The Corporation own the building and they're letting me have it at a nominal rent. The editor of the local rag is stage-struck and is giving me the most fantastic publicity. I've got the club license and the liquor license and have all the students and layabouts working for me touting membership from door to door. Here's how it stands at the moment. The decorators will be in until the end of January. I'm held up at the moment over some secondhand cinema seats (I only want

200, they want to sell me 300) but expect the curtain to go up February 10th. First production "Look Back." At the moment rest of the program as follows—"Journey's End," "Waiting for Godot," "The Seven Year Itch," and a double bill of "The Chairs" and "The Proposal." Each show to run about 3 weeks. Club membership only. Drinks served during the show. Posh salad bar for meals before or after. Here's the offer: you to play in "Look Back," "Journey's End," "The Itch," and to direct "Godot" and the double bill. Money shocking, eleven pounds a week. BUT am renting a huge house for storage, scene painting, etc., and the company can live there free. May even hire cook to provide meals. One more thing. Terry Baines is doing the sets but he needs an assistant and suggested Sally. She's too talented not to be doing it but would she be interested? And would *you* be interested? For obvious reasons will let you get in touch with her, but either way *let me know*. We need help immediately tarting the place up. Will ring you to discuss on Monday at 6 P.M. Wire if inconvenient. If all this excites you then would like you up here at once because there's plenty to do and I'm getting hysterical.

Yours,
MISCHA AUER

P.S. This letter does not constitute a contract.

That afternoon Sam walked up to the post office and wrote two lettercards, both brief, one to Sidney confirming that he would be waiting by the telephone on Monday, the other to Sally conveying Sidney's offer. He posted them both without hesitation.

As with all the important decisions of his life, he didn't know whether he had made up his mind out of great strength or great weakness. Was he looking forward or looking backward? He had no idea. He had simply decided. He was returning to the theater again. He would not be as idealistic as he had been, which is to say he would not expect so much; probably he would be the more useful for it. Nor would he ever be as fervent on behalf of a play (and as nervous on a first night) as he had been for *The Duchess of Malfi*, which meant that he was learning to dispense with heroes, a difficult thing for an actor. But it was enough to have had the experience of that production, on any score remarkable, more than some actors derived from an entire career. The people he believed in believed in him. What more had he a right to expect?

Though he had been waiting for it, when the telephone rang on Monday night it startled him. He jumped to his feet and ran downstairs to interrupt its forlorn and rather ominous pealing. "Go ahead, Darlington," said the operator. Sam was panting slightly. He guessed that Sidney, too, must be feeling as he was, a few of the misgivings of commitment. Did they really have the faith in each other they had always pretended? The venture could cost them a friendship (though friendship wasn't much if it couldn't embrace such risks). They both talked bravely on the phone, and by the end had effected mutual conversions to an almost unflawed enthusiasm.

Sally's letter arrived the following morning. It was brief and to the point, a careful imitation of the style of his own letter, which made him laugh. "The money will be all right because we'll have two salaries," she had written, but the money side of it had been the thing that least concerned him. The previous week he heard from Australia that he was to derive an income from his mother's estate. He had thought it might see him through teacher's training college. Now it was to be put to its proper use. His mother would continue to help him in his career, just as she had fought his cause when she had lived with his father in the big Vaucluse house. "We decided to stay together for your sake," she had once told him. He remembered the silent meals and the forlorn months of her trips abroad. Sometimes it seemed she had spent the rest of her life making up for it.

Sam and Sally: the conjunction of their names still had the embarrassing ring of adventuring tots in a children's story, but that could not be helped. On Saturday he picked her up with her luggage in a taxi, and that afternoon at half past five, with the lights coming up early and the misty expectancy of winter like breath upon the city, they caught the train north.

MY LIFE WITH NOËL COWARD

Graham Payn

with Barry Day

includes: **The Never Before Published Theatre Writings of Noel Coward**

"An engrossing portrait of this world famous and immensely gifted man, chronicled so frankly by his closest friend:A most vivid account of Noël Coward's career after the Second World War."

–John Gielgud

"I greatly doubt if anything written about the Master will ever be as fascinating, as perceptive, as amusing or as touching as Graham Payn's loving portrait."

–Richard Attenborough

"Graham Payn knew Noël Coward better than anyone:stories I never heard before bringing Noël Coward vividly to life."

–Lauren Bacall

BOOK/CLOTH $24.95• ISBN: 1-55783-190-4